STAND-IN
GROOM

STAND-IN GROOM

PLANNING THIS WEDDING
WILL BE NO HONEYMOON

KAYE DACUS

BARBOUR
PUBLISHING

Published by Barbour Publishing, Inc., P.O. Box 719, Uhrichsville, OH 44683, www.barbourbooks.com

Our mission is to publish and distribute inspirational products offering exceptional value and biblical encouragement to the masses.

ecpa Member of the
Evangelical Christian
Publishers Association

Printed in the United States of America.

DEDICATION

To my two most loyal readers, Mom and Mamie; and my hero, Daddy. Thanks for believing in me even when I didn't believe in myself.

ACKNOWLEDGMENTS

This book is the product of more than four years of work, and it would be impossible to acknowledge everyone who's had a hand in it. Special recognition goes to my two grad school mentors, Leslie Davis Guccione and Barbara Miller, who shaped my writing and guided me through the revision process; and to my agent, Chip MacGregor, for working so hard and patiently to help me get it published.

CHAPTER 1

*N*othing like running late to make a wonderful first impression.

Anne Hawthorne left a voice-mail message for her blind date, explaining her tardiness, then crossed her office to the gilt-framed mirror that reflected the view of Town Square through the front windows. At a buzzing jolt against her waist, she flinched, smearing her lipstick.

Great.

The vibrating cell phone chimed out a wedding march. A client. She reached for a tissue to repair her mouth while flipping the phone open with her left hand. "Happy Endings, Inc. This is Anne Hawthorne."

"I can't do it! I can't marry him!" Third call today.

Why had she agreed to be set up on a date the Thursday of a wedding week? If it were just the regular weekly dinner with her cousins, she could skip out and get some work done. "Calm down," she said to her client. "Take a deep breath. And another. Let it out slowly. Now, tell me what happened."

Fifteen minutes later, still on the phone, she pulled her dark green Chrysler Sebring convertible into a parking space in front of Palermo's Italian Grill. She sat in the car a few minutes—air conditioner running full blast—and listened to the rest of her client's story.

When the girl paused to breathe, Anne leaped at her chance. "I completely understand your concern. But sweetie, you have to

7

remember most men aren't interested in the minute details of a wedding. Just because he doesn't care if the roses are white variegated with pink or solid pink, don't take that to mean he doesn't love you anymore. Which ones do you like the best?"

"The variegated roses," the bride-to-be sniffled into the phone.

Anne turned off the engine and got out of the car. The heat and humidity typical for the first day of June in central Louisiana wrapped her in a sweaty embrace. "Then get the flowers you like. He will be happy because you're happy. Do you want me to call the florist in the morning?" One more change the day before the wedding. Saturday couldn't come fast enough.

"Do you mind?"

"That's what I'm here for." She opened her planner and made a note at the top of the two-page spread for tomorrow. "Feeling better?"

"Yeah. Thanks, Miss Anne. I've got to call Jared and apologize."

"See y'all tomorrow." Anne made sure her phone was set to vibrate-only mode and entered the most popular new restaurant in Bonneterre. Maybe she should have left the planner in the car, but she would have felt naked, incomplete, without it.

The heavenly aroma of garlic, basil, and oregano mixed with the unmistakable yeasty scent of fresh bread and wafted on the cool air that blew in her face when she opened the door. Her salivary glands kicked into overdrive, and her stomach growled. She really needed to stop skipping lunch.

Winding through the crowd of patrons awaiting tables, Anne scanned faces for the man her cousin Jenn had been *absolutely dying* to set her up with for months. She'd made a point of watching the local news broadcast on Channel Six last night so she'd know what he looked like. Her right heel skidded on the slatelike tile and she wobbled, her foot sliding half out of the black mule. Anne hated shoes that didn't stay on her feet of their own accord, but they were fashionable. She righted herself and arrived without further incident at the hostess station.

"Miss Anne!" A young woman in a white tuxedo shirt and black slacks came out from behind the high, dark wood stand and threw her arms around Anne's waist.

She recognized the girl as a bridesmaid in a wedding she'd coordinated just a month or so ago. What was her name? "Hey, sweetie! It's so good to see you. How are you?"

The bubbly brunette stepped back. "I'm great. I'll be getting my degree in August, and I already have job offers from advertising agencies in Baton Rouge and Houston."

Anne smiled, remembering the girl in a pewter, floor-length straight skirt with a corset-style bodice. The bride had let each of the girls choose which style top they were most comfortable in. Gray bridesmaids' dresses. Purple and lavender florals and bunting. The Garrity-LaTrobe wedding. Six female attendants. Of course! "How exciting. Congratulations, Carrie."

"Thanks. Are you meeting someone here?"

"I am, but I don't see him. The reservation was for seven fifteen under my name."

The girl ran her french-manicured acrylic nails down the waiting list and stopped at a crossed-out line. "Here you are. They were getting ready to reassign your table, so you got here just in time. Follow me, please."

Walking through the packed restaurant behind the slender, petite young woman, Anne tried not to feel self-conscious. At nearly six feet tall and doing well to keep herself fitting into a size eighteen, she hated to imagine what others thought when they compared her to someone like this little hostess—five foot fourish with a waist so small she could probably wear Anne's gold filigree anklet as a belt. When working, Anne rarely thought about her stature or size. In public, though, all the comments and teasing she'd received when she'd reached her full height at age thirteen rushed back into her memory. If only she'd had some athletic ability, she might have been popular and not fallen for a man who'd strung her along until he didn't need her anymore.

"Here we are." Carrie gave a bedimpled grin and bounced away.

"Thank you." Anne chose the chair facing the entry and set her purse on the floor and her planner on the table. She glanced at her watch again. Seven thirty on the nose. Surely her date wouldn't have given up waiting on her after only fifteen minutes.

"Still waiting on someone?" The young waiter—probably a student at the Bonneterre branch of the University of Louisiana—handed her a thick, faux leather–bound menu.

Not that I want to be. "Yes. He's probably just running a little late."

"Can I go ahead and get you something to drink while you wait?"

"Sprite with a cherry and twist of lime, please. Are Mr. and Mrs. Palermo here tonight?"

"Yes, ma'am, I believe the owners are here. Is anything wrong?" Worry etched the young face.

She gave him the reassuring smile she'd perfected over the years of working with nervous brides and frantic mothers of the bride. "No. I'd like to discuss planning a few events with them. But only if they have time. If they're busy, I can come back early next week."

His relief obvious, he grinned and nodded. "Yes, ma'am. And I'll be right back with your cherry-lime Sprite."

She turned her attention to the menu, pleased to see the broad range of selections.

The waiter returned with her soda. "Here you are. Can I get you an appetizer while you wait?"

She probably shouldn't, but—"I'd like the fried calamari and crawfish tails, please, with the cayenne-Parmesan dipping sauce."

"Excellent choice. My favorite."

She listened to the specials, making a mental note of the eggplant roulade—"Fried or grilled rounds of eggplant smothered in a spicy cream sauce with crawfish, bacon, and fresh spinach"—and the jambalaya alfredo—"With chicken, andouille, and traditional Cajun seasonings in the cream sauce."

"I'll be back with your appetizer in a little bit." He glanced at the still-empty chair across from her but didn't comment before walking away.

Anne set the menu aside and zipped open her camel-colored leather planner. Taking out a legal pad and pen, she reviewed her notes all over the two-page spread for today and the notes for tomorrow, then wrote out a to-do list of what she still needed to accomplish before her eight o'clock meeting with the bride, groom, and minister in the morning.

"Anne Hawthorne?"

She looked up at the voice and stood to hug former clients. She chatted with the couple for a few minutes before they continued on to their table.

Anne had just regained her seat when another former client came over. Anne hugged the young woman around the bulge of her pregnancy as she asked Anne to plan her baby shower. They looked at Anne's calendar and set an appointment to discuss ideas and dates.

The waiter returned with the calamari and crawfish tails and eyed the empty place as he set the dish on the table. "Do you want to wait until your companion arrives before you order?"

Maybe she should call to see what was going on. "Give me a few minutes?"

He nodded. "Enjoy the calamari."

"Thanks."

"Sure."

Grabbing her purse but leaving the planner on the table, Anne crossed the restaurant to the quieter lobby area outside the restrooms. She dialed and pressed the small cell phone to her ear.

Without ringing once, his voice mail picked up. His outgoing message gave his office phone number, which she repeated in her head while waiting for the tone. "Hi, this is Anne Hawthorne. It's. . . a little after eight, and I've been at the restaurant for a while and just wanted to see when you think you might be getting here." She left her number and disconnected, then called his office phone, which rolled into voice mail after three rings. Rather than leave another message, when given the option, she hit the number 0. After a couple of clicks and an ad for the TV station, someone picked up.

"KCAN newsroom. How may I help you?"

"Hi, I'm trying to get in touch with Danny Mendoza."

"Is this Anne Hawthorne?" the female on the other end asked.

Frowning, Anne started to pace. "Yes."

"I'm so sorry I didn't have time to call you before now. Danny got called in on a breaking news assignment and will be out in the field for the rest of the evening. He asked me to let you know he wouldn't be able to meet you but that he would call you tomorrow."

She squeezed her eyes closed and rubbed her forehead. "Thanks for letting me know. If you talk to him again this evening, tell him—" What? *Thanks for standing me up?* "Never mind. I'll just leave a message on his cell phone."

"Okay. Listen, I'm really sorry I didn't have time to call you."

"Don't worry about it." Anne ended the call, hooked the phone back on her waistband, and returned to her table. The aroma from the fried squid and crawfish on the plate in front of her tantalized her taste buds.

"Any word?" The waiter returned and tipped his head at the empty chair.

"Yes. He got called in to work so won't be coming."

"Oh. I'm sorry. Do you want me to box this up for you?"

"If you could bring me a box, that would be great, because I'll never be able to eat all this and a meal, too."

"You mean—you're going to stay?"

Anne tried not to laugh at his surprised expression. "Of course. I've been waiting to eat here for a month. I'm going to have the eggplant roulade—with the eggplant grilled instead of fried."

"Yes, ma'am. I'll go place your order now and bring you another drink."

"Don't forget the box for this." Anne served a few pieces of crawfish and calamari onto the small appetizer plate. Jenn always liked Anne to bring home leftovers after dining out, to see what other restaurants were doing.

At the thought of her restaurateur cousin, Anne shook her head. This was the third time Jenn had set Anne up on a blind date and the third time it hadn't worked out. Jenn had a habit of setting Anne up with men of Jenn's taste rather than Anne's type. At five foot six, Jenn didn't have to worry about towering over her dates. Five inches taller, however, Anne wanted to date someone who was at least six feet tall so she didn't feel like quite such an Amazon beside him. But it seemed as though *tall*, single Christian men over the age of thirty were hard to come by.

Of course, every man Anne had gone out with in the past who had matched her ideal of the Perfect Man had ended up being Perfectly Wrong for her. Maybe she needed to stop focusing on the physical type and just get out and have fun meeting new people.

She spent her life making others' dreams come true. Well, it was time for Anne Hawthorne, wedding and event planner extraordinaire, to start creating her own happy ending.

❧

George Laurence perused the menu, surprised to find the wide variety of dishes listed. His experience with Italian restaurants in midsized American cities primed him to expect spaghetti, lasagna, and fettuccini. So far, Palermo's Italian Grill in Bonneterre, Louisiana, appeared promising.

"So, George, where do you hail from in England?" Across the table, his employer's local lawyer shook out the folded fabric napkin and laid it in his lap.

George closed the menu. "I spent my childhood in London. My late teens and early twenties in Edinburgh."

"University of Edinburgh, huh? Heard that's a great school." Forbes Guidry handed his menu to the waitress and placed his order.

George considered his response as he ordered crawfish-stuffed manicotti. He'd wanted to live in America because he'd always heard that people weren't judged by their family background, wealth, or education. After five years of working for one of the wealthiest people in the country, he'd learned otherwise. The social prejudices in England and America differed but still existed. When most Americans found out he'd never attended college, they made assumptions about his intelligence and ranked him lower in their estimation.

He handed his menu to the server and returned his attention to the lawyer. "I wouldn't know about the university. I never had the opportunity to attend. I started working when I was sixteen." First, there would be an awkward silence, then a mumbled apology—

"I'm impressed." Forbes took a sip of his water, seeming un-flustered. "Just from talking on the phone this afternoon, I would have guessed you had at least a master's degree if not a PhD."

George opened his mouth, but nothing came out. No one had ever given him such a compliment. Although, he had heard lawyers in Louisiana weren't to be trusted. Was this man, with his tailored suit, expensive haircut and manicure, and impeccable manners, just one of those Artful Dodgers who could charm his way out of any situation? Or was he as genuine as his Southern accent and friendly demeanor indicated? George hoped for the latter. He'd never pretended to be someone else before and needed an ally, someone who knew his true purpose and identity.

"Thank you." No other response came to mind. Instead of putting on false modesty or being arrogant by focusing on his own merits, George returned to a previous conversation. "You said a housekeeper has been hired?"

"Yes, but since no one's been in residence, she just goes by every so often to dust and let the exterminators in, that kind of thing. The house was built like a typical English manor, or so I'm told. There are two bedroom suites in the basement beside the service kitchen. I figured you'd take one and Mrs. Agee would take the other. Now, to business." Forbes reached under the table and retrieved a document from his briefcase.

The document. The addendum to George's work contract—the contract he'd never wanted to sign in the first place. The rules by which he would have to live his life while in this quaint Southern city. He clenched his fists under the table. If keeping his work visa didn't depend on this. . .

"I assume your employer discussed the details of the addendum with you." Forbes handed the contract across the table.

George nodded, guilt clenching his gut. "Yes."

"As his legal representative, it is my responsibility to remind you of the confidentiality clause. Should you reveal to anyone, including the wedding planner, the identity of your employer or that you are not Courtney Landry's fiancé, your employment will be terminated. As you know, if you lose your job, you will be in violation of your work visa and must return to England."

The only reason why George had agreed to this charade. "Yes, I understand."

"Take it with you and read over it tonight. Any questions you have can be discussed when we meet tomorrow at ten."

George tucked the document into his own attaché case. "Very good."

"Whew. Now that that's over, we can enjoy our dinner."

"Yes, indeed." George needed a neutral topic to have time to take his mind off the fact that he was about to spend the next five weeks living a falsehood. He still hadn't figured out how to do it and maintain his Christian values. "Have you lived in Bonneterre all your life, Forbes?"

Over the salad course, the lawyer talked about Bonneterre as it had been during his childhood. George consciously made eye contact every fifteen or twenty seconds while also looking around the restaurant decorated to resemble a Tuscan villa.

Movement at a nearby table caught his attention. A waiter stopped, two fancy desserts perched precariously on his tray. With great ceremony and flourish, he placed the sweet delights on the table.

What was it about the patron that made him stand out? The fork in the young man's hand trembled, and he never took his gaze off his pretty companion. Neither could be much older than twenty. The lass took a couple of bites of the chocolate confection, but her fork stopped when she went for the third. She frowned, then dug something out. A small box. A few moments later, she let out a high-pitched gasp and threw her arms around her beau's neck. The lad dropped to one knee, and the crowd broke into applause.

George hoped the two young people had given this decision prayerful consideration. He hadn't been much older than the newly engaged couple when he'd prepared to propose to his first love. Praise God he'd learned her true nature before making a complete fool of himself.

Forbes clapped with enthusiasm. "Good for them."

"Are you married, Forbes?"

The lawyer held up his left hand and wiggled the empty third finger. "No. Don't know if I ever will be, either."

George sat back, surprised.

Forbes laughed. "Now, before you go getting the wrong idea about me, let me explain. I don't know if I'll ever find a woman my sisters and mother will find suitable for me. They've been trying for years. But the ones they like, I can't stand."

"And the ones you like?" George raised his brows.

"Humph. That's the problem. I can't even find one to bring home for them not to like." He sighed. "I suppose when God's ready for me to fall in love, He'll throw the right woman into my path."

"Hopefully you won't be driving at the time." George kept his expression serious.

Forbes blinked, then threw his head back in laughter, drawing the admiring gazes of several nearby female diners.

The waitress arrived with their meals. George glanced at the proposal-couple's table. A woman in an aubergine suit knelt between the two, listening to the animated young woman, her focus earnest and interested. Her blond hair was caught up in a french twist, and even from this distance, he could see a sparkle in her electric blue eyes. Everything about her—from her smile to the way she put herself below the level of the young couple—bespoke someone who put others before herself. The kind of woman he'd always dreamed of finding.

"George?" A frown etched Forbes's celebrity-caliber face.

George nodded his head toward the beautiful woman still kneeling beside the other table. "Who do you suppose that is?"

"Well, well, well. I knew she had other plans tonight; I just never imagined. . ." Forbes's smile took on a warmth usually reserved for a man's mother, wife, or sisters—or sweetheart. "She's a professional wedding planner. Right now, she's listening to all the young woman's childhood dreams of what her wedding should be like. When she meets with them in her office sometime next week—and don't worry, they'll be there—she'll already have a preliminary budget worked out."

George's heart sank at the woman's title. "Wedding planner? Is she—?"

"She is. She's going back to her table now." Forbes leaned to his left to watch her progress over George's shoulder. "If I can catch her before she leaves, I'll introduce you."

George nodded, keeping his turmoil under tight control. This would have been a lot easier if she'd turned out to be some old, grandmotherly type. How would he ever convince this wedding planner he was the bridegroom when he found her so utterly attractive? *God, what have I gotten myself into?*

CHAPTER 2

As soon as she returned to her table, Anne wrote down all the details of her conversation with the potential new clients. Of course, if they really wanted to get married in three or four months, she might not be able to take them on. Her schedule was so full now she rarely got more than four or five hours of sleep every night of the week. Just about the only remnants of her personal life she hadn't given up were church, Sunday dinners with the entire extended family, and Thursday night dinners out at Jenn's restaurant with the cousins.

In five years, her business had gone from operating out of the second bedroom of her apartment to allowing her to lease a storefront on Town Square. Six months ago, she'd purchased the Victorian-turned-triplex, where she'd lived in the second-floor apartment for nearly five years. Never in her wildest dreams had she imagined she'd be so successful. Of course, the article about her in *Southern Bride* back in January had helped.

Satisfied vindication filled her. Her ex-fiancé might have taken her for all she was worth ten years ago, but she'd still been able to get out of debt and make something of herself.

Good grief. Why did she still feel she had something to prove to *him*? Just because she'd supported him until he'd become a mega-movie star whose photo graced the front cover of every gossip magazine and tabloid known to man. Just because she'd dropped out of graduate school to go to work full-time to be able to send him rent money out in Los Angeles—

"Here you go."

She jumped at the sound of the waiter's voice and quickly closed her planner and put it on the floor. "Thank you. It looks wonderful."

"Enjoy."

Pushing aside the memories of her first and worst relationship, Anne determined to enjoy her meal and not let the past interfere with the present. The only thing she could do was make sure she never let another man use her and dump her again. She deserved better.

As she savored each bite of the eggplant roulade, she let her gaze wander across the restaurant to make sure she didn't miss seeing or speaking to anyone else she knew. Casual conversations with acquaintances could turn into referrals. At the sight of her cousin Forbes, with his dark good looks, halfway across the room, she paused. Women young and old turned to cast admiring glances in his direction.

Who was he with? Seated, the other man appeared to be about the same height as Forbes with a more slender but still athletic build, while his slightly too-large nose and sharp chin gave him a distinct profile.

Something stirred inside Anne that she hadn't felt in a long time— interest. He wasn't conventionally handsome—nothing compared to her cousin—but the way his sharp features softened when he smiled at the waitress created a tingling sensation in her stomach that she hadn't felt since high school. He had medium-brown hair but looked like he was graying a bit at the temples, adding a distinguished air. She should go over and speak to Forbes so she could meet this handsome stranger. But if they hadn't tried setting her up with him, he might be married—

"Is everything okay with your dinner?" The waiter replaced her half-full glass of soda with a fresh one.

"It's lovely, thank you. My compliments to the chef. There's just no way I can eat such a generous serving in one sitting."

"I understand. Can I get you another box?"

"Yes, please. And if you can go ahead and bring my check, I'd appreciate it."

"Yes, ma'am. Can I interest you in a dessert to go? Tiramisu, maybe?"

She smiled and shook her head. "I'll have to pass."

In a few minutes, she boxed up the remaining half of her meal, all the while keeping tabs on Forbes's table to make sure they didn't leave before she managed to get over there or catch his eye. She left enough cash in the black folder with the receipt to cover a generous tip and picked up her purse, planner, and to-go boxes.

She crossed the room, stopping twice to speak to acquaintances and see baby pictures or leave a few business cards for any newly engaged couples they might know. Keeping her attention anywhere but on the handsome stranger proved difficult. She must learn his identity.

When she drew near, Forbes glanced in her direction. "Here's someone you should meet," he said to his dinner companion. Forbes stood to draw her into a hug, his grin creasing the corners of his grayish blue eyes.

"Hey. I didn't want to interrupt, but I couldn't just leave without stopping to speak to you." She turned and smiled at the stranger, who'd also stood. He was a couple of inches taller than she, but more slender than the men she usually found attractive. She gazed into eyes the color of light-roast cinnamon hazelnut coffee, and her heart fluttered. Fluttered! Like some addlepated schoolgirl.

She regained control of her senses and extended her right hand. "Good evening. I'm Anne Hawthorne."

His grasp was firm, his skin soft. He worked indoors, probably at the law firm with Forbes. Then why hadn't she met him at the office Christmas party?

"George Laurence, ma'am, at your service."

Tingles danced up and down her spine. A British accent! She'd always dreamed of marrying a man with a British accent.

Get ahold of yourself, girl! You're thirty-five years old, not some starry-eyed teenager. "It's very nice to meet you, Mr. Laurence. So how do you know Forbes?"

The Englishman cleared his throat and looked at her cousin. She frowned.

Forbes rested his hand on her shoulder. "George. . .represents someone I work with."

Hopefully he wasn't in town briefly for a trial or something like that. "So you're a lawyer, too, Mr. Laurence?"

"Not exactly." Had he grimaced? Frowned? Grinned? The expression was there and gone before she could be certain.

"It's complicated, Anne." Forbes squeezed her shoulder. "I thought you were waiting on someone, or we would have asked you to join us. How was your dinner, by the way?"

Okay, obviously this guy was working on some case that was so confidential they couldn't even discuss it in front of her. "The food was great. I hadn't planned on eating alone tonight, but you know, 'the best-laid plans. . .' " Her cheeks burned as she was conscious of George Laurence standing next to her. Time to try to make a graceful exit. "Well, I'd best be going. As I said, I didn't want to interrupt."

"George, if you'll excuse me for a minute, I'd like to walk Anne out to her car." Forbes herded her toward the front door, stopping with alacrity, although only for a moment, when a family acquaintance recognized them. On the way past the hostess stand, Anne took one more peek at George Laurence, now sitting by himself at the table. Handsome, British, and at least six foot two.

She bit her bottom lip to contain her grin and braced herself for the heat as the air-conditioning chased them out the door. "Why haven't I ever met him before?"

"Because he just arrived in town today." Forbes tucked her left hand under the crook of his elbow, then took her food boxes and planner. "All kidding aside, what happened with your date, Annie?"

"I don't know. I was running a few minutes late, and when I arrived, he wasn't here. After I'd been here awhile, I called to check to see when he was coming, and some gal at his office told me he'd gotten called in for a breaking news story. So I had dinner by myself—" Her left heel caught in a crack in the cement parking lot and the shoe twisted out from under her. Thank goodness for Forbes's supporting arm, or she would have fallen face-first onto the pavement—which would have been a fitting end to a night like this.

"Maybe it just wasn't meant to be."

"He left word that he'd call me tomorrow." She stopped at her car, pressing the unlock button on her key-fob remote, and took her food and planner from her cousin. Forbes opened the door for her, and she ducked in to set her things atop a stack of files on the passenger seat. She narrowly missed hitting her head on the door frame as she stood. "Of course, I can't imagine why he'd rather go out with me and not with Jenn."

Forbes placed his hands on her cheeks and pulled her close to kiss her forehead. "Because you are a beautiful and interesting woman, Anne. Any man would be lucky to have you. If we weren't related—" He waggled his well-groomed eyebrows.

She groaned. "Forbes! I really wish you'd stop saying that. It's bad enough that half your coworkers think I'm your wife because you take me to every office party." If they weren't related, he'd never have given her a second glance. Not someone as good looking and popular as he'd always been. Of course, she had somehow been noticed by—

No. She'd already determined not to think about that tonight. That part of her life was long over and done with. "Tell me about this George guy."

"He's not for you, Anne."

"I didn't notice a wedding ring."

"No." Forbes ran his fingers through his short, dark auburn hair. She narrowed her eyes and crossed her arms. Forbes never touched his hair for fear of messing it up.

"Just take my word for it. He's—not available."

"Oh, so he's—" She stopped when he pressed his fingers to her lips.

"Not available. Leave it at that, please?" He kissed her forehead again. "Now, go home and get some rest. I'm sure you have a very busy day tomorrow."

"Rest?" She kept from snorting as a rueful laugh escaped, but just barely. "Do you see the stack of file folders on the passenger seat? It's a wedding weekend, honey. I wouldn't have taken the time to do more than pick something up at Rotier's on my way home tonight if Jenn hadn't insisted I go out with—" She snapped her fingers, her mind drawing a blank on her no-show date's name.

"Danny?" Forbes prompted.

"Yes. With Danny." She opened the car door. "Oh, and Forbes?"

"Yes?"

"Should your friend George ever become not *not available*, you'll let me know, right?"

"You'll definitely be the first person I'll tell. Good night, Anne."

She waved as he walked away, then got in the car and put the top down to enjoy the evening air.

Whatever Forbes meant by "not available," God hadn't let her cross paths with George Laurence for no reason. For the first time in her life, she wasn't just going to take Forbes's word.

❧

George sipped his water. *Anne Hawthorne.* Something about her just wouldn't let him be. She was pretty, yes. Tall for a woman, with a striking figure as well. But he'd met hundreds, perhaps thousands of beautiful women in his life. No, it was something in the expression of her eyes—something real that he wasn't used to seeing.

Setting his goblet back on the table, he took a deep breath and blew it out. *Lord, how did I get rooked into this scheme? I only signed the first contract five years ago because it ensured me a work visa and job security. This is the first time since then I've truly resented anything my employer has asked me to do. How can I live a life pleasing to You if I'm practicing deception? Yet how can I refuse when it means going back to England? If You can just get me through the next seventeen months until I can apply for citizenship—*

The chair across the table scraped against the ceramic tiles. George conjured a smile for Forbes. How did this man know Anne Hawthorne?

"Sorry about that. Dessert?"

George declined. "You know the wedding planner well, then?"

"The—Anne? Yes, I've known her all my life. She's my cousin."

His cousin. George kept his grin in check. Whether she was his cousin or his sweetheart shouldn't matter. She was still beyond his reach. The contract addendum litigated that. Maybe once his employer revealed the truth at the engagement party. . .

But by then, George would have been lying to this woman for more than a month. She would hate him, and her hatred would be well deserved. By then, he would probably hate himself as well.

To keep from dwelling on such thoughts, he turned his attention to his dinner companion. "When will the plumbing be repaired so Mrs. Agee and I can move into the house?"

"A few days more—probably next Monday or Tuesday. When does Miss Landry arrive?"

"Sunday evening. She has planned to lodge with a childhood friend while in town."

"Good." Forbes folded his napkin and laid it beside his empty plate. "Although it's not generally known who owns the house, it's better if she is seen only with and around people she's known all her life. Less suspicion will be raised that way."

"Would it be better if I stayed elsewhere?" Although he loathed the idea of spending the next five weeks in a hotel, better that than reveal his employer's secret before the time of his employer's choosing.

"No. I think you'll be fine staying out there. The rumor around town is that the property was purchased by a wealthy out-of-towner, and you'll serve as the mysterious, eccentric new owner for the time being."

"Does Mrs. Agee know—?"

"Who her real employer is? No. She signed a contract with a confidentiality clause, but we felt at this time she didn't have a need to know. When the time is right, she'll be informed."

George nodded at the waitress to take his dinner plate and waved off the dessert menu. "And Ms. Hawthorne? If she were to sign a confidentiality agreement?"

"No." Forbes's expression became courtroom-caliber serious. "She is not to be told until the day of the engagement party. I don't—she doesn't need to know you aren't Courtney Landry's fiancé. Of course, that means you will have to handle some details yourself."

Some details? George nearly laughed at the understatement. How was Anne Hawthorne supposed to pull together an engagement party when seeing the invite list might tip her off as to the true identity of her client? And what about the invitation itself? It couldn't have the name George Laurence on it. He'd have to do that, too. The more he thought about the event, the more tasks he discovered would fall to him to accomplish.

At least the next few weeks wouldn't be boring.

As she climbed the back stairs to her apartment, Anne juggled her duffel bag, attaché case, purse, stack of files, and the cup of gourmet coffee she'd stopped for on the way home. As soon as she dropped everything but the coffee cup on the kitchen table, she realized she'd left the food in the car.

She jogged back downstairs, retrieved it, and went up to the apartment on the third floor where, as she expected, the door was unlocked. In the dark kitchen, she found a grease pencil in a junk drawer, wrote a note on the lid of the top Styrofoam box, and put them both in Jenn's refrigerator.

Back in her own apartment, she turned on the computer in the guest bedroom, started the music media software, and filled the apartment with the dulcet tones of crooners such as Frank Sinatra, Ella Fitzgerald, Bing Crosby, Kay Starr, and her favorite of all, Dean Martin.

Singing along with Dean's "Ain't That a Kick in the Head," she returned to the kitchen and retrieved her mail from the floor where Jenn or Meredith had slid it under her back door.

She'd be surprised if George Laurence was any younger than forty.

Astonished by the wayward thought, warmth washed over her at the memory of the intensity of his gaze earlier.

Since her broken engagement ten years ago, every time she'd felt the least attracted to a man, her internal alarms had gone off. She trusted the instincts born of experience to keep her from being hurt again. But the entire time she'd stood there talking to George Laurence, all she'd felt was a profound sense of interest in getting to know him better.

God, what are You trying to tell me? Is he the one? Is this finally the answer to my prayer for a husband?

No answer came to her over the soft warbling of Frank Sinatra crooning "The Coffee Song." The fact that her mind had instantly jumped to wondering if George Laurence was her future husband did bother her a bit. After everything she'd been through, the desire to maintain her independence—as a person and as a professional— kept her working eighteen to twenty hours nearly every day. Yet deep down, she just wanted to fall in love with someone and experience his falling in love with her in return. Not wanting anything from her, just loving her.

George Laurence seemed like the kind of man who had everything together. His expensive suit and shoes, grooming, and impeccable manners stood as proof of an established man comfortable with himself and those around him. So many of the men she'd gone out with at her cousins' behest were still trying to "find" themselves, even into their late thirties or early forties, and wanted to be with a woman who would have a stabilizing influence on them.

Anne, however, didn't want that kind of turmoil in her life. She wanted a man who knew what he wanted out of life, a man comfortable with himself, and with simple tastes—classic music and movies, dining out—who didn't mind the hours she put into her business.

Her phone chirped the *Pink Panther* theme. She unclipped it, flipped it open, and pressed it to her ear. "I wondered when you were going to call."

Meredith laughed. "I didn't figure you'd be home any earlier than now, but if you were still on your date and having a good time, you wouldn't answer. So?"

She filled her cousin in on the evening, and by the time she got to seeing Forbes, she heard Meredith's SUV pull up the driveway. Although she trusted her completely, something kept Anne from telling her about how she felt when she met George Laurence. Anne wasn't sure herself what her feelings meant. She needed time to pray. . .and time to get to know him better.

"Do you want to come up for a few minutes?" Anne asked, crossing to the kitchen window that overlooked the carport.

"You working tonight?"

"Yeah."

"Just for a minute, then—Jenn sent some peach cobbler for you."

Anne opened the door and closed the phone. Meredith Guidry's strawberry blond head came into sight in the dim stairwell. Anne met her on the landing and accepted a plastic tub of the still-warm dessert while leaning forward to kiss Meredith's cheek.

"Did y'all have fun tonight?" She ushered Meredith into the kitchen.

"Turned out to be just Jenn, Jason, Rafe, and me. Seems it was a big night to have other plans. How much work do you have left to do tonight?"

"A few hours. What was Rafe's big announcement?" Anne closed the door and leaned against the kitchen cabinet. Meredith, Forbes, and Jenn's younger brother piloted the private jets owned by their parents' commercial real estate and investment corporation.

"He took a job with Charter Air as a senior pilot or something like that. He said he wanted to do more flying and less paperwork—Daddy had him working in the capital ventures office when he wasn't flying. Since Mama and Daddy aren't traveling as much, they decided to sell off the two company jets and sign a contract with this charter service."

Anne's stomach churned at the thought of flying.

"Of course, that means Rafe will be gone a lot more now," Meredith continued. "Most of his flights will be single-day round-trips, but occasionally he'll be gone overnight. He's going to get to fly bigger planes, too. Not the big commercial planes, but the kind that carry about thirty passengers—"

Bile rose in the back of Anne's throat, and clamminess spread over her skin. That was the same size plane. . .

"Oh, Annie, I'm so sorry. I didn't mean to remind you of—here." Meredith pulled over one of the tall, ladder-back chairs from the table. "Sit down and put your head between your knees."

Anne sank into the chair, drew a few deep breaths, and tried to smile. "I'm okay. It's been a long time since I've had that kind of reaction just from someone talking about planes."

"You sure you're okay?" Meredith crossed the kitchen, took a glass out of the cabinet, filled it with water from the refrigerator door, and handed it to Anne.

Anne sipped it and pressed the cold glass to her forehead. "I guess I'm just tired. You'd think after twenty-seven years and thousands of hours of therapy, I'd be over the fear."

Meredith gave her a sympathetic smile and rested her hand on Anne's shoulder. "I'm so sorry."

Patting Meredith's hand, Anne set the glass on the table and rose, her knees not too weak to support her. "I know you are. If you talk to Rafe before Sunday, tell him congrats from me."

"I will. Good night, Anne."

"Sweet dreams, Mere."

Shutting the door behind her cousin, Anne took a few more deep breaths and tried to put the images and sensations from a lifetime ago out of her head. The best way was to concentrate on something else.

Work.

For the next two hours, she focused on entering data into the software her cousin Jason had written for her to help with organizing seating arrangements at events, then moved on to making lists of everything that needed to happen in the next forty-eight hours—not just for the wedding on Saturday, but for weddings coming up in the next few weeks as well.

Why was George Laurence in town, and why was Forbes being so secretive about it?

She shook her head and returned her attention to the half-finished checklist on her computer screen—and saw she'd typed George Laurence's name. She deleted it and continued working, only to have the memory of their brief encounter pop up when least expected.

At 2:00 a.m., she finished the last list, saved everything, e-mailed the files to herself at work, and shut down her computer. When she finally climbed into bed, she grabbed her burgundy fabric–covered prayer journal and fountain pen filled with purple ink from the nightstand:

June 1—Lord, I know there's a reason why You had me meet George Laurence tonight. I've never felt this way about any other man I've only just met. Could he be the one You've had me waiting on for so long? I don't know what Forbes meant by "not available," but I do intend to find out. You showed me tonight that I need to take that first step on my road to my own happy ending. Thank You, Lord, for the confirmation I've made the right decision.

She set the journal aside and pulled out her worn, black leather Bible, flipping it open to where the ribbon held her place from this morning. She'd read the twenty-seventh Psalm many times in her life, but this night, the last two verses stuck in her mind: *I would have despaired unless I had believed that I would see the goodness of the Lord in the land of the living. Wait for the Lord; be strong and let your heart take courage; yes, wait for the Lord.*

She closed her eyes and cleared her mind. "Lord, I've been waiting for a very long time. Please let this be the answer to my prayer. Let George Laurence be the one."

CHAPTER 3

The bell on the front door of Anne's office jingled at 9:50 Monday morning. She looked up from Saturday night's invoices, which she'd been entering into her expenses spreadsheet. Her heart thudded. Dressed in a dark gray suit, a white button-down, and a colorful tie, George Laurence cut a dashing figure. More slender than she'd remembered from last Thursday, but with broad shoulders that suggested he worked out.

She saved the Excel document and went around the desk to greet him. What was he doing here? Had he gotten her office address from Forbes? Had his "not available" status changed over the weekend? And who was the young woman—"Courtney? Courtney Landry?"

The beautiful brunette stepped forward and extended both hands. "Miss Anne! I was so afraid you wouldn't recognize me."

Anne clasped the girl's hands, and they exchanged kisses on the cheek. "How could I not? Your sister Brittany's wedding was only last summer. You'd just graduated from high school, if I remember. Did you enjoy your first year of college? UCLA, right?"

Courtney's perfect, homecoming-queen features glowed. "Right. It was *awesome*. I loved it. It seems like a long time since you used to come over and babysit and tutor me in—well, everything." She squeezed Anne's hands. "I set up the appointment for today because I want you to plan my wedding. There isn't anyone else in the world I trust more than you to pull it together exactly the way I imagine—like, even better, I'm sure."

"Your—" Anne's heart dropped into her left big toe. She glanced over Courtney's shoulder at George Laurence, who stood in profile looking at photos of previous events on her wall. The name Landry was all that had downloaded from the request form on her Web site for ten o'clock Monday morning—now. "Wait a minute. Are you telling me that you—that you and he—" She swallowed hard. "Congratulations, Courtney. Why don't we sit down and discuss your ideas."

She couldn't meet George Laurence's gaze as she waited for him and Courtney to be seated on the Chippendale-style sofa under the picture window. "Can I get anything for either of you? Coffee? Tea? Water?"

Courtney shook her head as she sat. George also declined. He lowered himself onto the love seat a good six inches from Courtney.

Odd. Without exception, every couple who'd sat across from her in their initial consultation couldn't keep from touching each other—holding hands, his arm around her, her hand on his knee, some kind of contact. George Laurence, however, was as stiff as Courtney was animated when she started talking about her ideas for a grand outdoor wedding at a plantation home down on River Road. Could be a cultural difference. She'd never had a British client before.

Thursday night, she'd been so sure he was "the one." How could God have put that attraction in her if He hadn't meant for her to be with this man? She had to stop thinking about him. Focus on the wedding. His wedding. She swallowed hard and realized the girl had stopped talking. "That sounds lovely. Have you determined a budget yet?"

Courtney cast a furtive glance at George, her cheeks turning a becoming shade of pink. "Um, there really isn't, like, a set limit on what we can spend."

Anne frowned. "I'm not certain I understand what you mean." She looked at George, but his bland expression betrayed nothing.

"I mean, Cl—" Courtney broke into a coughing fit, bringing a delicate hand up to cover her mouth.

Anne leaped up and went around to the small refrigerator hidden in the base of one of her built-in cabinets. She took two bottles of water back with her and handed one to Courtney. George waved off the one she offered him as he pressed the blue silk handkerchief from his coat pocket into Courtney's hand. The expression on his face showed more fatherly concern than romantic interest.

Yes, that was part of it. Part of what bothered her. The age difference. George Laurence had to be older than Anne herself, while Courtney wasn't quite twenty. What was he thinking, marrying a girl half his age?

"I'm so sorry," Courtney said after taking a swig of the water. "Must be allergies or something." She looked at George before taking a deep breath and continuing. "Anyway, what I was saying is that my fiancé, well, I don't even know how to say this without sounding, like, stuck up, but he has, y'know, a lot of money."

Anne couldn't look at him. Why was he leaving this all up to Courtney? Why couldn't he come out and say it himself?

"He told me I could have anything I wanted, no matter what the cost." Courtney's eyes took on a dreamy quality. "Miss Anne, do you think it would be wrong of me to get married in a pink dress? I saw a picture in one of the magazines—I should have brought it with me—some actress or singer who just got married wore a green dress because green is, like, her favorite color. My favorite color is pink, and I've always dreamed of getting married in a pink dress like the one Princess Aurora wore at the end of *Sleeping Beauty*, y'know?"

Pink? Anne still tried to fathom the idea of a budgetless wedding. "I'm positive we can find the perfect dress for you." She turned to George, sitting so erect his back hardly touched the sofa cushion, hands clasped in his lap. "I realize you've told Courtney she can have whatever she wants no matter the cost, but can you give me a ballpark figure so I can start working up a plan of action?"

"I've—it's just as she said: whatever she wants, no matter the cost."

Really? Anne bit the inside of her cheek to keep her grin intact. Going to play that way, huh? Well, his "no matter the cost" would be put to the test as soon as she could sit down at the computer and start working up a plan based on everything Courtney said she wanted. No calling in favors from childhood friends on this wedding. If he really meant what he said, all of her vendors—*all* of them—would be rewarded for every discount, freebie, or no-charge delivery they'd ever given her. And for the first time, she might actually get her full fee, on time.

She picked up her planner. "Let's talk dates."

"Third Saturday in October," Courtney said. "That's the date we've chosen. Oh, but we want to have an engagement party the Friday after the Fourth of July."

Five weeks for the engagement party and four and a half months for the wedding. If she truly had unlimited financial resources, no problem. Anne had planned to take the weekend after the Fourth off, but for a commission this size. . .

"Let's see. That would be Friday, July seventh. . . ." She marked the date in July, then flipped to October. Nothing else on her calendar for that week. "Both dates look good." She closed the planner. "Now here's what we do next: I'll work up a proposal, complete with a budget, based on what you've told me, as well as a contract. If I can get an e-mail address, I can send both to you for review before our next meeting. Can you come in at three o'clock Thursday?"

George pulled out a touch-screen PDA and tapped away at the surface with a stylus. "Thursday afternoon looks clear." He clipped the thing onto his belt and reached into his shirt pocket, withdrawing a business card.

Anne took the card, hoping to get some idea of who this guy was. Against a plain white background, all she saw was GEORGE F. LAURENCE in the middle with his mobile number—a New York area code—at the bottom left and an e-mail address at his own dot-com on the right. Aha. If he had his own Web site, she could look it up and find out more about him.

Standing, she gave each of them one of her cards. "If you think of anything else you'd like me to figure into the plan, please call."

Courtney came around the coffee table to hug her again. "Thank you, Miss Anne. I know I'm going to have so much fun working with you."

"I'm delighted to have the opportunity." She walked arm in arm with Courtney to the door. "I'm serious. Call me if you think of anything. I'm available all hours, not just when I'm in the office."

"Thanks." Courtney grinned.

Anne turned and extended her hand to George. "Mr. Laurence, it was nice to see you again."

He shook hands with firm brevity. "Ms. Hawthorne." He bowed his head slightly and opened the door for Courtney.

She kept her smile pasted on until they were past her front windows, then spun on her not-too-high heels and crossed to her computer. If he had his own dot-com e-mail address, he must have a Web site. She opened a new Internet window and entered the address. The high-speed cable connection paused for a moment; then an error message popped up on the screen: WARNING! YOU DO NOT HAVE PERMISSION TO ACCESS THIS PAGE. She tried refreshing the page, but the same warning came up. So she did a Google search for his name. Lots of genealogy sites with George Laurences listed, but nothing that seemed to point toward the man who'd just shattered her girlish hopes and dreams of the past several days.

She slumped forward until her forehead touched the screen. "God, why are You doing this to me? Why did he have to turn out to be some kind of eccentric millionaire who's into much younger women? Why couldn't he have turned out to be a nice, simple British guy who likes old movies and Dean Martin?"

❧

"I don't think this plan is going to work." George turned down the volume of the Rat Pack & Friends satellite radio station and adjusted the hands-free earpiece of his mobile phone.

"What happened?" Digital static crackled through Forbes Guidry's voice.

"She thinks I'm some sort of debaucher of young women."

"What?"

George had to smile at the astonishment in Forbes's voice. "She didn't say it in so many words, but I could tell from her expression when she first realized why we were there."

"From Anne's expression? She's usually so good at hiding what she's thinking, even from those of us who know her best."

"I think Ms. Hawthorne is suspicious of the nature of my relationship with Miss Landry. And with every right to be so. Why would a man forty-one years old be marrying a girl half his age— less than half his age?" *Especially a man like me at whom no woman would ever look twice?* George shook off the negative thought and turned the leased Mercedes Roadster convertible into the driveway that should lead to his employer's nineteenth-century home.

"Anne's pretty open-minded. I mean, she does have high morals, but when she takes on clients, she doesn't let things like age differences in the couple interfere with her job."

Enormous oak trees lined the narrow road, creating a canopy over-head that allowed no sunlight through. George removed his sunglasses and slowed the car. After five nights in a hotel, he hoped all the plumbing repairs were indeed completed. He didn't want to wake up in the middle of the night with water dripping on his head, as Forbes told him the leak had been over the basement service quarters.

Anne might be open-minded, but he'd seen the look of pure astonishment in her eyes for a split second before she'd slipped into her professional persona. "Look, mate, she's your cousin, and you know her better than I do. I just don't want to see anyone get hurt because of this."

The tree-shaded drive rounded a corner to reveal a magnificent mansion, just like the kind used in movies about the American Civil War. "Love a duck," George breathed, stopping the car to drink in the view.

"I beg your pardon?" Humor laced Forbes's baritone voice.

"Oh, sorry. I've just seen the house."

"Pretty amazing, isn't it?"

"I'll say." Red brick with a white-pillared porch dominating the front, the manse loomed ever larger as he drove closer.

"Listen, you focus on getting settled in and don't worry about Anne. If she has a problem with you or the situation, believe me, you'll know about it. With Anne, you don't have to guess."

George bade the lawyer farewell, ended the call, and followed the paved carriageway to the separate garage building in the back. The land sloped down toward a large pond, exposing the basement level of the house. Mrs. Agee, the housekeeper, had moved in yesterday, but when George tried the main service entrance, it was locked. He punched in the security code Forbes had given him on the panel beside the door and entered.

"Hello?" His voice echoed through the shadowy interior of a cavernous kitchen fitted out with enormous commercial-grade appliances set in redwood cabinetry with gray granite countertops.

"Someone there?" A woman's voice came from a hall to his right, and bright lights blazed, momentarily blinding George.

"Mrs. Agee?"

An African-American woman entered the kitchen—tall, softly built, her gray hair kept back from her angelic face with a flowery scarf. "I've been expectin' you for a couple of hours now." She crossed the room, right hand extended. "I'm Keturah Agee, but you can just call me Mama Ketty."

Now he was almost certain he'd stepped out of real life and onto a movie set. He shook her hand. "George Laurence."

"Let's get you settled in, baby, and then we can discuss business matters."

He followed her through the stone-arch doorway into a hall with gleaming wood floors. The corridor extended the same short distance to the left and right of the doorway.

"I've taken up residence in the suite on the left." She pulled a key out of the pocket of her khaki pants.

The antique brass key was heavy in his hand. "Is locking the doors necessary inside the house?"

"It will be if there's ever a party here and this lower level is swarming with caterers and day-hires." She looked at the gold pendant watch hanging from a long chain around her neck. "It's nearly three. Can I make you some tea?"

Teatime really wasn't until four. "I'd love some."

She smiled, showing a full set of straight, white teeth and dimples in both cheeks. "I'll put the water on while you get yourself settled in."

By the time he'd gotten his two suitcases and hanging bag out of the car, the teakettle whistled, drowning out Mama Ketty's humming. She winked at him as he wheeled the luggage through the kitchen. He paused at the door to his room, hoping it was large enough that he wouldn't be tripping over the end of the bed, as in his room in the New York town house.

The door swung open on silent hinges. The dark wood flooring continued into a long but very narrow room. Well, if he was going to have to stay in the tiny space, at least it had a large window overlooking the back lawn and the pond. He opened the door to his left, expecting an equally small bath, and entered a second, much larger room.

In relief, he sank onto the queen-size bed that sat on a plain metal frame under another large window. Dark wainscoting gave way at waist height to walls painted hunter green. Two more doors revealed a walk-in closet and a large private bath.

He'd have to go furniture shopping, but the size of the suite more than made up for being sent into exile for nearly five months.

The sweet aroma of cinnamon and vanilla drew him back out into the kitchen. He sat in one of the tall chairs at the bar on the back side of the island. Mama Ketty set a white cup and saucer in front of him along with a dessert plate piled with sweets and pastries.

He'd just bitten into an oatmeal cookie when a chime reverberated through the room.

Mama Ketty looked perplexed. "Someone's at the front door."

"I'd best go see who it is." He stood, then looked around. He didn't know how to access the main portion of the house.

"Beyond the pantry." Mama Ketty indicated the opposite side of the kitchen from their suites. "Enter the security code before you open the door at the top. The upstairs is on a different zone than down here."

He jogged up the enclosed wooden staircase and found himself in another kitchen—smaller but still well appointed. He crossed to the swinging white door and exited into a wide foyer. The hall ran the length of the house, the front door on the opposite end. Two figures stood on the other side of the etched oval glass; he entered the security code and slid the dead bolt lock open.

"Miss—"

"George!" Courtney stepped forward and hugged him. "Mama had to come by and see the house." She gazed at him with wide eyes begging him to maintain his fictitious identity.

Forcing a smile, he stepped back and motioned the two women in. The only similarity between daughter and mother was their chestnut hair. Courtney, about average height, possessed a natural grace and a dancer's figure. Her mother, however. . .

The cloying odor of an entire flower garden preceded the woman into the house. Dressed in a bright pink sateen jogging suit, she sported overly large sunglasses, which she pulled down to the tip of her nose with claws painted to match her outfit.

"Mrs. Landry." He took her proffered hand, hoping her nails wouldn't impale him. "It is nice to finally meet you."

She looked him over from head to toe and raised her painted-on eyebrows. "So you're the cause of this. To think, my own daughter springing a surprise like this on me. She used to tell me everything, you know. Humph. I expected you'd be—"

Younger. So had Anne Hawthorne.

"Taller." Mrs. Landry brushed past him.

Courtney shrugged and cocked her head to the side in an apologetic gesture. He followed along behind as Courtney explored the house with her mother. He'd served in some of the largest estates in Britain yet was impressed by the obvious care taken in the restoration of this property.

"Oh, I have the perfect pink faux-fur rug for this room. It would make such a cute nursery." Mrs. Landry gave George a significant look over her shoulder from the doorway of the last room on the third floor.

He shuddered internally as he inclined his head toward the woman who fit the stereotype of nouveaux riches every person in the service industry feared working for.

Courtney checked her watch. "Oh, Mama, we need to go if you're going to have time to get ready for the homeowners' association meeting tonight."

He stepped out on the front porch with them, astonished to see a Rolls-Royce in the driveway. The chauffeur scrambled out and opened the back door.

"Mama, you go on. I need to speak with George for a moment." Courtney watched her mother climb into the car. As soon as the door closed, she turned back to look up at George. "I'm so sorry I sprung that on you without any warning. My friend I thought I was going to stay with ended up going to Australia for the summer, so I'm having to stay with Mama instead."

"And she didn't know you were engaged?"

"Not until I told her at breakfast this morning right before you and me went to meet Miss Anne. Mama wanted me to go to the beauty salon with her and was like, 'Where are you going?' And I was all, 'I have plans.' But she was like, 'You just got here—how can you have plans?' and got all up in my face until I blurted out where we were going. It wasn't exactly how I wanted to tell her—I wanted her to find out when everyone else does at the engagement party." She grabbed his hands and stood on tiptoe to kiss his cheek.

"Thanks for playing along."

Mentally, George added elocution lessons to the etiquette he planned to teach Courtney between now and the engagement party. "That's what I'm here for."

"Come to dinner with us tonight?"

"Of course."

She gave him directions to the restaurant, although he'd Map-Quest it as soon as he got inside. He waited on the porch until the car disappeared between the tree rows, then leaned against the front door after closing it and resetting the alarm. The deception had just gotten a little bigger. Now Courtney's mother believed he was the fiancé. But concealing the truth of his identity from the wedding planner had felt much worse than this.

The wedding planner.

He cut off all the lights and descended toward the service level. Anne Hawthorne.

When he'd seen her at the restaurant, he'd immediately wanted to get to know her better. No one had affected him like that in a very long time. And he must lie to her to protect his employer's identity and keep his job.

He shook his head as he regained his seat at the island. The next five weeks were going to be, *like*, the longest of his life.

Chapter 4

"What in the world is wrong with you, Grumpy McGrouch?"

Sitting at the large table in the back room of her cousin Jenn's rustic seafood restaurant Monday evening, Anne thought she was doing a good job of hiding her emotions. But Jenn was right: Anne had been in a bad mood ever since Courtney and her fiancé had left her office that morning. *Not available*. Just wait until Forbes got here!

"No joke," chimed in Meredith. "All you've done since you walked in is shred every napkin on the table. Was the wedding this weekend really that bad?"

Anne glanced around at the blizzard of white paper on the table. "I'm sorry, y'all. I asked for us to have dinner tonight instead of Thursday, and here I am being completely unsociable. It's just been—a stressful day."

Meredith squeezed Anne's shoulder. "No, we're sorry for teasing you."

Jenn flopped into the chair on her other side. "Hey, you were going to tell us about that guy you saw. The one having dinner with Forbes the other night. Forbes is running late. So tell us."

Anne snorted. "Well, when I first saw him, I thought he was handsome—and I seriously felt like maybe God had finally answered my prayers." She crossed her arms and slouched down in the plush red chair.

"But something changed?" Meredith prompted, pushing back a piece of hair back from Anne's face and letting her hand rest on Anne's shoulder.

"He's *engaged*. He and his fiancée were my ten o'clock consultation this morning."

"Oh, Annie." Jenn vigorously rubbed Anne's other shoulder.

"That's not the worst part. The worst part is that his fiancée is Courtney Landry."

Meredith cocked her head. "Courtney. . .which one is she?"

"The baby. The one who's barely nineteen years old. I mean, this guy has to be at least forty. You'd think Forbes—"

"Did I hear my name?"

"Speak of the devil." Jenn stood to allow her oldest brother to take the chair on Anne's left.

"Devil indeed." Anne punched him in the arm as soon as he sat down. *"Not available?"*

"Ouch! Wha—?"

"George Laurence! I felt like such an idiot this morning when he and his fiancée walked into my office. The least you could've done was tell me he's engaged. Then I wouldn't have—" Oops, she'd almost said too much.

Forbes stood and shrugged out of his suit jacket. "Wouldn't have what?"

She scrambled for something believable. "Wouldn't have acted so surprised when they walked in."

"You didn't have their names written down in your calendar?" Forbes sat and shoved the pile of shredded napkins to the middle of the large round table. "Really, Anne, you're usually so much more organized than that."

That little half grin, dimple, and sparkle in his blue eyes weren't going to work this time. "When the information downloaded from the Web site, all it had was her last name, which is pretty common in this state, if you haven't noticed. I arranged the appointment by e-mail, and she never signed her name to any of the correspondence."

"But it's going to be worth it, huh?" He nudged her with his elbow.

"Hrrrrr." She groaned, smiled, and shook her head. "Yeah, it's going to be more than worth it—if they're telling me the truth."

Forbes's left eyebrow shot up. "What leads you to believe they're not telling you the truth?"

"No limits to what can be spent? Come on. Everyone has their limits."

"Oh." He loosened his tie and turned to look over his left shoulder. "Hey, Jenn?" he called across the room to his sister.

She waved at him but didn't turn from her conversation with two of her servers. When she was finished, she rejoined them. "What's up?"

"That new music come in yet?"

"Yep—even those tracks Annie wanted me to order." Jenn poked Anne's shoulder. "And I just want you to know, those were hard to come by, too."

"Thanks. I've got to expose y'all to the classics. All this new music—"

"Good grief!" Jason, a younger cousin to all of them, flopped into the chair beside Meredith. "Karaoke hasn't even started, and she's already griping about modern music."

Anne laughed along with them. She'd save the lecture for the next couple choosing their reception music. Once the other cousins arrived and the food was served, they cajoled Jenn into opening up the microphone an hour early.

"You'll have to get up and do a couple of those songs you want us all to hear so much," Forbes said.

Anne shook her head, and her stomach flip-flopped. "No. You know I can't sing in front of a crowd."

"Once you're up there with the spotlight on you, you can't see anyone. Just concentrate on the words going across the TV screen, and you won't think about anyone else being here." Jenn jogged across the restaurant to the stage.

The rest of her cousins caught on to Forbes's suggestion and started chanting Anne's name. A bit of feedback quieted the now-packed restaurant. Anne angled her chair to see the stage better.

"Welcome to the Fishin' Shack, where every night is family-friendly karaoke." Jenn's announcement and following dialogue with her patrons got the crowd riled up. "Now I see the sign-up list is already pretty full." She pointed at the small whiteboard beside the stage. "And I usually open it up to the first person on the list. But tonight, we have a special request from the large party in the back." She cupped her hand around her mouth and whispered, "That would be my crazy family."

The men at the table stood and cheered as if their football team had just scored a touchdown.

Jenn's eye-roll was easy to see from across the room. "Anyway, if you've looked at the new music list tonight, you may have noticed some strange titles. Anne—why don't you come up here and entertain us with one of them?"

Anne's cheeks burned. She hated being put on the spot—especially when it meant public humiliation. The cousins started chanting her name again. She narrowed her eyes and grimaced at them before rising and crossing the dining room. She took the list from Jenn and picked out the first song title she recognized, pointing out the number to the sound guy.

Jenn hadn't been lying. Once she stood on the platform, she couldn't see anything but dark shadows beyond the bright spotlight.

The trumpet blast that started Dean Martin's "Ain't That a Kick in the Head" drew whoops and cheers from the crowd. She smiled and started singing—nervous at first, then with growing confidence as she lost herself in one of her favorite singer's signature songs.

She didn't do it justice, but she did have fun. The audience cheered and clapped when the music ended. The next person, an older gentleman, took the microphone from her but stopped her with a hand on her arm. "I haven't heard that song since the last time I saw the Rat Pack on stage in Vegas. Good choice."

Several people stopped her on her way back to the table to let her know how much they'd enjoyed the song.

❧

"And we ought to see if that Elvis impersonator Sara had at her reception is available. You don't want your uncle Billy Joe doing it once he gets into the beer."

George coughed and reached for his water glass. Since sitting down for dinner at the upscale restaurant, one absurd comment after another had spewed forth from Mrs. Landry's mouth, nearly bringing the half-chewed food back out as well.

If Courtney's shoulders drooped any lower, she'd be under the table. His heart twisted with compassion for the young woman. To be so browbeaten by a woman with such poor taste. He steeled himself to do what he'd been dreading all evening—living up to his namesake and facing the dragon.

He drew in a deep breath, wiped his mouth on the white cloth napkin, and laid it beside his plate. "Mrs. Landry, while I thank you for making suggestions for the wedding, I would ask that you cease now. Your daughter has hired a professional wedding planner to take care of all those details."

Mrs. Landry's mouth hung open, exhibiting the remains of the pasta she'd been chewing. "I beg your pardon!" She slammed her fork down hard enough to make the glassware on the table tremble and clink together. "Courtney, are you going to sit there and let him talk to me like that?"

Tears brimmed in the girl's eyes. "Mama, please. You're making a scene."

"He started it." Mrs. Landry pointed across the table at George.

How had Courtney turned out to be so delightful? He had to get her away from the harpy before Mrs. Landry ruined this experience for her. He dropped a hundred-dollar bill on the table, then stood and offered his hand to Courtney. She folded her napkin beside her plate and rose, not looking at her mother.

"Mrs. Landry, dinner was—enlightening. I will take Courtney home." He gave the sputtering older woman a curt nod and led Courtney out of the restaurant.

Outside, Courtney threw her arms around his waist. Taken aback, he froze, hands hovering away from his sides.

"Thank you so much. I've been wanting to tell her all afternoon to shut up. She offered to pay for part of the wedding, but probably only so she can have some say in what happens."

He patted her back. "Do you want her involved in the planning process?"

"No!" She released him. "I don't even want her *at* the wedding, much less having any say about it."

"Now, miss, she is your mother."

Once again, tears threatened to overflow the innocent brown eyes. "That's just it. She is my mother, and she knows exactly how to get under my skin. I don't know how I'm going to last four months in her house."

"You don't have to." The valet arrived with the car. George held the door for her, then went around and climbed in. "You're going to direct me to her house, and you are going to pack your bags and move into your fiancé's home."

Her full lips started to form into a smile. "Mama will flip when she finds out."

They'd been at the house nearly twenty minutes, and Courtney was halfway through moving her clothes from the bureau to a suitcase, when her mother stormed into the room. "Just what do you think you're doing?"

"Packing, Mama." Courtney continued arranging the folded T-shirts in a layer on top of the blue jeans.

George moved in between them as Mrs. Landry reached out to grab Courtney's arm. He intercepted her hand. "Kindly allow Miss Courtney to continue what she's doing."

Mrs. Landry gasped and jerked away. "How dare you come between me and my daughter!" Her voice rose to a pitch that would soon have all the dogs in the gated, exclusive subdivision barking. "Where do you think you're going to go? To live in *sin* with *him*?" She practically shrieked the accusatory words.

"Mama!"

"Mrs. Landry, that is quite enough." George used every ounce of training and past experience to keep his voice even and low. "Courtney is going to move into one of the third-floor bedrooms. I will be staying in a room in the basement—beside the housekeeper's room. Nothing untoward will happen."

"If you're not—then why—?"

"Because it's obvious she cannot stay here one moment longer."

"Well, I never!" Mrs. Landry folded her arms across her ample— and most likely not natural—chest. From the way her face screwed up, she seemed to be trying to conjure some tears. "I can't believe you're going to choose him over me! Is that what you really want? Because if you leave here, that's what you're doing. I'll. . .I'll never speak to you again."

Courtney kept packing; but her hands shook, and she tossed items in the suitcase haphazardly. George mirrored Mrs. Landry's movements to stay between them.

"Court?" Mrs. Landry glared at him when her daughter didn't answer. She planted her fists on her hips. "Fine. But you'll come back here begging my forgiveness before too long." She turned and flounced out of the room.

"I'm through here." Courtney slapped the lid of the suitcase down and zipped it closed. "If I've left anything behind, we can come back for it tomorrow when she's at the tanning salon."

Although happy to be leaving, George dreaded going downstairs and walking through the house again. Gold-plated cherubs and low-quality reproduction Greek and Roman statuary crowded every inch of space possible.

The wheels of the suitcase caught on the faux tiger-skin rug—at least he *hoped* it was fake—that covered Italian ceramic tile in the front foyer. He heaved the bag up and carried it to the door.

Her baggage barely fit into the car trunk.

"I'm so sorry about my mom." Courtney rested her elbow on the windowsill but leaned toward him as the cabriolet ragtop closed. He didn't want to take any chances with the thunder growling in the distance. "She always wanted to be rich—I remember she and Daddy used to argue all the time about how she wasted money on junk. Then after he died. . ."

He started the car and left with all due haste. "How long ago did your father pass away?"

"Ten years ago in April—an accident at work. Mama got a lawyer, and the chemical plant settled out of court for millions of dollars. Mama finally had more money than she could spend on all of the chintzy junk she'd always wanted. Lucky for me, she decided to send me to a private prep school, where I lived on campus nine months out of the year."

That explained how she'd escaped unspoiled. "I've seen enough people like her in my time. You don't have to apologize for her actions or words."

Thank God his employer's home lay on the other side of the city from her mother. Unfortunately, Mrs. Landry had been to the house and could probably find her way back should the fancy strike her. His stomach churned—although it could have just been hunger pains since he'd only eaten a few bites of his dinner before making the grand exit with Courtney in tow. "You don't think your mother will show up on the doorstep, do you?"

"Nope. There's no way she could find it again. She didn't pay attention on the way over, and she fired that driver this afternoon because he didn't change lanes when she told him to."

At the front door, he taught Courtney the security code to get in. She insisted on carrying two of the smaller suitcases, while he managed the large one and the hanging bag. Why had he decided to put her on the third floor? The second floor would have been much easier on his knees than climbing all these stairs.

Courtney chose the room at the end of the hall—the one that would make a "perfect nursery," and one of the few that had a full set of furniture. Pale pink walls and white and pink linens hugged the room in femininity. Perfect for the very feminine creature who stood beside him—whose stomach emitted a roaring growl.

She rubbed her tummy and grinned at him. "I'm kinda hungry. Think we can raid the kitchen?"

He returned the smile, his own stomach feeling grumbly. "I'd like to introduce you to Mama Ketty, the housekeeper and, for now, cook."

As he'd hoped, Mama Ketty cooed over Courtney and insisted on cooking dinner for her, even given the late hour of nine o'clock—Mama Ketty's normal bedtime. Mrs. Agee bustled around the kitchen in her bathrobe and slippers, silver hair mounted on enormous curlers and covered with another colorful scarf.

"Show me your room, George." Courtney slid off the barstool.

"There isn't much to show." He ushered her down the hall, opened the door, and motioned for her to enter.

"This can't be your bedroom. No, you'll have to move into one of the upstairs bedrooms."

He laughed. "No, this is just the antechamber."

She opened the second door and looked around. "Well. It's big enough." She disappeared through another door. "And the bathroom is great—better than mine at Mama's house." Coming back out, she pinned him with an amused gaze. "Tomorrow we go furniture shopping. I know you have a budget to furnish your room—I heard that part of the conversation at least. I know all the best places where you can get nice stuff cheap."

Furniture shopping with Courtney would help seal his assumed identity. He pushed aside the guilt that threatened every time he thought about the untenable situation he'd allowed himself to become entangled in. How was this going to reflect on his witness as a Christian when the truth finally came out?

"Now, George, it won't be as bad as what you're thinking—no, I can tell by your expression you don't like shopping. But it'll be fun; I promise."

He immediately composed his expression and bowed his head toward her. "As long as I don't end up with a pink faux-fur rug, I would appreciate your help."

Laughing, she tapped his arm with her fist. "Not funny."

"You two 'bout ready to eat?" Mama Ketty stood in the doorway, arms folded.

They followed her back out into the kitchen and sat at the bar, where she'd put plates piled high with scrambled eggs, bacon, sausage, and hash browns. Beside the main dish sat smaller plates with a stack of pancakes dripping with butter and syrup.

"Breakfast food's my specialty. Coffee's on—decaf—and I"—she paused to kiss Courtney on the cheek—"am going"—she kissed George's cheek—"to bed."

"Good night, Mama Ketty."

"Thank you so much, Mama Ketty," Courtney said around a bite of pancakes.

George poured coffee while Courtney wolfed down the food. She was halfway through when her cell phone sounded a familiar tune. Her eyes lit up, and her countenance glowed. To give her some privacy, he took his plate and coffee into the staff dining room—an octagonal chamber with a round, eight-person table as the centerpiece.

He'd no more than sat down when Courtney squealed with excitement and rushed into the room, phone still pressed to her ear. "Can you take me to the airport tomorrow? Charter terminal?"

He frowned but nodded. "Of course."

She jumped up and down a little bit and returned to the kitchen.

He ate slowly, enjoying the disparate flavors of the foods—the briny crisp bacon, spicy link sausage, eggs oozing with cheddar cheese, all washed down with rich, dark-roast coffee.

"I'm going to New York—and then he's taking me to Paris to

51

buy me my trousseau." Courtney leaned over him from behind, hugging him around the neck.

She'd needed something to take her mind off the scene at her mother's home. "I know you'll enjoy that."

"He also said something about apartments for me, and you could give me the addresses?"

"Of course." Three months ago George had signed leases on town houses in both cities when his employer decided to propose but wanted to keep the relationship a secret. Besides, she wouldn't have stayed in his apartment with him anyway. She wouldn't risk her reputation that way. "When do you expect to return?"

"In about three weeks."

"Three—" His mouth went dry.

"Yeah. Sorry to leave at such a crucial point in the planning, but this is the only time his schedule will allow—probably the only time we'll be able to see each other much before the wedding." She kissed his cheek. "Well, I'm off to bed. I rinsed my plates and cup and put them on the counter by the sink."

"That's fine." His mind reeled. Three weeks. The three most critical weeks for planning the engagement party—scouting out a location, securing a band, selecting invitations, creating the list. . .

And he'd have to do it alone with the most attractive woman he'd ever met.

CHAPTER 5

*L*eft on his own after Courtney's departure, George found getting out and about in Bonneterre eye-opening. The mental image he'd created of a midsized city in central Louisiana had been built solely on anecdotes of his employer's childhood and a few films he'd seen supposedly set in the area.

He hadn't quite believed he'd hear Cajun-French spoken in the stores and zydeco music on the radio or see alligators swimming around in swamps, but he also hadn't expected a teeming, modern minimetropolis, either.

Using his need for furniture as an excuse for leaving the house early each morning and not returning until late in the evening, he explored the city on his own. Although Mama Ketty fed him well, he discovered Beignets S'il Vous Plait, a chain of cafés around town that only served the powdered sugar–dusted, fried french puff pastries and the best coffee he'd ever tasted. The last three mornings, he'd started out his jaunt with a tall chicory coffee and a plate of three beignets.

He really wanted to explore Old Towne, Town Square, and the Riverwalk, but being in the vicinity of Anne Hawthorne's office with the possibility of running into her stopped him.

Slipping into the café's men's room, he washed the stickiness from his hands and checked his shirt for any signs of white dust from his morning snack. He'd have to go back to the house and change clothes before meeting with Anne this afternoon. Khaki pants and a navy polo shirt weren't his idea of a professional appearance.

He turned the air conditioner up to high when he got back in the car. Ten in the morning, and the Mercedes' external temperature gauge registered eighty-eight degrees. If only Bonneterre were located farther north—*much* farther north—he could call it ideal.

His cell phone began to play Nat King Cole's "Mona Lisa." Smiling, he turned down the radio to answer the call.

"Good morning, Miss Landry. How may I assist you?"

"George, I just got off the phone with Anne. She's going to make some changes to the contract and have you sign it. Can you pull together the address book so we can get a mailing list to her for the engagement party?"

"I believe it would be better if I handled the invitations. Since Miss Hawthorne is supposed to believe I am your fiancé, she would find it rather odd when my name isn't on the announcement, wouldn't she?"

Courtney giggled. He'd come to enjoy that sound so much. "Okay. Well, can you tell her that when you see her?"

"Yes, miss." She never demanded. She always requested. "Have you settled into the apartment?"

"Oh, it's so cool—I have the best view of Central Park from my window. And I'm in walking distance of all of the fabulous designer stores in Manhattan." She giggled again. "Oh, and George, thank you."

Heat rose in his cheeks. "What for?"

"For the pink and the lace and the ribbons. I know you had to be the one who had my room decorated for me."

"You're welcome, Miss Courtney."

"Speaking of decorating—how is your furniture shopping going?"

"The stores you recommended were wonderful. I think you'll approve when you return."

"I can't wait to see it. Oh, the car's here. Gotta run."

"Good-bye, miss."

"G'bye, George."

After losing track of time exploring a few shopping centers near the large enclosed mall, George returned to the house, stomach growling. He parked in back and headed for his room to shower and rid himself of the sticky feeling from running in and out of stores in the heat and humidity. He was going to have to rush to be on time for the three o'clock appointment with Anne.

The cell phone rang again while he stood in the closet, peeling off the sweaty clothes. "Hello, George Laurence here."

"Mr. Laurence, this is Anne Hawthorne. I wondered if we might push our appointment back to three thirty. I've had to take care of an issue with a vendor and will be late returning to my office."

The longer he could put it off, the better. "Three thirty will be fine."

"Thank you so much."

George ended the call and jumped in the shower. Then, although he hated to do it because of the heat, he dressed in black summer-weight wool trousers, a long-sleeved shirt, and a tie.

His phone beeped. A message from his employer. He grimaced at his reflection as he straightened his tie. Oh, to be able to turn off his cell phone and not have to jump to do someone else's bidding at any time of the day or night. Whoever had invented the mobile phone should be publicly executed.

He listened to the message and made notes on tasks he needed to do, e-mails he needed to send, and plans he needed to make on his employer's behalf. All of it could wait until later.

The luxury convertible twinkled at George in the shimmering sunlight as he approached it. Too bad he couldn't keep this indulgence. When his employer arrived, George would have to hand over the keys of this beauty and find something more in keeping with his own income.

Crosstown traffic was heavy for midday. He thought he noticed a group of women seated at alfresco tables outside of a coffeehouse admiring him, but he didn't want to turn around and look. He never ceased to be amazed at how the appearance of money could make women pretend to find him attractive.

He'd never had any delusions about his physical appearance. He'd been a slight lad growing up—a slight lad with an angular face, big nose, and unevenly spaced teeth. Although his teeth had straightened out somewhat as he grew up, he still tried to keep them hidden as much as he could. His nose, large to begin with, had been broken in a school rugby game when he was fourteen, so was a bit asymmetrical, too. His shoulders were broad, and he was tall; but if he didn't work out with weights at least four times a week, he could hide behind a lamppost just by turning sideways. He kept his light brown hair short, and several years ago, he'd started to develop wrinkles around his eyes.

Put him in an expensive Mercedes, and the women would look. Stand him beside someone like his employer or Forbes Guidry, and no one saw George Laurence.

"Lord, I know this has been a recurring theme in my prayers, but You know how much I would like to marry and have a family. I cannot ask a woman to live with the kind of schedule I must keep for my current employment. Please show me a way to do something else and still remain in this country." George looked around to make sure no one saw him talking aloud in an otherwise empty car. What did it matter? It wasn't as if he were talking to himself. He was talking to Someone more important.

He pulled into a car park just off Town Square. When he stepped out, the air wrapped around him like a sweaty gym sock. Why anyone would choose to live in these conditions baffled him. He'd take the clammy weather of northern England any day.

Following the sidewalk into the traffic-free square, he admired the original late-Victorian architecture. The row houses facing the large central commons had long ago ceased to be residences and were now stores, restaurants, and other businesses. The obvious attention to historic preservation made the commercial area feel more like a small English village and less like the large American city it really was.

Just before he reached Anne's office, he paused and drew in a deep breath. *Lord, again I ask, please help me to keep my word to my employer without having to lie to this woman. And please help me to overcome the growing attraction I feel for her.*

❖

Anne's skin tingled when George Laurence—and only George Laurence—entered her office. *He's engaged, he's engaged, he's engaged....* "Good afternoon, Mr. Laurence."

"Good afternoon, Ms. Hawthorne." Today he wore a light blue button-down with black dress pants. The multicolored tie looked expensive.

"Is Courtney running late?"

"She is in New York. Shopping. She asked me to come in her stead and begin work on the events with you."

She swallowed hard. Working alone with George Laurence. *God, what have I done so terribly wrong that You're punishing me like this?*

Sharp pain shot through Anne's left temple as she looked down at the paperwork on her desk. She knew better than to skip meals, but she'd been so busy this afternoon that lunchtime had completely passed her by.

She motioned for George to have a seat at the small round conference table beyond the sofa and wing chairs, biting back a smile when he waited until she sat before he did. She moved the vase of purple tulips aside and placed the file on the table facing him. "Here's the adjusted contract. Negotiated items are printed in blue ink. Items that incur an additional consultant fee are in green."

He read through the detailed list of services to be provided. "You label and stuff the invitations yourself?" He looked up at her without raising his head.

Bedroom eyes, grandmother would have called the cinnamon-colored orbs burning holes into Anne's self-consciousness. He was quite a handsome man, in spite of his being *engaged*.

"Yes. I'm also the copywriter, and I will design the programs for the ceremony, as well as other services."

"We can strike the invitations for the engagement party from the list. I will take care of those myself." He pulled a black metallic pen out of his shirt pocket and crossed through the line item.

He would do it himself? Was the budget monster rearing its head? "I'll remove that from the final version, then." Her stomach churned, and her head throbbed. She knew if she didn't get something to eat soon, she'd be in serious danger of passing out.

Before she could stop herself, she asked, "I know this will sound like an odd question, seeing that it's after three thirty, but have you had lunch yet?"

An audible rumble answered her question before he could speak. "No, I have not had lunch yet."

She couldn't be certain, but she thought he might have actually blushed. She suppressed her smile. "Would you be interested in walking over to The Wharf with me? I need to talk to the owners about the date for the rehearsal dinner, as it was one of the restaurants on the list Miss Landry e-mailed me yesterday. While we're there, you and I can discuss the contract and some other paperwork I'll need you to fill out."

As they walked across the park in the middle of Town Square, she found herself glad George was just a bit taller than she. Being full-figured was bad enough, but towering over men made her even more uncomfortable. She hadn't met a man who didn't find her height intimidating until she'd met Cliff Ballantine in eleventh grade. . . .

No. She wasn't going to go down that road right now. She was trying to stay positive. "How long have you lived in the United States, Mr. Laurence?"

"Five years."

STAND-IN GROOM

"And do you like it?"

"I'm not overly fond of Los Angeles or New York. Montana is very nice, as is New Mexico. Alaska was beautiful. Las Vegas is garish and noisy. And I find your city charming. I've been to many other places. Each was unique in its own way."

His response was the most words Anne had heard him string together since meeting him. She watched him from the corner of her eye as they crossed the cobblestone street. He carried himself regally, broad shoulders high and proud, chin parallel with the ground, eyes forward. He wasn't a lawyer. He "represented" a client of Forbes's. Some kind of an agent, maybe?

"You've seen a lot more places than I have," she admitted with a sigh.

"It's part and parcel of the job. I go where my employer needs me. Since my current employer roams the earth, I must make sure he lands in the correct spot." He opened the front door of the restaurant and motioned for her to enter ahead of him.

The hostess hugged Anne. "Hey, Miss Anne. You haven't been in for a couple of weeks. We've been worried about you."

"Hi, Sarah. It's June—you know, the busiest month for weddings."

The college student giggled. "I know." Sarah looked over Anne's shoulder, and her eyes widened when she saw only George standing there. "Table for *two*?" the college student asked with a grin.

Anne shook her head, exasperated, but smiled. "Yes, please. By the back windows if there's anything available."

"Right this way."

From the expression on the girl's face, Anne knew that before the server came around, the news that Anne Hawthorne, the spinster who planned everyone else's weddings, had come in with a man would have gotten back to the dishwashers. She fully expected a slow but steady progression of employees past the table in the next fifteen or twenty minutes. Never before had she come in with only a man. Usually she came in alone to eat and meet with one or both of the owners to discuss events. Sometimes she would bring in clients

59

who weren't familiar with the restaurant. Speculation would run wild.

"Sarah, can you let Samuel or Paul know that I'll need to talk to them after we have lunch?"

"I'll do it, Miss Anne." The hostess's blond hair bounced as she made her way to the kitchen.

By the time Anne and George placed their meal orders, four different people had come to the table to make sure they were being served. Anne could barely contain her laughter. She hated to think how many it would have been if they'd come in after the five-thirty dinner shift came on duty.

"Now that we have a few minutes," she said, taking a fresh yeast roll from the basket George offered, "I'd like to go over a few of these forms I'll need you to fill out." It was all she could do to be polite and cut the roll open, spread butter slowly onto it, and leave it sitting on the bread plate rather than stuffing the whole thing in her mouth.

❦

George anointed the steaming roll with cold butter. His stomach rumbled at the yeasty aroma as he tore off a bite-sized piece and brought it to his mouth. The saltiness of the butter mingled with the sweetness of the bread and melted on his tongue. He had to stop himself from sighing in contentment.

The shuffling of papers across the table drew his attention back to Anne.

"Now that the terms of the contract have been agreed upon, there are a few fact-finding forms I need filled out." She handed him a packet of several pages stapled together. "This is the registration form."

He glanced over the first page. Bride's full name, groom's full name, maid of honor's name, best man's name, number of brides-maids, number of groomsmen. . . . Guilt robbed him of his appetite. *Lord, how am I going to keep up this charade?*

"Some of the items on this list are going to be very important to me as I work on the final budget next week. I would appreciate it if you could get the information back to me by Monday morning."

Another server stopped at the table and asked if they needed refills of their mostly untouched beverages. George didn't quite understand the smile on Anne's face when she declined the offer. He found the constant interruptions somewhat annoying.

As they ate their meals, he unobtrusively but carefully watched the wedding planner. Her manners were impeccable—better than those of most of the aristocracy he'd served over the years. She took small bites, laid down her fork between them, kept her left hand in her lap, and maintained a straight posture without looking stiff. She might be able to help him give Courtney a few lessons before the formal parties, just to keep Courtney from being so nervous about her social skills.

The waitress was just clearing their plates when an older man with dark hair approached the table.

Anne stood and received a kiss on each cheek. George stood as well, laying his napkin beside the silverware.

"Sarah mentioned you were here." The man's decidedly Irish accent surprised George, though he didn't show it. "You fell into a bit o' luck, darlin', as I didn't know myself that I would be here today."

"I have a new event I'm planning, and I hoped to check some dates with you."

"Aye, I knew you were here for more than just our fine food." The restaurateur turned his attention expectantly toward George.

"Samuel Maguire, this is my client George Laurence."

George shook hands with the Irishman. "It's a pleasure to meet you, sir."

Pulling a chair over from another table, Maguire joined them. He put a black, leather-bound planner on the table, winked at Anne, and then turned to George. "Our little *cailín* here is the best businesswoman in town. If I'd known her ten years ago, I'd have retired from being a surgeon then and started my restaurant with her as my partner."

George gave the man the smile he knew was expected but didn't say anything. As he watched her interact with the restaurant owner, he was impressed by her ability to make the negotiation sound like casual, friendly conversation. From the obvious shorthand between them, they had a long-standing relationship, and George got the feeling the restaurateur would do anything within his power to accommodate whatever she requested.

The date Courtney wanted the restaurant for the rehearsal dinner had been booked for months. Anne showed no outward sign that this bothered her at all.

"If they happen to cancel, call me; but for now, let's go ahead and reserve it for that Friday night instead, and I'll discuss the date change with the bride." Anne made a notation in her file. "When can you meet to discuss a menu?"

Maguire consulted his calendar. "How about. . .next Tuesday afternoon?"

Anne looked across the table at George. "Mr. Laurence, are you available next Tuesday afternoon?"

George knew he would be, but pulled out his PDA just to put the appointment in his schedule. "What time?"

"Is three o'clock all right?" The Irishman looked from George to Anne and back.

"That should work well in my schedule." George notated the appointment.

The waitress returned to the table with the check for the meal. Maguire whisked it from her hand before Anne could take it. He stood, leaned over, and kissed her on the cheek. "It's on me, darlin'."

"Thank you, Samuel."

"My pleasure, Anne." He extended his hand to George. "Mr. Laurence."

George stood to shake hands. "Mr. Maguire. Thank you for your hospitality."

The owner escorted them to the front door of the establishment. "We'll be seein' you next week, then."

Outside the restaurant, Anne handed George the second file folder she had with her. "These are all of the forms I'll need back by next Monday. Can we meet around ten?"

"Ten on Monday morning will be fine."

"Very well."

He thought he could sense a stiffness in her body language but couldn't be sure. One thing about this woman that continued to impress him was that she could mask her feelings as well as or better than he could.

As she walked back toward her office, he couldn't help but admire her shapely figure. That combined with his growing admiration for her could be dangerous. Very dangerous.

CHAPTER 6

*G*eorge stared at the form he'd been trying to fill out for two days, then tossed the pen on the desk and stood to pace the tiny antechamber. How had he gotten into this position? He had signed a contract agreeing to lie about his identity. Every scripture he'd ever read about the evils of lying jumbled in his head.

His gaze fell once again to the paperwork littering the desk. He couldn't face it any longer. Besides, why was he sitting alone in the house wasting this beautiful Saturday morning by becoming more and more frustrated with his job?

Tucking his keys and cell phone in the pocket of his jeans, George grabbed his sunglasses on his way out the door. He hadn't attended church last weekend and had a sudden need to find one to attend tomorrow morning. He consulted his city map and set out toward the shopping district, where he'd seen several churches.

After a quarter hour, he passed the large stone arch marking the entrance to the University of Louisiana. He could picture Anne Hawthorne as she must have been years ago as a student here—sitting on a stone bench in the shade, chatting with chums. . . .

The random thought surprised George. He couldn't let his fancy get the better of him. He had a professional role to maintain.

How gutted would she be when she learned the truth? He hoped she would be happy for the opportunity rather than upset, but the more he got to know her, the more he worried about her reaction.

"Father, give me strength. I do not want to hurt Anne Hawthorne. Not when I'm coming to care for her—" He let his prayer stop when he spied a large structure on his right. The pictorial stained-glass windows reminded him of St. John's Cathedral, and the architecture seemed to be based on Middle English design. How long had it been since he'd been home?

The name on the sign near the street was incongruous with the size of the building. Judging from the sprawling wings of the structure, Bonneterre Chapel was larger than any church he'd attended in California or New York.

He pulled up beside a few cars parked near a side entrance, hoping to slip in and take a quick look around. A florist truck pulled up halfway on the sidewalk near the door. George waited until the three men from April's Flowers entered the church, then followed them.

Inside, he removed his sunglasses and discovered he'd entered a room that reminded him of the lobby of a small but expensive hotel; for all that the exterior of the building recalled a long-past era, the interior was anything but old.

The mossy green carpet of the foyer gave way to rich dark blue in the sanctuary. He drew a deep breath, and the muscles in his shoulders relaxed. The bright sunlight from outside filtered in through the multicolored glass windows and the Bible-story images glowed in rainbow hues.

He started when a female voice broke the reverent silence of the worship center.

"Let's place the candelabra here. . .here. . .here. . .and here."

His gaze snapped to the altar at the front of the room. Although distorted by echoing throughout the cavernous space, Anne Hawthorne's voice was unmistakable.

As before, her blond hair was pulled away from her face into a clip at the back of her head. She had an open notebook cradled in her left arm, a pen or pencil in her right hand, and a roll of masking tape around her wrist.

Unlike their previous encounters, when she'd been dressed in conservative business suits, she wore khaki shorts and a sleeveless denim shirt. Even though she was slightly larger than what most men would consider to be beautiful, George admired her athletic hourglass figure.

Only the lights over the altar were on; George stayed concealed in the shadows under the overhanging balcony. He slipped into the end of the rear pew nearest him and sat, wanting nothing more than to watch her.

As she directed the three men from the florist shop on the exact placement of the arrangements on the stage and around the chancel, she also instructed two others on the placement of tall candlesticks at the ends of the pews that flanked the central aisle.

"I'll need you to start lighting those at two fifteen," she said. The two young men, probably university students, followed her like trained Labradors. "All of the candles should be burning with the hurricane glass in place by the time we start seating guests at two thirty." Her gentle voice resonated with authority. "I'll let y'all get started on those. I need to make a few phone calls."

"No prob, Anne," one of the men said with a mock salute.

Not wanting to be seen, George was about to stand and slip out of the room, but Anne headed toward him, making flight impossible.

Before he could prepare an explanation for his presence, she moved into a pew in the middle of the room and sat down. With her back turned to him, he could barely hear her, but from what he could make out, she called the bride, the groom, the maid of honor, and the best man to ensure everyone was on schedule. She then called the caterer, the bakery, and someone at the venue where the reception was to be held to check that everything would be ready at the right time.

Her voice was pleasant, and her laugh melodious. He could tell just by the number of calls she made that her workload today was stressful, although she didn't let stress manifest itself in her interactions with clients and vendors. He was impressed.

She was on the phone with what sounded like the limousine company when George heard her say, "Manuel, I hate to interrupt you, but I have another call coming in. Do you mind holding? Thank you." She took the phone away from her ear for a moment, pressed a button, and then put it to her ear again. "Happy Endings, Inc., this is Anne Hawthorne."

A moment's pause grew into a long silence. Anne's posture changed from relaxed to so stiff he could almost hear the bones in her spine protest. He wondered who could be on the other end of the connection and what that person was telling Anne to cause such a reaction.

After several long moments, he heard her say, "Yes, Miss Graves, I understand. However—"

He leaned forward and rested his forearms on the pew in front of him. Although her body language bespoke strain, her voice didn't betray it. He listened, fascinated.

"Yes, I have written it down. . .two hundred for the ceremony, four hundred for the reception. . .formal evening wear, black tie required. . . Yes, of course. . . . I will look into that for you. . . . Right now? Your wedding isn't for nearly a year. I haven't booked anything yet, but—" Anne paused. "I will let you know as soon as I do. Yes. . . I will call you first thing Monday morning."

Her shoulders raised and lowered as she took a few deep breaths. She listened to her client a little longer, then raised her left arm up to catch a beam of light on the face of her watch. "I will be finished here today around midnight. I won't be able to get back to my office until then, but I have the information you requested. I can e-mail it to you tonight so that you have it first thing in the morning."

She was willing to do that for a client? Go back to her office at midnight after working all day on someone else's wedding? He remembered his own complaints to God about his employer sending him here and felt lower than the belly of a duck.

Anne pulled out her well-worn tan leather planner. "Yes, Miss Graves. I can meet you tomorrow after church—"

Would she be willing to give up church for a client? How many Sundays had George had to leave services early or give them up entirely to attend to his employers' wishes?

"I'm sorry, Miss Graves, but I cannot meet you before twelve thirty. . . . Yes, that's fine. I will meet you at Beignets S'il Vous Plait on Spring Street at twelve thirty tomorrow." Anne closed her phone and remained still and quiet for a long time.

What could be going through her mind right now? George longed to join her and ask her more about her job, about why she was willing to give up so much time for other people, about how she found the strength to keep giving of herself and receiving nothing in return.

She jumped when her phone beeped and quickly looked at the display screen, and a noise escaped from her throat before she put the phone back to her ear. "I'm sorry to keep you on hold for so long, Manuel. . . ."

As quietly as he could, George exited the church and climbed back into the car. He'd left his PDA in the car to charge and the screen flashed, indicating he had voice mail. The display showed that Courtney had tried to ring him up three times while he'd been inside.

He gripped the steering wheel hard. He was supposed to be back at the house filling out the paperwork for Anne, not spying on her as she set up someone else's wedding. Over the past week, he'd indulged himself with his daily jaunts into town, putting off work he needed to do for his employer—hiring a few more house staff, creating the engagement party invitation for when Courtney sent the revised mailing list back to him. . . .

He could take lessons on professional demeanor from Anne Hawthorne. She worked harder to ensure her clients' happiness than any butler, valet, or majordomo he'd seen in the entirety of Britain, including his father.

Needing someone to talk with about the security concerns for when the party guests arrived, he called Forbes Guidry. He couldn't remember when he'd had time to build a friendship with another man. The lawyer had come to mind each time George prayed God would bring new friendships into his life. He liked the Southern gentleman, who was his best resource in town. Aside from professional considerations, though, he had to find out all he could about Anne. Because once he no longer had to carry on this charade, George planned to get to know her better, too.

CHAPTER 7

*M*ulticolored folders littered the top of Anne's desk Monday morning, each containing pieces of someone's dream. Dreams she shared but knew would never come true for her.

With a sigh, she rummaged for the red folder containing the list of vendors for her friend Amanda's wedding. She found it, stacked the rest, and pulled out a green ballpoint pen. Her gaze darted to the clock as she lifted the phone receiver and dialed. Fifteen more minutes and *he* would be here. Her heart beat a little faster as George Laurence's image formed in her mind. She shook her head and turned her attention to the phone as someone answered.

"Bonneterre Rentals."

"Hi, Joe, it's Anne."

"Hey, gal. How's it going?"

She chatted with Joe Delacroix for a few minutes. "I'm just calling to confirm delivery time of the tent, tables, and chairs for the Boutte wedding on Saturday."

"Amanda Boutte who went to high school with us?"

"Yep. She's finally giving up on the single life."

"Good for her."

Papers rustled on the other end as he looked up the information for her. She glanced at the clock again. Thirteen more minutes until George Laurence arrived. His milk chocolate eyes burned in her memory, as did his baritone voice and the accent that sent shivers up her spine every time he spoke.

What had he been doing at the church Saturday morning? She hadn't noticed him until after the phone call from Brittney Graves. She'd stood and turned to run down to the fellowship hall to get a bottle of water out of the vending machine. The retreating figure exiting through the wide-open doors had startled her at first. . .until she recognized the sharp yet enticing profile of her newest client.

Had he been checking up on her? Did he not trust her ability to handle a wedding as large as his? Dared she ask him? Her heart fluttered. Why did he have to be so handsome, so charming?

"Saturday at 10:00 a.m."

What was happening Saturday at 10:00 a.m.? "What's that?"

"Delivery of your rentals, goose. Isn't that why you called?"

Anne banged her forehead with the heel of her right hand. "Of course. Sorry, hon'. I just got distracted." She wrote the time on her list. "I'll see you then."

"All right. Look, don't work too hard, okay?"

She let out a rueful laugh. "I'll try, but that's the best I can promise. Talk to you later."

"Bye, Anne-girl."

She grinned at the nickname Amanda had started everyone using for her when they were teenagers. "Bye, Joey."

Hanging up the phone, she closed her eyes and took a deep breath. "Pull yourself together, woman!"

She shook her head and returned her attention to the file in front of her. Four vendors left to call and only ten—no, nine minutes in which to do it.

Aunt Maggie, catering Amanda's reception at cost, was filling Anne in on the latest family news when the bell above the front door chimed and George Laurence entered.

"I'll have to call you back later about Amanda's cake. B'bye." Anne hung up, stood, and extended her right hand across the desk, proud it didn't tremble. "Mr. Laurence, thank you for coming in today."

"My pleasure, Miss Hawthorne." He nodded, returned her firm grip, and then sat in the chair she indicated. "At this juncture of our work relationship, I see no need for us to be so formal as to use titles and surnames. I'd be pleased if you'd consider calling me George."

Tingles climbed up the back of her neck to her scalp at the sound of his voice. "Thank you, George. I agree." She closed the red folder and swapped it for a blue one. "Why don't we begin with the registration form?"

Why now, Lord? Did You bring him into my life just to taunt me? Why do I feel so attracted to someone I can never have? She swallowed hard as the prayer she'd repeated fifty times in the last two days ran through her mind.

She took the six-page questionnaire from him, surprised by how little he'd filled in.

"I know you were hoping for more information," George said, "but my. . .there are reasons I cannot discuss for withholding some data. I have included a preliminary head count for the ceremony and the reception. I have detailed Courtney's desires."

Anne flipped to the third page. "A formal, late-afternoon wedding with one hundred fifty guests, and a black-tie, invitation-only reception for seven hundred." She removed her reading glasses as she looked at him. "Are these solid numbers that I can use in my budget?"

He nodded—a quick, crisp movement, almost as if he were saluting her. "Yes, with a margin of error of no more than ten for the wedding and fifty for the reception."

Anne made a notation on the form. "I notice there are two names written down for Miss Landry's honor attendant. Does she plan on having two maids of honor?"

A slow smile spread over his face, bringing an indulgent twinkle into the Englishman's light brown eyes. "She. . .decided she couldn't do without both ladies in her bridal party. Is that problematic?"

"No, I've planned a few weddings with two honor attendants."

STAND-IN GROOM

She looked down at the form and turned to the fourth page. Indulgent. . .again, more like a father than a fiancé.

She choked when she saw the dollar amount written on the estimated budget line. Her eyes teared up as she wheezed and reached for her bottle of water. Surely he'd scrawled at least one too many zeros. He'd doubled her original estimate, and she hadn't counted on that number being true.

She cleared her throat and took another sip of water. She could work around her attraction to the Englishman. With what he was willing to pay for his wedding, her business's future was assured. And her business was the only future she could count on.

George leaned forward in concern as Anne took another sip of water. "Are you all right?" Her cheeks were flushed, and her eyes watered from the vehemence of her coughing.

She held up her hand in front of her and nodded. After another sip of bottled water, she took a deep breath and cleared her throat. "Just got a tickle," she said in a hoarse whisper.

Her azure eyes glittered as she returned her gaze to the paperwork in front of her. He felt like a schoolboy who had failed an examination, dissatisfied he couldn't give her complete information. He'd spent hours on the phone with Courtney yesterday trying to get her to make up her mind about the major details.

"Ten attendants each. Does that number include the honor attendants?" She looked at him, her fine brows arched high.

George's heart thumped. Her gaze could pierce a man's heart with its intensity. "Yes, that number includes the honorables."

She looked down, but not fast enough to keep him from seeing the corners of her mouth turn up in an amused smile. His face burned at the realization he'd gotten the terminology wrong.

"What's this list?" she asked when she got to the back page—his addendum.

"Those are restaurants in New York and Los Angeles my—we

73

would like for you to contact regarding specific food items for both the engagement party and the reception. I have not yet had time to research them to find the phone numbers and contact names for you, but listed under each is the item my—we would like shipped in."

She looked down the page. "Oh. I see."

Uneasiness settled in George's mind. He had to get over this attraction to the beautiful woman sitting opposite him. Twice he'd nearly slipped up and said "my employer." If he wasn't careful, his employer's name could pop out of his mouth before he could stop himself. Fear of losing his job if he slipped up and revealed too much made him sit straighter and try to reconstruct the barrier around his heart to keep Anne Hawthorne's big blue eyes from getting under his defenses.

He watched Anne carefully as she read through the details Courtney had given him over the phone. Most of the outlandish requests—such as having caviar flown in from an importer in San Francisco for the engagement party—were from his employer, not Courtney. Over the years, George had heard all about the extravagances other wealthy American couples had included in their weddings.

But while his employer wanted to best them all, he'd left the task of hiring a wedding planner in Courtney's hands. As much as George respected Anne Hawthorne's abilities, she might not be the correct person to pull it off. Although the article Courtney had shown him boasted of the number of weddings Anne Hawthorne had planned in her career, was she capable of organizing and executing an event of this magnitude?

She reached for her Rolodex and flipped through several of the sections before she stopped and pulled out a card. "I've worked with Delmonico's in New York before." She flipped through a few more sections. "And I know someone at Pskow Caviar Importers, too." She clipped both cards to the page.

His skepticism decreased a notch. "At the bottom are several local restaurants. Courtney wants some regional dishes included as well."

She continued to read, then opened her top drawer and withdrew a red pen, which she used to cross through one of the names on the list. "Pellatier's closed down six months ago."

"I will inform my. . .Courtney next time I speak with her."

"Thank you." She set the questionnaire aside. "This will allow me to work on a revised budget in the next few days. I may need to call you if I have questions on some of the items we did not discuss today, however." Her expression asked his permission.

"Please, call me anytime you need to."

Her responding smile was beautiful, but tight and forced.

She didn't trust him. The truth stung, but he didn't really blame her. He was being dishonest with her, after all. More than anything, he wanted to earn this woman's trust and respect to ensure she wouldn't hate him when the truth was made known.

Father God, after all this is over, how will I ever deserve forgiveness from either You or Anne?

He kept his tone light, positive, and helpful as they reviewed the remaining paperwork he'd labored over all weekend. To his relief, she had only a few questions, which he was able to answer.

The clock on the credenza behind Anne chimed ten thirty, and she set the paperwork aside. "Are you ready to go see some possible sites for the engagement party?"

He stood. "At your service, ma'am."

She smiled and crossed to the front door, yet did not exit. Instead, she locked it and turned over the sign hanging in the window to let passersby know the office was closed. She led him through the arched doorway at the rear of the office down a hall lined with boxes spilling their contents onto the hardwood floor. Silk flowers, fabrics, glassware, candelabra, and other decorative items glinted in the soft incandescent light.

"Most of this is for the wedding I have this coming weekend." Anne folded back a tablecloth dangling over the edge of a box.

He nodded, distracted by the lock of golden hair that had escaped her conservative french twist and skimmed the curve of her neck. He wanted to reach out and remove the Spanish-style comb holding her hair back. She was beautiful with it up, but he was sure when she had it down—

No. He clasped his hands behind his back as he followed her through a small kitchen and out the back door to the alley where her car was parked. He had to stay professional, at least as long as she thought he was the groom.

She used a remote to unlock the doors of a midsize American-made convertible.

Without thinking, he crossed to the car and opened the driver's door. She paused a moment, surprise flickering across her face. Although the expression disappeared in a split second, her cheeks remained a bit more pink than normal.

His own face flared with heat. "I beg your indulgence, ma'am, but in England, one always holds open a door for a lady."

She smiled. "No need to apologize. It's still a common practice here in the South, too. Thank you." She climbed in, and he secured the door.

As he went around to the other side, she started the engine and closed the roof. After he was situated inside, she handed him several packets of collated pages.

"Here is information on each of the sites we'll be visiting today. I thought you might like to know a little about each place before we arrive."

He regarded her from the corner of his eye as she reached behind her to put her case on the backseat, fastened her seat belt, slid on a pair of stylish sunglasses, and shifted the car into reverse.

Glancing through the brochures, he looked for the best aspects of each locale. He didn't want Anne to think he was focusing only on the negatives, but with the list of requirements Courtney had passed along to him this morning, he wondered if they'd be able to find a place.

By the time they left the third site, Anne was annoyed with him. He tried to be positive, but none of the three would be suitable.

The first, a privately owned park, was too close to the motorway and the airport. While they looked at the beautiful open pavilion, the owner's description of the amenities was drowned out by a jet coming in for a landing.

The second site, a converted nineteenth-century sugar refinery, had an impressive view of downtown Bonneterre, but the narrow, winding carriageway wasn't paved and wasn't conducive to the limousines or luxury cars the guests would be arriving in.

The third site, the courtyard of the university's horticultural gardens, was fine until the groundskeeper mentioned the building would be undergoing internal restoration beginning next week and would be inaccessible to the guests, necessitating portaloos—not acceptable.

Anne drove across the campus toward the fourth property, and George's hopes rose. The driveway was wide and well paved. The crepe myrtles that lined the drive were covered in bright pink blossoms—Courtney's favorite color.

"How long do the trees bloom?"

"All summer. Since it stays so warm here, they don't usually lose their color until October."

The building they approached resembled his employer's antebellum mansion, except on a grander scale, and sat on a bluff overlooking a small lake to the west and the college campus to the east, which should appeal to his employer's sense of the dramatic.

Anne parked near the building under one of the enormous shade trees that encircled the lot. A young woman—pretty with ginger hair—met them on the wide porch that wrapped all the way around the building.

When the two women exchanged a kiss on the cheek, George was struck by how much they favored each other.

Anne turned and motioned toward him. "George Laurence, this is Meredith Guidry, executive director of events and facilities for Boudreaux-Guidry Enterprises."

Mededith was slimmer and several inches shorter than Anne,

but her handshake was surprisingly strong. "Welcome to Lafitte's Landing, Mr. Laurence."

"Guidry. . . ?" He glanced from Meredith to Anne and back. "Are you related, by chance, to Forbes Guidry?"

Meredith smiled. "He's my brother."

"Which makes you two. . ." He pointed from one to the other.

"Cousins." Anne nodded.

Meredith swept her arm out to the left. "Why don't we walk around the building so you can get a feel for the views this site offers?"

George walked beside Meredith and tried to concentrate as she launched into the history of the building, which had originally been a plantation house, including what year it had been built and the subsequent fires, reconstructions, and expansions. When they'd made a full circuit of the building, she pointed out the magnificent vista of the lake.

The view was breathtaking. He couldn't find a fault with this site. . .so far. As a bead of sweat trickled between his shoulder blades, George reached up to loosen his tie but stopped and returned his hand to his side. Everything his father had taught him about maintaining a professional appearance no matter the weather rang through his memory.

"Would you like to see inside?" Meredith asked him, moving to open the double doors before he could do it for her.

Cool air poured out onto the porch, and George stepped in across the raised threshold. The interior of the building featured decor appropriate for the 1840s, the period in which it had been built, according to Meredith. The wood floors gleamed, the crystal chandelier in the wide entry foyer sparkled and threw rainbows around the room, and the enormous ballroom at the center would be large enough to hold the two hundred invited guests—with dining tables and a separate dance floor area. The cavernous, three-story-high room had wood wainscoting up to the windowsills and rough white plaster above. Tall windows let in plenty of light and all of the views surrounding the building.

As he turned to tell Anne he thought they should move this property to the top of the list, her cell phone rang.

"Please excuse me. I must take this call." She stepped back into the entry hall.

To fill the time while Anne was on the phone, Meredith recounted a few events the venue had hosted over the years.

Even though Anne had stepped into the entryway, George could still hear her voice and see her from where he stood near the entrance of the ballroom.

"Hello, Amanda. How is the bride-to-be? Only four and a half days left." Her posture and cheerful expression changed as she said, "Oh, honey, that's just prewedding jitters. I'm sure he'll—"

The caller interrupted her, and Anne's shoulders slumped as she raised her right hand to rub her forehead. She squeezed her eyes closed and grimaced as she listened to her client. Her voice was low and soothing when she continued. "Sweetie, I understand you feel like you're never going to be able to work this out, but I know David really loves you. Let's not cancel anything until we have a chance to sit down and talk about it. What time does he get off work? Six? All right. I'll tell you what. I'll call him at work. I want both of you to come over to the office this evening, and we'll sit down and discuss this. Okay, honey? You're very emotional right now, and I don't want you to make a decision you'll end up regretting. I'll see you tonight, sweetie."

George was so focused on Anne that he started when Meredith cleared her throat. "She is very good at her job."

"Yes, she is brilliant at her job."

As he listened to Anne on the phone with the disgruntled groom, he realized that not only was she a wedding planner, but she was as close to a marriage counselor as some couples would ever have. Her caring came from having genuine feelings for the people she worked for, not just a concern for her business's bottom line. He suspected that if she felt it would be in the clients' best interest to call off the wedding, she'd be the first one to tell them so.

He asked God to forgive him for ever doubting Anne's ability to plan this wedding. He just hoped when the time came and his true role was revealed, Anne would be able to forgive him, too.

CHAPTER 8

From the expression of pitying concern on George's face, Anne knew he'd overheard her phone conversations. She should have walked farther away. Following George and Meredith out of Lafitte's, she felt turmoil built up inside. If he had been checking up on her Saturday because he didn't trust her ability to plan his wedding, she needed to know. She'd prove to him she could do this as well as or better than anyone else.

Her thoughts returned to her more pressing situation as George took pictures of Lafitte's Landing with the digital camera in his PDA. She and Amanda had grown up together but had never really been friends until just a few years ago when they had run into each other at church. She'd been surprised when Amanda asked her to plan her wedding, knowing how tight finances were for the couple, as they were also purchasing a house.

What Amanda and David didn't know was that for their wedding gift, Anne was providing her services for free. Through her connections in town, she'd gotten deep discounts on nearly everything for the rehearsal dinner, ceremony, and reception. She hadn't asked them for a deposit check, and she was scheduled to have the final meeting with them tomorrow, when she planned on handing them her bill, marked PAID IN FULL.

Now she had to try to put all the pieces back together before her friends made a huge mistake by calling off their wedding. She wasn't worried about the logistics of canceling an event with such short notice—she'd done it several times before. But she knew deep down that these two people were supposed to be married. She just had to get them to see that.

She nearly bumped into George when she walked out the front door.

"Thank you for your hospitality." George shook hands with Meredith again. "I will speak with the bride by telephone tonight and hope to speak with you again tomorrow."

"Thank you, Mr. Laurence. I hope your fiancée likes Lafitte's Landing as much as you do." Meredith turned to Anne. "I'll see you later."

Anne hugged her cousin. "Thanks for meeting us up here, Mere. I'll talk to you soon."

"I'm sure you will."

Anne ignored the saucy gleam in Meredith's eyes and followed George to the car.

A slight breeze rustled the top of the canopy of trees. The buzz of cicadas resonated in harmony with the sound of the lake in the background and the birds chirping overhead. Lafitte's Landing was one of Anne's favorite places, and she recommended it to nearly every client with a large guest list. The fact that it was owned by B-G Enterprises and she could count on Meredith's help, as well as B-G's executive chef, Major O'Hara, helped a lot.

In the car, she turned up the air conditioner and looked at her day planner. They had appointments to visit two additional sites down in the nearby town of Comeaux but weren't scheduled to see the next one for nearly two more hours.

She fastened her seat belt and pulled out of the small parking lot. Her stomach clenched, reminding her that breakfast five hours ago had consisted of a banana and a small bowl of dry cereal, as she'd been out of milk.

Mr. Laurence—George—deserved to be able to stop for lunch, too. Just because she usually worked through lunch didn't mean she had to force him to do the same.

"Do you like seafood, George?" She stopped at the end of Lafitte's Landing's long driveway. She waited for his answer, since it would determine which direction she turned.

"Yes. And I have heard that the seafood in Louisiana is incomparable."

"Well, I think it's pretty wonderful, but I don't have much to compare it to." She turned right and headed south instead of back toward her office.

After a few moments of silence, George asked, "Is planning an outdoor event more difficult than indoor?"

"Somewhat. There are more variables—more things that can go wrong, more safeguards and alternatives that need to be planned. It's almost like planning two events in one." She glanced at him from the corner of her eye. Even though his posture was erect, his body language was relaxed, comfortable. She narrowed her eyes a little as she returned her focus to the road. She wanted to ask him why he'd been watching her Saturday morning, but the words wouldn't leave her mouth.

"I'm very pleased with Lafitte's Landing. I believe we've just secured the location for the engagement party. I'll send my. . . Courtney a message."

She glanced at him again and saw he was reviewing the digital pictures he'd taken of the location on the screen of his PDA. Whenever he spoke of Courtney, he tripped over her name. He never personalized the relationship—and if he ever did say "my," he always stopped himself as if not wanting to commit to saying "my fiancée."

Silence descended on them as she navigated lunch-hour traffic in midtown. Without thinking, she powered on the stereo.

Beside her, George started visibly when Dean Martin singing "That's Amore" blasted through the speakers. Embarrassed, she fumbled with the buttons and turned it off again.

"No, don't turn it off." George reached over and turned it on again but adjusted the volume lower. "Not many people listen to Dean Martin these days."

Her cheeks burned. Yet another example of how backward she was—she didn't even listen to contemporary music.

"They just don't make music like this anymore. It's a shame, really."

Was he serious or patronizing her? He'd leaned his head back against the headrest, and he looked fully relaxed. The CD moved to the next track, and he started to hum, then sing along with "Memories Are Made of This." Same taste in music to add to the ever-growing list of his attractions. He probably liked old movies, too.

Twenty minutes later, after being treated to George's perfect imitation of Dean Martin through several of her favorite songs, she slowed and passed an old-fashioned general store and gas station. "This is the town of Comeaux."

George craned his neck to take in the sights. "How far outside of Bonneterre have we come?"

"We're only about twenty miles from Town Square—about ten miles from the city limits. I know it feels like we're out in the middle of nowhere."

"How beautiful."

Anne glanced past George at the enormous, gingerbread Victorian house. "That's the Plantation Inn Bed and Breakfast. Some of my clients who can't afford big expensive trips for their honeymoons come down here. I've stayed here a couple of times, too, when I just needed to get away."

A few blocks down, she pulled into the gravel parking lot in front of a building sided with rough wood planks that featured fishing gear hanging from rusted iron nails as decorations.

The interior of the Fishin' Shack was dim and cool compared to the sultry sunshine of a June day in Louisiana. The aroma of sweet seafood and spicy Cajun seasonings hit her full force as she entered. Her stomach growled loudly.

"Anne, what are you doing here?" Jenn stepped away from a

table and met her at the door.

Anne hugged her cousin. "I'm in the area looking at venues and had to stop somewhere for lunch." She stepped out of her cousin's embrace before the younger woman spilled the iced-tea pitcher she held.

Jenn looked behind Anne, and her eyes widened when she saw George.

"Jennifer Guidry, this is George Laurence, my client." Anne stepped back to include George. "Jenn is the owner of this place."

"My pleasure, Miss Guidry." He paused, her hand still clasped in his. "Guidry. . .let me guess—another one of Anne's cousins."

"Yep, and proud of it." Jenn led them to a table away from the moderate-sized lunch crowd and placed the large laminated menus on the table as Anne slid into the booth. Jenn turned to George. "Since you've never been here, I'll let you know that our Cajun dishes are very spicy, but we can tone that down if you like. If you don't see anything on the menu that you like, just let me know, and I'll talk to the chef." She winked at him.

Anne held in her laugh as her cousin turned on all of her Southern charm for the handsome Englishman. When Jenn returned with their beverages, George ordered the traditional fish 'n' chips basket, while Anne ordered her favorite Cajun grilled shrimp Caesar salad.

As they waited for their meals, she struggled to think of a neutral topic of conversation but was saved from having to come up with appropriate small talk when George remarked, "Hawthorne isn't a name one would typically associate with Louisiana."

He wasn't the first person who'd pointed that out to her. "No. My father was from Boston but came here for college, where he met my mother." She'd explained this so many times over the years it was hard to keep it from sounding rehearsed.

"I've been to Boston. It's a very interesting city."

"So I've heard." Anne traced the ring of moisture her glass of tea left on the table as she took a sip.

"You've never gone there yourself? Not even to visit family?"

KAYE DACUS

"I. . .don't fly." Anne swallowed hard and raised her left hand to make sure her shirt collar covered the twenty-seven-year-old scar on the side of her neck.

"Why ever not?" As soon as the words were out of his mouth, he held up his hand in front of him. "No, wait. I apologize. That question is presumptuous. Please do not feel you have to answer it."

"It's all right." She took a fortifying breath. "You see, when I was eight—"

"Here's your lunch!" Jenn called cheerily as she swooped down upon them. She gave Anne a wink and floated away to visit with other patrons.

"You were about to tell me why you don't fly," he reminded her.

Anne lifted her napkin to dab the corners of her mouth and cleared her throat. "The only time I was ever on a plane was with my parents when I was eight. It was a commuter plane that held thirty people. The pilot tried to take off in the middle of a thunderstorm, but. . ." She took a deep breath to calm her voice and try to settle her stomach. "We crashed, and I was one of only five people who survived."

Silence settled over the table. He swallowed a couple of times. "I'm sorry."

She shook her head. "Don't be. It was a very long time ago. I tried to get on a plane when I was fifteen and had such a bad panic attack that they had to take me to the emergency room." She hadn't meant to reveal that to him. No one outside of her family—except for the airline and emergency room staff who'd helped—knew about it.

He nodded slowly, taking a moment to push a morsel of fish onto the back of his fork with his knife. Before putting the bite in his mouth, he asked, "Where would you have gone had you gotten on that plane?"

"New York with my grandparents and aunt and uncle." She pushed her half-finished salad toward the end of the table to let Jenn or the other servers milling around know they could take it away. She'd felt half-starved when they sat down, yet talking about her aversion to flying spoiled her appetite.

"And have you never tried to board a plane since then?"

Why had he decided to take such an interest in this topic? She leaned back against the padded booth seat and crossed her arms. "No. I'd love to see Europe, but I don't want to go through another panic attack."

"Hmm." It was a short sound from the back of his throat. "Have you ever considered taking a ship over?"

He was as tenacious as a coonhound that had treed its prey. Why wouldn't he just let it drop? "I've looked into it, but being self-employed, I can't be gone for that long. How often do you go back to England?" Hopefully he'd take the hint and let her change the subject.

"I've traveled to England several times in the past few years in the capacity of my job." He wiped his mouth with his napkin, then laid it beside his plate. "Do you mind if I ask, how did you come to the decision to pursue a career as a wedding planner?"

Not really the topic she wanted to discuss, but much better than talking about planes and flying. "When I left graduate school, I went to work as the event planner for B-G—yes, the job Meredith has now. After several years, I realized I enjoyed planning weddings the most and felt like God was leading me to start my own business."

A light Anne hadn't seen before sparked to life in George's eyes. "You felt *God* was leading you? I've always admired people who listen for God's voice and take the leaps of faith He sometimes asks of them."

Was George a believer? She wanted to ask but didn't want to embarrass him. "Faith is something I've struggled with my whole life. But I knew I just had to do it."

"What a blessing. . .to know what you're doing is God's plan." His voice sounded almost sad. "And you are good at it. I. . .I happened by the Bonneterre Chapel Saturday morning and watched you work. I should have made my presence known, but you were busy, and I didn't want to interrupt."

His admitting he'd been there was a surprise, but the words of affirmation floored her. "Thank you. What brought you by the church?"

"I was out for a drive and was drawn to it. I would like to find a congregation to attend regularly, since I will be living here until October. I noticed the door was open and let myself in. It's a beautiful church."

"Yes. It's a very easy place to hold a wedding. Not much in the way of decoration is needed, and the colors are neutral enough that they go with anything a bride could choose. Plus, I know practically everyone on staff—that's the church I grew up in."

"And do you still attend there?" Interest in the subject lent a new warmth to George's handsome features.

Anne's heart skipped a beat when his brown eyes twinkled. "I do, although sometimes it's hard to make it to Sunday morning service when I have a late evening wedding the day before. Are you—did you grow up going to church as well?"

He shook his head. "No, I prayed to receive Christ as my Savior about twenty years ago. The head of staff at my first professional position was a Christian. We read the Bible and prayed together every day before we started work."

"Do you still keep in touch with him?" She smiled up at the waiter who came by to clear their plates, then returned her focus to George.

"He passed away five years ago, just after I came to the States to work." George's eyes softened as he spoke of his mentor. "I couldn't attend his funeral, and while I do miss being able to speak with him, I know I'll see him again."

His openness made Anne even more uncomfortable. Every detail she learned about him served to reinforce her attraction to him. She couldn't allow herself to feel this way about a client. She wasn't sure what to say, and silence once again settled between them.

They were saved from a moment of awkwardness when Jenn

returned to the table. "How were your meals?"

"Very good, as usual," Anne told her cousin, but Jenn wasn't looking at her.

"The fish and chips reminded me of a pub in London we frequented when I was a boy." George smiled politely.

Even though she hadn't known him long, just from watching him carefully today and in their past few meetings, Anne was starting to be able to read his facial expressions. He was better at controlling his reactions and schooling his features than she, but his eyes gave him away. His beautiful eyes that were the color of sun-brewed iced tea. . . the very same eyes that were now looking at her askance.

"Anne?" Jenn nudged her. "Are you all right?"

"I'm fine. I just zoned out there for a second." Heat crawled up her cheeks.

Jenn removed the cap of her pen with her teeth to write something on her order pad. Speaking around the cap, she said, "I asked what site y'all are going to visit next."

"Oh. Comeaux Town Center. Then Benoit Hall."

"Lafitte's Landing has those two beaten, hands down." Jenn tore off the sheet she'd written on and put it facedown on the table in front of Anne. "George, great to meet you. Hopefully I'll see you around again soon."

He nodded noncommittally.

Jenn leaned over and kissed Anne's cheek. "Annie, I'll see you back here for dinner Thursday night."

"I should be here, but don't be surprised if I'm late." Anne picked up the ticket and slid out of the booth.

"I'll save you a seat."

"Thanks." She gave her cousin a quick hug. As soon as Jenn walked away, Anne reached into her small purse and pulled out a twenty-dollar bill, which she left on the table.

George reached for his wallet, but Anne stopped him. "I never make a client pay for a meal. Company policy."

He looked uncomfortable but didn't argue with her.

Anne looked down at the check. Rather than a receipt for their lunch, it was a note in her cousin's chunky, loopy script. She read it as she walked toward the door.

He's hot. Find out if he has a brother and let me know.

—J

Anne smiled and shook her head. When would her cousin figure out that she was a wedding planner, not a matchmaker?

CHAPTER 9

$\mathcal{A}$t eight o'clock Tuesday evening, fourteen hours since the beginning of her workday, Anne locked the front door of her office and turned off all the lights. But after two hours of draining mediation, Amanda and David's wedding was a go for Saturday.

Her back ached between her shoulders, and she rolled her neck to try to work out the stiffness. Next stop: home, where she would fill the spa tub with hot water and her favorite tea-therapy essential oils and try to release some of this stress. Her stomach rumbled, and she adjusted her plans to include running by Rotier's on the way to get her favorite grilled chicken club sandwich.

The sandwich never made it out of the car. In the ten minutes from the restaurant to the converted Victorian triplex, she'd wolfed down the club and most of the large order of french fries. Her eyelids drooped as she parked between Jennifer's red classic Mustang and Meredith's white, late-model Volvo SUV.

She'd rather hoped the girls would have gone out tonight so she could be sure of some private time to unwind. Even though each had her own apartment—Meredith on the ground floor, Jennifer on the third, and Anne in the middle—they rarely, if ever, hesitated to drop in on each other if the mood struck. Especially Jenn, who couldn't seem to comprehend why anyone would ever want to be alone.

Anne waved bugs out of her face as she fumbled to find the

key to the back door. Maybe they should replace the incandescent porch light with a bug zapper.

She smiled and crossed the threshold. With the deposit for the Landry-Laurence wedding safely tucked away in the bank, she could get an architect out to start redesigning this place back into a grand single-family home. She hadn't told the girls yet, just in case something fell through. But it was time for all of them to move on, live by themselves.

Thursday night at the family singles' dinner would be the perfect time. That way she wouldn't get fussed at for leaving someone out of the telling.

The wooden stairs creaked, and she winced, hoping neither of the girls would notice. The rear entrance opened into her kitchen. She snapped on the lights. . .and groaned. A couple of cabinet doors stood ajar, and half of her mixing and serving bowls sat on the previously empty countertop.

"Hey, Anne—" Meredith stopped in the doorway.

Anne dropped her bags on the kitchen table, shrugged out of her suit jacket, and waved toward the mess. "Jenn?"

Meredith nodded, stepped back out into the hall, and bellowed her sister's name. "She came down a couple of hours ago to 'borrow' some flour—and sugar and eggs and baking soda. I didn't realize she needed something to mix it all up in, too."

Anne leaned over to replace the stack of bowls in the cabinet under the sink. "Looks like she needed the mixer, too. How a woman who has her own business—"

"You rang?" Jennifer bounced into the room. "Oh, sorry. I was about to come down and put all that away, Anne."

Meredith sat at the table, and Jennifer hopped up to sit on the counter beside the refrigerator. So much for a quiet evening and a long, hot bath.

"So—are you going out with him?"

"Going out with—no, he's engaged!" Why in the world would Jenn ask that when she knew George Laurence was a client?

Jenn's pixie-esque face crumpled into a frown. "Danny Mendoza's engaged? Then what's he doing sending you flowers?"

"What are you—?" Anne turned and for the first time noticed an enormous floral arrangement in the middle of the table. She must be more tired than she thought to have missed it. Meredith plucked the card off its stick and handed it to her. The flap on the tiny envelope hadn't been sealed, thus explaining how Jenn already knew who'd sent them. Anne opened it and read the note:

Anne—
   Sorry I've missed you the last few times I've called. I hope to talk to you soon and look forward to getting to know you better.

Danny Mendoza

What was wrong with him? He'd stood her up a week and a half ago, and she'd been avoiding his calls since then. Why wasn't he getting the hint?

"Obviously he cares enough to drop a wad of money on flowers." Jenn cupped a stargazer lily and inhaled its spicy fragrance. "Are you going out with him again?"

"What *again*? I haven't been out with him *yet*." Anne concentrated on putting the card back into its sleeve. She worked with April's Flowers enough to know Danny had indeed "dropped a wad of money," as Jenn so eloquently put it. Over two feet tall and about as wide, the bouquet featured not only the dark pink and white lilies, but also deep red roses, purple delphiniums, pink gerbera daisies, blue phlox, violet veronicas, lilac blossoms, and white hydrangeas.

"How could you not see them when you came in?" Meredith fingered a velvety rose.

"Have you seen the two arrangements in my living room? I have two others at my office, in addition to the purple tulips I get from April's Flowers every time they get some in stock. The florist shops around here like me to keep them in mind when making recommendations to clients, so I get at least two or three deliveries every couple of weeks." She turned the vase so the large purple bow faced forward. "I don't think that going out with someone whose schedule is as hectic as mine is a good idea. When I meet the right man, I'll know it."

The image of George Laurence flooded her mind's eye. Why did he have to be engaged? She tried to stop the flutter in her heart, but the memory of their conversation over lunch yesterday—his gentle humor, his deep faith, his expressive brown eyes, his to-die-for accent—wouldn't go away.

"Oh, really, Anne!" Jenn slid down from her perch, arms crossed. "When are you going to give up on the idea of love at first si—" She jerked and grabbed for the cell phone hanging from her tiny waistband. "Sorry, gals, it's the restaurant." She whizzed out the door, phone to ear.

"Don't mind her." Meredith stood and stretched. "She and Clay Huntoon broke up."

Anne frowned. "Clay Huntoon? The sports reporter for Channel Six who sings at church occasionally? Did I know she was seeing him?"

Meredith smiled and shook her head. "That's how she met Danny Mendoza—Danny and Clay work together."

"I swear she changes boyfriends like socks." Anne fingered the waxy petal of one of the stargazer lilies. "Do you think maybe that's why she's so keen to find out if I plan to see Danny again? Do you think she might be interested in him?"

"Dunno. Maybe." With a shrug, Meredith crossed to the door. "Hey, have you heard from Major O'Hara the last couple of weeks?"

Anne shook her head. "No, why?"

"He asked about you this afternoon—mentioned we haven't worked any events with you recently, was wondering how you are, and said he'd probably give you a call to see if you have any small events he might pick up freelance."

"Really? Are things so slow there that he has time to cater non-B-G events? I mean, it must really eat into the time he gets to spend with Debbonnaire."

"You really are behind the times, Anne. Major and Deb broke up before Christmas. She wanted him to propose—after dating only two months, if you can believe that." Meredith pressed her lips together. "Well, I'd better get going. I'll tell Major tomorrow you'll be calling." Meredith pulled the door closed behind her. "Good night, Annie."

" 'Night, Mere. No, sweet dreams instead." She grinned when Meredith stuck her tongue out at their long-standing joke.

After putting her kitchen to rights, Anne slid the chain lock into place and put a pot of English toffee–flavored decaf coffee on to brew.

The news that Major O'Hara was once again available hadn't struck her the way it would have a few weeks ago. Twenty years ago, when he'd started working for Aunt Maggie, fifteen-year-old Anne had been sure she was going to marry him one day. Although he seemed to enjoy flirting with her, he never hinted he would consider asking her out. Then she met Cliff Ballantine and allowed her relationship with Major to fall into a comfortable friendship.

She forced Major's dimpled smile to replace George's sharp features and brown eyes in her imagination. If she was going to obsess about someone, better for him to be someone available. She concentrated on Major, trying to remember the last time she'd seen him. Hadn't it been at church a month or so ago?

Had George found a church to attend yet?

"Stop it."

She carried her laptop computer into the bathroom and set it on a low stool. Perching on the side of the tub, she held her hand under the faucet, and when the water reached a comfortable temperature, she measured out two capfuls of the black-tea-and-red-currant bath oil.

KAYE DACUS

Going back into the kitchen, she filled a latte mug with the richly scented coffee, doctored it with a bit of half-and-half and sugar, then went into the living room to grab a DVD. She hadn't indulged in a bath and movie evening in quite a while.

Not even twenty minutes into *My Fair Lady*, Anne stopped it and brought up the computer's media player to listen to music instead. Why did Professor Henry Higgins remind her of George? Was it his influence over Courtney that made her seem older than her nineteen years? Had he seen her as a diamond in the rough and fallen in love with her as he taught her etiquette? Or was he just a wealthy man who wanted a beautiful wife and decided to get one young enough that he could mold her into the kind of woman he wanted her to be?

How had they met? He self-admittedly had never been to Bonneterre before. In fact, aside from the New York area code on the business card he'd given her, she wasn't sure where he lived.

And where had his money come from? Probably some old, aristocratic family in England, with the legacy fortune passed down to and doubled by each successive generation.

Closing her eyes, she sipped her coffee as the strains of Frank Sinatra's "Come Fly with Me" wafted through the steamy room.

She'd opened up with him over lunch yesterday more than with anyone outside of Meredith and Forbes. Not even Jenn knew all of the details of Anne's parents' deaths or of why she had started her own business.

The next song started, and rather than picturing Dean Martin, she could clearly imagine George Laurence serenading her with "Return to Me," her favorite song.

She jumped out of the tub, not caring that she splashed water all over the rugs and tile floor, and turned the music off. Jamming her arms into her bathrobe, she fled to the kitchen, where she grabbed her planner and flipped to the address book.

"Please let him still have this number." She picked up her cell phone and dialed. It rang once. . .twice. . .

"Hello?"

"Hi, Major, it's Anne Hawthorne. . . ."

❧

Soft amber light pooled on the brick walkway from the faux gas lamp outside Anne Hawthorne's office. George stopped. Why had he come down this way? There weren't any restaurants on this side of Town Square.

He had to stop thinking about Anne Hawthorne. He was here to do a job, and once finished, he'd go away. She would stay here with her family and her successful business.

Maybe if he confided in her—no. If he told Anne he wasn't the groom, he would be breaking the contract, and it would put her in an awkward position with her cousin Forbes. Anne would ask questions George couldn't answer, and that would only make matters worse.

After lunch yesterday, though, he was hard pressed to deny the growing attraction he felt for her. He wanted to spend more time with her, wanted to be the one to whom she told all her secrets, in whom she confided her dreams and fears. Asking her to go out socially was out of the question as long as she thought he was the groom. He couldn't do anything to compromise his employment or Anne.

Why was he still here? Nothing he could do or say would justify his lurking outside of Anne's office at nine o'clock in the evening. He crossed Town Square toward the lights and music emanating from the Riverwalk. He fruitlessly wished Anne had still been working so he could have invited her to dinner.

He grimaced. Yes, a romantic dinner with someone he'd spent the last two weeks purposely deceiving. What a brilliant idea.

He chose an open-air café, and the hostess showed him to a small wrought-iron table. He took the chair that faced the river. Although his stomach clenched with hunger, his appetite was gone. Nothing on the menu piqued his interest. He ordered a Caesar salad and let the waitress talk him into trying their peach-flavored iced tea.

What did Anne do outside of her work? His own job was such that he was always on call, necessitating that he drop his own plans whenever his employer wanted something. Anne was self-employed. She could set her own hours. What interests did she pursue? Did she have hobbies?

He'd had a glimpse of that outside life yesterday when she turned on the music in the car. To hear the strains of his favorite singer coming from her stereo. . . He'd never met another woman who enjoyed listening to the classics. Most women thought he was odd for not enjoying the latest noisemakers.

With whom did she spend her free time? Obviously, she had family in town. He shook his head, remembering her cousins. Jennifer Guidry—pretty, young, and flirtatious—had mentioned seeing Anne again on Thursday night. Not for the first time did he wish he had a group of friends or relatives to spend time with. Although he guarded his personal space and private time jealously, he still needed fellowship and companionship.

Lights from the buildings behind him twinkled on the surface of the river. He leaned forward, resting his elbows on the small table.

Are you testing me, God? Is this attraction supposed to be a test of my ability to keep my word to my employer while not lying to Anne? How am I supposed to do both?

He gave the waitress a tight smile as she set the glass of tea down. Absently, he lifted it and took a sip, then groaned. It had taken him years to learn to enjoy cold tea, but he'd forgotten restaurants in the South always overloaded theirs with sugar.

He flagged down another server and requested a glass of water with no ice and a slice of lemon.

He envied Anne. She'd found what she enjoyed doing and had created a flourishing business. He was jealous of Jennifer Guidry's precocious success as a restaurateur. The girl couldn't be thirty years old yet had built a restaurant that seemed to thrive in an out-of-the-way town when the chances for failure in the food-service industry were high.

Both women had found a way to make their dreams come true, while his still remained only a fantasy. Maybe he wasn't praying about it often enough or listening for God's answer hard enough.

"George?"

George started at Forbes's voice. He stood and extended his right hand. "Good evening, Forbes."

The lawyer smiled, his eyes reflecting the glow of the Japanese paper lanterns strung around the café. "I'm glad to see you're getting out and enjoying Bonneterre."

"Yes. The city has many charms." George glanced around at the women gaping or batting their eyelashes at Forbes. "Won't you join me?"

"Ah, I'd love to, but—" Forbes nodded toward a nearby table at which sat a breathtaking redhead. He grinned. "It's a business dinner, but that doesn't keep her from wanting my sole attention."

George smiled. "If you have to do business over dinner, at least the company is pleasant to look at."

"Speaking of dinner company, do you have plans Thursday night?"

"Not particularly. Just work."

"Now, George, you know what they say: All work and no play makes George a dull boy. I know you've got a reputation to protect, so bring Courtney along with you, if you don't think that'll make things too uncomfortable."

"Miss Courtney is in Paris." George's mind raced. Thursday was the night Anne and Jenn were supposed to be having dinner.

"Then you must come. I'll make sure no one asks you any probing questions. You can't just sit around at home by yourself for the next four months."

"Just how many will be at this dinner?"

"Oh, five or six others—Anne, my sisters Jennifer and Meredith, a few other miscellaneous cousins." Forbes squeezed George's shoulder. "Say you'll come. Anne will never forgive me if she finds out you're spending the night by yourself when you could be with us."

"When and where?"

"The Fishin' Shack—it's Jenn's restaurant. Take River Road south out of town and go about twenty minutes to the town of Comeaux—"

George held his hand up with a smile. "I've been there once already, so it should be no trouble to locate again."

"Excellent. We'll see you there around seven Thursday night."

George sank into his chair. He'd get to see Anne in a social setting and meet more of her family. Would she be happy to see him? She seemed to enjoy the time they'd spent together yesterday—

No, he was deluding himself. The attention Anne showed him amounted to nothing more than professional courtesy. She thought he was a client—someone who was getting married—but he was letting it go to his head, thinking that somehow, deep down, she must know he wasn't the groom, imagining she was as attracted to him as he was to her.

The story of his life—he liked a woman he couldn't have because of his social status or job. He had to find some way to cure himself of the attraction and refocus on the job at hand.

CHAPTER 10

With a wave and return greeting, Anne swept past the hostess and made her way through the crowded restaurant to the large round table in the back. She wasn't the first to arrive, as several cousins sat around talking and laughing over their iced tea and hush puppies.

Meredith scooted out the chair beside her for Anne, who slid into it gratefully. "Working late?"

Anne nodded. "Probably would have worked straight through dinner if Forbes hadn't called me to tell me he was leaving the office later than usual. I didn't tell him I was still at work myself."

"Big wedding this weekend?"

"Yeah, so I'm going to have to eat and run."

"I'm just glad you've been able to make it to as many dinners this summer as you have. When you're not out on dates, that is." Meredith winked.

Anne grabbed a glass and filled it from the pitcher of sweet tea in the middle of the table. Thursday night dinners with the family were easier to work into her schedule than dates with men she didn't know and didn't particularly want to meet. With her family, she could be herself; she could put aside the persona of the outgoing, vivacious professional woman everyone else wanted to see her as. She could let her vulnerabilities show, could let someone else support her for a little while.

"I'm a little surprised Forbes isn't here yet." She looked over her shoulder toward the door. "If he left downtown around the same time I left. . ."

Meredith turned to answer a question from one of their cousins, leaving Anne to her own thoughts. Oh, to meet a man she could feel as comfortable with as she did her family. To be able to talk to him like she had with George here in this very restaurant three days ago.

She wasn't supposed to be thinking about him in that way. He'd already made his choice of partner, and she'd no more try to win him away than she would try to break up a married couple. She had to overcome these feelings. She *had* to.

"Oh, Anne, did you ever talk to Major?" Meredith asked.

"I did. We're having dinner—so I can go over a couple of up-coming events with him to get bids on catering them. That's all." At least, Anne told herself, she didn't have any other motives for getting together with the handsome chef whom longtime Bonneterre residents still remembered as a high school and college football star.

"Hey, y'all."

Forbes's voice startled her. She hated sitting on this side of the table where she had her back to the main part of the restaurant.

"I've brought a guest tonight."

Anne twisted around and nearly fell off the seat. Behind Forbes stood George Laurence, looking handsomer than ever in a cobalt blue button-down and khakis. The shirt hugged his muscular shoulders, and the bright blue hue turned his eyes from cinnamon brown to a deep chocolate.

Anne had to tear her gaze away from George before he caught her staring at him as Forbes introduced him around the table. When Forbes had called her half an hour ago, she'd been begging God to take away the attraction she felt toward her client. God hadn't answered her prayer.

"We're so glad you could join us, George," Meredith said after shaking hands with him. "I believe the seat beside Anne is unclaimed."

No! Anne wanted to yell at her cousin. The last thing she needed was to spend time with George Laurence outside of work.

She was forced to paste on a smile when George looked at her. She couldn't be rude to him. He was her most valuable client, after all. "Yes, please. There's always room for one more."

George sat next to her; Anne's nerves crackled like a live electrical wire. He had some kind of magnetic aura that pulled at her soul, drawing her to him, making her want to know him better. She buried her nose in the menu and tried to calm herself with a few deep breaths.

"Hey, y'all. Sorry I'm late."

The final member of the party, Rafe Guidry, tall and slender with strawberry blond hair like his older sisters, arrived and took the last available seat beside Forbes.

Before Forbes or Anne could make the introduction, Rafe half stood and extended his right hand to George. "Rafael Guidry."

George stood. "George Laurence."

"What kept you?" Jenn leaned over Rafe's shoulder to hand a menu to her younger brother.

"Meeting ran late." Rafe didn't even look at the menu before he handed it to the server while giving his food and beverage order. "Forbes, I now understand why you decided to go to law school instead of taking over the family business."

"Rafe—no business talk at the table, please." Forbes gave him a look only an older brother could get away with, then turned to George. "Our parents are the proprietors of Boudreaux-Guidry Enterprises—the company that owns most of the convention spaces and several hotels and buildings in town. We got our fill of shop-talk around the dinner table when we were kids."

"Which is why Forbes and Jenn got out." Meredith's entry into the conversation surprised Anne, as she usually let Jenn and Forbes overshadow her around nonfamily members.

"But not you." George leaned forward a fraction, though his posture remained perfect.

103

Anne recognized the same interest in his expression he'd had when their conversation had become personal over lunch the other day. Annoyance filled her for being disappointed her cousin could illicit that reaction from him, too. The man was already engaged to someone else; any interest he'd shown in her had been strictly on a professional level.

Meredith's mouth twisted ruefully. "I decided to major in art history in college. Needless to say, since I didn't want to teach, there really weren't many opportunities out there, so I started working as Anne's assistant at B-G. I took over when she left to start Happy Endings."

George turned to look at Anne. "I'd be interested in hearing, sometime, why you decided to start your own company."

"Anytime." She tried to still the fluttering in her stomach at his intense gaze. At thirty-five, she was far too old to have a schoolgirl crush on a man who was completely unattainable.

"George, do you find Bonneterre to your liking?" Meredith asked.

George answered, and Anne let out a relieved breath. She hated when everyone's attention was on her.

With each word that came from his mouth, Anne's pulse skipped and jumped like a kid on the last day of school. *He's engaged. I'll never work in this town again if word gets out that I've fallen in love with a client. Lord, please help me!*

"All right, George, we're all curious," Rafe interjected, shoveling crawfish cheese dip onto a small plate. "What do you do for a living?"

When George didn't immediately answer, Anne's gaze snapped to him. Why would being asked about his job cause his smile to vanish, his posture to stiffen? She hadn't asked him personal questions because she was afraid that the more she knew about him, the more she'd like him.

He cleared his throat. "I am a household manager and personal assistant."

Anne frowned. Not what she'd expected.

"Okay. . ." Her cousin Jason drawled the word. "What does that mean?"

She was torn between throwing her spoon at her cousin and thanking him for voicing the question in her own mind. She didn't want her family to alienate George and make him decide he didn't want her to plan his wedding, but she really wanted to know everything about him.

"I oversee and attend to all of my employer's personal needs—such as travel plans, social calendar, household organization, setup for entertaining."

"So you're familiar with event planning?" Meredith asked.

He smiled, and his posture eased a bit. "Quite. My employer entertains large numbers of guests at home frequently."

"What a great help for you, Anne." Jenn slipped into her seat as the servers arrived with the entrées. "Who do you work for, George? CEO of a major corporation? An ambassador? A Hollywood megastar? Come on, fess up."

He shook his head, the lines around his eyes tightening. "Part of my job is maintaining discretion."

"I know who it has to be," Rafe said, winking at Anne. "I'll betcha he works for Mel Gibson."

Everyone laughed, and Anne saw George's posture ease again.

"Sean Connery? No? Tom Hanks?" Rafe continued teasing.

Eating gave a much-needed diversion for everyone's attention. Jenn had to excuse herself twice and disappear into the kitchen, and Rafe and Meredith talked shop for a few minutes.

Exhaustion rested heavily on Anne's shoulders. She'd only gotten about four hours of sleep the last three nights. She picked at her crawfish étouffée, eating only the chunks of meat.

"Hey, Annie." Jason speared a shrimp from Jenn's unattended plate. "I talked to Mom on the way over here. She said that she may have to bring the cake for Amanda and David's wedding earlier than planned on Saturday, since she has a birthday cake she has to finish for someone else that afternoon."

"I'll call her first thing in the morning. But it shouldn't be a problem." Anne was keenly aware of George listening to their conversation.

He had a thoughtful expression on his face when she glanced at him. "You have a family member who makes wedding cakes?"

She nodded. "My Aunt Maggie. I would like to set up a time after Courtney gets back in town to do a tasting so y'all can choose the flavor of the cake and the fillings."

"I will check the calendar to arrange a time." He pushed a chunk of salmon toward the edge of his plate and speared a few pieces of romaine and a crouton. "Do you work with your aunt often?"

"I've worked with her since I was nine years old. My first paying job was as her catering assistant." Anne dug the fingernails of her left hand into her palm. Why did she always run on at the mouth whenever he asked her a question?

His smile was inscrutable. "So, in essence, you entered the family business as well."

She blinked a couple of times in surprise and then couldn't stop her smile. "I've never thought about it that way, but I guess you're right."

"But she's bossy, so she wanted to be the one telling everyone else what to do." Jason swiped another shrimp off Jenn's plate. "That's why she started her own business."

"I'm not bossy." Anne laughed as Jason waggled his eyebrows at her. Six years her junior, he'd only been three when she'd come to live with his family after her parents' death. "Okay, maybe I was a little bossy growing up."

Jenn, Meredith, and Rafe scoffed.

Forbes leaned forward to look at her around George. "I hate to be the one to break it to you, my dear, but you do like to be the one in control. . .at least when it comes to your weddings. That's why you work around the clock to make sure everything's up to your exacting standards."

"But that's what makes you so good at what you do." Meredith could always be counted on to defend her.

Anne laughed to keep from groaning. What kind of an impression was George Laurence going to have of her after tonight? Would he still respect her in the morning?

"Anne was featured in one of the bridal magazines a month ago." Jenn jumped into the conversation, slapping Jason's hand away from her plate as she regained her seat. "She's gotten calls from brides all over the country since it came out. Of course, now we can get away with calling her an 'obsessive perfectionist' since it appeared in print from an objective outsider."

"Jenn!" Heat crawled up Anne's cheeks.

"Yes, I saw the article."

George's admission startled Anne.

"That is why Miss Hawthorne was hired to plan this wedding," he continued. "The bride was very impressed by her credentials and the portfolio of photographs from other weddings that were featured."

"So your fiancée decided to get married here just because she read an article about Anne?" Rafe asked.

George shook his head. "No. The bride is originally from Bonneterre and wished to get married in her hometown."

"So that's how you ended up here." Jenn gave George an appraising glance. "You know, George, I'm going to keep bugging you about who you work for until I get it out of you."

The servers returned to the table to remove their dinner plates and offer a dessert menu.

"No dessert for me," Anne said as she handed him her plate, "but I would love a hazelnut cappuccino."

"Brilliant idea." George's voice was soft, as if meant only for himself. "I'll have one of the same, please," he told the waiter.

The talk around the table turned to travel. Anne listened with unbidden fascination to George's descriptions of the distant and exotic places he'd visited. She fought the desire to ask her own questions about his personal life. What had led him into his profession? For whom did he work? Was it someone famous or just wealthy? And how was Courtney—

She gasped, nearly choking on her cappuccino. *His employer!*

Coughing, she grabbed her napkin as Meredith pounded her on the back. "I'm okay—just went down the wrong way," she assured her cousin, her voice raspy. She breathed a little easier when George excused himself from the table.

What he said he did for a living didn't sound like a job that would make him try to shroud his wedding with mystery. What if it was his employer and not himself he was trying to protect? What if he did work for someone famous like Rafe had been teasing about, and that person was embarrassed by George's marrying a girl so much younger?

She needed to go down to the Blanchard Leblanc bookstore, grab as many gossip magazines as she could find, and do some research. If his employer was someone famous, maybe there were pictures of him or her at some event with George hovering in the background—a movie premiere, a black-tie fund-raiser. . . . The coffee scalded her tongue, but she didn't care. Somehow, she had to find out who George Laurence really was.

Yes. Focusing on figuring out who he really was might help her overcome her growing attraction to him.

The house lights lowered. Anne glanced at her watch. How had it gotten to be nine o'clock? She really needed to go back to the office and finish her to-do list for the next two days.

She leaned over to grab her purse from under the table but snapped back upright when the strains of "Volare" started—sung by someone who sounded so close to Dean Martin, chills danced up and down her arms.

She blinked twice just to make sure her eyes weren't playing tricks. Entranced, she couldn't move, couldn't breathe. George Laurence stood on the karaoke stage—now crooning the song's bridge in Italian—sounding just like Dean Martin and giving every indication this was something he not only enjoyed doing, but did often.

Tears burned her eyes. Everything. Every detail about this man fit her long-held mental image of her soul mate. Cliff's weaknesses, the things about him that had driven her crazy, were George's strengths: his ability to socialize with grace, his discretion, his apparent good stewardship of his money. . . . She had a feeling George would never pretend to be in love with a woman just to gain his own end, the way Cliff had used her.

How could God do this to her? Bring the perfect man into her life only to force her to help him marry someone else?

She fled the restaurant. Her car's engine came to life with a roar. But instead of putting it into gear and driving away, she pounded her fists on the steering wheel.

"This is my punishment, isn't it, God?" she cried. "You're punishing me because I've never been able to forgive Cliff Ballantine for what he did to me, aren't You? I don't want to forgive him! He ruined my life. I dropped out of graduate school to work and send him money, and then he dumped me so he could go off and become a famous movie star and I could work myself practically to death to pay off all the debt I went into for him. Why is it fair that You're punishing me by showing me what I can't have, and he's had everything go right for him?"

She slammed the car into gear and screeched the tires pulling out of the parking lot. Taking a deep breath, she tried to calm down. "Lord, I know You have a plan for my life. But if it includes forgiving Cliff Ballantine, I'm not sure I can do it."

CHAPTER 11

$\mathcal{T}$he coffee shop inside the Blanchard Leblanc bookstore was Anne's favorite place to unwind on a Sunday afternoon. She sipped her caramel-hazelnut latte and claimed one of the overstuffed armchairs near the front windows. Heavy rain pelted the glass, drowning out the low buzz of noise from the other customers.

She set the stack of magazines she'd just purchased on the floor and pulled *People* off the top. Most of the publications she'd purchased were running celebrity wedding issues, serving dual purpose as research materials. She retrieved an empty folder and scissors from her attaché to save any interesting articles or photos.

Usually she just flipped through the pages, not paying attention to anything but the wedding articles and pictures. Today she scrutinized every photo, read each caption in hopes of seeing George Laurence's name.

The more she saw, the more thankful she was that she hadn't married someone who was always in the public eye. She'd seen the shows on TV about how photographers stalked celebrities. They never got a moment's peace.

She choked on her latte when she flipped a page and was faced with a double-spread layout of photos of Cliff Ballantine. Pushing aside her distaste for the man, Anne found the long caption at the bottom of the page: *Hollywood is abuzz with rumors that America's most eligible bachelor, and this year's "Sexiest Man Alive," is no longer eligible. According to sources close to the actor, his recent solo appearance at premieres and events may be due to a relationship he's managed to keep out of the tabloids.*

A few months ago, she'd thrown the local newspaper across her office after opening it to see Cliff's face in full color on the front page when he'd come to town for his college fraternity's one hundredth anniversary. Thank God his visit had coincided with her trip to Shreveport as an exhibitor at a bridal show. She didn't know what she would have done or said if she'd run into him while he was in town.

She chewed the inside of her lip as she looked at the photos of Cliff at different red-carpet events in Hollywood and New York. His hair was shorter than he'd worn it ten years ago, his body more sculpted, his wardrobe top-of-the-line. But he was still the same full-of-himself Cliff with the smile that had charmed her out of all good sense. . .and thousands of dollars. To think that she was the one who'd enabled him to become what he was today—but no, she didn't want to go there.

The surprise came from seeing him alone in all the pictures. In the past when the magazines featured him on the cover so that she couldn't avoid seeing him, he had a buxom blond starlet hanging off his arm.

Anne shook her head and turned the page. She was tempted to send a letter to the editor expressing her condolences to the anonymous girlfriend.

Her cell phone began playing the theme song from *The Pink Panther*. She grabbed it out of her briefcase. "Hey, Mere. What's up?"

"Didn't see you at church this morning and you didn't come to family dinner, so I wanted to make sure you're okay," Meredith said.

Anne arched her back to ease her bunched muscles and found a more comfortable position in the cushy chair. "I overslept, so I slipped into the back, and then I had lunch with David and Amanda before they left town."

"Stayed up too late partying last night, huh?" A crackle of static sounded through the phone connection as lightning flashed outside.

"It's not every day one of my friends gets married. Even a wedding planner is allowed to cut loose once in a while." Anne tore out a page that listed restaurants that had catered celebrity events.

Meredith chuckled. "It was a gorgeous wedding. I thought it was so sweet that David got choked up when he was repeating his vows."

"It was the first wedding in a long time where I've shed a few tears. They're so cute together." She pressed the phone to her ear with her shoulder to free her hands and cut out a photo of a gorgeous wedding cake that Aunt Maggie would adore trying to recreate.

"Hey." Jenn's voice replaced Meredith's. "Do you have plans for dinner tonight?"

"I'm not going on another blind date." Anne pulled the magazine closer to try to see someone in the background of a picture.

"What makes you think I'm trying to set you up on a blind date?" A hint of laughter betrayed the falsely innocent tone Jenn tried to adopt.

"Because you asked if I have 'plans for dinner.' That's what you always say when you're trying to set me up. What an awful dress." Anne tore the page out of the magazine for her file of what *not* to do.

"What are you talking about?" Jenn asked.

"Oh, it's a celebrity who got married in a dress that looks like strips of toilet paper strung together with silver shoelaces."

Jenn's laugh mixed with the static crackling through the phone. "Annie, he's a really nice guy. He works in Forbes's law firm."

"No, Jenn. I. . ." Why not? She wanted to get married, didn't she? Then why did the thought of another blind date set off her panic alarm? "This is the busiest time of the year for me. You know that. I don't have time to think about dating right now."

"Okay. You just remember that was your excuse this time. Come fall, you won't be able to use that one."

Anne laughed. "I'll remember. I'll think of a better excuse by then."

"I know you will. We'll catch ya later, gal."

"Bye." She closed the phone and dropped it back into her bag.

Outside, thunder rumbled, vibrating through the building. Anne nestled down into the chair and sipped her latte, amused by the amount of money celebrities were willing to spend on simple items. Dresses that cost more than most normal people's entire weddings. Florists who charged more for one event than most flower shops' annual incomes. Imported crystal and china. Flamboyant gifts for attendants. And all of this for marriages that would last only a few years before they did it all over again with someone else.

Lord, thank You that Cliff broke off our relationship before we actually got married. I don't think I would have survived a divorce. It was a painful reminder that people aren't trustworthy, but I'm glad I learned it sooner rather than later.

"May I join you?"

Startled out of her prayer, she looked up. George Laurence stood in front of her, a shopping bag tucked under one arm, a grande cup in his free hand. His hair was damp, and he wore jeans, a dark T-shirt, and a long-sleeved denim shirt. Water spots on his shirt and pants betrayed his lack of preparation for the unpredictable Louisiana weather. Anne swallowed hard. He was even handsomer dressed down than in his expensive, tailored suits.

Her skin tingled. She should say no. She should remind him that he had a fiancée. She should insist their meetings be chaperoned. "Yes, please do."

"Catching up on some reading?" He nodded toward the stack of magazines beside her chair.

She showed him the wedding-themed front of the one in her hand. "Research."

"Ah. No one gets married like the rich and famous." He settled down onto the adjacent love seat.

"Been to many celebrity weddings, have you?" She had to know who this guy was and for whom he worked. Coming right out and asking wouldn't work.

"I've witnessed several—shall we call them events?—in my time." He grinned, and Anne tried to keep her heart from flipping out of her chest. "Of course," he continued, "the weddings here are much different than those I've seen in England."

"Did you do the same type of work there?" She laid the magazine on her lap and sipped her latte.

He crossed his legs, his left ankle resting on his right knee. "In a way. Working for a member of Parliament is much different than working for someone. . .not in government service."

He didn't work for a politician. She hadn't thought so, but it was nice to know for sure. "Which do you enjoy more?"

His expression turned thoughtful. "It's hard to say. In the years since I've worked at this level, I've enjoyed postings because I liked the person I worked for, or I've enjoyed postings because of where I lived, or I just haven't liked postings at all."

"Postings? Does that mean that you get assignments as to whom you're going to work for?"

"Oh, no." He sipped his coffee and pulled a hardback book from the shopping bag. "I suppose it's just a difference in British and American terminology. A posting is the same as a job, a position."

She grinned. "I'll bet there're a lot of differences in what you're used to in England and how we do things here." To see him like this—relaxed, casual, and chatty—was addictive. She could imagine spending every Sunday afternoon like this with him. *He's engaged to Courtney Landry.*

"Most of the cultural differences are minor. Though the distances one has to travel to do anything—and the lack of public transport in most places—was a rather difficult transition."

Anne slipped off her shoes and pulled her feet up under her. "What would you say is the strangest thing you had to get used to over here?" *Get up. Leave now. He's not available. He's already spoken for.*

"Drive-throughs."

She stared at him a moment. "Drive-throughs? Restaurants? You don't have drive-throughs in England? But haven't all of the American fast-food places opened up over there?"

The lines around his eyes deepened; the corners of his lips pulled up with such warmth Anne nearly started fanning herself. "They have, but you walk in and either dine there or order takeaway. And I'd never heard of such a thing as driving up to a window to collect dry cleaning or even prescriptions."

She laughed, her heart racing. She really needed to get out of here. "Yeah, that's the old, lazy American mentality at work. Drive-through everything, pizza and groceries delivered to your door—and now we don't even have to go out to rent movies. Just get online and click a button and wait for it to come in the mail. Same thing's happening to our language. Laziness has turned to ignorance, and what used to be incorrect is now 'acceptable usage'—" She stopped, embarrassed, at the odd expression on George's face. Why did she become such a geek around him, running on about something that no one she'd ever known—outside of her professors—had ever shown the least interest in?

"Please continue. Your conclusions are fascinating. It sounds as if you've spent a lot of time thinking about this."

Her pulse did the jitterbug. Was he serious? "I used to. My master's thesis was on the impact of the popular culture of the 1970s and '80s on American English."

"You've a master's degree in English?" George set his book aside, shifted to the edge of his seat, and leaned forward, elbows resting on his knees.

She tried to swallow the emotion that threatened to cut off her breath. She'd ventured into treacherous territory; he belonged to someone else. *I have to get out of here. I have to put an end to anything but a professional relationship between us.* "Linguistics—though I was about ten hours from finishing when I had to leave school for financial reasons."

"I'd be interested in reading your thesis sometime. The study of language has always fascinated me." He couldn't be for real. No one—not even a family member—had ever asked to read her work.

The sincerity and warmth in his gaze made Anne want to cry. "I'll see if I can dig it up."

He leaned back again. "I enjoyed dinner with your family Thursday evening."

"I'm sorry they gave you such a hard time with all those questions." Her cheeks burned in memory of some of the things said at dinner a few nights ago.

"Don't fret about it. My brothers would probably be much worse. Do you eat together every week?"

"It's a long-standing tradition. Forbes, Meredith, and I started it a couple of years ago to help support Jenn's restaurant." She remembered Jenn's request. "How many brothers do you have?"

"Two, both younger."

"And do they both still live in England?"

"Henry just moved to Australia. Edward still lives in London. My mum writes occasionally to say they're doing well."

"It must be hard to be so far away from your family." She would never want to live anywhere but within a short drive of her relatives.

He shrugged, and the sadness in his gaze tore at her heart. "I left home at sixteen for a live-in apprenticeship. Henry and I have grown closer since the advent of e-mail, but I don't have much contact with Mum or Edward."

Stop asking him personal questions. "Have you gotten to know Courtney's family?"

He looked away and cleared his throat. "No. Since I moved Courtney out of her mother's house, we've had no contact with her family."

Her heart constricted. "You. . .you're living together?"

"We are living in the same house, yes."

Anguish choked her, and she struggled for breath. She stuffed the magazines into her bag. "You must not have read the entire contract. I'm sorry, but I'll have to resign as your wedding planner. The morals clause states that unless the wedding is to be immediate, I don't plan weddings for couples living together." Standing, she flung the strap of her briefcase over her shoulder.

"Wait—let me explain." He jumped up from the sofa, panic edging his voice.

Grabbing her empty cup from the floor, she stuffed her unused napkins into it, unable to meet his gaze. If she looked at him, the moisture burning her eyes would turn into full-fledged tears.

"I had to get her out of her mother's house. You've met Mrs. Landry, yes?"

Anne nodded.

"Then you understand why I couldn't leave Courtney there. But you must believe me—there is nothing untoward happening. She is staying in a room on the third floor, while my suite is in the basement—right beside the housekeeper's room."

"Right beside. . . ?"

"The housekeeper's room. So you see, even if Courtney weren't currently in Paris, we have a chaperone. There is no need for you to resign. I would—I know Courtney would be most distraught if she discovered my decision to get her away from the negative influence of her mother caused you to break the contract."

He'd thought of everything, hadn't he? Could he be a more perfect gentleman? She swallowed hard. "I see. Well, in that case, I suppose we should set a time to meet this week and finalize the plans for the engagement party, since it's only two weeks away."

Based on several bids still out, she scheduled George for Wednesday afternoon, at which time she planned to have her presentation for the engagement party finalized. She just hoped the plan wasn't too ambitious to pull off in less than fourteen days.

She had to get out of here. "Oh, wow, look at the time." She rummaged for her keys. "I've got to run." Keys found, she extended her right hand. "George, it was good to see you. I'll see you Wednesday. Don't forget you can park in the alley and come in the back door."

His warm, smooth hand wrapped around hers. "I'm glad I ran into you. Cheerio."

Anne tried not to look back as she exited the store but did take a peek over her shoulder as she reached the door. He'd sat down again, his back to her.

She wanted so badly to go back, to sit and talk to him as if they were the only two people in the world. . .like they had for the last hour. *Walk away. Don't give in to temptation. Lord, give me strength.*

She opened the exterior door and got a face full of rain. She'd left her umbrella on the floor beside the armchair. Unable to face him, she ran to her car. She didn't start the engine but leaned forward and rested her dripping head against the steering wheel.

"God, why are You torturing me like this? Please, please take away these feelings I have for him. Why is it that the only men I've ever been attracted to haven't felt the same way for me? Lord, what have I done wrong? I do the best I can—every task You've ever put before me, I've poured myself into one hundred and ten percent. Why are You asking me to plan a wedding for a man I'm falling in love with? What are You trying to teach me?"

A tear burned down her cheek as she visualized George standing under a floral-bedecked arbor, awaiting his bride. . .and it wasn't her.

⋇

Forcing himself to stay seated and not run after Anne was the hardest thing George had ever done in his life. He'd nearly blown his cover this afternoon by revealing more of his feelings than he should.

He gave her a few minutes to drive away, shoved the copy of the latest spy thriller from his favorite author back into the bag, and edged around the coffee table. He tripped and looked down to see her red and black University of Louisiana umbrella tangled between his feet.

Grabbing the umbrella, he headed for the exit. He pulled out his phone, scrolled to the entry for Forbes Guidry, and selected his mobile number. Anne's umbrella came in handy as he splashed through the parking lot to the car.

Thunder nearly drowned out Forbes's baritone voice. "George? Is everything all right?"

"I need to speak with you. About Anne."

Leaden silence transmitted through the phone for a moment. "I had a feeling. Come on over to my place, and we can sit down and figure this out."

Since George couldn't stop to write down the directions, Forbes stayed on the phone with him until he pulled into the driveway of the redbrick row house not too far from Town Square.

The front door opened to reveal the man who could be either George's enemy or his ally in sorting out the mess he'd gotten himself into with Anne. He dashed up the front steps, glad to take the thick green towel Forbes held toward him.

Forbes led him down the shiny, dark wood–floored hall into a masculine leather and wood–furnished study. "Make yourself comfortable. I can put on some water for hot tea. Or coffee, if you'd prefer."

"Nothing for me, thanks." George spread the towel over the leather club chair before sitting. He leaned forward, elbows braced on his knees. Now here, he didn't know how to start the conversation.

Forbes sat in a stiff-looking blue Queen Anne wing chair.

Queen Anne. Yes, she had all the makings of royalty.

"I was afraid when I first met you that things between you and Anne might get complicated." Forbes templed his fingers, looking as if this were a casual Sunday call rather than one of the most important meetings of George's life.

"Complicated? Bit of an understatement. I—" He glanced down at his clenched hands. "I cannot continue being dishonest with her. I respect her too much to continue the charade."

"And that's how I know you're perfect for her."

Surprise rushed through George. "Excuse me?"

The younger man nodded. "You'll find that I haven't been completely forthcoming with you, George. You see, I wanted to be able to observe you for a while. I'm very protective of my cousin. She's been through a lot in her life."

George bolted out of the chair and paced the perimeter of the room. "Yes, she's told me some of what she's been through."

"Such as?"

"Her parents' deaths, having to quit graduate school for financial reasons, the decision to start her business. . ." George stopped pacing and braced his hands against the frame of one of the tall windows. "Do you think she'll be affronted when she learns I've been deceiving her?"

"Probably. But she'll get over it quickly. She's not one to hold a grudge. Well, in one case, but otherwise I've never known her to be unforgiving. And I think she has good reason to want to forgive you quickly." Forbes's voice took on an amused tone.

George studied the pattern of the rain washing down the paned glass, his emotions in turmoil. Fear balled in the pit of his stomach. "If I tell her I am not getting married, I'll be in breach of contract."

"I'll handle that part. By this time tomorrow, that part of the contract will be null and void."

"How?"

Forbes held his hands up in front of him. "I've known your employer a very long time. Suffice it to say I do have some measure of influence with him."

A glimmer of hope burned in George's soul. "I'm unsure of how to tell her."

Forbes rose and crossed to join him at the window. "Don't worry. When the time's right, you'll know."

"What if I blow it? What if the time isn't right?"

"Tulips. Purple ones. Lots of them."

CHAPTER 12

With a couple of hours before the meeting with George Wednesday afternoon, Anne headed upstairs to what used to be bedrooms in her converted Town Square row house. She sang along with Nat King Cole's "Unforgettable" while she rearranged supplies in the larger of the two storage rooms. She loved having music piped through the building over the stereo system her cousin Jason had installed last year. And the five-disc CD changer she'd bought on his recommendation kept her from having to change them but once or twice a day.

The machine cycled to a new track. "I've got you under my skin," she sang along with Frank Sinatra. She stopped singing. The lyrics fit exactly how she felt about George. She clamped her lips shut and refused to let the words affect her. Was she going to have to stop listening to everything because it reminded her of George Laurence?

She kicked off her black pumps and got up on the stepladder to move her Christmas decorations on the top shelf. Last Christmas had been her first in the Town Square Merchant Association, and she had joined with the rest of the members in decorating her storefront in the Victorian Christmas theme. With her love of literature, she'd tried to make hers as Dickensian as possible.

Would George have liked it?

No! She couldn't allow herself to think about him, nor be worried about his likes and dislikes.

Sinatra faded out to be replaced by Dean Martin crooning "I Can't Give You Anything but Love." Anne tossed a wreath onto the top shelf, jumped off the ladder, and ran downstairs. She yanked the CDs out of the changer and replaced them with more innocuous classical music. Hopefully that would help keep her mind from wandering down treacherous paths.

Strains of Mozart, Strauss, Beethoven, Handel, and Chopin filled the office. With renewed determination not to think about George Laurence, she returned to the storage room and tried to lose herself in organizing.

As she cleaned, she mentally laid out the tables at Lafitte's Landing for the Landry-Laurence engagement party. She still couldn't understand why George didn't want her to send out the invitations, but with as much other work as she'd had to do in the past two weeks, his insistence turned out to be a blessing.

The first few notes of "The Blue Danube" came over the speakers. She shook out the eight-yard length of tulle even as her feet started the one-two-three pattern of the waltz. She usually tried to get her clients to incorporate this piece into their reception music. Most under the age of forty didn't.

Letting the music fill her, she twirled around the room, a cloud of yellow fabric billowing about her. If only—

"May I have this dance?"

Anne yelped and spun toward the door. The fabric tangled with her feet and sent her sideways into a tall metal shelving unit. Hand over her pounding heart and cheeks burning, she righted herself and turned to face George Laurence. "I didn't hear you come in."

George stepped forward and took the hazardous material from her, rolled it into a ball, and deposited it on a shelf beside her. Turning, he bowed and extended his right hand. "May I?"

No. She shouldn't. It wasn't appropriate. She placed her hand in his and let him whisk her around boxes and stacks of fabrics and bunches of silk flora.

His cinnamon eyes burned into hers. She wanted to look away, to regain some control over her actions and reactions. She couldn't. The heat of his gaze held a future that would never come true. He belonged to someone else. He spun her as the song swelled to a close, then ended with a dip. As he brought her upright, still tight in his embrace, his breath caressed her cheek.

Fire swept through her. She wanted him to kiss her more than anything she'd ever wanted in her life.

He reached up to brush back a lock of hair that had fallen over her forehead.

As soon as he touched her cheek, she pushed away from him. "I'm sorry." She took several steps back and tried to catch her breath.

He moved toward her, but she held her hands out to stop him.

"George, I can't. . . . I don't think I can continue as your wedding planner."

"That's what I came here to speak to you about." His deep voice was soft, comforting. "You are not *my* wedding planner. I am not getting married."

Lava-hot tears burned the corners of her eyes, and her chest tightened. He wasn't getting married—

Oh no. If he'd broken off his engagement because of her, she'd never be hired to plan another wedding again. She shook her head. "No. Please don't tell me that. I can't—"

"Let me explain."

She shook her head. He wasn't getting married? She didn't want to believe him. The possibility of making more money in four months than she had netted in the last five years vanished. She turned and escaped downstairs to the kitchen. She pressed her back against the cool wall above the air conditioner vent in the floor, her head swimming.

He descended the stairs at a more civilized pace. "Anne?" He reached for her hands. "Anne, we need to talk."

She loved the way he said her name: *Ahhnne*. No. She wasn't supposed to find any pleasure in this situation. She needed to

123

be professional. To express her condolences and cut off all communication with him in the future. But never to talk to or see him again. . . ?

She pulled away. As she yanked, though, he let go and the momentum threw her off balance. She reached for the wall to steady herself.

Lord, what do I say to him? I don't know what to do. Help me, please. She took as deep a breath as her constricted chest would allow and turned to face him.

His eyes were soft, like melted milk chocolate. "Are you all right?"

She nodded but looked away. Why couldn't she resist this attraction?

"Until yesterday, I've been bound by a contract my employer asked me to sign."

My employer. When would he just be forthright and honest with her? She tried to speak, but her voice came out as a squeak. She cleared her throat and tried again. "I'm sorry things didn't work out for you. I'll call all of the vendors we've already signed this afternoon and let them know to cancel the contracts."

He frowned. "No, no. You don't understand. I'm not the groom. I never was. The groom is my employer. He wants to remain anonymous—to keep the wedding plans out of the media. He sent me here as his stand-in—to plan his wedding by proxy."

Stand-in. . . Anne's knees buckled, and the ivy-stenciled walls started to go dark in her peripheral vision. She felt an arm around her waist, and suddenly she was sitting on a hard chair with her head being pushed down.

She waved her arms above her head and knocked his hand away. "I can't breathe." She sat up and wished she had done it slower, pressed her hands against her temples, and closed her eyes.

"Can I get you a glass of water or something?"

She opened her eyes. George knelt in front of her. *George.* She'd wished for this all along. He wasn't getting married. "I think I'm having a nervous breakdown and hallucinating all at the same time."

Chuckling, he reached for her hands, folded them atop each other, then held them between his. "You're not hallucinating. Nervous breakdown, maybe. I didn't mean for it to happen this way, but now you know."

Anne's heart connected with the imploring look in his eyes. "Let me make sure I'm clear on this. Everything we've discussed—the vendors we've booked, food we've tasted, venues we've visited— none of that was for you?"

The skin around his eyes crinkled in the way she loved as his smile grew. "Correct."

Concentration on the subject at hand was hard when he looked at her that way, but she persevered. "The contract *you* signed with me isn't for *you* but for someone else?"

"Yes." He leaned forward.

Anne shifted to her right a bit so her knees didn't impede him from getting closer. "And you couldn't tell me before, but now you can?"

He shrugged. "I should have found a way to tell you from the beginning. But my—"

"I know. Your employer." She tried to ignore the tingles that climbed up her arms from the way he rubbed his thumbs against the backs of her hands. If George was here on behalf of his employer, and George and Forbes had been working on something together— this wasn't just a case of George withholding his identity from her. Both of them had been lying to her for nearly three weeks.

She pulled away from him and crossed the kitchen to lean over the sink, just in case her churning stomach decided to give up its contents.

"Anne?"

"Forbes has known all along, hasn't he?"

"Known? Yes. He is the one who presented me with the con- tract." George's voice faded out as if he realized he was revealing too much.

She backed away, holding her hands out in front of her, palms out. "I don't believe this." She closed her eyes. "I don't know what to believe anymore."

She should have known better. She'd forgotten the only thing Cliff had ever taught her—never trust anyone.

❧

George moved closer. Anne's Wedgwood blue eyes turned a stormy gray, her cheeks went pale, and she wouldn't make eye contact with him. "Anne, it's not what you're thinking."

"You have no idea what I'm thinking." Anger, quiet but potent, laced her words.

He should have known it wouldn't go well. "I'm sorry. Can we sit down and talk?"

"No. I just need you to leave." Her smooth alto voice was emotionless, flat. She gave him a wide berth and opened the back door.

Fear—deep down and abiding—took root in George. Only once before had he ever fancied himself in love. That had been a mistake. Looking at Anne, he now knew the true nature of love. He couldn't risk losing her.

"Anne—" His cell phone interrupted him with Courtney's ring. He ignored it. He had to talk to Anne. To explain. To apologize. To beg her forgiveness. To have her look at him again with the longing in her eyes even her best expression of professionalism hadn't been able to mask.

"Please leave." Tears escaped onto her porcelain cheeks.

His heart ached. He'd caused this pain. "Anne, I'm so sorry." His voice cracked and he cleared his throat. "Please. I'll do anything to make this up to you."

She wouldn't look at him, just turned her flooded eyes toward the floor.

Rather than stay and cause more damage, he opened the glass storm door and trudged down the steps. The door clicked shut behind him with a crack that ripped through his heart like a bullet.

God, what am I going to do? No immediate answer came.

The carriage house–style lights lining Main Street flickered past as he drove down the wide, tree-canopied boulevard. How happy he could have been here! Even with the nearly unbearable heat and humidity, Bonneterre was the first place in more than twenty years that had truly felt like home.

For the second time in his life, he'd taken someone else's advice on how to tell a woman he had feelings for her. The first time, he'd merely been embarrassed by the outcome. He could only pray this time he hadn't ruined the chance for future happiness for both of them.

He couldn't leave things like this. He grabbed his PDA and scrolled down to Anne's number. He was immediately connected to her voice mail.

"This is Anne Hawthorne. I am sorry I cannot take your call at the moment. Please leave me a message, and I'll get back with you as soon as I can. Thanks!" Her cheerful recorded voice twisted his innards with guilt.

"Anne, George here. Please call me back. I desperately need to speak with you. Words cannot express how terrible I feel about what transpired this afternoon. I know you're angry and have every right to be so. But please, you must let me explain—"

A tone sounded and the connection cut off. He quickly dialed her number again. "Please, Anne, call me. It doesn't matter what time. We need to talk."

Later that evening, although he prepared for bed and turned off the lights, George couldn't sleep. He stared at the small black phone on his nightstand, praying it would ring and he'd hear Anne's voice.

He jumped out of bed and paced, chewing on the tip of his thumb. Why didn't she call? The grandfather clock in the upstairs entry hall chimed twice. They'd parted more than ten hours ago.

The rattle of plastic against wood startled him. His phone vibrated, then started to play "I Can't Give You Anything but Love."

Anne!

He leaped for the phone. "Anne? I'm so glad you called."

"George, it's Forbes." The lawyer's voice was gravelly. "Has Anne contacted you? Do you know where she is?"

George dropped to sit on the edge of the bed. "No, I haven't heard from her. How are you calling me on her phone?"

"I'm at her apartment. Her cell phone was here. She had your number programmed into it. I'm calling everyone on the list. She didn't show up for church tonight, which isn't like her at all."

"She's not home?"

"That's what I just said." Frustration clipped Forbes's words.

"Where might she go? Is there a friend she might stay with? Another of your relatives?" Where was it she'd said she liked to go when things got hectic? "Your grandparents?"

"Meredith has already driven out there. No one's talked to or seen her since this morning. What happened this afternoon?"

George ignored the accusation in Forbes's voice. "I told her the truth—not all of it, just my role. She didn't react well."

"How 'not well' did she react?"

"She asked me to leave, wouldn't look me in the eye, went dead quiet." He rubbed his forehead. That day they'd driven down to Comeaux to view sites, what was it she'd said about getting away from it all?

"That's what I was afraid of."

"Does she have another mobile? One that she uses for personal calls rather than business? Might she have that phone with her?" George stood and resumed pacing.

"I don't think so. At least, none of us has the number if she does." Forbes sighed. "I'm so sorry things turned out like this, George. I guess I didn't realize she'd be so sensitive about it."

"The fault is not yours to bear alone. Is there anything I can do to help in the search?" He stopped and rested his forehead against the armoire.

"Pray."

CHAPTER 13

$\mathcal{G}$eorge rolled from his stomach to his back, kicked the duvet off, and shifted onto his right side. The glowing hands of the alarm clock stood straight up and down. Six in the morning, and still no word. Where could she be?

"Please, dear Lord, please let her work through this and forgive me."

He sat up. Perhaps that prayer had already been answered. He hadn't prayed for her to be found. Rising, he shrugged into his robe. Pink light edged the blinds. He grabbed his Bible, journal, and phone and went out through the kitchen to the veranda. Sinking into the plush deck lounger, he breathed deeply of the early morning air and soaked in the colors of the sun rising over the duck pond behind the house.

"Heavenly Father, You are all-knowing and all-seeing. I have faith You are protecting Anne. She's a rational woman. If she needs this time to herself, don't let us find her before the right moment. When I do see her again, please give me the appropriate words to say to gain her forgiveness." The stress of the night melted away, and he rested his head against the thick cushions of the chaise.

When he woke, his neck was stiff, and the sun was well risen in the sky. A glance at his watch confirmed he'd been asleep for over an hour.

Comeaux. What was it Anne had said when they were in Comeaux that day? As they'd driven to the restaurant. . .a large Victorian house. . .the Plantation Inn Bed and Breakfast.

"I've stayed here a couple of times, too, when I just needed to get away," she'd said.

He picked up his phone and dialed information. He let the computer automatically connect him with the inn. His heart pounded as the proprietress answered.

"Plantation Inn Bed and Breakfast. How may I help you?"

"Good morning. I'm a friend of Anne Hawthorne's, and I was calling to see if she got checked in all right yesterday." He held his breath, praying he'd guessed right.

"She did. Would you like me to connect you with her room?"

He pounded his fist against his leg as he tried to control his relief. "No, I don't want to wake her if she's still sleeping. Thank you."

"Would you like to leave a message for her?"

"Oh no, that's quite all right. Good day."

"B'bye, now."

He disconnected and rushed inside to dress. It would take him nearly twenty minutes to get out to Comeaux, and by then, Anne should have had sufficient time to get out of bed. He had to talk to her before her family found her and made more of a mess, but he couldn't leave them in suspense. He called Forbes.

"Did you find her?" Forbes answered without preamble.

"I know where she is. I'm on my way to go see her."

"Where? I'll meet you."

"No. I need to see her alone." George grimaced, imagining what Anne's reaction would be at both of them showing up at her secret getaway. "I'll have her call you after we have our chat."

Silence met him from the other end of the connection. George checked the phone just to make sure the call hadn't disconnected.

"Fine." The single word betrayed Forbes's frustration. "I'll talk to you later." The line went dead. George hadn't realized until now just how much Forbes liked to be in control of everything and everyone around him.

He didn't take time to shave but brushed his teeth, then wet his hands and ran his fingers through his hair. It was probably his imagination, but there appeared to be a few new gray hairs mixed in with the brown this morning.

At a quarter of eight, he drove into Comeaux. The inn sat on the corner two blocks north of the Fishin' Shack; he turned onto the side street and into the driveway, pulling up behind Anne's dark green convertible and leaving her no room to pull out.

The aroma of bacon, coffee, and whatever sweets the inn was serving for breakfast made his stomach rumble. Perhaps they could converse over breakfast.

He wasn't sure whether to knock or enter until he saw the DINING ROOM OPEN, PLEASE COME IN sign. The door swung open into an entryway much like the one at his employer's house. He heard soft voices to his left and closed the door to reveal the dining room. A few tables were filled with patrons who looked like they'd stopped for breakfast before work. Anne wasn't among them.

"Good morning, and welcome to Plantation Inn. Just one for breakfast?" A middle-aged woman wearing a pristine white apron over a flowered dress approached him from the other end of the entry hall. She carried a silver coffeepot.

"I'm looking for Anne Hawthorne."

"Oh, Anne is taking her breakfast on the back porch." She motioned with her nearly gray head over her shoulder toward the french doors at the end of the hall. "Can I bring you anything?"

"A spot of coffee would be lovely, thank you." Walking down the hall at a civilized pace was hard, but he eventually made it to the doors. Taking a deep breath, he swung them open and stepped outside.

❖

Anne drew her gaze away from the blue jays fighting in the birdbath when she heard the doors open. George stepped out onto the porch, and her heart leaped. She shouldn't be happy to see him. Her hand shook a little as she reached for her coffee cup.

Finally, he turned toward her. She fought to keep from smiling back at him. She returned her gaze to the birds in the yard, his presence too unsettling for her peace of mind.

He strolled over to the table. "May I join you?"

"It's a free country." Yeah, that was a mature thing to say.

He walked around the small scrolled-iron table and sat in the only other chair, which happened to be immediately to her left. If she stared straight ahead, he was in her peripheral vision. She wanted to look at him, to memorize the contours of his face, to gaze into his brown eyes. But she was still mad at him.

"Anne, I cannot begin to express to you how utterly sorry I am. I never set out to hurt you—that is the very last thing I would ever want to do."

She closed her eyes and tried to swallow. His voice was so soft, his accent so endearing. She'd picked up the room phone to call him three times during the night to demand an explanation. She'd wanted to hear his story, to understand what had happened. "George, I—" She stopped when his hand covered hers on the table.

"Please, allow me to say this. I came to Bonneterre expecting to meet a middle-aged woman who wouldn't question anything I said to her. Instead, I met you, my beautiful Anne. I wanted to tell you the truth from the beginning, but I was bound by the contract my employer made me sign that I wouldn't reveal to anyone my true role. I was legally bound to pretend to be Courtney's fiancé. They thought it would be easier, thought there'd be fewer questions that way." He paused, and she could feel him searching her face for some reaction.

"Who's 'they'?"

He cleared his throat. "My employer. . .and Forbes."

Her cousin had a lot of explaining to do.

George rushed to continue. "But that was before I'd met you. As I started to get to know you, the deception was already in place. When Forbes realized that I had. . .come to care for you, he interceded on my behalf with my employer and got that clause removed from the terms of my contract. He told me you would understand."

"I'm sorry Forbes misled you. He knows how I feel about people lying to me."

"I'm not here to talk about Forbes." George made lazy circles on the back of her hand with his thumb, sending shivers up her spine. "I'm here to apologize for not telling you the truth from the beginning and to beg your forgiveness, even though I don't deserve it."

Part of her jumped at his words, ready to forgive him and move on to explore what their relationship could be. The other part kept her silent for a long time. Her confidence in him was shattered. She'd always dreamed the man she fell in love with would be as honest with her as she always tried to be with everyone around her. Would George lie to her again if his employer told him to? The whole situation didn't do much for her opinion of his ethics.

The slight whoosh of the doors opening broke the silence. Cheryl appeared with a coffee service tray, which she set on the low side table behind them. "Y'all doing okay?" she asked. "Hon, are you sure I can't bring you anything more than coffee?"

"I'm not certain how long I'll be here," George answered.

Anne finally turned to look at him. She sighed and shook her head. "Cheryl, go ahead and bring him your breakfast special. We're going to be here for a while."

He continued to hold her hand but didn't say anything while they waited for his food. There were so many things she wanted to say to him, so many questions.

After his food arrived, she gave him a few moments' peace to start eating while she pushed the remainder of her omelet around the plate. The birds in the centuries-old oak trees that shaded the large yard provided background music, and a light breeze brought the fragrance of roses and honeysuckle.

When he stopped to spread Cheryl's homemade strawberry jam on his toast, he broke the long silence. "Whatever you're thinking, whatever questions are on your mind, I can handle it."

She rested her fork on the edge of the plate and folded her hands atop the white napkin on her lap. "How am I ever supposed to trust you again?" She'd meant to lead up to that question, not just blurt it out. She didn't take her gaze away from his face, though.

He grimaced, then let out a slight chuckle. "That's my Anne, always straight to the point."

She tried to stop her heart from fluttering at being called "my Anne" but wasn't entirely successful. She was woman enough to admit to herself she was enjoying watching him eat breakfast. He was so fastidious. Not a crumb hit the table as he bit into the toast.

He swallowed and wiped his mouth with the napkin. "The irony of the situation is if I promise I will never lie to you again, you won't know whether or not to trust me. So all I can do is promise to try to earn your trust and regard." He reached for the coffeepot and leaned closer to refill her cup. "Will you allow me to do so?"

He smelled wonderful. And the stubble on his face gave him a rugged look she'd never imagined. What was he wanting her permission for? Oh yes, he wanted to try to regain her trust. "Yes, I'll allow you to do so."

His grin tugged at her heart. "Excellent." He lifted her left hand from her lap. "Now, more to the point, will you forgive me for deceiving you?"

Charm is deceitful. . . . Was he for real, or was he trying to charm himself back into her good graces? But she couldn't call herself a Christian and not forgive someone when asked. "Yes, I forgive you."

He kissed the back of her hand. "Thank you. You have no idea what it means to me."

The silence that fell between them brought a sense of comfort. He returned to his food, and she picked up her coffee, watching him over the cup's rim. "How much of what you told me about yourself is true?"

He frowned and cocked his head to the side as if surprised by her question. "Everything. I've never lied to you about anything—other than who the groom is."

"How did you do it? I mean, didn't it bother you to have to live a lie?"

"Yes. It bothered me very much. There were times I couldn't sleep at night, when I almost called you at 3:00 a.m. to tell you the whole truth."

"I wish you had." She set her cup down and started to relax. He hadn't lied to her about anything else. . .if she could believe his statement. She wanted to. "How did you know where to find me?"

"You told me the day we were out here you occasionally escape to the inn. How is it none of your family know you come here?"

"My family?" Anne frowned. "Why would they need to know?"

Instead of answering, he handed her his phone. "Call Forbes. He was sick with worry looking for you last night."

"He could have called me."

"You left your mobile at home."

She groaned and accepted his, immediately dialing Forbes's number. It didn't ring twice before he picked up.

As soon as he heard her voice, he said, "Anne? Where are you? Do you realize how much you've upset Meredith and Jennifer by disappearing like this?"

"I'm sorry I worried everyone." Her guilt over the concern she'd caused her family was tempered by anger at the way Forbes had handled the entire situation. "After family dinner tonight, you and I are going to have a long talk."

"So you're going to be at dinner tonight?"

"Practice begging my forgiveness between now and then."

Forbes laughed. "Will do, Anne-girl."

When she finished with Forbes, she dialed her own number to check her voice mail. Several from Forbes, which she deleted. Then one from George. She glanced at him as she listened to it. He sounded even more distraught than her cousin had.

She waited until he finished refilling their coffee cups to hand him the phone. "Why were you so frantic to find me?"

He reached up to cup her face. "You were upset, and I didn't know what you were thinking. I couldn't bear to think you might hate me and would never want to see me again."

Emotion gathered in her throat. "I was upset, yes, but not like that."

He glanced at her; then his cinnamon-hued eyes scanned the yard. "Why don't we take a walk?"

She nodded and stood. George assisted with her chair, then offered her his arm. When she slipped her hand into the crook of his elbow, she could feel his tension. "George, there's more to this than your worrying about me being mad at you, isn't there?"

He led her down one of the many gravel paths that led to the gardens hidden beyond the tree line. "It's not important."

"You're going to try to regain my trust by being honest with me, remember?"

He grimaced and patted her hand. "Right." Their shoes crunched on the gravel path, and the daytime symphony of locusts, birds, grasshoppers, and other insects started to warm up as the sun grew hotter. He stopped at a marble bench hidden beneath an enormous oak tree. They sat in silence for a few moments.

George took a deep breath. "This isn't the first time deception has nearly ruined my life. A very long time ago, I fancied myself in love. Felicia was unlike any woman I'd ever met. We were both too young—I nineteen and she seventeen. I'd been forced to leave home three years before, give up my dream of attending university, and start working to support my mother after my father suffered a debilitating stroke. I'll admit I was as attracted to the idea of the daughter of a duke falling in love with me as I was to Felicia herself, but I convinced myself I was in love with her, despite our youth, despite her immaturity."

He picked up a leaf and twirled it between his fingers. "She talked about eloping, running away together, and then surprising her parents. I told her I couldn't bear lying to her parents and insisted on going to them and telling them everything." He let out a rueful laugh. "I know now that she never wanted to marry me. She was just trying to manipulate her parents into sending her to Paris for the summer. The man she really loved—an earl, married with three children nearly her age—summered there and wanted to set her up as his mistress.

"Of course, my employment was terminated immediately, much to Felicia's amusement. Felicia was sent to Paris in the care of the governess who'd introduced her to the earl in the first place." He dropped the leaf on the bench, rose, and paced, hands clasped behind his back.

"What did you do?" Anne retrieved the leaf and pressed it between her hands.

"Rumor spread amongst the aristocracy as to what had happened—all from the point of view that I'd lead dear, innocent Felicia astray—and I couldn't find employment anywhere. I went to work for a British actor. That gave me entrée into other circles and allowed me opportunities for travel and employment I wouldn't have gotten elsewhere."

"Thank you for telling me." She couldn't meet his gaze. Dare she trust him enough to confide her own story of falling for someone who was only using her for his own end?

George knelt in front of her. "I've never told anyone else—aside from my mother and brothers—about it. I'm glad you know."

"I'm sorry I frightened you by disappearing." The thought of opening up old wounds with George when the new ones weren't yet healed kept her from sharing that part of her past with him.

"I trusted God would keep you safe. I prayed He wouldn't let us find you until the time was right." His brown eyes sparkled. "Was the time right?"

She couldn't resist his grin. "Apparently so."

"Speaking of time." He glanced at his watch, then stood and offered his hand. "If we're going to finish planning *my employer's* engagement party, we'd best be going."

"It's a good thing I cleared my calendar for today." She got a schoolgirl thrill when he intertwined his fingers with hers as they walked back up to the inn. Cheryl had cleared the table and left the check anchored under the vase of fresh-cut roses.

George reached for it, but Anne snatched it from him.

"Anne, please, it's the least I can do."

"The least? George, you've already paid enough in worry and stress for this date. It's the least I can do."

He nodded his agreement. As she settled up with Cheryl, his phone started to beep. He winked at her, then stepped out onto the front porch to answer the call. After paying for breakfast and her room, she went upstairs and quickly threw everything into the bag she'd packed in haste last night before her getaway.

When she joined George outside, he was still on the phone, deep frown lines etching his forehead and mouth. "Yes, sir. I understand. Yes, she called me last evening. . . ." His frown dissolved into a smile. "No, I did not plan on calling them. . . . I agree, sir. I will run anything like that past you before any calls are made. . . ." He reached his free hand out toward Anne and she took it. "Yes, I believe I will be able to speak with the wedding planner about it sometime today. Good-bye, sir." He ended the call and clipped the device back to his belt. Over her protest, he took her bag from her. "My employer. Courtney called me last night and asked if we could call to see if Cirque du Soleil would perform at the reception."

Anne laughed. "Really? And was your employer putting the brakes on that?"

"Fortunately, yes." He opened her car door for her. Before she could get in, he leaned close and kissed her cheek. "I'll meet you at your office." His voice was caress-soft.

On the drive back into town, Anne had plenty of time to think about everything George had said. Although she wanted to be upset with him for deceiving her, her relief he wasn't a client and her attraction to him made it easy to rid herself of her anger. And since he'd been burned once in love before also, he'd understand why she would want to take their relationship slowly.

George got ahead of her going through a couple of lights she got stuck at and was sitting on her back steps when she pulled up in the alley behind her office. Her heart fluttered in anticipation of being with him and not having to hide her feelings.

CHAPTER 14

$\mathcal{F}$orbes skipped out on Thursday night dinner. But by the time she sat down with her family—and George—at Jenn's restaurant, Anne was the happiest she'd been in a very long time. George had agreed they needed to take their relationship one step at a time while he tried to rebuild her trust.

Her other cousins' reactions ranged from bland astonishment to squealing excitement from Jenn and Meredith. And every single one of them insisted George attend Sunday dinner with the whole family.

George twined his fingers with hers as he escorted her from the restaurant. "I think they like me."

The twittery feeling in her stomach intensified. Was it okay to hold hands if they were taking things slowly? "Yeah, I think so, too."

"Which is good, as I plan to be around them for a long time."

A long time. She reminded herself she was thirty-five and not fifteen as her heart jumped up and down like an entire championship-winning Little League team. She barely knew this man, and he didn't have a great track record for honesty.

He opened the door to the convertible Mercedes and offered his hand. She caught the tip of her tongue between her teeth. *God, don't let this be too good to be true!*

Pointing the car back toward Town Square, he reached across for her hand and lifted it to kiss the back. "What time shall I call for you Sunday morning for church?"

Her whole arm tingled. "What? Oh, uh, service starts at eleven, but we'd better leave my place around ten thirty."

"Will you be tied up all day tomorrow and Saturday with your clients?"

"I probably won't get home until well after midnight Saturday."

"You put so much time and energy into your work. Is it that rewarding for you?"

She nodded, stifled a yawn, and leaned back against the leather headrest. "I love my work. I never imagined I'd find planning other people's weddings so fulfilling. It's not a profession I'd ever dreamed of entering—although I did it as a maid of honor in a couple of weddings in college. I always planned to be a college professor."

"Yet you had to drop out of graduate school."

"Not by choice. I—I had to quit school to go to work full-time. Cl—the guy I was dating at the time—had moved elsewhere to pursue his career and borrowed a lot of money from me." She glanced at George, whose sharp profile reflected the lights from the instrument panel in front of him. He'd been honest about his relationship. "He asked me to marry him. Since I figured I could continue graduate school after his career took off, I withdrew from school and went to work full-time for my aunt and uncle at B-G. But even that wasn't enough. I had to give up my apartment and move back home—back with Uncle Errol and Aunt Maggie—just to be able to afford to pay for my car and insurance and the minimum on all the credit cards I'd taken out that year to help support him."

"What happened?" Soft, deep concern resonated in George's voice.

"His career took off, and once the money was flowing in, he didn't need me anymore. I made excuses for his inattention for a long time, but he finally called me two days before the wedding was to take place to call everything off. I haven't heard from him since." She sincerely wished she didn't hear *of* him all the time, too. She was probably the only person in the country who didn't idolize

Cliff Ballantine, mega–movie star, humanitarian, and most eligible bachelor with the charming Southern accent.

"I wish I could say I'm sorry."

She raised her eyebrows. "But you can't?"

"No." He turned and grinned at her. "Because if you'd married him, we never would have met."

Her insides turned to jelly. She hadn't thought of it like that.

In the alley behind her office building, George came around and assisted her out of the car, then turned and opened the door of her car for her. He reached for her hands and once again kissed the backs. "Good night, my Anne."

No good-night kiss? She pushed her disappointment down. *Slow, remember?* "Good night, George."

❦

Sunday, Anne spotted Forbes as soon as service ended and beckoned to him across the crowded sanctuary with her crooked finger. She wasn't going to let him off easy.

He enveloped her in a bear hug when he reached her. "I'm so glad you're okay. Don't ever do that again. Or at least take your phone with you next time."

"While we're on the subject of things never to do again. . ." She cocked her head toward George. "No more surprises, please."

Forbes raised two fingers. "Scout's honor."

She pulled his hand down. "You were never a Scout."

"Same difference." He kissed her forehead. "I'm sorry, Annie. Really, I am."

"Forbes, may I speak with you a moment?" George's voice matched his serious expression.

Her cousin immediately switched from big brother to lawyer mode. "Certainly. Out in the vestibule?" He motioned toward the back doors of the sanctuary.

Anne frowned as they walked away. Something was going on or George would have said whatever he needed to say to Forbes in front of her. Fighting her desire to follow them, she slipped out of the pew to make her way up front where Jenn was holding court, surrounded by several guys from the singles' group.

"Anne, I was so hoping to see you today." A former client stopped her. "I wanted to ask if you would speak at this month's Bonneterre Women in Business luncheon."

"Speak?" Her heart quickened. "About what?"

"About being an entrepreneur. About being a small-business owner in our city. What it took to start your own business. You've been a BWB member for years now. Every month, we get suggestion cards requesting to have you speak."

More than a hundred women attended those lunches. Anne had barely made it through the required public speaking class in a college class of thirty. "Let me get back to you?"

The woman handed her a business card. "Call me at my office anytime this week. I'll need to know by Thursday."

Anne nodded and tucked the card into her planner. She'd almost made it to Jenn when she was stopped again.

"I'm so glad I found you, Miss Anne." A blonde who could grace any fashion runway in New York or Paris gave her a quick hug. "I wanted you to meet my fiancé, Heath."

The young man she shook hands with looked like he'd stepped right off a magazine cover. He was fashionably dressed with boyish, curly golden hair, hazel eyes, and a grin that could melt steel. "It's nice to meet you, Heath. Congratulations. You've found yourself a wonderful bride."

"I know." He put his arm around Elizabeth's miniscule waist and gazed down at his fiancée in a way that twisted Anne's heart with envy. "God has truly blessed me."

Elizabeth's color was high when she pulled her gaze away from Heath. "And thanks to your advice, we're getting married the first weekend in August. Would you have time to work with me? I can't afford much, but I'd really like your help, since it's so soon and you have all the connections."

"Of course." Anne rested her hand on Elizabeth's shoulder. "And don't you worry about the cost. We'll work around what you can afford."

The young woman's eyes filled with quick tears, and she threw her arms around Anne's waist again. "Thank you so much—for everything."

Laughter bubbled up in Anne. "Of course. Call me this week, okay?"

"Okay."

Oh, to be young and in love. Anne shook her head and turned, only to be practically tackled by Jenn. Ending the hug, Jenn slipped her arm around Anne's waist as they strolled toward the exit. "Did I see you and George come in together this morning?"

"Yes. He came and picked me up this morning. We've worked a lot of stuff out this week." But even though he'd promised he wouldn't lie to her again, he was holding something back. He and Forbes had been gone a long time.

"Is that a blush I see?" Jenn teased. "Did you ever find out if he has a younger brother who's as good looking as he is?"

Anne rolled her eyes and shook her head. "Is that all you ever think about?"

"What?"

"Men!"

Jenn laughed. "What else is quite so entertaining?"

Meredith joined them from the direction of the choir room and gave Anne a long, gentle hug. She didn't ask questions like her sister. Emotion lumped in Anne's throat. Meredith's deep understanding of her need for quiet or space was one of the reasons they were so close.

Anne put her arms around her cousins' much smaller waists. "I guess we should head out for Uncle Errol and Aunt Maggie's."

Jenn gave Anne's arm a light pinch. "Is George coming?"

"Yes. Do you think he would dare risk offending any of you?" The rest of the family was going to have a field day with him. If he thought Jenn and Rafe had given him a hard time at dinner Thursday night, once again trying to pry his employer's name from him, he was in for a surprise.

The brass chandeliers overhead went dark, casting the sanctuary into dimness accented by the light flowing through the windows. She'd tried to talk several of her brides into leaving the majority of lights off in this sanctuary to showcase the beautiful stained-glass images of scenes from Jesus' life, but so far, none had. If she got married in this church. . . Anne stopped her fantasy as soon as it started. The faceless groom she'd seen dimly for so many years had been replaced by George Laurence. *Slow, remember.*

"There you girls are." Forbes's voice echoed from the rear of the nearly empty church. "We've been waiting for you out in the foyer."

Her heart skipped a beat at the sight of George, who stood in the doorway with Forbes. She took a deep breath and pushed her emotions back. She couldn't let her feelings get the better of her. When she reached him, his closed expression set her ill at ease.

Her skin tingled when his hand cupped her elbow. Forbes took her other elbow and started to lead her across the vestibule.

She stopped and pulled away from both men. "What have you two been talking about out here?"

"Nothing." Forbes gave her his most charming smile.

Anne wasn't buying it. She turned to George. His mouth was set in a grim line, and he wouldn't meet her gaze. "George? Remember what we talked about Thursday morning? About honesty and trust?"

He closed his eyes and nodded, then turned and rested his hands on her shoulders. "It's just some business I needed to take care of with Forbes for my employer."

"That's all?" She hated to doubt him but couldn't help it.

"That's the truth." His voice, soft, deep, and holding promises she hoped would come true, settled her doubts.

She nodded and took his arm. "All right, then, let's go."

How was he going to tell her the truth? Anne deserved to know what she was in for when the identity of the man she was planning this wedding for broke in the media. On his way to pick her up this morning, his employer had called to warn him that reporters were starting to bug his publicist with questions about the rumor of his engagement. He had returned to New York, leaving Courtney in Paris to eliminate the risk they would be photographed together.

"George?" Anne's mellow voice broke into his worries.

Some of his anxiety ebbed away when he locked gazes with her. He squeezed her hand. He loved that she'd taken it without hesitation as they walked through the very modern part of the church building.

Her fine brows drew together in a frown. "What were you thinking about so intently?"

She didn't like surprises, but he couldn't breach what remained of the confidentiality clause. He needed, however, to be as honest as possible. Forbes, Jennifer, and Meredith had walked faster and disappeared around a corner.

He bit his bottom lip and took a deep breath. "I'm worried that my employer's confidentiality about his relationship with Courtney may have been breached." He paused, and she turned to face him. "If anything happens and I have to suddenly disappear, please don't hold it against me. If anyone connects me with Bonneterre or Courtney Landry, all may be lost."

"I still don't understand the need for such secrecy. What would happen if someone found out why you're here?"

He stepped in front of her to open the door to the parking lot. "If my employer's secret engagement leaks to the press because of me, I would most likely lose my job, which means I would have to return to England."

"Would that be such a bad thing? To go home after so many years?" Anne looked like a movie star when she slipped on a stylish pair of sunglasses and ran her fingers through her hair to push it back from her face. The late June sun and steamy humidity never seemed to affect her.

How long would he have to live here to become acclimated? He probably wouldn't get the chance to find out. "Given the dwindling need for full-time personal assistants with the advent of modern technology, it would be difficult for me to find a position that's the equivalent of what I have now. Aside from that, it's not really the occupation I'd like to keep for the rest of my life."

"Well, just from what I've seen in the short time I've known you, I know you'd do well as an event planner wherever you decide to settle."

"Thank you." *Wherever you decide to settle. . .* Disappointment attacked him through her words. He'd hoped she'd want him to settle here, maybe even go into business with her. They would make a perfect team—her connections and his attention to detail. If he went into business with her, he could get his work visa changed. . . or he could marry her and get a green card. There were much worse fates than being married to a woman he was already attracted to.

They reached the car, and he used the remote to unlock it. He opened the door for her.

She lowered her glasses and winked at him. "Have I warned you about my family? Almost all of the extended family will be at lunch. And they can be somewhat overwhelming."

He winked back. "I have survived a couple of dinners with Jennifer and Rafe."

She laughed. "Oh, they can't hold a candle to the whole family being together."

George followed Anne's directions through town. What had she meant by "overwhelming"? He'd experienced many large dinner parties and gatherings throughout his career—of course as someone who had to service the guests—so he couldn't imagine a meal with her family would be that different.

He was going to meet the rest of her family. He and Forbes

had formed a strong friendship in the short time since they'd met. He also enjoyed the weekly dinners he'd attended with Anne's cousins. Not all of them came every week, but they accepted him and offered him friendship even when he couldn't divulge much personal information to them.

From the examples he'd seen in Anne, Forbes, and the others, her family was the epitome of his image of Southern charm. Anne, never ruffled, always had a smile and encouraging word for everyone she met. Forbes played the dapper gentleman for whom chivalry was a way of life, not an ancient fairy tale. Jennifer, the flirtatious Southern belle. . . He laughed. Henry would love Jennifer. His youngest brother would definitely fall for the beautiful charmer with the strawberry blond hair.

The sunlight barely peeked through the dark green foliage that canopied Oak Alley Drive as they traveled through the garden district toward midtown. She instructed him to turn left on Tezcuco Avenue before reaching the commercial district. Deeper into the heart of the residential area, the smaller houses on Oak Alley gave way to large, immaculate Victorians set far back from the street and surrounded by lush green lawns shaded by oaks, magnolias, and other trees he didn't recognize.

Another left onto Destrehan Boulevard, and the lots grew larger, the landscaping more elaborate. Homes ranged from sprawling Victorians to enormous Greek-revival manses, red brick with fat white columns lining the front.

The first indication that this "family dinner" was beyond what he'd imagined was the number of cars lining the street in front of the multi-gabled, three-story house Anne had him stop in front of.

"This is Aunt Maggie and Uncle Errol's house. They bought this house after I went to college, but it's still home."

He helped her out of the car, and she led him up the driveway toward the sidewalk that snaked across the yard to the wraparound front porch.

Maggie and Errol. He was about to meet the people who'd

stepped in to raise Anne after her parents' deaths. His heart pumped a little faster. He hoped to make a favorable impression on them. If he was going to spend the rest of his life with her—but no, he couldn't indulge in that kind of thinking yet. She needed time to get to know him better, and he had to regain her trust.

His thoughts were interrupted when the front door flew open and an older woman—who bore a remarkable resemblance to Anne—stepped out onto the porch.

"It's about time," the woman called as George and Anne approached the house.

"What are you talking about?" Anne looked at her watch. "It's only twelve forty-five. We never eat dinner before one."

"You're thirty-five years old. It's about time you brought a man home for Sunday dinner!"

CHAPTER 15

*J*ust when she'd thought her family couldn't possibly embarrass her any further. . .

Anne stepped up onto the porch and bent forward to accept Aunt Maggie's kiss on her cheek. "Good afternoon to you, too, Mags." She turned. "George, this is my aunt, Maggie Babineaux. She's the vendor I suggested to you for the wedding cake."

He nodded, brown eyes twinkling as he took Maggie's hand and lifted it to his lips. "The pleasure is mine, Mrs. Babineaux. I've heard much about you from Anne."

Maggie regarded him with calculation in her gaze. "I wish I could say I've heard more than rumors about you, George Laurence." With a wink at Anne, she took hold of his arm and directed him into the house. "But we'll remedy that today, won't we?"

Anne shrugged and wrinkled her nose in an apologetic grin when George glanced at her over his shoulder. She nearly laughed at the expression of trepidation in his eyes. He'd never experienced anything like a large Cajun family gathered for Sunday dinner. This afternoon would be a trial by fire of his professed feelings for her.

She inhaled deeply as she crossed the threshold into the house. The aroma of roast beef and fresh yeast rolls brought instant images of her childhood to mind. Aunt Maggie and Uncle Errol had bought this house not long after Anne had left for college, but every time she walked in, she was *home*. Her happy memories from childhood started the day she moved in with Maggie, Errol, and their four sons twenty-seven years ago.

The buzz of voices from the back of the house created a tingle of anticipation in Anne. Would George, mostly estranged from his own relatives, understand the importance of family to her? She grinned. Would he survive her family?

❧

George refrained from turning to make sure Anne was still behind him as her aunt led him through the large, well-appointed home. The food smelled wonderful, and even though breakfast had been more than satisfying, his stomach rumbled in response to the tantalizing aromas.

Beside him, Maggie Babineaux kept up a constant chatter about the family, trying to tell him the connections of everyone he'd meet today. She lost him after the name of her oldest son, daughter-in-law, and grandchildren.

The front rooms were formally furnished and appeared rarely used. From what he could see, each room had wood floors covered with expensive, probably antique, Oriental rugs. Anne came from money. He shouldn't be surprised by that, given her education and refinement. He fought disappointment. He'd assumed her background was more like his—enough income in the family to meet their necessities, but not a lot left over for luxuries.

Anne gained his attention with her hand on his arm. "Mamere, I'd like you to meet George Laurence. My grandmother, Lillian Guidry."

He swallowed his surprise as he took the petite, dark-haired woman's hand in his. "It's very nice to meet you, Mrs. Guidry."

"We're pleased you could join us for lunch, Mr. Laurence." She turned to Anne, who leaned over to receive a kiss on each cheek. "You look beautiful, Anne Elaine."

The two women couldn't be more opposite in appearance—Anne, tall, curvaceous, and blond; her grandmother, petite, thin, and brunette. As he watched them converse, he did notice similarities around their eyes and mouths. Each was beautiful in her own way.

"George!" Forbes clasped his shoulder and shook his hand. "Get out of the kitchen before they put you to work."

He looked around for Anne.

"Don't worry, ol' man. She'll join us when the aunts finish questioning her about you, which they can do better if you're not around." Forbes introduced George to his parents, aunts and uncles, siblings, and cousins as they crossed the crowded family room to a sunny, glass-enclosed porch beyond.

Jason, Rafe, Jennifer, and Meredith stood to greet him. George let out a relieved breath when he sank into the thick cushions of an oversized wicker club chair, glad to be around people he knew.

Meredith perched on the ottoman in front of him and leaned forward, her hands clasped in front of her. Genuine concern gleamed in her gaze. "I assume by the fact that you're here that you were able to work things out with Anne?"

He shrugged. "Somewhat. We've agreed to take things slowly and get to know each other better."

The ginger-haired woman nodded slowly. "Good." She stood, then leaned over and pressed her cheek to his. "Because if I ever hear that you've lied to her again, you'll have more than just Anne to answer to." She kissed his cheek, held his gaze for a long moment, then crossed to sit beside Forbes on a leather love seat.

He held his grin in check. The love Anne's family displayed pleased him. Like him, they wanted only the best for her. But he could see why she needed a secret getaway.

"By the way, how did you find Anne the other day?" Forbes loosened his tie and stretched his arm across the back of the sofa behind his sister.

"I simply recalled something she'd told me while we were out visiting sites one afternoon." He returned Forbes's courtroom stare with a challenge of his own. There was a reason her family hadn't known where she was, and it wasn't his right to reveal the location to them.

Before Forbes could interrogate further, two twentysomething women bubbled into the room: a strawberry blonde who turned out to be a younger sister to Forbes, while the other, with brunette hair, belonged to yet another branch of the Guidry family. After being introduced to George, they retreated to a corner to flip through magazines they'd brought and converse in whispers.

After a few minutes, the two young women flittered across the room and dropped something into Forbes's lap. "I knew you weren't telling me the truth the other night," the redhead said.

"Where did you get my high school yearbook?" Forbes reached for the large volume, but the young woman held it out of his grasp.

"From that old trunk of stuff that's still in Mama and Daddy's attic. You told me you didn't know Cliff Ballantine when you were in high school. But how come there's a picture of the two of you together?"

Forbes's expression tightened. "Let it go, Marci. We were on student council together. That doesn't mean we were friends or hung out together."

"But you *knew* him."

George caught sight of Anne from the corner of his eye as a relative waylaid her from entering the sunroom.

Meredith snatched the yearbook from her younger sister. "Marci, please don't bring up his name again."

The uncharacteristic vehemence in Meredith's voice surprised him. What had happened between this family and Cliff Ballantine?

"You know. . ." Marci sighed and stood, hands on hips. "One of these days I'm going to find out what all the secrets in this family are." She put her arm around her young brunette cousin. "We're not children anymore. We deserve to know."

Forbes took the book from Meredith. "When the people in the family who have those secrets feel like telling you, you'll know. Until then, try to keep to your own business. That includes not invading my personal property."

The two young women left in a huff.

Anne stopped them in the doorway. "Marci, Jodi Faye, what's the matter?"

"Ask Forbes." Marci's full lips were set in a pout when she glared over her shoulder at her oldest brother. "He seems to know everything."

Anne's fine brows wrinkled into a frown when she entered the room. "What's going on?"

Forbes held up the school annual and tossed it onto the coffee table in front of him, where it landed with a thud. "They just wanted an ancient history lesson, and I wouldn't give it to them."

Her blue eyes widened at the sight of the book. "Oh." Her shoulders drooped for a moment, then squared; her lips pressed together, then turned up at the corners. "Well, no sense in letting the past spoil the present, right?" Her gaze seemed to search her cousin's for reassurance.

Forbes nodded. "Right. You survived the aunt gauntlet?"

She blushed, and her eyes turned toward George for a brief moment. "Standard questions—who is he, what does he do, when are you going out again. . . . You've been through it before."

"And will probably go through it again. That's why I rescued George and brought him out here, so he didn't have to witness the mayhem."

A ringing echoed through the house, like the triangle and clapper that cooks used as a call to dinner in all the old Western movies. The exterior door flew open and children flooded the sunroom from the backyard.

"Dinnertime." Anne extended her hand to George with a warm smile. "Papere—my grandfather—will say grace, and the children's plates will be served. Once they're all situated in the breakfast room, we'll get our turn."

He rose and placed his hand in hers—even as two children ran between them. They joined the rest of the family, congregated in the great room and kitchen. The feeling of Anne's hand in his offset

155

any feelings of discomfort he had from being surrounded by such a crowd of people. It might take him years, but he could probably learn to love attending Guidry family gatherings.

The dining table's length hindered conversation with anyone other than those immediately surrounding him. With Anne on his left, Forbes on his right, and Meredith, Jason, and Rafe across the table, George found Sunday dinner not much different than the Thursday night suppers he'd attended. And the food. . . He stopped at two servings of roast beef and mashed potatoes with gravy, green beans, corn, and what Anne said were collard greens. He did take a third yeast roll, however, and followed Forbes's example of dipping the bread into the gravy that remained on his plate.

Forbes laughed and took the fork out of George's hand, then put a piece of roll directly between his fingers. "You can't sop like a Southerner if you're using your fork and knife."

George glanced around the table and did see he was the only one not using his hands. "This is called what again?"

On his left, Anne laughed. The sound sent tingles up his spine. "Soppin'. You're soppin' up the gravy with your roll." Her eyes twinkled at him.

"And this is appropriate dinner-table behavior?"

"It is in this family." Across the table, Meredith held up a piece of roll between her fingers. "You might not want to do it at the Ritz in New York, but you'll find pert-near everyone in Bonneterre won't fault you none for soppin' up your vittles."

"I'm flabbergasted as to what you just said, but"—he took the piece of roll and sopped up some of the gravy on his plate—"I'll take your word for it."

When everyone finished eating, the women, including Anne, rose and cleared the plates from the table. When George started to push his chair back and offer to help, Anne stopped him with the gentle pressure of her hand on his shoulder. "It's family tradition," she whispered in his ear. "The women clear the table and bring dessert. The men do the dishes afterward."

As soon as the women were out of the room, Anne's grandfather, Bonaventure Guidry, an imposing, tall man, spread his arms to rest his palms on the corners of the table. "Well now, Mr. Laurence, what are your intentions toward our Anne?"

George sputtered to keep from spitting out the water he'd just sipped. He swallowed and wiped his mouth with the blue fabric napkin. "Sir?" He glanced around the table. Without exception, Anne's male relatives stared at him, awaiting an answer to the preposterous question. "My intentions. . ." He cleared his throat. "My intentions toward Miss Hawthorne are honorable, I assure you, Mr. Guidry."

Beside him, Forbes burst into laughter, and the rest followed suit. "They're just giving you a hard time. Means they like you."

Not sure he understood, George nodded and smiled. He was saved from any further embarrassment by the reappearance of the women. He started to stand, but Forbes stopped him with a hand on his shoulder. "They're going to serve dessert, so you'll just be in the way if you do that."

"I see." He edged his chair closer to the table.

Maggie directed the presentation of the desserts on the sideboard. A white cake with strawberries on top became the centerpiece, surrounded by pies, dishes of petits fours, and other confectionaries.

"Coffee?" Anne leaned over his right shoulder with a carafe and a cup.

"You know me." He winked at her.

She set down the cup and poured. "This is the real thing—genuine Louisiana coffee with chicory. Dark roast." Her voice held a hint of warning.

He sipped the dark, rich, bitter liquid. "My favorite. Although I haven't had it quite this strong anywhere else."

"That's the way Aunt Maggie likes to make it." She squeezed his shoulder and moved on to serve coffee down the table.

Meredith placed a square plate in front of him with a sampling of each of the desserts, arranged on the plate as he would expect to see in a fine restaurant. Maggie did this for a living. Anne had suggested her aunt to make Courtney's wedding cake. If what he'd seen today was what she did for a regular family gathering, he'd love to see what she could do for a reception for seven hundred guests with no holds barred on the price.

He stood and held Anne's chair for her. "Everything looks wonderful. I'm not even certain what all of it is."

Anne picked up her dessert fork and used it as a pointer. "White amaretto cake with strawberries and raspberry filling. Banana pudding. Chocolate petits fours—some have a berry filling, some are vanilla crème, and some are mint—I'm not sure which kind you got. Lemonade icebox pie. We don't usually have this many desserts. Aunt Maggie catered the Junior League tea yesterday afternoon and had all this left over."

"Annie, did Madeline catch you at church this morning?" one of her aunts asked as she leaned between them to refresh their coffee.

"Yes. I figured you were one of the key people who put her up to asking me to speak."

Forbes handed George the cream to give to Anne before she had to ask for it. She answered her relatives' questions about the invitation to speak at the Bonneterre Women in Business luncheon but fidgeted as if uncomfortable with the focus of attention on herself. As soon as the discussion turned to something else, she stopped twisting her napkin in her lap, sipped her coffee, and nibbled at her desserts.

❧

Anne smiled at George when he brought the carafe of coffee over to refill her cup before following the rest of the men into the kitchen to help clean up. As soon as the kitchen door stopped swinging, her aunts and cousins exclaimed over him—his sweetness, good looks, charm, impeccable manners, and especially his British accent.

"Is it serious?" Aunt Maggie's question brought everyone else to attention.

STAND-IN GROOM

Anne shrugged. "Not really. Less than a week ago, I thought he was marrying someone else."

Meredith leaned forward. "But could it be serious?" Her expression told Anne what answer she wanted to hear.

"I'm really not sure. I haven't even known him for a month. I know y'all want me to find someone and settle down, but give us some time, please." She smiled at the women staring at her to soften her words. "I promise you'll be the first to know if it turns serious."

Each of the younger single women was then given the opportunity to be the center of the aunts' appetite for romance. When the masculine voices and laughter in the kitchen grew louder than the clank of dishes being washed, the women's conference ended. Anne took the opportunity to slip off to the powder room.

On her way back, one of her younger cousins waylaid her at the entrance to the sunroom and pulled her back into the now-empty kitchen.

"What's up, Marci?" Anne reached over and pushed a lock of the twenty-four-year-old's honey-streaked red hair back from her face. She knew the young woman was struggling to get her parents and even Jenn, Mere, and Forbes to recognize her as an adult. But there was a lack of maturity in the way she acted around her family, compounded by the fact that she still hadn't chosen a college major after five years, that kept her a perpetual child in their eyes.

"Annie, you're the only person in the family who'll tell me the truth."

"Of course I will. What do you want to know?"

"Earlier, when I asked about Cliff Ballantine, I know Forbes was lying to me about not knowing him. Did y'all know him in high school?"

Anne's stomach twisted. She didn't want to lie to her cousin, but she also didn't want the story to get beyond the family. She crossed her arms and leaned against the edge of the island. "If I tell you, you have to promise me it goes no further. There's a reason why he's not discussed by anyone, and that's because of me. I've asked everyone in the family to keep my secret, which has become harder as he's gotten more famous." She took a deep breath. "Yes, we knew Cliff in high school. I tutored him in English and helped him write several papers."

"Even though you're two years younger than him?"

Anne harrumphed. "He was only a year ahead of me in school, but I was in advanced placement classes. He wasn't. When he started college, I kept helping him. You have to understand—I was very shy as a child and had very low self-esteem from all the teasing I got because I hit a growth spurt and was nearly six feet tall by the time I was thirteen. I never had a boy show the kind of attention to me that he did just for doing something I was good at. When I got to college, though, I wasn't just helping him with English—it was all his classes: history, anthropology, even his drama classes. When I told him I didn't have time to continue, he really turned on the charm. We started 'dating.' " She made quotation marks in the air with her fingers. "I'll spare you all the gory details. But when Cliff moved out to Hollywood my first year of graduate school, I sent him money every month to help him make ends meet. It got to the point where I was getting every credit card I could and maxing it out with cash advances just to have money to send to him. When the loan company threatened to repossess my car, I told him I couldn't afford to send him any more money. That was when he suggested we get married. I was naive and wanted to be married, especially to someone as handsome and talented as he, so I agreed. I quit grad school and went to work full-time as the event planner for B-G."

"The job Meredith has now?"

"Yes. I started planning my wedding. It was going to be small, just our families. We couldn't afford much, and I didn't want to ask Uncle Errol and Aunt Maggie for money because they'd already helped me out by giving me a loan to pay off all of my past-due bills and letting me move back in so that I could use my rent money to pay them back. Half of each paycheck went to them, half to Cliff in

California. We set a date. I reserved the chapel, the reception hall, worked out the menu with Maggie, and had a gown on layaway at Drace's."

"What happened? I mean, obviously you didn't end up marrying him. . . *did you?*"

Anne had to laugh at Marci's incredulity. "No, I didn't marry him. Two days before the wedding, he called me and told me to cancel everything. He'd gotten a callback on a movie role he'd auditioned for and would have to stay in California another week."

"What a pig."

"Yeah. So I canceled everything and lost most of the money on nonrefundable deposits. For a month, I didn't hear anything from him. The next thing I know, I see a photo of him with some blond bombshell of an actress on the front cover of one of the gossip rags at the grocery store. Time went by, and eventually I gave up hope that I'd ever hear from him and accepted the fact he'd only been dating me to get me to do stuff for him."

The glaze of admiration for the actor in Marci's eyes had been replaced by disillusionment at the revelation of the man's character. "It's no wonder you don't want anyone else in the family to talk about it. Did he ever pay you back all the money?"

Anne shook her head. "Nope. Never saw a penny. I suppose I could have blackmailed him by threatening to run to the media and show them all the canceled checks with his signature on the back, since he takes great pleasure in telling everyone how he struggled to make it on his own in Hollywood until he got his big break. It was a hard lesson to learn."

"What lesson is that?"

"Don't pour all of your emotions and energy into a relationship unless both parties are willing to give one hundred percent to it. Cliff was a taker, and he was willing to take whatever I was stupid enough to offer—my skills and education, my emotions, and my money. I'm just glad he's out of my life."

CHAPTER 16

*H*ow could you not tell me?" George brushed past the secretary who'd opened Forbes's office door to announce his arrival early Monday morning.

Forbes gave his assistant a curt nod and laid his gold pen atop the paperwork on his desk. "And what is it I'm supposed to have told you?"

Although the woman closed the door behind her, George strained to keep his voice low. "That Anne was engaged to be married to Cliff Ballantine!" He crossed the office and leaned on the desk, his hands on either side of the desk blotter. "Have you lost your senses? How do you think she's going to feel when he arrives in town next week for the engagement party and I turn around and say, 'Surprise, you've been hired to plan your ex-fiancé's wedding'?"

"It wasn't my place to tell you."

"Not your—" Fury clogged George's throat. Was it all just a game to Forbes? He liked Anne's cousin, had thought they were getting on famously and becoming fast friends. But now. . .

"You are the only person in this farce who knows all the players and their roles. How could you let Anne take on this contract?"

The lawyer leaned back in his chair, his fingers steepled and resting on his chin. "Are you more upset because you didn't know or because of how you think this might affect Anne?"

George straightened and dropped his hands to his sides. "Don't play the barrister with me, Forbes." His so-called friend's calm exterior only fed his anger. He wanted to see some kind of emotion, some kind of remorse or embarrassment. He took a calculated risk. "Did it make you feel powerful, knowing that you could manipulate this situation? Or do you hold some kind of shares in Anne's business to make you trick her into taking this wedding on just to increase the return on your investment?"

Forbes exploded out of his chair, and it slammed against the credenza behind him. "There are a lot of things I'll put up with." Menace edged his low voice. He braced his fists against the edge of his desk. "But being insulted isn't one of them. A hundred years ago, we would be headed to a field with dueling pistols about right now."

"And gladly would I have defended Anne's honor and my own." George matched his pose, trying not to let the other man's larger build and height intimidate him. "I've read about the corruption of lawyers in Louisiana, but I never expected to see it in you. To use your own flesh and blood—"

Forbes grabbed the front of George's shirt and nearly dragged him onto the desk. "You have no right to accuse me of wrongdoing. I love Anne, and I would die before I brought her harm or unhappiness."

Some of George's anger dissipated at Forbes's passionate speech. "Then tell me everything. Make me understand. Because from where I stand, you look guilty as sin. And I don't want to be caught in the middle."

Forbes released him, and George stumbled back a step. Balance regained, he smoothed his shirt and tucked it back into his trousers.

Letting out a low growl, Forbes straightened his tie and raked his fingers through his hair. He pulled his chair forward and sank into it with a sigh. "I never meant for you to be caught in the middle, George, and I apologize if you feel that way." He motioned for George to sit. "How did you learn of Anne and Cliff's engagement?"

George perched on the edge of one of the leather armchairs, guilt nibbling away at his anger. "I did not come by the information honestly. I overheard Anne telling the story to your younger sister yesterday, after you'd already left your aunt and uncle's home."

"Then to answer your first question. . ." The lawyer had replaced the outraged man again. "I didn't tell you about Anne and Cliff because it wasn't my secret to share. Just as you swore to Cliff not to reveal his identity to anyone, I swore to Anne I would never tell anyone she had a relationship with him."

"But. . ." Logic and reason failed George. A man had to honor his promises. That still left the second issue. "Why didn't you counsel Cliff against hiring Anne as the wedding planner?"

Sheepishness overcame Forbes's professional demeanor. "Cliff doesn't know Anne is the wedding planner. As you may have experienced, he's leaving the details up to Ms. Landry." He spun his pen on top of the papers that were now strewn across the desktop. "Anne needs to plan this wedding. I think it'll be cathartic for her."

George frowned. "How is planning the wedding for the man who bilked her for thousands of dollars and practically left her standing at the altar going to bring her healing?"

"Two ways. She needs to forgive him; but until she gets closure, until she's able to show him what she's made of herself—and maybe say a few things to him that she's had locked up inside of herself for years—she'll never be able to close that chapter of her life."

Manipulation for Anne's own good. It still didn't sit well with him, but was easier to understand. "And the second way?"

"How much is he going to end up paying her to plan this wedding?"

Understanding rolled in like a London fog. "So she gets closure and revenge all at the same time."

"Oh no, not revenge. . .just what he owes her—with interest." Forbes gave him a conspiratorial wink. "Now was there something else you needed to see me about?"

❧

George left Forbes's office with twenty minutes to get from downtown to Town Square to meet Anne at her office.

Anne had been engaged to his employer. Wanted to marry him. Loved him enough to drop out of graduate school so she could support him. Thought he was *handsome* and *talented*. She would have gone through with it. She would have married Cliff all those years ago if he hadn't gotten his big break and discarded her like a used tissue.

Oh, Anne. . . The disillusionment she must have suffered from being so ill used. No wonder she'd reacted with such vehemence when she discovered his own deception of her. . .on behalf of Cliff Ballantine.

The old adage couldn't be truer than in this situation: *What a tangled web we weave when first we practice to deceive.*

If she'd been so angry at him for simply pretending to be getting married, how angry would she be when she discovered whose wedding she was really planning? And would that anger, justified though it would be, destroy any chance of their relationship growing into something serious?

By the time he reached her office, he dreaded walking in and looking her in the eye. Would she see his misgivings? Would she sense something amiss? He needed to distance himself until the truth came out. If he allowed himself to fall in love with her and then lost her when she found out about Cliff, his heart would never mend. "Above all else, guard your heart, for it is the wellspring of life," King Solomon had written in Proverbs. And Solomon had had his own issues with women, so he knew from whence he wrote.

George parked in the alley behind Anne's office and killed the engine. With trepidation, he mounted the steps to the back door. He crossed the threshold into the kitchen, and cool air washed over him. Making his way from the kitchen through the hall to the front office, he could hear voices. He didn't want to interrupt and stopped out of sight of the doorway.

His skin tingled at the sound of her voice. She would be sitting in the wing chair facing the bow window, her sapphire blue eyes sparkling as she discussed wedding details with her clients.

He leaned against the wall and enjoyed listening to her guide the potential clients through the same questionnaire he'd been given to fill out at Courtney's first appointment. When he heard the telltale jingle of the bell over the front door, he entered the front office.

Anne rose; the intensity of her gaze nearly unraveled him.

"I am so glad I heard you come in." She dropped into the wing-back chair. "I'm not sure I want to sign a contract with the couple who was just here. They can't make a decision to save their lives, and all she did was ask me about Cliff Ballantine. If I didn't know any better, I'd think they were undercover reporters trying to dig up some kind of scandal from his past." She cut her gaze at him. "Of course, if that were the case, why would they come to me?" Her laugh had a nervous quality to it.

What had she said about honesty? If she wanted him to be honest with her, she needed to grant him the same courtesy. He needed to know she was over Cliff, that she'd forgiven him and could move on with a new relationship without the specter of being hurt in the past coming between them in the future.

"What's wrong?" She stood and crossed to stand in front of him, resting her hand on his crossed arms. "I do declaiyah, you look jus' like an ol' thundahcloud."

He loved it when she put on that thick Southern accent. His tension started to melt, and he smiled at her. "Nothing's wrong. It's just been a busy day already."

She gave his arm a gentle squeeze, then went around her desk to retrieve her handbag and keys. "You ready to go to the rental lot and choose decor for the engagement party?"

Cliff's engagement party. The event where Anne would learn the true identity of her client. The thundercloud returned to his heart, but he schooled his expression to mask it. "Certainly. Lead on."

He let her make the decisions on what columns, greenery, linens, tables, and chairs to rent. The only thing he ordered was the gold flatware and table service, per Courtney's request. Anne laughed and chatted with the proprietor, a friend of hers from childhood, as she completed the paperwork and George paid with the expense-account credit card.

Headed back toward her car, Anne's stomach growled. "Where do you want to go for lunch?"

"I. . ." He had to get away. Distance. He needed distance to guard his heart. In one week, she might decide she never wanted to see him again. "I can't. I'm interviewing for several house staff positions this afternoon and need to get back." The interviews didn't start for another three hours but made a convenient excuse.

"Oh. How about brunch on Friday? It's the Fourth of July, and I'm officially taking the day as a holiday. . .except for the wedding I have to set up at noon." She unlocked the car doors with the remote on her key chain. "Then later you can join us for our family Fourth of July celebration."

He slipped into the passenger seat. How could he say no to her when she caressed his face with her azure gaze? "I'll check my schedule and get back with you."

❧

For the next three days, George vacillated between his desire to spend time with Anne and his fear of ending up with a broken heart. The only person he could talk to about it was Henry, and his brother had been no help whatsoever.

"Just tell her the whole tale and have done with it," he'd said. "Honor be hanged."

George couldn't let go that easily. He'd given his word and signed a contract. He couldn't go back on that. But he agonized over the thought of spending time with Anne, because he wanted to lay before her the whole of his situation, especially the part about Cliff, so he could learn her true feelings.

The days dragged. Thursday, as he had every day that week, he went into the study on the main floor to work on the travel arrangements for Cliff and Courtney's party guests. Most had their own personal assistants, but he had a lot of information to convey to get the two hundred guests from all over the world into Bonneterre, Louisiana. He'd started a spreadsheet to track the RSVPs and now used it to enter travel itineraries.

The data swam on the computer screen, and after mangling three entries, he gave up and turned the leather executive chair around to stare out the picture window. The gray clouds and pelting rain matched his mood.

He couldn't do it. He couldn't face her. He picked up the phone and dialed Forbes's private number. The line didn't ring but went straight to voice mail, thank heavens. Forbes would ask too many questions.

"Forbes, George Laurence here. I'm calling to let you know I won't be attending dinner tonight. Something has arisen that I must handle. Please make my apologies to. . .everyone." He ended the call and let the cordless receiver drop into his lap.

The rhythm of the rain lulled him into a semiconscious state. He imagined every possible scenario of how Anne would react. She might be absolutely nonplussed at the revelation. She could be angry enough to break the contract.

"Baby, are you all right?"

George started when he realized Mama Ketty stood over him.

"I'm sorry, but you didn't answer when I knocked on the door." She clucked her tongue. "You're too young to be bearing such a heavy weight. Tell Mama Ketty all about it." She settled into one of the chairs across the desk.

He blinked. She didn't budge. Words tumbled out of his mouth—he couldn't stop them. He told her everything, including his fear that Anne might never want to see him again.

She sat very still when his verbal torrent ceased, her dark face not revealing any hint of her thoughts. She closed her eyes for a moment, and when she opened them, warmth flooded him. Her soft voice drowned out the storm outside. " 'For thus the Lord God, the Holy One of Israel, has said, "In repentance and rest you will be saved, in quietness and trust is your strength." ' I'm thinking Isaiah knew what he was talking about when he wrote that. Until you find peace with God, you ain't gonna have happiness with yourself nor no one else around you." She stood and smoothed her floral dress over her ample figure. "Now come into the kitchen and have some of my snickerdoodles."

Who did she think she was coming in here and telling him— exactly what he needed to hear? The words had been given to her by God, and they convicted him to the core of his soul. He had to heal his own scars before he could give his heart to someone else. He picked up the phone and dialed Anne's cell number. Until he figured his life out, he needed to keep her at arm's length. She didn't answer. He left a message canceling their brunch date tomorrow. He would go to her family's Independence Day celebration in the park. She wouldn't be there until late, and they'd be buffered by the number of people surrounding them.

The aroma of cinnamon and baked goods rolled over him. He inhaled deeply. How had he not noticed before? He rose and followed the amazing smells downstairs.

Mama Ketty bustled about the kitchen. "You just set down at that bar and don't move a twitch. Mama Ketty's gonna put some meat on them bones if it's the last thing I do." She placed a plate of cookies and an enormous glass of milk in front of him. "I know you haven't been eating any of my cooking. How long's it been since you ate proper?"

When was the last time he'd had a decent meal? Sunday afternoon at Anne's aunt and uncle's home. "Awhile."

She clucked at him again. "Uh-huh. I suspected as much. Sit tight, and you'll have a meal that'll stick to your ribs."

Contentment settled into him along with the milk and cinnamon-dusted cookies while he watched her work. "Mama Ketty, do you believe that everything happens for a reason?"

"Baby, I believe that nothing happens without God knowing about it. And when things do happen, if we turn toward Him, He'll make the best of the situation, be it good or bad." She set a plate in front of him. "This here's a good Louisiana-raised, sugar-cured ham steak, fresh corn on the cob, purple-hulled peas from my son's garden, tomatoes from there, too." She turned back to the stove and lifted a small pan. She glopped something akin to porridge onto the plate. "Those are the finest grits in all of Louisiana. They'll stick with you, too. No one leaves Mama Ketty's table hungering after they've had some of my grits."

George had heard of the Southern delicacy but hadn't really thought he'd ever have to eat them. With Mama Ketty's hawklike gaze on him, though, he didn't dare leave a morsel of food on the white ceramic plate.

Seasoned with butter, salt, and pepper, the grits melted in his mouth. She'd salted the tomatoes to bring out their full flavor, and butter dripped down his fingers as he bit into the crisp, sweet corn. The ham steak was among the best meat he'd ever put in his mouth.

She took the plate as soon as he laid down his fork. "Now you get on out of here and let me get back to work." She shoved a small plate of cookies into his hands when he stood. "And take these with you. You children these days, wanting to be skin and bones." She shook her head and mumbled to herself.

He carried the cookies back up to the office to start over on the spreadsheet. His position as head of the household staff had just become an empty title.

Instead of getting straight to work, he opened the Bible program on the computer and searched for the verse Ketty had quoted. Isaiah 30:15. "In repentance and rest you will be saved, in quietness and trust is your strength." He printed the verse, cut it out, and taped it to the bottom of the monitor.

"In quietness and trust is your strength."

"Father, help me to be quiet and trust You for strength. You know I'm going to need it."

CHAPTER 17

"George is acting weird." Anne tipped her wide-brimmed hat forward to better shield her face from the midmorning sun. She couldn't show up at the church with a sunburned nose.

"Hmm?" Meredith's distracted voice came from behind a biography of Claude Monet.

"I said George is acting weird."

Meredith slipped a bookmark in to keep her place and scooped her strawberry blond hair over her shoulder. "Define *weird*."

"Ever since he came to lunch last Sunday, he's been. . .acting funny—not like himself, like I've said or done something that offended him and he doesn't know how to tell me." Once again, she went over everything that had been said and done at Maggie and Errol's Sunday afternoon, trying to figure out what might have upset him.

"Have you asked him about it?"

"I haven't had a chance. He's been avoiding me all week." Something tickled her ankle, and she jerked her foot out of the inflatable kiddie pool. A leaf from the ancient oak tree overhead careened away on the wake caused by her movement. She put her foot back in the tepid water. As long as it wasn't a bug.

"Maybe he's just been busy with getting ready for his boss coming into town for the engagement party next week." Mere fanned herself with her straw hat. "Jenn better get back soon with that ice.

It's gotta be nearly a hundred degrees out here. But at least it's not raining like last year."

"He didn't come to Thursday dinner last night and canceled brunch with me today."

"Do you think maybe someone said something to him when you weren't around Sunday? Something that scared him off?"

"Are you kidding me? With as much as the whole family wants to see me married?" Anne paused. "Maybe *that's* what frightened him. Maybe they tried to pressure him into making a commitment."

"Or he could've overheard you telling Marci about Cliff, and he's scared he can't compete with a movie star."

"Bite your tongue!" Anne splashed water toward Meredith with her foot. "I can't stand Cliff Ballantine. He's nothing compared to George. He's nowhere near as kind, considerate, funny, caring, compassionate, generous—"

"Okay, okay," Meredith splashed back. "I get the picture. Sheesh. All George needs is a dragon to slay to ensure his sainthood."

Anne smiled, but it faded quickly. "I hate Cliff Ballantine. If it weren't for him, I never would have dropped out of school. I'd be Dr. Anne Hawthorne now, teaching English at some fantastic, quaint little four-year college, redbrick buildings covered with ivy. . . ."

"Yeah. . ." Meredith's voice had the same dreamy quality Anne's had taken on. "Instead, you have your own business, you're a leader in the community, you love what you do." She leaned across the low table between them and poked Anne's arm. " 'God causes everything to work together for the good of those who love Him.' God has blessed you, Annie."

"Did someone send for ice?"

An avalanche cascaded over their shoulders and into the shallow water.

Meredith yelped and yanked her feet out of the pool. Anne laughed and kicked hers to mix the ice in with the warm water.

"That was a twenty-pound bag." Jenn flopped into the third chair, breathless. "And the only one Bordelon's Grocery had left.

I'll take the coolers out to the restaurant and fill them from the ice machine there for tonight." She kicked off her sandals and dunked her feet into the cooling water. "You know, if our landlady would get the real swimming pool fixed, we could be floating around on inflatables instead of sitting around a wader like three rednecks."

"I told you before that there's no way I could get someone out here on the Fourth of July." Anne scooped up a few ice chips and tossed them in Jenn's direction. "Besides, I wouldn't be able to do more than this even if we could use the pool."

"What time do you have to be at the church?" Meredith tested the water with her toes, then slipped her feet in with a sigh.

"I have to be there at noon to get the setup started, then I'll run out to the park to meet the caterer and get them situated. I'll be running back and forth all afternoon." She glanced at her watch. She needed to leave in half an hour. "I'm so glad Jason agreed to help out. He's a natural, but he insists on staying a cop instead of joining me as my assistant."

Meredith laughed. "You know him. He wants to be chief of police someday so that if Forbes ever gets elected mayor, the two of them can work together to make all the changes they think this city needs."

"You have so much work, you need to hire a full-time assistant, not just temporary part-timers." Jenn dug a piece of ice out of her glass of tea and rubbed it across the base of her neck.

Anne sipped her tea and resumed fanning herself with her book. "I've been thinking about that. I've got George's wedding in October—"

"His employer's, you mean." Meredith winked and flashed a grin.

She shrugged. "Same difference. Between now and then, I have a wedding, engagement party, or other event every weekend but two. Then the mayor's wife called me about planning the fall debutante cotillion in September. That's on top of a couple of reelection events for her husband's mayoral campaign and the LouWESA conference

173

Labor Day week in Baton Rouge."

"Louisa conference?" Jenn asked.

"Louisiana Wedding and Event Specialists Association. That's the week before the cotillion."

"Speaking of debutantes," Jenn said as she crunched ice from her tea, mouth open the way that made Anne's skin crawl. "You'll never guess who I ran into at the grocery store."

Anne didn't bother guessing—Jenn would tell them anyway.

"Patsy Sue Landry." Jenn drawled out the name, imitating the middle-aged Southern belle. "She remembered me from when I used to babysit her younger girls after you started college, Anne. She asked about you."

Anne cringed. She hoped the woman wasn't going to call her again. She didn't know if she could avoid the woman's questions without lying to her about George and the plans for Courtney's wedding.

"She said she's leaving for the Riviera next week and will be gone four or five weeks."

"Thank goodness."

"While we were chatting, I saw on one of the local rags on the magazine stand that Cliff Ballantine might be coming to town next week. Something with his fraternity, they figure."

Anne snorted. "I'll make sure to be on the lookout so I can avoid him, then."

"Don't you think it's time you forgave him?" Meredith's sincerity and concern soothed Anne like a squirt of lemon juice in the eye.

"Look at the time." Anne jumped up from the lounger. "I'm going to be late." She rushed inside and took the stairs to her second-floor apartment two at a time. *Coward.* The passage she'd read from Matthew in her quiet time that morning came back to haunt her. "For if you forgive men for their transgressions, your heavenly Father will also forgive you. But if you do not forgive others, then your Father will not forgive your transgressions."

She had no right to withhold her forgiveness from Cliff for

what he'd done to her. After all, Jesus was willing to give His life to forgive her for all of her sins.

She slammed the apartment door behind her. "Okay, Lord! I forgive him! Does that make You happy?" She felt stupid even as she yelled at the ceiling. Of course her outburst didn't make Him happy. She said the words, but her heart wasn't in it. She just wanted the Holy Spirit to leave her alone with the whole guilt thing.

Halfway through changing clothes, she sank onto the edge of the bed. "Jesus, You're going to have to teach me how to forgive him, then give me the strength to do it. I'm not going to be able to do this on my own."

George's image flashed in her mind. "I can't be with George until I rid myself of Cliff once and for all. I don't know what's going on with him right now, Lord, but give me the strength to resist my attraction to him until I've worked through the Cliff issue and can approach the relationship without baggage."

❦

"Why don't we go back to the church for your car later?" Jason handed Anne her duffel bag. Behind them, the wedding reception limped on, not as much fun for the guests now that the bride and groom had left. "We're already at the park, so we might as well take my Jeep over to the pavilion, have dinner, watch the fireworks, and then get your car on the way home."

Her change of clothes was in her tote bag in the backseat of Jason's vehicle. She glanced at her watch. "You're right. Papere would have fired up the grill about half an hour ago, so the first hamburgers and hot dogs should just now be coming off." She slung the duffel's strap over her shoulder. "Let's go."

On the other side of Schyuler City Park, she dashed into the public restroom, changed, and then tossed everything into the open-top Jeep. Mamere reserved the same pavilion every year for their Independence Day cookout—the one between the playground and the privy, with an unobstructed view of the fireworks.

Her mouth watered at the smoky barbecue aroma that wafted over from Papere's huge charcoal grill. She jogged straight toward the gaggle of children running amok in the grassy field.

"An-Anne! An-Anne!" Seven girls under the age of ten surrounded her.

"We saw the wedding people when we drove into the park." Ten-year-old Jordyn Babineaux hooked her arm through Anne's. Slim with long dark hair, the tween would be unintentionally breaking hearts in a few years. "Was it a beautiful wedding?"

She tweaked the girl's nose. "Of course it was. I planned it, after all."

"An-Anne, when are you gettin' married?" eight-year-old Kaitlyn Guidry asked.

"Probably not for a long time, sweetie." At a tug on her shorts, Anne turned.

Six-year-old Megan's brown eyes beamed up at her. "But Mama said you're gonna marry Mr. George, sooner better than later."

Kaitlyn covered her younger sister's mouth none too gently. "Shush, Megan. You don't know what you're talking about."

Anne's cheeks burned. She knew if the girls' parents had been discussing her at home, the rest of the family was, too.

"Do you like him?" Jordyn ducked her head and kicked at something in the grass.

"Sure I like him. He's a very nice man."

The adolescent heaved a dramatic sigh. "That's not what I mean. Do you like. . .*like* him?"

Good grief! Even the children were getting in on the matchmaking. "I'm not sure, Jordy. I need to get to know him better."

"He's here." Megan tugged on Anne's shorts again. "Over there with the boys, fishin' in the lake."

Anne shielded her eyes against the setting sun. Her heart thumped. George sat on a pier between Cooper, seven; and Christian, four; kicking his feet back and forth in the water. The boys giggled and yelled as the water sprinkled them.

Lord God, I want this man to be the father of my children. She stopped dead in her tracks. Never in her life had she given serious thought to having children of her own. Just the opposite. She'd *never* wanted children of her own.

A bell clanged at the pavilion. With war cries Geronimo would have been proud of, the girls beat a path to go get their supper.

George sprang lightly to his feet and helped the boys gather their fishing poles, shoes, and tackle box. She should turn around now and go into the pavilion. Shoes tucked under his arm, he stopped when they made eye contact.

She smiled and raised her hand in a weak greeting. She couldn't let him see how he affected her. She had to remain distant until she got the rest of her life sorted out.

He smiled and angled over toward her.

What to say to him? Should she tell him about Cliff? What if Meredith was right and he'd be jealous or upset to hear it? He was within a few feet. She had to say something. "There aren't any fish in that pond, y'know."

He shook his head and laughed. "I'd surmised as much. But there's more to fishing than catching fish." He motioned toward the pavilion.

She fell in step with him. "More than catching fish? I thought that was the whole point." What an inane conversation. . .inane but neutral, casual, easy.

"For a professional fisherman, yes, I suppose that would be the general idea. However, for the man of leisure, fishing is an exercise in relaxation, in getting to know oneself and one's companions better."

She laughed, relaxing. "Except for the accent, you sound like one of those fishing show hosts on TV."

"You don't fish?" He clasped his hands behind his back.

He clasped his hands behind his back. Five days ago, he'd taken hold of her hand as they'd walked out of church. Something *had* changed between them. *Focus. Keep things casual.* "I've only been on one fishing trip with my family, and I got yelled at for talking too much when we were sitting there in a boat in the middle of the lake. How can you get to know your companions better if you can't talk?"

He chuckled, a deep, rich sound that tugged at her heart. "Men don't need words to bond."

"Ah, so it's a male-bonding ritual, then." She stopped when they reached the edge of the crowd gathered in the pavilion.

"Precisely." In the waning sunlight, his eyes took on a coppery glow.

Papere called the family to order to say grace, for which she was grateful. Around them, everyone joined hands. George enveloped hers in his. She hadn't noticed Sunday how large and strong his hands were. During the prayer, she stole a glance at him. *Don't you hurt me, George Laurence. If I give you my heart, please be the man who's going to watch over me and protect me from pain. Don't break it the way Cliff did.*

When the prayer ended, Jenn and Mere grabbed her by each arm. "How'd you do it? You said no one could come out today." Jenn waved at someone over Anne's shoulder.

Anne laughed. "I called in a favor."

Meredith pursed her lips. "Let me guess. . .a classmate from high school."

She shook her head. "Nope, college. I didn't tell you earlier because he didn't know for sure if he'd be able to come out today."

" 'Grief, Anne, you know everyone in this city. We should have known you'd know someone who could fix the swimming pool." Jenn kissed her cheek. "Thanks. We enjoyed it this afternoon. It sure was hot outside."

"Tell me about it. I had an outdoor reception to work—" She shoved Jenn when her cousin rolled her eyes. "Quit rubbing it in. I plan to make full use of it tomorrow and Sunday."

When she'd filled her plate, she turned and scanned the long tables under the open shed. George stood and waved her over. She laughed when she got closer. On each side of him were his two fishing buddies. She went around and sat opposite the threesome.

"Mr. George, can you help me with this?" Cooper held up a hamburger hemorrhaging ketchup from all sides.

"Of course." With a plastic knife, he scraped away the excess condiments, then cut the sandwich in four pieces. "Better?"

"Yes, sir!" The boy did his best to shove one of the wedges into his mouth whole.

George turned to his right and did the same for Christian and his hot dog.

"You're going to be a wonderful father someday." She'd said it out loud! She couldn't take it back. She might as well have come out and told him how she felt.

"Thank you, Anne." George's gaze burned into hers.

Embarrassed, she dropped her attention to her plate. So much for being low-key.

The boys vied for his attention, leaving Anne to eat in peace. . . and to fall in love with him a little more with each passing moment. *God, You're supposed to be helping me* resist *him! Not making him more irresistible.*

Peace didn't last long. After less than fifteen minutes, leaving mangled bread and soggy chips behind, Christian and Cooper left the table to expend their now-refueled energy.

"Where's Forbes tonight?" George consolidated the remains onto one plate and stacked them.

"He'll be here shortly. Some kind of emergency conference call came up at work." They were watching. All her relatives. Their gazes bored into her. She glanced around, and no one seemed to be looking in her direction. But she knew what they were thinking and hoping and plotting.

He pushed the plates out of the way and leaned on the table on his crossed arms. "Tell me what to expect tonight."

"Well, about eight thirty, Papere will read the Declaration of Independence. We'll sing 'America, the Beautiful,' 'My Country,

'Tis of Thee,' and the national anthem, and if we've timed it right—which we usually do—the fireworks should start."

"No stage show?" Disappointment furrowed the space between his well-groomed brows.

"Stage show?"

"A concert by the local philharmonic while the fireworks are being shot."

"Oh, they have that up at the amphitheater. But it's always so crowded on that end of the park, so we crank it up on the radio—the public station broadcasts it."

"How big is this park?"

"It's triangular—about two miles long and about a mile wide down here at the base. The north end is only about two hundred yards wide. That's where the stage area is. They shoot off the fireworks from about halfway between." She rested her chin on her hand. "How many Fourth of July celebrations have you been to?"

"I witnessed the Washington, DC, celebration last year because my employer was in town—for work. I've seen it in New York, too."

"Is it strange for you to watch us celebrate our independence from England? After all, what we're celebrating today is basically the declaration of war between our two countries."

The twinkle in his eyes was as addictive as hazelnut crème lattes. "We Brits have taken on a very pragmatic attitude toward the countries that were once a part of the British Empire. As long as no one is currently declaring war on us, we don't mind people celebrating wars that happened centuries ago."

Around them, everyone headed for the field. George took her plate to throw away, and she took his cup to refill with Diet Sprite, no ice. They joined Jenn, Meredith, Jason, and Rafe, who'd overlapped the ends of two quilts on the ground.

Forbes flopped down beside Anne as she got settled. "Miss anything?"

She returned his kiss on the cheek. "Just dinner."

"George came?" he whispered.

Odd question. "Of course. Why wouldn't he?"

"Oh, I thought—never mind." Forbes leaned forward and greeted his sisters by pulling their hair.

After he finished reading the Declaration of Independence, Papere led young and old alike in singing, "America, the Beautiful." Anne added her alto to Forbes's tenor, Jason and Rafe's bass, and Jenn and Mere's soprano. The dumbfounded expression on George's face ended their harmony with laughter.

Forbes held up his hand. "We know, we've heard it all our lives: 'You're just like the Von Trapps from *The Sound of Music.*' "

George recovered himself. "Not exactly what I was thinking, but it did sound nice. Pray, continue."

When they segued into "My Country, 'Tis of Thee," Anne made the mistake of looking at George to see what he thought of the co-opted British national anthem. He leaned over and sang low in her ear, "God save the Queen!"

"You're bad," she whispered.

"I'm bad? Your ancestors stole our song, and I'm bad?" He shifted position, turning his torso toward her, their noses almost touching. A few inches, and they would be kissing. His grin faded. Emotion flooded his gaze. "Anne, there's something—" With a whoosh of breath, his forehead banged hers.

"Ow!" She rubbed her head and leaned away. "Hello, Christian, Cooper."

The two boys hung from George's neck, one in his lap, the other on his back.

The boys' mothers rushed over. "Oh, George, Anne, we're so sorry. Boys, come on with us."

He waved them away. "It's quite all right, Andrea, Keeley. Let them stay. We've been bonding today."

The second time he was with her family, and he'd remembered everyone's name so far. Each moment she was near him, he revealed even more how he fit the image of her perfect mate.

Forgiving ol' what's-his-name didn't seem so hard all of a sudden.

Chapter 18

It had to be you," Anne sang with the music flooding her office. She smiled, recalling the warmth in George's cinnamon-hazelnut eyes as he'd talked at length with her grandfather Friday evening at the picnic. He'd been such a good sport to put up with the ribbing Papere and the uncles had given him. But he still had to prove himself. She couldn't just fall head over heels for him because he got along with her family.

She wound pink tulle onto a heavy cardboard bolt, pulling the fabric yard by yard out of the white trash bags that nearly filled the floor of her storage room. Her bride Saturday afternoon had taken the wedding from *Steel Magnolias* as her model, with pink bunting draped over anything that would stand still. Anne's own wedding would be much more sophisticated—

Whoa. Thinking in terms like that could only bring disappointment. Sure, she liked George now, and he seemed to like her, but what if the glow wore off? What if she discovered him lying to her about something important again?

The future without George Laurence in it looked dim and dismal. But it was a possible reality she needed to face. At thirty-five, she was too old to indulge in a crush. She couldn't pin her hopes on him. She could, however, have fun exploring the possibility of something permanent.

The room filled with Frank Sinatra's voice crooning "I Get a Kick Out of You." Anne sang along, swirling around in the tulle. She wished more brides would choose standards for their receptions. Easier to dance to, the words and music also spoke to a larger audience than the inane pop music of the moment her clients tended to choose.

George listened to the same kind of music, and oh, how he could croon it! But could he dance—more than just the waltz they'd already shared? If not, they could always take ballroom dancing together. She knew a few—the waltz, the fox-trot, and the cha-cha. She spun around, her feet tangled in the tulle, and she fell, landing on the soft pile of bags of fabric.

The bell on the front door echoed throughout the town house. Oh no, her ten o'clock consultation! She struggled to her feet and managed to reach the door. "I'll be with you in a moment," she called. Her own laughter didn't make extrication from the pink cloud easy. Once out, she had to dive back in to find her left shoe and hair clip. She slipped into the eggplant-colored pump, then crossed to check her reflection in the mirror on the back of the storage room door. She ran her fingers through her hair, tossed the clip on the nearest shelf, opened the door, and rushed down the stairs.

The couple seated on the love seat under the front window stood. He was in his late thirties, slender, just over six feet tall, well dressed, wearing expensive shoes, and would look good in a single- or double-button coat, charcoal or black.

"I'm sorry I kept you waiting." She extended her right hand to the bride first. "I'm Anne Hawthorne."

"Kristin Smith. I'm so glad you were able to fit us into your busy schedule. This is my fiancé, Greg Witt." Kristin looked several years younger than her fiancé. She stood about five and a half feet, with shoulder-length blond hair that would look good in an updo and a crown headpiece, and a pink skin tone that would look best with pure white.

Anne shook hands with the groom, then motioned for them to sit. She grabbed her planner off her desk before taking her place in the armchair across the coffee table from them. The purple tulips were starting to wilt a little. She'd have to call April's Flowers to see if they'd gotten in another shipment.

"Let me start by saying congratulations. I know this is an exciting time for you as you start planning the biggest event of your life. My job as a wedding planner is to take the stress off of you on the administrative end so that you can relax and enjoy your day." As she did with all potential clients, Anne reviewed her business credentials, association memberships, and certifications. Almost every potential client came in with a list of questions from the Internet to ask. Every list started with questions about the planner's professional qualifications. She found most clients relaxed more if she got that information out before they had to ask.

"We saw the article about you in *Southern Bride*. That was one of the reasons I wanted to come to you." Kristin tapped a black Waterford pen against her pink notepad. "How many weddings do you coordinate in an average month?"

"During the summer, I typically handle three to five weddings per month—about one a week. Some of those are just consultations—I help the bride plan ahead of time, and she handles everything the day of the wedding—while with others, I handle everything for the bride, allowing her to sit back and not have to worry about coordinating anything. Of course, during the fall, winter, and early spring, I don't have as many clients. Did you have a wedding date in mind?"

"We're looking at a couple of dates in the fall—October maybe?" The young woman pulled out a well-worn, checkbook-sized calendar.

Anne flipped to October in her planner, nodding. "October's a good month, especially if you're thinking about an outdoor wedding. I have a couple of events already on the books for the first and third weekends but would be able to assist you either as a consultant if you choose one of those weeks or as your on-site planner any other week."

Both bride and groom made notations in their calendars. "Do you have an assistant or someone who can fill in for you if something happens and you're unavailable on our wedding day?" Kristin asked.

"Yes, if something happens and I am unavailable, I will line up a substitute to work with you at a discounted cost, although I have never missed a client's wedding, so that shouldn't be an issue."

Kristin made another note and continued down the list of standard questions, becoming more open and chattier as Anne answered each concern. With the interview list complete, Anne guided the couple into talking about their ideas for what they wanted. She took copious notes, including the fact that neither seemed locked into any firm decisions. That could be good if they would be open to her suggestions. Bad if it meant they were indecisive.

When their half hour was almost up, Anne set her planner on the coffee table. Time to close out the consultation with chatty conversation. "So are both of you from Bonneterre?"

"No."

"Yes."

Anne blinked and glanced from bride to groom.

"What Greg means is that he's not from Bonneterre but I am." Kristin's explanation was rushed, her tone embarrassed. "What about you?"

"Bonneterre born and raised. Where'd you go to high school, Kristin?"

"Governor's Academy." The boarding school that cost more per year than an Ivy League university. "What about you?"

"Acadiana High."

Kristin exchanged a glance with her fiancé. "Really? Were you there when Cliff Ballantine went to school there?"

Of course. Everyone always asked that when they heard what school she'd attended. "He was a year ahead of me. But it's a really big school." Her standard reply.

"I read somewhere that he's getting married here." Kristin gave her a sly grin. "You wouldn't be planning his wedding, would you?"

Anne forced a smile. "I hadn't heard he was getting married."

"I just think it would be awesome to know what his wedding's going to be like. It's going to be the social event of the year, no matter where he gets married. But could you imagine planning his wedding? Whoever that wedding planner is, she's set for life." Kristin tucked her notepad and calendar into her pink gingham purse and stood.

Anne shook hands with the couple and walked them to the door. "Please let me know if you'd like me to write up a contract."

"Oh, we'll be in touch soon."

Anne stood at the front door and watched as the couple crossed the square toward the restaurants on the other side. For a newly engaged couple, they weren't very affectionate with each other. Oh well. Everyone showed their love in different ways. Odd that they didn't even hold hands, though.

Where had they heard that Cliff was getting married—and in Bonneterre of all places? She prayed that wasn't the case, although if it was true, it would have been on the front page of the *Reserve*. Planning his wedding, indeed. Besides the fact that he would never hire her personally, he would never stoop to hiring a local to plan what Kristin had aptly called *the* social event of the year. He probably had some overpriced Beverly Hills event planner on retainer—someone like the character Martin Short played in the remake of *Father of the Bride*: pretentious, foreign, and way overpriced.

The phone rang and interrupted her ponderings.

"Happy Endings, Inc. This is Anne Hawthorne."

"Good morning, Anne." George's silky accent brought her fully to the present.

She sank into her chair and leaned her elbows on the desk. "Good morning, yourself. I guess you got my message?"

"I did. I would love to have dinner with you tonight. Shall I meet you or pick you up at the office?"

Her heart did a happy dance. "Actually, I'm coming to you."

A warm chuckle melted through the phone. "I'd love to cook

for you some night, but with no advance notice and Mama Ketty's not being here. . ."

"The chef will be there at four o'clock to start cooking."

"The chef?"

She laughed. "Major O'Hara, the executive chef for Boudreaux-Guidry. Tonight is the only time he has available to do a tasting menu for the rehearsal dinner. Since you didn't have a chance to taste his food before agreeing to his catering the engagement party, I hope to set your mind at ease tonight."

"Ah. And here I was thinking you were trying to surprise me with a romantic, home-cooked dinner."

Were he standing in front of her, he would wink and give her that enchanting crooked grin of his. She bit her bottom lip and took a calming breath. *Have fun but don't indulge.* "I'll see you at six o'clock."

❦

The caterer arrived at four. After a brief interview, George turned him loose in the kitchen and returned to his quarters. Less than two hours before Anne arrived. Plenty of time to get ready.

He rummaged through shopping bags until he found the table linens. He hadn't expected the enormous discount store to have quality linens, but the ivory fabric with an embossed pinstripe was at least as nice as what he could find at the local department stores. He ironed the creases out of the tablecloth and napkins and carried them into the small room off the kitchen that would serve as the employees' dining and break room, once he hired a full house staff.

Covering the large round table with the cloth, he placed a glass vase of lavender tulips in the center. He'd gone to nearly every florist in town trying to find Anne's favorite flowers, eventually securing the last two dozen at April's Flowers—finalizing the purchase just as someone else called in looking for some.

He opened the french doors onto the promenade that ran the length of the back of the house. The small iron café table with a glass top and two matching chairs, which he'd found at a locally owned hardware store, made for a perfect alfresco dinner for two. He whistled as he arranged the table, finishing with the second vase of tulips and two taper candles.

Distance, remember. Don't let's get in too deep, aye, old boy?

His watch beeped. Five thirty. He'd taken too long with the decorations. He left a book of matches on the table and closed the doors to keep the cool air inside a little longer.

He moved the rest of the spoils of his quick shopping trip into the walk-in closet. He made up the bed with sheets freshly laundered by Mama Ketty, a new duvet, and pillows. In the extra bathroom, he put out the towels Mama Ketty had insisted on laundering before being used. The navy and gold colors were the same he'd used in his quarters in Cliff's two other homes. His brother Henry would laugh and call him set in his ways. He liked to think of himself as consistent.

He showered, then dressed in gray pants, a blue button-down, and a colorful tie. His short hair dried quickly. He leaned close to the bathroom mirror. The dark brown around his temples seemed to sprout new grays every day, and it needed trimming.

He heard a sound and realized it was his phone playing "I Can't Give You Anything but Love." *Anne.* His heart leaped, then stalled. She couldn't be calling to cancel. "George Laurence here."

"Anne Hawthorne here." Her voice sounded amused. "I'm pulling up to the house now, but I thought I should ask—should I come to the front door or. . . ?"

Only someone else who worked in a service industry would even think about that. "Since my employer is not in residence, the front entrance is fine."

"Okay, I'll see you in a sec."

George switched the phone to silent mode, then snapped it into the holster on his belt. He needed to know if Cliff or Courtney called but didn't want dinner disturbed. He straightened his tie, then headed to the front of the house. Through the etched glass in the door, he could see Anne, hand raised to knock. He opened the door and ushered her inside.

Her tremulous smile betrayed a surprising nervousness, given this had been her idea. "This is for you—a kind of housewarming/host gift."

He took the white gift bag from her, surprised by its weight. "Thank you." He kissed her cheek, then turned and made a sweeping gesture with his free hand. "Welcome to my employer's home. Would you care for a tour?"

She smiled. "Maybe the upstairs part. I'm pretty familiar with the ground floor. Aunt Maggie used to cater events for the Thibodeauxes here a few times a year. Once I was old enough, I came out to help with setup, service, and cleanup."

"Ah. That's why you asked about the service entrance."

She stuck her head in to glance around the formal front parlor. "This is the first time I've ever come in through the front door."

He took her by the hand and led her upstairs. "Obviously, it's not fully furnished yet. I expect a shipment later in the week, and once Courtney returns"—he winked at Anne—"she will address decorating the guest bedrooms."

"And the thought of that frightens you?" She glanced in each room as they wandered through both upper levels.

"Not so much as the thought of her mother doing it." He should have known she'd see through him. He opened the door at the top of the service stairs at the back of the house to take her down to the kitchen. "The one time Mrs. Landry came into the house, she suggested a pink faux-fur rug for one of the upstairs rooms."

Her laughter resonated like chimes in the enclosed stairwell. "Hopefully she's not planning to give Courtney the one that's in her own house as a wedding present. Maybe you should find an interior designer to recommend to her."

"I'm meeting with three on Thursday."

The chef turned when they entered the kitchen. "Hey, Anne." He wiped his hands on the red-and-white-striped towel draped over his shoulder and crossed to embrace her.

"Hey, Major. I've been looking forward to this dinner all day."

He cut his gaze toward George. "I'm sure you have."

George wasn't sure how to read the look that passed between Anne and the caterer, who was not wearing a wedding band. George led her out of the kitchen. "How do you know him?"

"Major? He started working for Aunt Maggie when we were in high school."

George smiled and shook his head.

"What's so funny?"

He led her through the dining room and opened the french doors. "I grew up in London. For the last five years, I've shuttled back and forth between Los Angeles and Manhattan. I knew Bonneterre was smaller, but with a quarter of a million population, it's not a village. Yet listening to you, seeing how you cannot go outside of your office without seeing someone you know. . .it's very quaint." He held her chair as she sat.

She looked over her shoulder with a grin. "It used to be a lot more 'quaint' than it is now. The city has nearly doubled in size in the last ten or fifteen years."

He sat as she told him about how Bonneterre had changed over her lifetime. At the first lull in the conversation, he stood. "May I offer you a beverage?"

"Oh, that reminds me, you never opened your gift." She pushed the white bag on the table toward him.

"Quite so." He reached through the tissue paper and wrapped his hand around something rectangular and solid, with a smooth surface. Drawing it out, he grinned when he saw it. "Is this a hint for later?"

"I thought you liked flavored coffee." Her protest was over-shadowed by the laughter lacing her voice.

"Yes, but if I guess correctly, hazelnut caramel is your favorite flavor."

She bit her bottom lip, and her smile grew wider. "Busted."

He loved her laugh. "Would you like some now?"

"No, save it for dessert. I could really go for some iced tea."

"The only kind we have is without sweetening."

"That's fine. I can drink it either way." She started to stand.

He stopped her with his hand on her shoulder. "No. You're my guest. Stay there and let me serve you."

Anne's blue eyes sparkled, and she squeezed his hand. "Thank you."

The dinner Major O'Hara put before them was nothing short of perfection, from the spinach salad with muscadine vinaigrette to the medium-rare London broil with Cajun garlic mashed potatoes and sautéed baby asparagus.

"I hope this sets your mind at ease," Anne said after O'Hara cleared their dinner plates. "Major is one of the best chefs I've ever worked with. He's done a ton of catering for me over the years."

George reached across the table and covered Anne's clasped hands. "I'm happy you came."

The candlelight glittered in the sapphire pools of her eyes. "I'm happy you didn't mind the intrusion."

Slow. Take it slow. "Your presence would never be an intrusion." He leaned closer to her.

They both turned at the sound of a cleared throat. "Are you ready for dessert?" O'Hara stood in the doorway, a silver tray balanced on one hand, a coffee service cart beside him.

Anne groaned dramatically. "I don't know how I could eat another bite. What is it?" She leaned back to make room on the table as he stepped forward.

"White chocolate crème brûlée with raspberries." He put the individual dishes in front of them. "The coffee is hazelnut caramel."

George couldn't stop looking at Anne. The chef poured the steaming, fragrant liquid into fine china cups, set the silver coffeepot on the sideboard, and withdrew.

She closed her eyes and sighed as she savored the first bite of the custard dessert. Tonight had been a revelation to George. When she wasn't in business mode—when she was relaxed and not on a time schedule—she truly enjoyed the experience of dining.

"What?" She'd caught him staring.

"I just like watching you." He was going under deep and fast. Was the pleasure of falling in love with her tonight worth the risk of losing her in a few days?

Her cheeks glowed in the candlelight. "Why?"

"Because you're beautiful." He sipped his coffee.

She laughed and shook her head.

"Yes, you are." He set down his cup and reached over to lift her chin, forcing her to look him in the eye. "You *are* beautiful, and I don't know who would have told you otherwise."

She didn't speak for a moment, her gaze never wavering. "It was never in so many words." She put her spoon down. "But the intent was the same."

"Well, I'm here now—and I'm right, so you'd best believe me."

The smile he'd become addicted to returned. He tweaked her chin between his thumb and forefinger, then lifted his dessert spoon.

The symphony of crickets, frogs, and other indigenous fauna filled the silence between them. The sky turned red and purple as the sun set on the other side of the house.

Anne sighed and cradled her coffee cup between her hands.

"What is it?" Although his father would have been appalled, he propped his elbows on the edge of the table and leaned toward her.

She swallowed and blinked a few times. "It's just been a really long time since. . ." Her voice caught and her bottom lip quivered.

"Since?" Now that he had her to himself, he wasn't about to let her clam up.

She shrugged, her gaze fixed on the horizon. "Since I stopped to let myself enjoy a quiet eve—" She flinched and reached for the phone clipped to the waistband of her pants. Her shoulders fell when she looked at the caller ID. "I'm so sorry. It's my client who's getting married next week."

He stood and kissed her on the forehead. "I need to go speak with Mr. O'Hara anyway."

The chef turned as George entered the kitchen. "Is everything all right?"

"Yes. It was a wonderful dinner. My compliments—"

"George, I have to run." Anne breezed into the kitchen. "There's a problem with the wedding dress, and I have to go find out if it's something I can fix or really a problem."

"I'll walk you out." He helped Anne into her suit coat and rested his hand on the small of her back as he escorted her to the front door. "What seems to be amiss?"

"I'm not sure. She was so hysterical she wasn't coherent. So I'm driving out to her house to see what's wrong. Hopefully it'll be an easy fix. If not. . .well, I have a few days to figure out what to do." She stopped at the door and turned toward him. "Thank you for a lovely evening. I'm sorry work interfered."

"Thank you for making it a lovely evening." He brushed back a lock of hair that had escaped to fall across her forehead. How was it possible that no man had claimed this wonderful woman? "I'll ring you tomorrow about the final arrangements for the engagement party." He flinched as the vibrator on his phone startled him. He reached for it as he kissed her on the cheek.

"Good night."

She graced him with another full smile. "Good night."

Cliff's number scrolled across the phone's screen. He waved good-bye to Anne and lifted the phone to his ear. "Yes, Mr. Ballantine?"

"Courtney may have blown our cover. If any reporters show up there in the next few days, you have to let me know immediately. We'll have to change all the plans."

CHAPTER 19

*B*y Wednesday, George started to relax. No news of the engagement or wedding had appeared in the celebrity press. Cliff had announced he'd be giving a press conference in Bonneterre on Friday, and a private service had been contracted to provide security that night since Cliff didn't want the local police brought in. Courtney would arrive tomorrow, ostensibly to attend a friend's wedding.

"George, dude, what is up with you tonight?" Rafe's voice brought him back to the present—the Fishin' Shack, where Anne's cousins had gathered for dinner a night earlier than usual so both Anne and George could attend this week.

"Sorry. I've lots on my mind tonight. What did I miss?"

"We were wondering where Anne is. We thought she was coming with you."

"She had a last-minute meeting with a client. Something about a dress fitting. She assured me she would arrive by seven." George glanced at his watch. She was nearly twenty minutes late. "Obviously the meeting ran longer than she expected."

The restaurant's back room partially muffled the sound of the large dinner crowd in the main dining room. Jenn fluttered in with a couple of baskets of the fried balls of seasoned cornmeal they called hush puppies. When he'd asked about the name last week, Jenn had spun a tale about Southern soldiers in the American Civil

194

War feeding bits of fried meal to their dogs to "hush" them from giving their position away to the enemy.

He'd researched it that night on the Internet and hadn't found a more definitive answer—just a few other tall tales. Whatever their origin, he enjoyed Jenn's version of the savory pastry, even though cornmeal didn't rank high on his list of favorite flavors or textures.

"You gonna try something different tonight, sugar?" Jenn asked, resting her hand on his shoulder. "I'm proud that a real Englishman likes my fish 'n' chips so much, but. . ."

He closed the menu and handed it to her. "I'll make you a deal, ducky. Bring me your favorite dish—on or off the menu."

The delighted gleam in Jenn's eyes amused him. "Oh, George, we're going to have so much fun teaching you to suck crawfish heads!" She left the room without taking anyone else's order.

"George, you're going to get a trial by fire tonight of what it means to be in Louisiana." Jason watched Jenn as she flitted from table to table.

"My dear fellow, you forget that I am British. I've eaten haggis in Edinburgh and jellied eels in London. I've also traveled extensively and eaten so-called delicacies ranging from insects to parts of animals that were never meant to be eaten. Crawfish presents no challenge I cannot overcome."

The expression on Jason's face said he believed otherwise, but the young man held his tongue.

"Hey, y'all. Sorry I'm late." Anne slid into the vacant chair beside George before he could stand and offer his assistance. Although smiling, the tight lines around her eyes betrayed her heightened stress level.

"Did everything work out all right?" Forbes, on her other side, put his arm around her.

Anne blew out a long breath and rolled her neck from side to side. "No. I'm taking the bride dress-shopping next week. She decided she didn't want to pay the dress shop to alter her gown and instead asked a coworker to do it. Unfortunately, the coworker didn't measure correctly, and rather than leave extra fabric to make corrections with, she trimmed all of her seams down to less than a quarter of an inch. Now the dress is too tight and too short and can't be let back out. I know. I tried." She rubbed her forehead, then reached into her purse and withdrew a small bottle of aspirin. "George, may I?" She pointed at his water.

He handed his glass to her. "How will she afford to purchase a new dress if she couldn't afford to pay for alterations to the first one?"

Anne swallowed two pills with a big gulp of the water with no ice. "I can't tell you. It'll make Forbes mad."

Why would Forbes care how one of Anne's clients paid for a dress?

"Please tell me you're not letting her take it out of your final fee." Forbes's voice had a growl to it that didn't sit well with George. How Anne conducted her business was just that—her own business. Yet who was he to step between her and her cousin?

"If I don't tell you, will you let the matter drop?" She sounded tired—defeated.

"Anne, the contract you sign with your clients is as much for your protection as it is for theirs. I drew it up specifically to make sure that if something went awry, you would still be paid. The more you do this, the more people are going to hear and take advantage of you."

She rested her fists against the edge of the table. George wished there was some way he could help. Without knowing her any better than he did, he wasn't sure if she would see any action or words on his part as support or as butting in.

"Forbes, I know for you, as a lawyer, this is going to be hard to understand. My client's happiness matters more to me than if I get paid next Saturday or if I get paid in miniscule installments for the next six months. It's not as if I'm hurting for income now like I was a few years ago. This girl is a nursing student who works part-time as a waitress." As she talked, her voice got softer, her words faster. "She's already spent more money on the wedding than I advised because she's trying to make both mothers happy, even though they've refused to pay for anything. What should I tell her, Forbes? What?" She shrugged and held her hands up toward him. "Should I tell her she should just wear her next-best dress? Maybe see if she can borrow a friend's old wedding gown? Tell me. You apparently know better than I do how to run my business."

Stunned silence filled the room. Jason and Rafe stared at Anne, mouths agape. Jenn dabbed at the corners of her eyes with her napkin, moved to emotion either by Anne's story or by the conflict between her cousin and older brother. Meredith glared daggers at Forbes. George suppressed a smile, proud of Anne for taking a stand.

Forbes cleared his throat. "Anne, I apologize. It's not my place to lecture you on how you run your business. I know if you wanted legal advice, you'd come to me. I just don't want to see you lose that business because you let clients overspend their budgets and then not pay you."

"I have never had a client not pay me everything due, including my fee. Sometimes it just takes longer." She rested her hand on her cousin's arm. "How do you think I got as successful as I am? Not because I was a hardnose about people paying me every penny the moment I thought it should be paid. My brides recommend me to their friends because I'm willing to work with them and do what it takes to make their weddings the most joyous events of their lives. I'm so sad for this young woman because the happiness that she should be feeling this week has been overwhelmed by the fact that she made an error in judgment and her dress was ruined. Forbes, what if it were Mere or Jenn or Marci or Tiffani? I can be a blessing to this girl, show her the true generosity of Christ's love, and maintain my integrity and my conscience. We've already worked out a payment plan that she can afford."

Forbes rested his hand on the back of her neck and pulled her close to kiss her temple. "I am so happy you never decided to become a criminal defense lawyer."

KAYE DACUS

Lafitte's Landing echoed with the hushed tones of student workers late Thursday afternoon. Anne dropped her duffel bag on the floor just inside the main ballroom. Her cousins Kevin, Jonathan, and Bryan and several of their friends approached her.

"Thanks for coming, guys. Here's the deal. Within the next couple of hours, I expect several deliveries of large items. I'll need y'all to help unload the trucks and bring everything in. Once it's all here, then we'll worry about where it goes. Any questions?"

"Yeah—what time's dinner?" Bryan elbowed one of his friends and winked.

"Pizza. Six o'clock. On me." Even though she was paying them to be here, college boys couldn't go but an hour or two without eating. Instant gratification to keep them happy until they received their paychecks next week. "Oh, and there's a big ice chest full of sodas in my car if one of you will go out and get that."

Footsteps reverberated from the tiled entry. She tingled from blond hair to pedicured toenails. George strolled in, twirling his key ring around one finger. How could she not have noticed his muscular physique before? His snug, heather gray T-shirt clung to the contours of his shoulders, chest, and upper arms as if he should be on a TV commercial for exercise equipment. His worn-in jeans looked like they'd been tailored to fit. He'd had his hair trimmed since she last saw him, and his milk chocolate eyes sparkled when their gazes met. He had no right to look so utterly sensuous when she was trying to maintain a safe emotional distance.

"Hello! Delivery!"

Anne jerked out of her trance at the shout from the opposite end of the building. She grinned at George. "Looks like you timed your arrival perfectly."

His forced frown couldn't quite draw down the corners of his perfectly shaped lips. "And here I'd hoped I'd missed all the manual labor and would be able to stand back and direct."

198

"Nope. That's my job." With a sweeping motion of her arm, she invited him to join the boys, who trooped toward the service entrance. "What was it you said earlier this morning on the phone about doing whatever I need you to do?"

"You thought I was serious?" He tucked his hands into his pockets and rocked from heel to toe.

That dangerous grin of his nearly dismantled her resolve. " 'Deadly serious,' if I recall correctly."

His laughter filled the cavernous room. . .and her heart. "You've got me there. I'd best go see where I can lend a hand, then."

To keep from watching him walk across the room, she turned to her bag and withdrew several CDs. She'd gotten keys to everything in the building from Meredith, including the cabinet containing the sound system components. She dropped five discs into the CD changer, switched on the surround sound, and enveloped the hall with the classic tunes and sultry vocals of Dean Martin, Frank Sinatra, Dick Haymes, Bing Crosby, and Nat King Cole.

"Annie, these are so cool." Jonathan and three of his buddies grasped the corners of an enormous board. She'd gone through thousands of stock photos of Mardi Gras to find images that would add ambience. Each had been enlarged, cut into four pieces, and mounted to twelve-feet-wide-by-eight-feet-high boards and would cover the walnut paneling of the room, stacked two high.

"They should be numbered on the back, so put the face against the wall." She directed them toward the far corner as George and the other three boys carried in another.

"What's this music?" one of the boys asked, but a sound pelting from her three cousins stopped him from further comment.

"Guys, I'll tell you what I've told these three." Anne put her arm around the shoulder of the boy who'd asked and drew the others in with her gaze. "If you really want to woo a woman, don't play any of that hip-hop, R&B junk. Show her you have style. That you appreciate the finer things in life—like the classics. This is the most romantic music in the world. And it's a lot easier to dance to."

"Don't laugh," Jonathan chimed in. "It really works. How d'you think I got Kelli to go out with me?"

Anne laughed with them as they trooped out to bring in the next two boards. She pulled out the diagrams she'd composed with the designer, along with her measuring tape.

"Looking for a carpenter?" A woman about ten years Anne's elder entered, juggling two-by-fours more than twice her height.

"Hey, Pamela! The pictures look fantastic." Anne reached for the end of the boards. "I'll help you bring the rest of this in."

"Nah, Trevor came with me to help. You just get to marking where everything goes, and I'll get to work on these brackets."

Following the measurements on the chart, Pamela and her husband installed the mounting boards, which would be removed and the holes filled and stained to match the paneling afterward. They used an impressive arsenal of power tools and laser levels that shot a line all the way down the length of the room. Anne took the thumbnail printout of the pictures around and slapped the corresponding panel numbers up where she wanted them, using the high-tech tools of a Magic Marker and sticky notes.

She hummed along with the music, singing when she didn't have to concentrate so hard.

The rented ironwork arrived as the last of the mural boards were unloaded. "Just stack those up there in front of the stage area. We have to get the pictures up before we can do anything with those."

"I hope you're going to take lots of pictures of this for your Web site, Annie." Bryan kissed her on the cheek. "I can't wait to see what it looks like all put together."

"Don't worry. You'll have plenty of opportunities to see the photos." George cuffed the younger man around the back of the neck and escorted him back out the door.

She frowned, trying to figure out what that comment meant. His employer was supposed to be media shy, given that he'd gone to great lengths to make sure his wedding planner didn't know for whom she was working.

Her timer beeped at a quarter after five as she posted the last two numbers. Time to order pizza. She snagged her planner and phone and perched on top of the ice chest to call her favorite Italian restaurant. No fast-food pizza for this crew, with as hard as they were working.

She stood when George and the boys approached, pointing at the cooler. "What do y'all want on your pizza?" A cacophony of answers showered her and she reduced it down to one word: *everything*.

George fished his wallet out and handed her a credit card. "Expense account."

Excellent. One less thing for her to have to keep track of. "Thanks." With the boys' chatter, Pamela and Trevor's power tools, and the music, which the guys had turned up to hear over the rest, Anne stepped into the office and pulled the door closed behind her. She ordered from Giovanni's all the time, and they always accommodated her, no matter the volume of food she needed.

When she opened the door, all she could hear was music and voices—no power tools. Hopefully Pamela hadn't run into a problem. She hurried down the hall into the ballroom.

The seven college boys swayed back and forth, arms around each other's shoulders, singing "That's Amore" at the top of their lungs, doing their best to drown out Dean Martin. Pamela and Trevor Grant waltzed across the empty parquet floor, sawdust and all.

"See, *that's* what I was talking about." Anne had to raise her voice for the guys to hear her. "That's romantic music." She gasped when George grasped her hand, pulled her out onto the dance floor, and twirled her around.

"Yes, it is." His breath tickled her ear as he drew her close and swung her around the room.

The grace she'd only had a taste of that afternoon when he'd surprised her in the supply room proved to be greater than she'd suspected. Heat burned through her T-shirt at the small of her back where he held her. Muscles rippled under the gray cotton fabric where her hand rested on his shoulder. Her trainers squeaked against the shiny wood floor.

Then he started to sing. No, not sing. Croon. Just like Dean Martin. Her knees wobbled. His gaze captured hers, and the rest of the world disappeared. The song ended, and he twirled her, then pulled her back into his arms and dipped her. Gently, he raised her until their noses almost touched.

His gaze dropped to her lips, and he swallowed hard. "We need to talk." His voice cracked.

"Yes." She allowed him to take her hand and used the silent walk to the office to regain her composure. Once inside the small room, she perched on the edge of the old wooden desk.

He closed the door and leaned against it. "Anne, there's so much I want to say to you, but. . ."

"But you're bound by your word to your employer not to." She smiled. "I know I've put you in a difficult place by demanding that you be completely honest with me. I don't expect you to tell me what you've sworn to keep secret." She dropped her gaze to her clasped hands. "We all have secrets." She had to tell him about Cliff. Before he found out from someone else. "Speaking of secrets, there's something I need to tell you." She glanced at him.

His relaxed posture encouraged her. "Anne, no matter what you tell me, it won't change the way I feel about you."

The way I feel about you. . .and that was? Her heart careened. Not what she was here to discuss with him. *Focus!* "Before we figure out what our relationship is, there's something in my past you should know. I. . ." It was one thing to tell a family member. Quite a different thing to tell the man working his way into her affections. "I've told you I was engaged to be married a little more than ten years ago."

His easy expression didn't change, except for a slight raising of his dark brows. "I never expected you wouldn't have broken relationships in your past."

Oh, it had been broken, all right. "That's not the whole story."

Trepidation coursed through her. "I was engaged to Cliff Ballantine. Back before he was 'Cliff Ballantine.' "

"And?"

"And. . ." She shrugged. "I just thought you should hear it from me before someone else in the family slipped up and let it out."

He nodded, seeming to contemplate her words. "May I ask you a question?"

"Of course."

"Do you still. . .have feelings for him?" He crossed his arms and leaned his head to the left.

"If contempt counts as having feelings for him, then yes. You know what happened—he took advantage of me and then left me in the lurch when he didn't need me anymore." At his silence, she dropped her gaze. Meredith had been right. The truth about her past upset him.

The tips of his athletic shoes appeared beside hers. He cupped her chin and raised her head. "Then he's the biggest fool in the world." He leaned forward and kissed her, his lips warm, soft, and electric.

Tears burned twin trails down her face. She touched his cheek, and he trembled. He raised his head, gave her another quick kiss, then pulled her into his arms. "Oh, I've wanted to do that for so long."

Lightning bolted through her when he kissed the side of her neck. "I've wanted you to do that for a long time." She stepped back. "But George, until I've figured out how to forgive Cliff, I'll never be over him. I've been praying about it, but I just can't seem to get over the anger."

He took a tissue from the box on the desk and dried her face. "Perhaps if you talked to him."

"Ha!" She shook her head. "There's no way I'd ever be able to get in touch with him. He's probably surrounded by people whose only job is to keep commoners like me away from him."

George traced the contours of her face with his fingertips. "You'd be surprised what God can bring about."

"You're such an optimist." She stepped back into his open arms and relaxed into his embrace. "The only way I'd be able to talk to Cliff Ballantine is if he were to walk through those doors."

A sound rumbled in George's chest. "Stranger things have happened."

CHAPTER 20

*H*eadlights flashed in Anne's rearview mirror. Who in the world would be pulling into her driveway at three o'clock in the morning? She parked and cut off the engine, then reached into the center console for her pepper spray.

The car pulled up beside her, and she released a shaky breath when she recognized Jenn's classic Mustang. Wearily, she climbed out and fumbled with her keys to locate the master for the back door.

"You just getting in?" Jenn called in a hushed voice.

Anne nodded. "And I feel guilty about leaving when I did. There's still so much to finish tomorrow—I mean today."

Jenn skirted her car and put her arm around Anne's waist. "If Fridays weren't one of my busiest nights of the week, I'd offer to help."

"I know. Thanks. How come you're getting in so late?"

"I went out with some of the staff for midnight breakfast after closing. Sort of a celebration. We scored a ninety-eight on our latest health inspection."

"The surprise inspection? Jenn, that's great." Anne looked down to find the right key for the back door.

"So was George there tonight?" In the yellow glow from the porch light, mischief glimmered in Jenn's eyes.

Anne's cheeks burned, and she focused on getting the door unlocked.

"Anne?" Jenn grabbed the keys. "Something happened tonight, didn't it?"

The memory of George's kisses—the one in the office and his good night just a few minutes ago—sent goose bumps racing up and down Anne's body.

"Oh my goodness. He kissed you, didn't he?"

Was she that easy to read? She nodded, unable to speak.

Jenn hopped up and down, her blond-streaked red ponytail bouncing about her shoulders. "I knew it! I knew it! I knew the first time I saw him he was the one for you."

Anne laughed. "Jenn, the first time you saw him, you thought he was a client I was planning a wedding for."

She shook her head. "Nope. Even then. I knew somehow the two of you would end up together. He was too interested in you to be engaged to someone else." She waved her hand to fend off a dive-bombing june bug. "Meredith and I started making plans as soon as she met him."

"Making plans?" With Jenn's attention on avoiding the bug, Anne unlocked the door into the hall that connected all three apartments to the back porch.

"Yeah—for your wedding."

She dropped the heavy key ring on her foot and stifled a yelp. Her *wedding*? She hadn't let her own mind go down that path. She didn't want to be disappointed again when things didn't work out.

"I mean, it's not like we've actually gone out and booked the Vue de Ciel or anything. We just started looking at dresses. . .and flowers. . ."

Crazy. Mad as hatters. Her cousins— "What did you just say?"

"What? That we were looking at dresses and flowers?"

"No, before that."

"The Vue de Ciel? Could you imagine having your reception there? Of course it would have to be at night when all the stars are out." Jenn's tone turned dreamy. "Being on the top floor of the tallest building in downtown; surrounded by glass overlooking the city; the moon and stars glittering like diamonds on velvet. . ."

Anne dropped the keys she'd just retrieved and grabbed her phone, speed-dialing George's number as she raised it to her ear.

Jenn stopped gushing about the location. "Who are you calling at this hour?"

Come on, George, I know you can't be at home in bed yet. As soon as she heard the click of connection, she started talking. "George, I've got it. I know Courtney was disappointed that we can't have the reception at Jardin. But I know where we can do it."

"Slow down. Breathe. What brought on this sudden inspiration?"

She smiled in reaction to the barely suppressed laughter in his voice. "Oh, a conversation I was having with Jenn. Next week we'll go see the Vue de Ciel."

"Is it large enough?"

"A long time ago, I planned a served dinner for nearly a thousand attendees and still had room for a dance floor and bandstand." Fatigue faded as ideas started to take shape. With approximately seven hundred guests, she could have the room set with a mixture of two-, four-, and eight-person tables. The long head table would go on the west side, so they'd have the best view of the city—

"Anne? Are you still there?"

"Sorry. Just formulating some ideas. I need to get it down on paper while I'm thinking about it." She bent down and picked up her keys.

"Are you going to get any sleep tonight?"

"Probably not. I may try to grab a thirty-minute nap tomorrow afternoon when I know everything is going smoothly." Black and white linens with mirrors and candles as centerpieces. Only candlelight— no ambient lighting to distract from the view.

"Do try to get *some* rest, please?"

Well, a bit of electric lighting so it wasn't so dark people would trip and hurt themselves. "I can't make any promises, but I'll try."

"See you at seven for breakfast?"

The enormous cake, fabulously made by Aunt Maggie, would

grace a large table on the south wall. Of course, the photographer would have to figure out how to do the pictures surrounded by so much glass. "Yes, seven at Beignets S'il Vous Plait on Spring Street."

"Good night, then."

"G'night." She flipped the phone closed and started up the stairs.

"Annie? You okay?" Concern laced Jenn's voice.

"Yeah. I've just got to get this all written down before I forget." She turned and kissed her cousin on the cheek. "I probably won't see you until Saturday."

"Bring George by the restaurant Saturday night if he's available. Y'all need to go on a real date and have some alone time."

Somehow, the two of them going to dinner at Jenn's restaurant didn't sound like "alone time" to Anne. "I'll mention it to him and see if he can get away."

"You got in awful late last night."

George gratefully took the blue ceramic mug full of Mama Ketty's chicory coffee and sank onto a stool at the kitchen island. "We had to leave quite a bit undone to get home at that hour." The rich, slightly bitter, extremely hot liquid woke up his mouth. Hopefully the rest of him would follow suit soon. After only three hours of sleep, he felt every one of his forty-one years. . .and then some. He'd gotten soft. Many times in the past few years, he'd had to attend to tasks for Cliff late at night and still be up at six in the morning to keep up with both their schedules. Two months away, and he'd lost the ability to hop out of bed without a minimum of seven hours of sleep when the alarm first sounded. "What time did Mr. Ballantine get in last night?"

" 'Bout an hour before you. He was mightily fearsome when he found out you weren't back yet." Ketty covered her bread dough and set it aside. "Did that young man never learn how to pick up after himself?"

George snorted. He'd picked up Cliff's discarded couture clothing from the bedroom, bathroom, and dressing-room floors this morning. "Apparently not. But it keeps me in cash."

"You gonna clean up after the little miss like that, too, once they're hitched?"

"In the three days she's been back, have you seen her put anything down where it doesn't belong?" His brain started clicking better as the caffeine took effect. "No, Miss Courtney appreciates the fact I have enough to do with looking after Mr. Ballantine. She hardly allows me to do anything for her." *And treats me like I'd always hoped a daughter would. . .* That poor girl. Did she know what she was getting herself into? He had no doubt Cliff was head over heels in love with her. But as soon as Cliff announced their engagement, the media would pursue her as they had Princess Diana. George hoped he'd be able to protect Courtney from the worst of it.

"I s'pose y'all will be getting in late again tonight." Disapproval dripped from Mama Ketty's words.

He caught her about her thick waist as she tried to brush past him. "I'm terribly sorry, lovey. I know you worry."

The muscles in her cheeks twitched as she tried to hold on to her scowl. "Don't go tryin' to butter me up. I told you when you first came here that I work better with a regular schedule. Now you got people coming and going at all hours. . . ." She harrumphed, kissed the top of his head, and continued to the pantry.

"Sorry, what people coming and going?" He checked his watch. Six thirty. He needed to leave in a few minutes to meet Anne for breakfast—and coffee. He swirled the bit of black liquid still remaining in his cup and chuckled. He needed a cup of coffee to wake up enough to go to a coffee shop for breakfast. He really was getting old.

"Them movers that came yesterday after you left."

Frowning, he followed her into the storage room. Fresh spices and dried herbs mingled with the odor of the onions and garlic cloves in the wire basket suspended by a long chain from the high ceiling. "What movers?"

Mama Ketty balanced near the top of the stepladder. She glanced over her shoulder and handed him a large sack of cornmeal. "They came to the service entrance and knocked. Said they had furniture for the upstairs that they was to deliver to Mr. George Laurence. I figured since you and Mr. B. weren't here it was okay, so I let them in. I had Miss Courtney's dinner just coming out of the oven, and I came back to the kitchen. But when I checked on them half an hour later, they weren't moving any furniture, and one of them was coming out of the office. Said he was leaving you a note that they had the wrong furniture and had to go back to the store."

"Oh, love a duck!" The pantry door slammed against the wall in response to George's hasty retreat. Had they been reporters? Had they found anything? He hadn't thought it would be necessary to lock the office when he was out of the house. He kept the file cabinets locked unless he needed something out of them.

The dark wood door swung open at his touch. Nothing appeared to be out of place.

The computer. He dropped the bag of cornmeal and turned the machine on. It didn't require a password to get into the main operating system. Most of his files were encrypted, but what if they'd copied them and had a computer elsewhere that could get into them?

"What's wrong?" Ketty wheezed, out of breath from running after him. "Did I do something I oughtn't have?"

He stared at the blue WELCOME screen. How difficult would it be for them to figure out his password for the confidential files was anne0608? The "anne" part they might figure out if the perpetrators knew Anne was planning the wedding. What they didn't know was that he'd first met her on June 8.

The image of the Big Ben clock tower with a purple evening sky behind it replaced the start-up screen. A yellow bubble popped up in the right corner. YOU HAVE FILES WAITING TO BE WRITTEN TO THE CD. TO SEE THE FILES NOW, CLICK THIS BALLOON. His heart sank when the window opened and he saw the list. Five files. The RSVPs and travel arrangements for the engagement party. The guests for the wedding ceremony. The invite list for the reception. And the detailed questionnaire he'd filled out for Anne.

He hoped the thieves had been thwarted by the unreliable CD burner. But half the time when he used it, that message popped up even after the files had been successfully copied to a disc. He closed his eyes and rubbed them with the heels of his hands, hard enough to see stars.

The dulcet chime of his Westminster clock marked forty-five minutes past the hour. Mama Ketty's warm hand rested on his shoulder, and she leaned over him to look at the screen. "What's all that?"

He let out a defeated breath. "Confidential documents about the wedding. Those blokes weren't movers."

"Oh, honey, I'm so sorry. I knew I should've called you when they showed up. But they knew your name. . . ." She squeezed his shoulder. "Do you s'pose they're reporters?"

Nodding, he shut down the computer. "I'm certain of it." He patted her hand. "Our saving grace is that Mr. Ballantine will make the announcement just a few hours from now. If they can get through my password and figure out what the files mean, we can only hope they try to keep the information for themselves. After the press conference this afternoon, everything will be public knowledge, and they'll lose their exclusive story. Just pray they can't break those passwords."

⌘

Anne checked her watch again and flipped open her phone. She didn't even have to look at the keypad as she punched in the code to speed-dial George. He was always on time. She hoped he hadn't overslept. Too much still needed to be accomplished before the florist arrived at noon.

After one ring, he answered. "Good morning. Sorry I'm running behind schedule a bit."

"I was starting to worry about you. What's your ETA?"

"I'm turning onto Spring Street as we speak. As soon as I overtake this lorry that's pootling down the lane, I should be within sight of the coffee shop."

She laughed. "*Pootling*? That's a new one on me." She craned her neck to see down the road. "Ah, there you are. See you in a bit."

"Toodle-oo."

Taking a deep breath to calm her racing pulse, Anne tucked the phone in her pocket. Would he regret his actions last night? They'd spent so much time trying to avoid the attraction between them, she didn't know how easy showing affection for each other would come for either of them. Yet as she watched him unfold his lanky frame from the low-hung convertible, she wished he'd stop *pootling* and get over here and take her in his arms and—

She tried to control the size of her smile as he approached.

He clasped her hands and gave her a quick kiss on each cheek. "Good morning."

Disappointment surged, but she tamped it down. Standing on the front porch of one of the most popular coffee shops in midtown probably wasn't the best place for the kiss she'd hoped for. "Good morning. You look tired."

"And you, m'lady, look fresh as if you'd just returned from a long holiday." He tweaked her chin, then motioned her toward the door. "Shall we? I don't know about you, but I could use a lot more coffee this morning."

"More? As in, you've already had some?" Anne reached for the door handle, but George was faster. She loved being treated like a fine lady. . .especially by him. Her male cousins were all gentlemen, but sometimes they forgot to open doors or allow her to enter ahead of them. George never forgot. More often than not, he asked her to wait for him to perform his chivalrous duty.

He gave her half a grin. "I had to or I was afraid I might fall asleep driving here."

"Good morning, Anne!"

She turned and greeted the three young women behind the counter, introducing George. While he read the menu board, one of the girls handed Anne her usual.

"That looks good." George leaned over and took a whiff of the enormous muffin.

"This is a tall caramel vanilla latte with a splash of hazelnut and a glorious morning muffin, still warm from the oven." Her stomach growled at the aroma of the dark bran pastry filled with raisins, grated carrots, walnuts, and dates, not to mention the cinnamon, nutmeg, brown sugar, and honey. She took a sip of her coffee and closed her eyes as she imagined the tingle of the caffeine rushing to every nerve in her body. She'd have to have at least one more of these before she'd have enough energy to get anything accomplished this morning.

The three baristas gave Anne a pitying look when George ordered a "large coffee, black." She rather liked the fact he was a no-frills kind of guy. Forbes had probably given closing arguments in court that were shorter than the description of the specialty espresso he drank.

Melted cheddar cheese oozed from George's croissant, and the salty fragrance of the ham made Anne wish she'd ordered that instead. Oh well. Maybe next time. She found an unoccupied table on the back deck that overlooked Schuyler Park and pulled out her list. Halfway through, though, George's attention seemed to be elsewhere.

She set the notepad down on the table and pinched off a chunk of her muffin. "What's going on, George?" She popped the bite in her mouth and savored the chewy sweetness.

The faraway glaze slowly left his eyes. "I'm sorry, what were you saying?"

"Just trying to find out why you haven't heard a word I've said since we sat down." She really didn't have time for him to be unfocused today.

He sipped his coffee and dabbed the corners of his mouth with the white paper napkin. "I do apologize. Pray, continue."

She shook her head. Keeping secrets again? Or just fatigue? Maybe she was overreacting, but she couldn't take that chance. Disheartened, she took a swig of her latte to try to wash down the lump in her throat. She didn't know him well enough to discern if his blue funk was because of her or something else he didn't want her to know about. Truth be told, she hardly knew anything personal about him. She wanted to remedy that, but when he wouldn't open up to her. . .

Exhaustion pushed her emotions to their limit, and she blinked back sudden tears. She'd gone and done exactly what she'd feared—given in to her feelings and made herself vulnerable to him. Just like before, she'd end up with a broken heart after he'd gotten everything from her that he wanted. Just what did he want from her?

She jolted when his fingers touched hers. She pulled her hand away and rested it in her lap, focusing on the now unappetizing lump of muffin on her plate.

"Anne? Anne, I'm sorry. I don't mean to shut you out." He let out a deep breath. "I discovered this morning that some confidential documents may have been stolen from my computer. Documents containing information about the wedding."

Her gaze snapped to his. "Someone hacked into your computer at home?"

"Not exactly. Someone got into my office and may have copied the files onto a CD. I don't think they can do anything with them. But. . ."

She no longer felt sorry for herself, but for him. "Oh. George. What happens if they figure it out? Will you lose your job?"

He shrugged. "There's nothing for it now. We can just pray. . . ."

"Yes." She nodded and reached across to take his hand. "Let's pray. That's why everything feels so overwhelming to me. I didn't start my day in the presence of God." She closed her eyes and bowed over the small round table. George lowered his head, his forehead nearly touching hers. She took a deep breath and cleared her thoughts. "Most merciful and gracious Father, only through the grace of the blood of

Your Son, Jesus Christ, can we come before Your throne. Humbly we give You thanks for Your goodness and mercy, for the blessing of life, and most especially for Your grace and love. Please give us strength today to do what needs to be done, to put aside fatigue and concerns, to make this the best event for the client. Help George to set aside his worries over the crime committed against him. We ask that You keep the thieves from ruining his employer's special day and endangering George's employment. Help me to be a conduit of Your Spirit of love and hospitality with everyone who crosses my path today. Amen."

George squeezed her hand. "Almighty God, I come before You with a humble heart this morning. Grant that I may be able to put aside all anxiety to be prepared to be of service to You and to Anne today. Help us to trust Your guidance and not be carried away by our own plans or preoccupations. Drive away wrong desires, incline our hearts to keep Your law, and guide our feet in the way of peace; that, having done Your will with cheerfulness throughout the day, when the night comes, we may rejoice and give You all the glory. Amen."

CHAPTER 21

"Have you seen George?" Anne looped a gold-beaded garland around her neck and picked up a string of white twinkle-lights.

"Not recently." Her cousin Bryan came down a few rungs and reached for the end of the light cord. He scrambled back up the ladder to complete the faux starry sky. "You might try in the office. Last time I saw him, he was griping about not being able to get a good signal on his cell phone. He might've gone in there to use the landline."

What could possibly be so important as to take him away from the work he'd promised to help with? "How long ago?"

"Probably more than an hour ago."

"Thanks." She crossed the ballroom to deliver the strand of beads to the student workers decorating the parade float. Continuing through the heavy pine door, she tried to get hold of her anger. How could he disappear on her like this? She'd hoped to turn things over to him for half an hour so she could sit down and regroup— and maybe close her eyes for a few minutes. She was getting too old to keep these kinds of hours. With her business's financial future secure, she needed an assistant—or a partner.

The office door stood open. No George. Frustrated, she dropped into the tall executive chair behind the desk, picked up the phone, and dialed his number.

He answered on the third ring. "George Laurence here."

"Where are you?" She grimaced at the accusation that managed to slip into her voice despite her best efforts to affect a light tone.

"I am in the hot sun at the top of a very tall ladder trying to hang purple, gold, and green garlands while talking on the phone without plunging to an early and grizzly demise."

Embarrassed relief washed through her. "Oh. I thought. . ."

"Anne." His deep voice caressed her jumbled emotions. "I promised I would be here for you. Unlike. . .other people, I always hold true to my word."

Her throat tightened. His ability to understand what she was thinking continued to amaze—and comfort—her. "I'm sorry I doubted you."

"No apology necessary. Why don't you close the office door and rest for a few minutes? I'll fetch you should any problems arise."

The idea of being "fetched" by him like a stick by a golden retriever brought her to irrepressible laughter. She couldn't explain her mirth to him at his inquiry. She repeated his "Ta-ta for now" and hung up.

Indecision hit her when she crossed to the door. Three o'clock, and so much left to do. Could she afford to disappear for fifteen minutes? Or, being honest with herself, could she depend on George? Happy Endings, Inc., and her reputation as an event planner represented what she valued most in life, outside of her family.

She closed the door. If the relationship between them stood any chance of developing into. . .something, she must learn to trust him. Besides, what could happen in the few minutes she needed to get her second—or was she already on her third—wind?

⊰❈⊱

At five o'clock, George found Major O'Hara and asked him to bring all of the workers together in the break room behind the kitchen. Cliff's press conference would begin in half an hour, and George wanted the staff to be made aware of the ground rules for tonight's event.

He found one of Anne's cousins in the crowd of student workers. "Have you seen Anne recently?"

Jonathan shook his head. "Not for a couple of hours. I thought maybe she'd gone to run some errands."

"Thanks." George asked O'Hara to keep everyone together until he returned. He jogged across the ballroom-turned-French Quarter and down the hall to the administrative office. He turned the knob softly and swung the door open.

Anne never stirred. Even when she was sound asleep, stress drew her forehead into worry lines. He eased the door closed and released the handle centimeter by centimeter until it latched. He wanted to reveal the guest of honor's identity to her in private anyway. Best let her get all the rest she could. She'd need it. As soon as he finished with the staff, he'd come back and tell her.

The buzz of voices in the break room stilled when George entered. "I know many of you have been curious as to whom this event is for. That's why I wanted to call you together. Our guest of honor this evening is Mr. Cliff Ballantine."

Astonishment swept through the room, and the initial gasp turned to excited whispering, especially among the females. He held his hands up to regain their attention. "Obviously I don't have to explain who he is. There are, however, some ground rules everyone must agree to before his arrival. If you cannot agree, or if you break any of these rules, you will be asked to leave."

He pulled a manila folder from his bag. "First, Mr. Ballantine will not be signing any autographs tonight. Please do not approach him with any such request. He has been kind enough to supply autographed photos for each of you instead." He passed the stack of black-and-white head shots to the young woman at his right. "Second, you may not, under any circumstances, call anyone to let them know he will be here tonight. You are more than welcome to talk about it after the event to whomever you please." He reached for a cardboard box on top of a stack of chairs. "Please deposit your cell phones in this box. They will be locked in the office until the end of the event."

Excited twittering turned to groans. George gave them his sternest look. "If you cannot abide by these rules. . ." The thud of phones dropping into the box drowned out the complaints. "Third, there will be many other people here tonight whom you may be tempted to ask for autographs. Don't. After the event is over, if they offer to sign something for you, that is permissible. But don't solicit them. Finally, for those of you who will be greeting guests at the door, if they do not have an invitation, please call me over the radio before allowing them admittance."

A hand shot up at the back of the room.

"Yes?"

"Even if it's someone we recognize, we're not to let them in?"

He didn't want any of the guests offended, but he didn't want any paparazzi or reporters gaining entrance, either. Most of the guests would understand. "Please call me no matter what." He pulled another stack of papers out of his bag, split it in half, and started them around the room. "This is a release stating that you have heard and understood the guidelines I've just enumerated for you. Please sign it and return it to Mr. O'Hara or me, and then you can go back to your duties."

They were signing the releases when Anne's cousin Jonathan burst through the doors. "George, I think you should come outside."

He left Major to gather the paperwork and ran across the building. His phone beeped and he pulled it out to answer the call from Cliff's publicist.

"We were on our way to the hotel in downtown, and Mr. Ballantine decided he wanted to have the press conference at Lafitte's Landing instead." Tracie's voice betrayed her state of near-panic. "You'll need to figure out a podium and some sound quickly." A black stretch limousine, followed by innumerable vehicles, wound its way up the long drive toward Lafitte's Landing.

"Oh, my sainted aunt!" He spun and ran back inside. "Keep Mr. Ballantine in the car until we get everything set up," he called into the phone, then disconnected and clipped it back in place.

One of the staff directed George to a storage room where he found a large lectern and portable sound system. As the boys who'd worked with the equipment before rushed to get everything plugged in, George arranged the stanchions and black velvet rope, originally set out to line the red carpet leading to the entrance, as a barrier to keep the reporters and cameras out of Mr. Ballantine's face. Like locusts, they swarmed toward the building, but the college students did an admirable job of keeping them behind the barricade.

After a thumbs-up from Jonathan, George descended the porch steps and crossed to the limousine. Blinding flashes combined with yelling reporters competed for Cliff's attention as George opened the door and the movie star stepped out.

What was he wearing? Blue jeans and a University of Louisiana baseball jersey? George shook his head. If he hadn't been here all day. . . But he'd promised Anne.

Anne! She still didn't know. He whirled to return to the building and find her before she woke up and walked out into the middle of her worst nightmare.

Cliff grabbed George's shoulder to stop him. "Tracie, call the hotel and have them send over any other reporters still waiting for me there. Laurence, show me what's been done inside."

No, no, no! He had to get to Anne. He had to tell her himself. *Please, dear Lord, let her sleep through this. Let her stay in the office until I can get to her.* "Yes, Mr. Ballantine."

The diminutive, dark-haired publicist stepped up to the lectern to announce that Mr. Ballantine would give his statement in approximately fifteen minutes.

As soon as his eyes adjusted to the dim interior, George's gaze scoured the room for the statuesque blonde he'd come to love in the last month. He sighed when he couldn't spot her.

Like a politician, Cliff greeted the college students still working on the decorations, table settings, and final preparations. George kept his eyes trained on the door at the back of the room. When Tracie gave him the word, he'd get Cliff back out front and go tell

Anne. He couldn't let her hear this from someone else.

Standing in the middle of the ballroom, Cliff turned in a full circle, nodding his head. "Looks great, Laurie. Good job."

"I can take no credit, sir. Your wedding planner, An—"

"Why aren't any of them asking for my autograph?" A fierce frown marred Cliff's world-famous face.

Oh no! A worker, with the box holding everyone's cell phones under her arm, went through the door at the back of the room. George moved to stop her, but Cliff grabbed his shoulder again. *God, please don't let Anne wake up!* "Everyone working here tonight signed a release that they wouldn't. We gave them signed head shots a few minutes ago."

The frown melted into relief. "Oh. Good. I thought I was losing my touch for a minute there." He inhaled deeply. "Take me to the kitchen. I want to sample what we're eating tonight."

Yes. The kitchen. Anne probably wouldn't go in there.

The frenetic preparations in the kitchen came to a dead stop when Cliff entered. Major O'Hara commanded them all back to work and came toward him, his face a study in granite.

"As I live and breathe, Major O'Hara." Cliff extended his hand jovially.

The caterer's smile seemed forced. "Cliff Ballantine. It's been a long time. Welcome."

"So what's on the menu?" Cliff seemed not to notice the frosty reception.

George followed them as Major allowed Cliff a taste of each of the dishes. He knew why Anne and her family would give Cliff a frigid greeting. What had happened with Major O'Hara?

Tracie beeped through on his phone while Cliff taste-tested the jambalaya. George stepped to the double doors and peered out into the ballroom. No sign of Anne. "Tracie, please tell me everyone is here and we can get started."

"Yes. The natives are getting restless. They're ready for the human sacrifice."

"I'll have him out there in a moment." He had to wait for Cliff to finish slurping down a glass of iced tea. Through the doors and fifty feet across the ballroom, and Tracie would take over. He pushed the swinging door open, and it bumped someone on the other side.

"I beg your pardon—" Not now! Not when he was so close to success.

"It's okay. Oh, hi, George." The beautiful, trusting smile that crossed Anne's face broke his heart.

"Thanks, guys, everything looks great!" Cliff called over the din of kitchen equipment.

George's shoulders dropped. "Anne, I was going to tell you—"

"No!" She shook her head and backed away from him. "No." The dead calm of her voice worried him more than the shock on her face.

"Laurence, why—" Cliff stopped beside him and muttered a surprised expletive under his breath. "Annie Hawthorne. I never thought I'd see you again."

George clenched his hands into fists and bit the insides of his cheeks. "Mr. Ballantine, may I introduce your wedding planner?"

"Wedding planner?" Cliff looked from George to Anne. "You're kidding, right?"

Anne's face had gone pale, her posture so stiff George worried she might faint. His phone beeped again. "Sir, the press conference."

"Right. Anne—we'll talk later." Cliff brushed past her on his way out of the kitchen. She jerked away from him and exited into the ballroom.

When George came out of the kitchen, Anne stood with her back to him. "Anne. Anne, I wanted to tell you privately, but then he came here instead of going to the hotel, and. . ." He shook his head. "And things spiraled out of my control." He touched her arm.

She whirled to face him. "Cliff Ballantine? You work for *Cliff Ballantine?*" Her gaze shot electric blue anger at him. "Did you have a good laugh last night? I poured my heart out to you. I told you how much he'd hurt me. And you stood there and said nothing. Nothing!

If you really cared about me, you would have told me. Right then. *Stranger things have happened?* That's all you could say?"

Although she never raised her voice, he felt as though she'd yelled at him. He looked around the room. A few students working nearby quickly turned their attention back to their tasks. He clasped her elbow. "Let's go to the office—"

She yanked out of his grasp. "Afraid I'll embarrass you with my outburst?" She took a deep breath, and before he could blink, her expression changed from fury to calm professionalism. "If you'll excuse me, I have a job to do." She stalked away.

Oh, Anne, Anne! I'm so terribly sorry. He turned to exit the building. Now the truth had been revealed, Anne wouldn't want him here. His responsibility lay solely with Cliff and Courtney. . . and in figuring out how to convince Anne to forgive him. Perhaps after she got over the initial shock, she'd be more open to listening to his explanation.

❦

A red haze surrounded Anne. Cliff Ballantine. She'd been planning Cliff Ballantine's wedding. To see him standing there behind George. . . Tears burned her eyes. How could he do this to her?

He? Whom was she most angry with? George? Cliff? God? She hated to admit it, but of the three, Cliff's surprised expression at seeing her acquitted him of any guilt. He hadn't known about her any more than she'd known about him.

"Keep the walkways clear of streamers and confetti. We don't want anyone slipping and hurting themselves." The college students jumped to do her bidding.

George. She'd trusted him to be honest with her. She'd told him—

"Make sure to tape the plugs connecting those light strings so they don't come undone. Also, tape the extension cord down along the floorboard so no one trips on it. If y'all are finished with that, you need to go change into your uniforms."

God, how could You do this to me?

In response, her own voice echoed through her memory. *The only way I'd be able to talk to Cliff Ballantine is if he were to walk through those doors.* She hated it when God took her at her word.

Several students stood in the front hall, gawking through the windows on each side of the front doors. "If y'all don't have anything else to do, you need to go change clothes and get your stations ready."

They scattered, and Anne took their position at the window.

Had Cliff always been so broad through the shoulders? Between them stood George, hands clasped behind his back. Compared to his employer, he looked half his real size.

He glanced over his shoulder, and their gazes met. He turned and slipped inside. "Anne."

She stepped back, shaking her head. She opened her mouth but had no words. Pressing her lips together, she closed her eyes and turned away.

He moved closer. "Anne, I wanted to tell you last night, but I couldn't. I truly was going to tell you this afternoon, but he changed his plans at the last minute and came here instead of going to the hotel to give his press conference. He showed up just as I was coming to tell you."

The din outside rose in volume as reporters started shouting questions over each other. Anne stopped but kept her back turned to him. "I don't want to talk about this right now. I just want to get through tonight with as little drama as possible." She walked away, praying he wouldn't follow. The sound of the heavy front door closing gave her some relief.

She crossed the French Quarter at Mardi Gras–themed ballroom into the kitchen. Major O'Hara looked up from where he was supervising one of his cooks. She jerked her head toward the staff break room. He nodded and joined her a few moments later, closing the door on the noise and confusion of the final preparations.

"Did you know?" Major asked. He perched on the edge of a

stack of four dining room chairs. Ten years ago, Major had agreed to cater Anne and Cliff's reception for a miniscule amount of money.

She released the large clip at the back of her head and ran her fingers through her hair. "No. I can't believe George didn't tell me."

"Does he know you have a history with Cliff?"

"Not until I told him everything last night." She sank onto an ancient sofa and then decided she'd have been more comfortable on the floor.

"And he didn't tell you then?" Major crossed his arms, a familiar storminess coming into his expression. She'd forgotten what a short fuse he had when he thought someone he cared for had been wronged.

"He—" What was it she'd said to George last night just before telling him about Cliff? *I don't expect you to tell me what you've sworn to keep secret.* She leaned her head back and stared at the water-stained tile above her. "He promised Cliff he wouldn't tell anyone."

"Then why did he pull everyone together and tell all of us right before Cliff got here?"

Anger surged anew. Why indeed. "You're right. He could have told me last night. It's not like I'm going to go out and blab to some supermarket tabloid reporter. He should have shown me more respect than that. 'Stranger things have happened,' my foot! If he has so little respect for me, after tonight is over, he can just plan the rest of the wedding by himself."

CHAPTER 22

*S*he would put all the Hollywood royalty present tonight to shame.

George ran his finger under his collar, suddenly unable to breathe. Dressed in a modest floor-length, black column dress, Anne glided around the perimeter of the room, double-checking the readiness of each station and each server. If her idea had been to blend into the background, she'd failed miserably. He turned at a tug on his sleeve.

"George, how do I look?"

Courtney Landry stood before him, no longer a cherubic nineteen-year-old, but a grown woman dressed in a clinging, plunging silk gown the same electric blue as Anne's eyes. He wanted to drape his tuxedo coat about her bare shoulders and hold it closed just below her chin. He cleared his throat and reached for her hand. "Like a princess." He brushed a kiss on her knuckles.

She blushed and touched the chestnut curls piled up on top of her head. "He's introducing me to all his friends tonight. What if I trip? Or drop food down my dress?"

"Now, Miss Courtney, I know you paid more attention than that during our etiquette lessons. Chin up, shoulders square, make direct eye contact." She followed his commands like a well-trained soldier. "And remember, tonight is about *you*. Not Cliff, nor anyone else in the room. Now. . ." He tucked her hand under his arm. "It's

226

time for you to greet your guests."

Cliff stopped pacing when George arrived in the foyer with Courtney. "It's about time. Laurence, check my tie. I think it's crooked."

George squeezed Courtney's hand once more and stepped forward to pretend to adjust the perfectly straight knot of white silk at Cliff's throat. In his ear, a short burst of static came over the radio, followed by, "Mr. Laurence, a limo's coming!"

He touched the button on the side of the pack clipped to his belt. "I'll be right along." Returning his attention to Cliff, he brushed invisible lint from the lapel of the black Valentino. "If you're ready, sir?"

Cliff waved him away. "Yeah. Enough. Go. Don't keep people waiting."

"Wait!" Anne's voice stopped George cold. She ran into the foyer and skidded to a stop, breathless. "You forgot your jewelry, Miss Courtney." Anne's maternal smile as she clasped the diamond-and-sapphire-encrusted choker around the girl's throat curled George's toes. Yes, she would be a wonderful mother to their children.

She left without even a glance in George's direction.

"Laurence. I believe it's time to let the guests in." Cliff motioned toward the front doors.

"Yes, Mr. Ballantine." George stepped out onto the front porch, rolling his shoulders to release some of the tension.

Over the next two hours, he stood vigil on the porch, keeping the photographers beyond the ropes, welcoming guests, overseeing the valets, and, in general, trying to keep the chaos to a minimum. Every so often, Anne's voice came over the radio in response to one worker or another's panic. The calm reassurance in her tone acted as a soothing balm for everyone. Just the awareness that she had everything under control made the evening successful.

The radio crackled as she came over the connection. "George, I need your assistance. Please come to the administrative office." Something had to be terribly wrong for Anne to call him away from his post. But her voice betrayed nothing.

"I'll be right there." He motioned to Jonathan to take over supervision. Inside, around a hundred guests milled about, exclaiming over the decor and devouring the Cajun food. He looked around to check on Courtney. His heart thudded when he didn't see her, and he quickened his pace.

He pushed open the ajar office door. Courtney sat in one of the guest chairs, Anne kneeling on the floor in front of her. When the young woman saw him, she burst into tears, pulled away from Anne, and flung herself at him. He caught her in an embrace and looked over the top of her head at Anne. She shook her head as she stood.

"They hate me," Courtney wailed against his black waistcoat.

He patted her back, trying to soothe her. "No one could possibly hate you. What happened?" He directed the question at Anne.

"Apparently she overheard some not-so-kind remarks about herself in the restroom."

"They called me a gold-digging, trailer-park redneck." Courtney pulled away enough to look in his eyes. "I did everything just like you taught me."

"I'm certain you did." He disentangled himself and sat her in the chair again. He knelt on the tile floor in front of her while Anne perched on the edge of the other chair. "Courtney, I wish there were some way I could protect you from people saying terrible things about you. But this is the life you've chosen by agreeing to marry Cliff. You must become inured to being insulted for no reason."

Courtney's fine brows pinched together in confusion. He looked to Anne for assistance.

Her lips twitched, and she wouldn't meet his gaze. "What George means is that you have to get used to people insulting you. You're going to be in the public eye, and you're the envy of every woman in this country." What had it cost for her to say that? "Hell hath no fury like a scorned—or jealous—woman. I'm certain you remember what it was like when you were in high school. Everyone hated the girl who dated the most popular guy, and said horrible things about her behind her back, and made up stuff to make her look bad."

Courtney ducked her head and blushed. "Yeah. I remember. I was like that. I guess it's payback time now, huh?"

Anne patted her hand. "Whenever you hear or read bad things about yourself, just remember the people who love you and think you're one of the most wonderful people in the world—like us."

Courtney looked from Anne to George, moisture still glittering in her brown eyes. "Really?"

With a tissue, Anne dried the young woman's tears. "Really." She handed her a makeup compact. "Now. Powder your nose and go show those jealous biddies what you're made of."

Courtney giggled and did as instructed, then swept out of the office with her chin up, shoulders straight.

George tried to get Anne to meet his gaze. "You're very good at what you do, Miss Hawthorne."

"Thank you for your assistance. I don't know if I could have handled her on my own." She turned her back on him, reaching for the doorknob.

Disappointment filled him. He'd hoped when she called him in here that she might have gotten over her anger and decided to forgive him. "You would have managed one way or another."

❦

Anne surveyed the crowd milling in the ballroom, exclaiming over the genuine Mardi Gras parade float, admiring the life-size murals of the historic buildings lining the French Quarter, and devouring Major's excellent Cajun food nearly to the exclusion of the caviar and other delicacies she'd worked so hard to get brought in from the New York and Los Angeles restaurants. Of course, the list had been Cliff's idea. No way would Courtney have ever come up with that.

George came out of the kitchen, and her heart thumped even as she narrowed her eyes. How could she feel so torn about him? Part of her was ready to forgive him, while the other part never wanted to talk to him again.

Halfway to the front door, a vaguely familiar young woman grabbed George's arm.

"George, you have to introduce me to the event planner!" The girl's voice carried over the din of guests and the zydeco band playing their hearts out on the other side of the room.

His tight smile and the slight bow he made gave a good indication the girl wasn't an acquaintance of his. He led the girl to Anne. "Miss Alicia Humphrey, I'm pleased to present Miss Anne Hawthorne, who is solely responsible for planning this gala."

Embarrassment crept up to burn her cheeks. "I wouldn't say *solely* responsible." She smiled and finally recognized the young actress. "It's very nice to meet you, Miss Humphrey."

The girl, who couldn't be any older than Courtney, took Anne's proffered hand in both of hers. "I want to hire you to plan my wedding. Court's been telling me all about what you're doing for her, and I just have to have you do mine. I'm getting married at Christmas at home in Baton Rouge. With me living in Malibu, I can't do it myself."

Anne's heart raced. Another celebrity wedding meant another influx of income. She really would have to take on a partner. George bowed and excused himself.

George. She didn't know another person who possessed more experience in planning high-profile social events. He wanted to stay in America but disliked his current employment. Would he consider. . . ? More to the point, would she consider taking him on as a partner? Could she trust him?

"Miss Hawthorne?"

"I'm terribly sorry—my mind wandered there for a moment." She smiled at her newest potential client. "Tell me about what you want for your wedding."

Twenty minutes later, Alicia Humphrey floated away on her director-fiancé's arm, Anne's card in her hand. Although Anne didn't usually make house calls, nor appointments to meet with clients on Saturdays, she'd be visiting Miss Humphrey at her hotel at eleven tomorrow morning.

Throughout the evening, she made a point of speaking with the local VIPs in attendance, including the mayor and the state senator from their district, just so they might keep her in mind should they need any event-planning services.

As the locals began to leave, more of the Hollywood crowd trickled in. She walked past the food tables, pleased to see all the dishes were as full as if the party had just started. As usual, she'd been impressed by Major O'Hara's staff. All evening, she'd switched over to the frequency channel they'd chosen and listened to the constant chatter between the kitchen and the table staff. He'd also taken charge of the student employees working as servers and made them part of his battle-ready army.

At midnight, as the crowd waned, she signaled Major to pare down the savory foods and put out more sweets and coffees.

She stifled a yawn. Speaking of coffee. . . Slipping into the kitchen, she smiled at the sous-chef, then stopped at each of the four commercial coffeemakers and inhaled the fragrance of each.

There, the one that was still brewing. Cinnamon hazelnut. Had to be. Like a pro, she slipped the carafe out and slid a cup under the basket, not letting a drop of the precious liquid go to waste. She turned with her stolen treasure to find Major standing behind her, hands clasped behind his back like a drill sergeant.

"Hi."

"Anne Hawthorne, you know no one is allowed in my kitchen except my staff."

She held the mug toward him. "You don't happen to have any cream on hand, do you?"

He tried to stare her down, but she knew him too well. His frown broke, and he pulled a carton of half-and-half from behind his back. He even poured it and produced a spoon and crystal bowl of sugar. "I'd started to wonder how long it would be before you had to have a caffeine fix. You know I only make that sissy-flavored coffee because of you. Why a Louisiana gal like you can't be happy with good ol' chicory."

She leaned against the counter beside him. "Thanks, Major. I love you, too." She sipped her treat while he reviewed his evening. Around them, his staff cleaned up their work areas and packed away equipment, leftover food, and unused ingredients.

"I can return a lot of the unused items."

"No." Anne downed the last of her coffee and poured another cup, letting Major doctor it for her again. "Donate it to University Chapel's food closet. Put the cost for all of it on the invoice. He can afford it."

"He? You mean Cliff?" Major spat the name out.

Anne leaned into his side. "I know why I'm angry at him. Can I assume your bad feelings are on my behalf?"

"He stole my girlfriend." He put his arm around her shoulders.

"I was never your girlfriend."

"I wanted you to be."

"You never asked."

"I didn't think your aunt and uncle would approve."

"Aunt Maggie loved you like a son—still does, even though you're her competition now instead of her favorite employee."

"Am I going to have to hate this George character now, too?"

Anne leaned her head to the side to gaze at her friend. "What are you talking about?"

"I've watched him all night. He's in love with you, y'know."

She frowned at him. "Weren't you the one who sat there in the break room just a couple of hours ago, egging me on in being angry at him?"

Major quirked the left side of his mouth. "Yeah. But I've had more time to think about it. He was looking for you for a while before he gathered the staff together. I think he was planning to tell you privately."

Guilt started to replace the righteous indignation she'd used as a shield between herself and George all night.

"You don't know how hard this is for me to say, but you need to forgive him."

Tingles started at her toes and shot all the way to her scalp. "I know."

He crooked his elbow around her neck and pulled her close to kiss her temple. "See if you can convince this George fella to stay around. He sorta grows on a body."

She patted his arm where it rested across her throat. "Oh, I'll see what I can do."

❧

At 2:00 a.m., Cliff and Courtney's limousine drove away from Lafitte's, taking the last of the paparazzi with them. George pulled the radio earpiece off and let out a big sigh. "Wonderful job tonight, gentlemen. Let's go find Anne and see if we can call it a night."

"Amen to that," Jonathan agreed. "Fourteen hours is *way* too long to work in one spell."

George shook his head as the man twenty years his junior trudged into the building. Oh, to have to work only fourteen hours at a spell. Several of the service staff passed them, dressed in their shorts, T-shirts, and thong sandals. The boys ahead of him picked up the pace, ready to be released to go home.

Anne sat at one of the tables near the kitchen signing time cards. Major O'Hara straddled a chair behind her, his denim chef's tunic unbuttoned to reveal the UL–BONNETERRE T-shirt beneath, massaging her shoulders.

George tried not to be jealous, recalling they were old friends, and continued around to the coffee service cart beyond them.

"Plain coffee is brown; flavored is white," Major said, leaning his head back to tell him.

George lifted the brown carafe.

"Man after my own heart." The caterer raised his Styrofoam cup in salute.

George returned the gesture and sank into the chair on Anne's other side. She wrote the time and signed each card as fast as she could, trying to get the kids out as soon as possible. How many of them would leave here and go out now? He'd heard his valet-parking boys discuss some kind of big event going on tonight down on Fraternity Row. Knowing college kids, it would still be going on at this hour, if the police hadn't been called in yet.

Anne's makeup couldn't hide the dark circles beneath her eyes. Limp tendrils of her hair had come out of the french twist at the back of her head, and she tapped the fingernails of her left hand on the table as she worked. She wouldn't leave until everything was finished and the place locked down for the night.

"Are some of the staff staying to help clean up?" Major asked, looking around at the mess.

"We have a cleanup crew coming in tomorrow," George answered. "Meredith is supervising that so Anne doesn't have to come back up here."

She glanced up at him in surprise. "What? When was that decided?"

"Meredith and I discussed it last week. She said if they run into any problems, she'll call you. She talked to Pamela and Trevor yesterday and arranged for them to come remove the murals. You've already scheduled the rental company to come pick up what belongs to them, and I supplied Meredith with my copy of the list so she knows what to set aside. The rest belongs here, and it's her staff who will be working, so she didn't feel your presence would be necessary. I wholeheartedly concur."

Rather than argue, she surprised him with a smile—the first she'd given him since she'd walked into the kitchen and seen Cliff. "Thanks. I really wasn't looking forward to spending another full day up here."

Major rose and returned the coffee service to the kitchen. He returned a few minutes later, a large bag hanging from his shoulder. He leaned over and kissed Anne's cheek. "Great party, Annie."

"Wouldn't have been without you. Fax over that final invoice as soon as you have it, and George will write you a check." She patted the caterer's hand. "Won't you?"

George nodded. "Just ring me up when you have the total, and I can drop it off."

"I'll call, then. Probably Monday morning after I have a chance to do a complete inventory and go over my staff's time cards. Mere and I have that banquet tomorrow night, so it's unlikely to be any earlier."

"Monday's fine." Anne signed the last time card with a flourish and sent the student away. "I'll be talking to Mere next week about a couple of other projects we'll need you for."

"I look forward to hearing about them." Major's gaze shifted to George for a brief moment, then back to Anne. "And remember what I said."

Anne's cheeks reddened. "I will. Now get out of here so I can, too."

"Okay. Kitchen's locked down tight; lights are off. G'night, you two." Major beat a path out the front door.

Anne stood and stretched, then bent over to pick up her shoes from under the table. "George, I. . .I'd like to talk to you if you have a minute."

For her, he had hours, days, weeks, years. He followed her back to the office, where she shoved the shoes into her bag and pulled out her trainers. He grinned as she put the white athletic shoes on with the black evening gown.

When she finished tying the laces, she didn't stand but leaned back in the chair, her hands folded at her waist. "I wanted to apologize to you."

He raised his brows and leaned against the edge of the desk.

"I've treated you unfairly tonight. I was angry with you because you didn't tell me about Cliff. But I can't hold that against you, for the very reason you didn't tell me in the first place."

"I'm not sure I follow."

She rubbed her temples. "I'm not making any sense, am I? Too long without sleep. I guess what I'm trying to say is, will you forgive me for being mad at you for being an honorable man and keeping your word?"

Grinning, he knelt in front of her, took her hands in his, and kissed her palms. "Gladly and wholeheartedly."

Leaning forward, she wrapped her arms around his neck. "I'm sorry for being so hard-hearted. It was just. . .seeing Cliff like that with no forewarning. . . I guess I really have a lot to work on when it comes to forgiving him, because that isn't going to come easily. I know that now."

He held her for a few moments until his knees started to ache on the tile floor. He kissed the side of her neck, rose, and stretched as stress rolled off his shoulders.

She slouched back in the chair. "There's something else I want to ask you."

He perched on the edge of the desk facing her, curiosity aroused. "All right."

She bit the right corner of her bottom lip as she searched his face, then sat up straight, her knuckles turning white as she gripped her hands together. "I know we've only known each other for a little over a month. And during that time, we've had our share of misunderstandings and communication issues."

Her skill with euphemistic understatements would put a parliamentarian to shame. He nodded, encouraging her to continue.

"I feel like we have a lot in common, and we obviously work well together." She smiled nervously. "What I want to ask is: How about making this permanent?"

He nearly fell off the desk. Permanent? Had Anne Hawthorne just proposed marriage to him?

She rushed to continue. "As I said, I know it hasn't been that long. And I know you'll need time to think about making a major step like this."

Every fiber of his being cried out, *Yes! Yes, I'll marry you.* The miniscule part of his brain that clung to reason still controlled his tongue. "I'm flattered. But, Anne, have you thought this through? Are you sure this is what you truly want, and not just a reaction to seeing Cliff tonight?"

She frowned. "Cliff? What does he have to do with my asking you to be my business partner?"

Business partner? He chuckled and shook his head. Yet another example of their typical misunderstandings and communication issues. "Nothing, I suppose."

"I mean, you may not make as much in a year working with me if we're splitting the profits equally, but the cost of living here is a lot lower."

And he'd get to see her every day. He tapped his thumb against his lips a moment. If he were going to stay here, he wanted the whole package—and he meant to have it before Courtney's wedding. But given her nervousness at asking him to go into business together, convincing her to marry him would be a considerable undertaking. "Draw up a business plan, and I'll take a look at it. I'll have to look into the legality of changing jobs with my current work visa." Of course, being married to an American citizen, he wouldn't have to worry about work visas ever again. Not that where they would live mattered. He'd be happy living in a thatch-roofed hut in the bitter cold of Scotland, as long as he had Anne at his side.

CHAPTER 23

𝒜nne tried to ignore the pounding by pulling a spare pillow over her head. There. The noise stopped.

Something heavy hit her bed. She shrieked and bolted upright, nearly colliding with Jenn, who bounced up and down on her knees.

"When were you going to tell us?"

Anne glanced at the alarm clock. Not even eight o'clock. Less than four hours of sleep—again. Never before had she thought ill of a relative. But right now she hated the two auburn-tressed sisters staring at her like baby chicks waiting to devour a worm. She fell back against her pillow with a groan. "Go away! Let me get some sleep."

"I told you we should have left her alone," Meredith scolded her younger sister. "Come on, let's go."

"No. I want to hear it from her. Is it true?" Jenn crawled over and straddled Anne.

"Is what true?" She could very easily toss the skinny-minnie off the bed, maybe even out the window.

"You're planning Cliff Ballantine's wedding."

She could have gone all day without being reminded of that. "Go away." She pushed Jenn away, rolled onto her side, and covered her head with the pillow again.

"You're on the front page of the newspaper, Annie." Meredith's

238

soft voice filtered through the thick down covering Anne's ears. "You looked really nice last night."

She bolted upright again, this time bumping Jenn's nose with her forehead. She snatched the paper from Meredith. Below a giant color photo of Courtney and Cliff on the front porch of Lafitte's Landing was a smaller image of herself. When. . . ? Oh, she'd gone out to give Jonathan batteries for his radio pack.

"I'm surprised your phone isn't ringing off the hook." Jenn rubbed her nose.

"I turned the ringer off when I got home last night. I thought that would thwart anyone who might try to disturb me before I had a decent amount of sleep. I guess I'll have to start using the door chain."

"She would have just stood there pounding on the door until you opened it." Meredith came around and sat on the edge of the bed. "Did you know?" She pointed at Cliff's picture.

Anne shook her head. "No. George was under strict orders to keep his employer's identity secret. No one knew until just before the press conference."

"Hello?" Forbes's voice rang through the apartment.

"In here," Jenn yelled.

"What is it with you people and Saturday mornings?" Anne flipped the folded paper over to look at the top of the page again. BALLANTINE TO MARRY LOCAL GIRL, the headline proclaimed. Poor Courtney. She tossed the paper aside as Forbes entered her bedroom.

"Aren't you going to read the articles?" Jenn caught the section before it slid off the far side of the bed.

"I was there. I planned it. I think I know what happened." She propped a couple of pillows against her headboard and scooted up to sit against them. She reached for the tall paper cup of coffee Forbes held in his hand and took a big gulp before handing it back to him. "Ugh. Gross. Skim milk and artificial sweetener. I always forget."

"Everything okay?"

Why did he look so nervous? "Mostly." She cocked her head to one side. "Did you know anything about this? No, wait." She held up her free hand. "I don't want to know. Anything you say will probably just make me mad, and then we'll sit here all morning analyzing why I'm mad and I'll never get any more sleep. So now that everyone is reassured that I'm okay, can you please leave so I can go back to sleep?"

His relief palpable, Forbes leaned over and kissed her forehead. "Yes. Yes, we can do that."

Meredith patted Anne's knee through the quilt. "Yeah. Sorry we woke you up like that."

"Jennifer, let's go." Forbes stood at the end of the bed like a nightclub bouncer.

"But—"

"No buts. Now." He snapped his fingers and pointed at the door. He waited until his younger sister huffed out of the room, then turned back to Anne. "Rest up. If what they wrote in the paper is true, you're not going to be getting a lot of rest anytime soon."

As he walked out the door, Anne rearranged her pillows and curled into her favorite position. She yawned and closed her eyes. Ah, sleep.

If what they wrote in the paper is true. . . Forbes's words bounced through her mind. What had they written about her in the paper? The feature they'd done on her after the article in *Southern Bride* had been extremely complimentary and had driven most of this summer's business. But with whom had the reporter spoken last night?

Her head throbbed. She wouldn't worry about that now. She needed sleep. Sleep. She tapped her fingers on the mattress. Sleep. Yes, that's what she needed.

One professional photographer had been allowed in last night. George said Cliff's publicist, that very nice young woman named Tracie, would choose certain photos from inside the party to be released to the major entertainment magazines. Anne hoped she wasn't in any of them. She hated what the camera did to her already large frame.

Stop thinking about it. Sleep!

How many messages would she have on her voice mail at work? After the *Southern Bride* article, she'd changed her home number and kept it unlisted. But not only was her cell phone number on her business cards; she'd bought a display ad in the Yellow Pages this year. She was the only one out of the five planners listed in the category who'd done so. She was also the only one to ever be featured in a regional magazine. Or to have her own office in Town Square, just a few doors down from the store that did the most bridal clothing business in town. How much was this kind of national exposure going to grow her clientele?

She tossed onto her other side. She already had the answer to that in her appointment with Alicia Humphrey in a few hours. The girl was by no means a major star like Cliff, but her fiancé's latest film had won several awards at this year's independent film festivals. Buzz had already started about the possibility of an Academy Award nomination for best director. At least, that's what she'd heard most often last night.

What if Alicia wanted Anne to come out to California to meet with her? She rolled onto her back and stared at her high, white-plaster ceiling. No. Not even for a client could she board a plane. In this day and age, technology should allow her to do whatever necessary from here. Baton Rouge was only a two-hour drive, so that was no problem. But she had to make Alicia understand that Anne Hawthorne would *not* be flying anywhere.

All possibility of falling asleep again gone, Anne pushed up into a sitting posture and reached for the newspaper. The article contained mostly fluff. A truncated guest list. The reporter should have stayed later, as the most interesting names weren't on it. A reference to the Mardi Gras–themed decor with Pamela Grant and the Delacroix Gardens Nursery & Florist both mentioned. Excellent, free publicity for her vendors. When she found her name, she took a deep breath before continuing on.

> *The event was planned and executed by Bonneterre's own Anne Hawthorne, an event planner whose business, Happy Endings, Inc., is well known throughout Louisiana and the Southeast. Hawthorne has planned many high-profile events, such as the mayor's inaugural ball, the annual Bonneterre Debutante Cotillion, and the society wedding of Senator Hawk Kyler's daughter Aiyana Kyler-Warner.*
>
> *"I totally relied on Miss Anne for everything," bride-to-be Landry said. "She talked to me about what I wanted and then did everything just like I imagined. No, even better than I imagined."*
>
> *Hawthorne, a Bonneterre native, first appeared in the pages of the* Reserve *twenty-eight years ago as one of five survivors of a commuter plane crash that took the lives of twelve others, including her parents, world-famous photographers Albert Hawthorne and Lilly Guidry-Hawthorne.*
>
> *According to sources, Hawthorne and Ballantine knew each other as students at Acadiana High School and UL–Bonneterre. Neither Hawthorne nor Ballantine could be reached for comment.*

"Nor am I likely to comment." She tossed the paper aside. At least they hadn't written anything negative about the event or her company. She climbed out of bed and winced as her sore feet hit the hardwood. She hadn't even worn heels last night, and her feet still ached.

Thank goodness she'd set the coffeepot up without changing the timer before climbing into bed in the wee hours. She poured a cup of the chocolate-caramel-pecan-flavored brew, stirred in half-and-half and sugar, and padded across to her giant chair-and-a-half. Cradling the blue ceramic mug in her left hand, she grabbed the

TV remote and clicked the TV on. The screen came to life showing CNN Headline News.

". . .confirmed all the rumors when he announced yesterday he is getting married." The picture cut away from the cutesy reporter to footage of Cliff's press conference. She smiled to see George in his butler-esque stance behind him. If George agreed to go into business with her, he'd never have to debase himself the way she'd seen him do with Cliff several times yesterday.

She clicked up one channel. MSNBC. Same story, same footage. Click. Fox News. Different news story—but then the scroll at the bottom of the screen ran the announcement. Click. Regular CNN. A repeat of *Larry King Live* from earlier in the week—with the announcement of Cliff's engagement in the scroll at the bottom. Click. E! Entertainment Television. The *True Hollywood Story* of Cliff Ballantine. Couldn't be all that "true" since they'd never interviewed her or Aunt Maggie, his employer for four years. Click. The Style Network. The fashion critique of a movie premiere event last night—and chatter between the hosts about the engagement announcement "a few minutes ago." Click. Bravo Network. A repeat of *Inside the Actor's Studio* featuring Cliff.

Okay, maybe she needed to go to a different set of channels. She punched in the number for TBS. They usually ran romantic comedies on Saturday mornings. Commercials. She sipped her coffee. Hopefully something that would put her to sleep. The movie came back on. She squinted to read the caption in the lower right corner. "You're watching *Mountebank*."

She nearly threw the remote at the TV. Cliff's first movie. The one that had made him a star and her a nobody. She jumped out of the chair, crossed to the armoire-style entertainment center, and grabbed the blue box of the extended edition of *Return of the King*. Nothing like the Battle of Pelennor Fields and the destruction of the ring to get her mind off things—

"Anne, it's you!"

She glanced down at the TV. Cliff's face, ten years younger, filled the large screen. She recognized that expression. She'd seen it when he suggested they get married.

"Anne, you're the one I love. You're the one I want to marry—"

She turned the DVD player on, mercifully sending the TV to a blue screen while she inserted the first disc.

No wonder he'd gotten that part. He already had the fake emotions—and the lines he had to say—down pat from practicing on her. She slouched down in the deep cushions of the big chair.

What would his marriage to an overweight, provincial, home-town girl have done for his career ten years ago? He'd spent the past decade creating the image of a happy-go-lucky bachelor, only too happy to have a different starlet on his arm at every red-carpet event he attended. Women turned out in droves to see his action-adventure movies on opening night. Would he have become such a phenomenon with Amazon Anne on his arm at every event?

No. She sighed. Not only would she have hampered his rise to megastardom, she would have hated all the attention; and being honest with herself, the stress of living in the public eye would have driven a wedge between them. She was woman enough to admit they would have been divorced within a few years.

He had an ulterior motive for dating her all those years. Could he be marrying Courtney now to improve his image? He'd gotten lots of press about being a playboy, gracing the cover of several magazines as the Bachelor of the Year multiple years running. Which was fine as long as he made action films. According to several conversations she'd overheard last night, Cliff wanted to be "considered for dramatic roles." He'd never get those roles and garner an Academy Award nomination as long as he lived a life worthy of the cover of the *Enquirer*. And he'd wanted to win that particular award ever since she'd known him. He'd even practiced his acceptance speeches on her. "I'd like to thank the Academy, the wonderful casting agent who had the foresight to choose me for this role, the fabulous screenwriters who wrote this role with me as their model, the director who took my advice on every scene. . . ." She'd laughed then, not truly understanding the size of his ego.

Did Courtney really comprehend what she was getting herself into? Could the poor girl ever hope to compete with Cliff's first love—himself?

The struggle between good and evil on her TV screen no longer interested her, and she turned it off. She needed to have a heart-to-heart with Courtney Landry before things went any further. If the girl got in over her head and ended up brokenhearted when Anne could have done something to head it off. . .

She went into the kitchen and grabbed her cell phone from her purse. She scrolled down to Courtney's name and hit the button to dial.

No answer. Her voice sounded so young in her voice-mail greeting. "Hello, Courtney, it's Anne Hawthorne. I hope you enjoyed yourself last night. You looked beautiful, and everyone in America loves you already. I know—I saw it on all the news channels this morning. Listen, I wanted to schedule a time for the two of us to go to lunch this week. We've never really had a chance to sit down, just the two of us, and chat. We've got some big events coming up that I'd like to get your ideas for. So just give me a call." She left her cell, home, and office numbers and hung up.

Out of curiosity, she called into her voice mail at work.

"Ms. Hawthorne, hi, my name is Alaine Delacroix—you've worked with my family at Delacroix Rentals and Delacroix Nursery many times. I'm the social scene reporter with Channel Six—" Anne skipped forward and listened to the first few seconds of twenty-three more messages—all from reporters wanting exclusives about the wedding. She deleted them with no remorse.

She needed to go to her office and get her planning calendar. She hadn't picked it up yesterday morning as she didn't need it for the engagement party. But for her meeting with Alicia in an hour, she'd need it. So much for a leisurely shower.

She hopped in and out, put a little bit of makeup on so she didn't look like death warmed over, and drove to the office with the convertible top down so her naturally straight hair would be dry enough to pull into a clip at the back of her head.

She deactivated the alarm at the keypad just inside the back door. She didn't bother turning the lights on and passed through the dark hall into the front office, lightened enough to see from the bright sunshine outside. Shadows passed in front of the windows. *Lots of people out shopping today.*

She grabbed the leather planner and glanced out onto the sidewalk. Several people stood outside her storefront. People with huge cameras strung around their necks. Good thing they didn't have the back entrance covered.

She slipped out the back door and speed-dialed George as she drove down the alley.

"Good morning, Anne." His voice had an early morning, gravelly quality that sent shivers down her spine.

"You sound like you just woke up."

"Not exactly. I have to keep regular hours when I'm with Mr. Ballantine. Early morning is the only time I get to myself to read the Bible and spend time in prayer." He yawned and begged her pardon. "Did you get plenty of rest this morning?"

"Not exactly. Jenn, Meredith, and Forbes practically beat down my door at seven forty-five, wanting to make sure I was all right, waving the newspaper under my nose. I couldn't go back to sleep after that."

"You need to get away somewhere they can't find you."

"No kidding. Hey, speaking of not being found—I had to run up to the office to grab something for a meeting, and there were photographers hanging out on my front porch."

"At home?"

"No, at the office. They didn't see me. I went in and out the back. But I think you and I need to sit down with Tracie and come up with a game plan for how I'm supposed to handle the phone calls and paparazzi on my front stoop."

"Yes, we do. They'll lose interest as soon as Cliff leaves for New

York Tuesday. Or if not lose interest, all you'll have to deal with is the phone calls, as the photographers will follow him."

"Pictures of me aren't worth much, I gather."

"Not without either Cliff or Courtney with you. But that's good, yes?"

"Definitely." She turned into the hotel parking lot. "I'm at my appointment, so I'd better go."

"You're working?"

"Remember Alicia Humphrey? She wanted to sit down before she leaves for California this afternoon."

"Oh. Good for you. I'll talk to you later."

He sounded less than enthusiastic, but she didn't have time to ask why.

Toodles? You, too? No, I love you. . . .

She went with "Toodles" as if she were an old school friend. Oh well. She'd known going in that she needed to take this slowly. And, although empirically she'd thought forgiving Cliff would come easily, seeing him last night sent her back to square one without passing Go or collecting two hundred dollars.

An hour later, she dialed George as the elevator doors shut.

"How'd your meeting go?" he asked by way of greeting.

"Why didn't you forewarn me?"

"Didn't want you to think I'm a spoilsport."

"Her third engagement in less than two months? Is she trying to beat out Elizabeth Taylor for a most-broken-relationships award?"

George chuckled. "You never know. He could be 'the one.' You know how it is with those Hollywood types. So quick to move on to greener pastures. . ."

"Is that going to happen to Courtney? Is she 'the one' for Cliff, or is she just 'the one for now'?" She climbed into the car and started for home.

"Do you mean, is he using her to gain something? I'm not certain. If he were just looking for a token wife to, say, give him a more serious image, there are a lot of other women out there he could have chosen. He's opened himself up for some fierce criticism from the public by announcing he's engaged to a woman half his age." He sighed. "You know better than I how people marry for many reasons other than love. I do believe he cares for her. I know she cares for him."

"Will caring be enough, though?"

"Let me pose this: What's more important in a marriage? Being madly in love or having a strong friendship based on mutual respect and admiration?"

Anne had the funny feeling he wasn't talking about Courtney and Cliff anymore. "I'm not married. I can't answer that."

"Oh, you know the answer. You surprise me, Anne. I thought after so many years of working with couples—especially with as much counsel as you provide them—you'd have lost some of your ideals of romanticism."

Her heart thudded in her chest. What did he mean? Could he just be playing devil's advocate, as he did so often? "I think the best marriages are built on love that grows out of that strong friendship and mutual attraction." She'd seen the failure of too many couples' marriages because they'd fallen madly in love but never taken the time to get to really know one another. "But I want to be madly in love with the man I respect and admire when I get married."

His pause grew so long she checked to make sure she hadn't lost the connection.

"Well, how does a romantic dinner at a restaurant overlooking the lake sound as a start?"

CHAPTER 24

*A*nne watched Meredith over the rim of her iced-tea glass as she took a sip. She'd just finished spewing all the shock, anger, hurt, confusion, excitement, and flutterings of the past forty-eight hours. Fortunately, the second-story veranda at the Plantation House restaurant was empty except for the two of them. The sound of the river below and the light breeze rustling the ancient oak trees worked in tandem with Meredith's calm presence to soothe Anne's spirit.

"It sounds like George really is in love with you." Meredith pushed a chunk of tomato to the edge of her salad. "I know he would have told you about Cliff if he could have. I admire him for being a man of his word."

Warmth wrapped around Anne. "I do, too. And there's one other thing. That's one of the reasons why I wanted to have lunch with you before I see him again tonight." She put her glass down. "I've asked George to become my business partner. Now, I know I've always told you that I want you to be my partner—"

Meredith held up her free hand, a smile playing about her lips. "And there was always something in my heart that kept me from saying yes. It's not that I don't trust your ability as a businesswoman. And we've always enjoyed working together. But every time I would get to the point of agreeing, something held me back. Don't you see, Annie? God knew I wasn't the right partner for you."

"I hadn't looked at it that way." She smiled, skin tingling. "It's always so much easier for us to see how God works in others' lives than it is in our own, isn't it?"

Meredith grinned. "You know the family is expecting him to come to lunch tomorrow, right?"

"I'll have to find out his schedule now that his employer"—Anne cleared her throat and winked—"is in town. Who knows what all Cliff will have him doing."

"Speaking of, are you going to try to talk to Cliff about—well, about what happened between the two of you?"

The euphoria from thinking about George vanished. "I know I need to, but every time I think about it, I start feeling sick to my stomach. I don't want to dredge up the past if it's going to make him resent me and possibly fire me as the wedding planner. I can't do that to Courtney."

"Do you think he's told Courtney about y'all's relationship? I mean, really, she was only eight or nine years old when that happened, so it's not like she's a contemporary who would know that the two of you even dated."

"And now that the media knows about their engagement, they're bound to start digging into Cliff's history for dirt about past relationships. All it takes is one or two people outside of our family to mention we dated, and the reporters will be beating down my door wanting all the details. Can't you just see the headlines?" Anne held her hands up as if framing the words on a marquee. " 'Movie star Cliff Ballantine hires ex-fiancée to plan his wedding.' Wouldn't that make great publicity?"

"You can't worry about what some reporters might or might not do. You just have to make sure that your life is straightened out. If you don't talk with him, if you don't forgive him, how will you ever be happy moving forward in a relationship with George? That bitterness you hold inside of you toward Cliff will always be there, keeping you from fully giving your heart to George. Cliff will own you more fully than he did when you went into debt to support him back then."

"I know. I've gone through all of the arguments in my head. I know I have to talk to him."

"Knowing in your head isn't enough." Meredith set down her fork and reached across the table to grasp Anne's hand. "You have to know it in your heart, too. You have to ask God to break through those walls you've built up—whether from the teasing you got in school about being an orphan or losing your parents or finding out Cliff never really wanted to marry you. God can heal your hurts, but He can only do so if you choose to trust Him and forgive."

Tears burned the rims of Anne's eyes. No sermon could have come to a more laser-honed point. All her life, Anne had allowed every hurtful thing that happened to pile up like so much garbage in her soul. Then whenever someone came along and tried to get through to her vulnerabilities, she assumed she would be hurt again and turned away, isolating herself and blaming those who'd hurt her in the past.

"I'm not sure how to start," she whispered.

"You just did." Meredith squeezed her hand. "If you really want my opinion, I think that before you talk to Cliff, you should start with forgiving your parents."

"My parents?" Anne shook her head. "What do they have to do with George and me?"

"Everything if you're going to have a healthy relationship with him. Annie, every time we're with any of our relatives who have kids, I can see the hurt in your eyes. You think you hide it, but I know you better than most."

Not wanting to have an emotional breakdown in the middle of a restaurant, Anne gathered her wits—and defenses—took a deep breath, and dabbed the corners of her eyes with her napkin. "How did you get so smart?"

"Well, I do have a master's degree in art history, even though I don't use it most of the time. That's almost as good as a professional therapist, right?" Meredith grinned and took out some cash and laid it on top of the tray with the check. "I know this is a lot to handle over lunch on a sunny Saturday afternoon. And I didn't mean to push you so hard. But I also don't want to see you lose the best thing that could ever happen to you. So please, if you need help with any of this, come talk to me. You know I'm at your disposal twenty-four-seven."

"I know. Thanks." Anne put her money down, too. She hugged Meredith and kept her arm around her cousin as they left the restaurant.

Half an hour later, alone in her apartment, Anne pulled several storage boxes out of the large hall closet until she found the particular one she sought. Stacking the rest neatly in place, she heaved the large plastic bin into the living room, set it in front of the ottoman, and sat with it between her feet.

She stared at the blue plastic. Could she do this? She hadn't looked in this box since she'd given up hope on Cliff. Steeling herself—and rising to pull a box of tissues closer—she popped the clasps and laid the lid aside.

Like wild creatures released from captivity, memories ravished her as she recognized the items at the top of the container. The notebook she'd put together for the very first wedding she'd ever completely planned—her own. Inside the plastic front cover, a photo of her with Cliff—she smiling and looking like nothing would ever go wrong, and he practicing the smile that would grace the front of every entertainment magazine and supermarket tabloid for the next ten years.

Today wasn't the day to deal with that particular part of her past. She put it aside, along with the album of photos of the two of them during their nearly six-year relationship—well, more pictures of him in his various stage roles through those years than actual shots of them together. The one in the front of the notebook was one of the few when he wasn't hamming it up.

Next, she pulled out the scrapbook Meredith had created for her college graduation. Nostalgia and regret mingled as she set it down on the floor. The high school graduation scrapbook went on top of that.

Now she was getting down to it. She pulled out a red photo album with a brass spiral spine and gingerly lifted the cover. In her bad teenaged penmanship on the title page she read, *Trip to Baton Rouge and State Capitol Building. Anne Elaine Hawthorne, Freshman Civics Class, Acadiana High School.* One of the better memories from her earlier years. She closed it and added it to the stack beside her right foot.

Three more albums joined it until she finally got to what she was looking for. The padded cover had a faux wood-grain finish with a large script *H* engraved in a metal plate shaped like a shield in the middle. Her skin tingled when she opened it to see her mother's handwriting on the first page. *Hawthorne Family Photos. Copyright Lilly Guidry-Hawthorne and Albert Michael Hawthorne. Amateur photos by Anne Elaine Hawthorne.*

Her mother had written the beginning date—Anne's fifth birthday. Anne had written the ending date—the one-year anniversary of the plane crash four years later. Her throat tightened. She hadn't looked at these pictures since then, as her grandmother had become visibly upset every time she caught Anne looking at photographs of her parents the year she'd lived with them. And she hadn't wanted Aunt Maggie and Uncle Errol to think her ungrateful by making herself sad looking at them.

Like an old-fashioned television warming up, Anne's memory slowly faded in as she flipped through the album. She remembered her mother and father with cameras in front of their faces most of the time. Not little ones, but big black monstrous ones that made the most wonderful whirring and clicking noises. Her gaze rested on a photo of her father teaching her all the different parts of the camera. She couldn't have been more than six years old but knew all of the terminology—from f-stop to parallax to field flattener. Her first few attempts at taking pictures with the cameras she could barely lift followed on the next few pages. She'd helped her mother develop them in the converted-garage darkroom. For her birthday that year, she'd received her mother's first camera—a 1958 Kodak Signet 35mm—and twenty rolls of film. Her grandmother had taken a picture of her with her parents at the New Orleans airport before they left for some exotic locale like Bora-Bora, Nepal, or Taureg. Their parting instructions were to use all twenty rolls of film in the four months they'd be gone.

Apparently she hadn't had a precocious talent at it, as the scene when they sat down to critique her work popped into her mind with picture-perfect clarity. Only ten photos—out of the hundreds she'd helped her mom develop—made it into the album. After that session, seeing the disappointment in her mother's beautiful face and her father's bright blue eyes, Anne had carried the camera with her everywhere—until her first grade teacher confiscated it because she wasn't doing her schoolwork. When her grandmother gave it back to her after a week without it, Anne spent all of her free hours trying to practice what they'd taught her about focus, light saturation, contrast, and composition so that when they came back from taking photos sure to win them more national and international recognition, they wouldn't be disappointed again.

Examples of her "much better" work followed—a close-up shot of ladybugs on a leaf. The branch of an old oak tree dipping down into the creek behind Mamere and Papere's farmhouse. Uncle Lawson teaching Forbes to play chess. A wide shot of the entire family—except Lilly and Albert—eating Sunday dinner.

She flipped the next page and something slipped out. She caught it before it hit the floor, and her heart lurched. She unfolded the newsprint. There, on the front page, above the fold. A photo of the skeleton framework of the "tallest building ever to be built in Bonneterre" with which she'd won the newspaper's amateur photography contest. She had to admit, the composition was pretty spectacular, taken from the roof of a nearby office building. *Maybe now my parents will see that they can stay in Bonneterre to take pictures and still have them printed,* she had thought when she had found out about winning the contest.

The adult Anne snorted. At thirty-five, she knew why her parents had to leave to do their work. The child within her still wanted to know why they loved doing it more than being with their daughter.

Of course, they'd been thrilled. Had bought her a new camera. Had taken her out to dinner to celebrate.

Then the Smithsonian called. They wanted to display her parents' photography in a special exhibit in the months leading up to the announcements of the Pulitzer prize, which everyone in the country was sure her parents would win for their photo essay on a flood that ravaged a previously unknown village in the Appalachians. They wanted Lilly and Albert to be there for the opening.

Anne begged to go with them, now that she was an award-winning photographer herself. They laughed at her earnestness, but she got through to them because after a couple of days, they agreed she could go. They'd take a week and make it a family vacation. So many things for Anne to practice her photography skills on in Washington, DC.

Never having left Bonneterre before, Anne had been excited but tried to imitate her parents, to whom the trip was nothing out of the ordinary. She kissed Mamere and Papere good-bye at the gate at the Bonneterre airport—then just a small regional outfit—and followed her parents outside and up the steps into the small plane, lugging her heavy camera bag. The commuter jet had two seats on one side of the aisle and one on the other. She sat beside her daddy, in the window seat, the thrill of finally getting to go with her parents ready to boil over.

Her stomach lurched as she remembered the sensation of the plane picking up speed down the runway. She swallowed hard and closed her eyes. She was holding Daddy's hand, looking out the window at the buildings and trees whipping by. The front of the plane lifted up.

She swallowed again, cold sweat breaking out on her face.

Farther and farther back in her seat the g-force had pressed her as the plane lifted off the tarmac. Daddy pointed out the steeple of Bonneterre Chapel and the tree-shaded campus of the university. There was Town Square and the river.

The plane gave a sudden loud *pop* and jerked drunkenly to the right. Other passengers gasped. Daddy's hand on hers tightened. What was happening? She looked up at Daddy, who wasn't smiling anymore as he looked across the narrow aisle at Mama. The plane jerked again, and Anne could smell smoke. Something was on fire! A woman behind them started praying, calling Jesus' name over and over.

The memories came back so real, so clear; tears streamed down Anne's face, and she wrapped her arms around her churning stomach.

With a sickening screech, flames had erupted outside her mother's window as the engine exploded. Anne remembered screaming. With gathering speed the small plane hurtled toward the woods. Daddy wrapped his arms around her, tucking her head into his chest, whispering, "It's going to be fine, sugarplum. It's going to be okay."

Smoke filled the cabin; flames backlit her mom. *Mama, get away from the fire—you'll get hurt! Mama!*

Anne leapt off the ottoman and dashed to the bathroom just in time as her stomach emptied all its contents. She collapsed on the cool white tile, sobbing, trembling, her heart racing.

She'd woken up in the hospital three days later. Lilly had died instantly. Albert lingered a few hours—his chest impaled with a twisted piece of metal, the same piece of burning metal that seared a scar along the left side of Anne's neck. He'd protected her as best he could during the impact of the crash, shielding her from burning debris, but her injuries had still been extensive: her left foot and ankle crushed by her heavy camera bag, second- and third-degree burns where his hands and arms couldn't cover her, the gash along her neck into the shoulder muscle.

Her father had only been thirty-four years old, her mother

thirty-two. Still so much life ahead of them.

Why, God? She pulled herself off the floor and proceeded to brush her teeth. *Why did Lilly and Albert have to die? Why did I have to be deprived of my parents growing up? You could have saved them, but You didn't. I don't understand.*

She took some Pepto-Bismol to try to calm her stomach.

God was no more to blame than her parents for their death. Yes, He could have worked a miracle and stopped them from dying. But He hadn't. Accidents happened. She wasn't the first child to have lost her parents, and she wouldn't be the last. But she could take comfort in the knowledge that they'd believed in Him, had accepted that their salvation was only to be found in the blood of Jesus. They had been with Him from the very moment their lives here ended.

Leaving Anne to have to go on without them. To have the stigma of being the girl who had to depend on the charity of relatives for a place to live. The girl who was teased when changing clothes for gym class in the locker room because of all the burn scars on her back. No boy would ever want to be with a *monster* like her.

That legacy followed her through junior high into high school, combined with the fact that she had a burning need to please every adult she came into contact with, including all of her teachers. What other students saw as Anne trying to ingratiate herself by volunteering to help or getting the best grades had been no more than her need for approval by anyone in a pseudo-parental role—at least, that's what a friend had written in a psych paper about her in college. The teasing had followed her, too. Especially being nearly six feet tall at thirteen with no athletic ability whatsoever.

She returned to the living room and started replacing items in the box. The trip to Baton Rouge in ninth grade had been great because only the kids with the top grades—other nerds, geeks, and social outcasts like herself—had gone. No one had teased her about her height, her grades, her lack of "real" parents.

She cracked open her high school scrapbook. A photo of her

with her "older brothers" and Forbes slipped out. Maggie and Errol's three older sons, Whit, Andre, and David, along with Forbes had done their best to protect Anne from the worst of the teasing. But they'd had their own lives and couldn't be around all the time.

Tucking the photo back into the book, she continued flipping through. She stopped in the pages representing her junior year. A piece of paper with purple ditto-machine ink glared back at her:

ACADIANA HIGH SCHOOL
NOMINEES FOR JUNIOR PROM COURT

As a joke, someone had nominated her for prom court. She'd tried to make light of it, not to take it seriously. That was hard when Aunt Maggie heard, though. Since Maggie had no daughter of her own, she and Anne had a strong relationship. But Aunt Maggie couldn't understand why Anne wasn't excited about being nominated, until Anne finally confessed that she didn't have a date for the dance and knew no one would ask her to go.

Maggie had suggested Anne ask one of her cousins to go as her date. It was the only major argument she and Aunt Maggie ever got into. Anne won but felt terrible for disappointing her mother's sister, who'd been so kind as to take her into her home to live.

Once the flyers had been passed out among the junior class, the teasing intensified and started getting nasty when the chess team, chemistry club, and honor society started campaigning for her.

She could remember that worst day like yesterday. Three of the cheerleaders had cornered her outside the gym on her way out of PE—one of them was her cousin David's girlfriend. They threatened her with all sorts of retribution stolen straight from the Molly Ringwald movies they'd seen too many times. She was doing her best to get away when a masculine voice rang across the hall.

"Leave her alone!"

The three cheerleaders had squeaked and spun around.

Cliff Ballantine—tall, slender, and well liked, with dark hair and brooding good looks—stood over the three twits like an avenging angel. She'd only seen him in the school plays or across the room at assemblies. The cheerleaders scurried away, and Cliff had escorted her to her next class.

Anne didn't go to junior prom by her own choice. By the end of the school year, Cliff was working for Aunt Maggie part-time, and Anne was helping him with his English homework so he could graduate.

Maggie had taken every opportunity that summer to have the two of them work together. Although with every appearance of being outgoing and happy-go-lucky, Cliff let only a few people, including Anne, see his vulnerable, somewhat introverted side. She was the only girl at school who knew he lived with his mom in a trailer park on the edge of town instead of at his deceased grandparents' address that he used to be in the Acadiana High district—the school with the best drama program in town. He was the only person outside the family she ever told all of the details of the plane crash to. She also recognized that he used his good looks and charm to get people to do what he wanted. She'd confronted him about it the year before he graduated from college, but he just laughed, patted her cheek, and asked her if she could go to the library and find him some books for a sociology research paper he had to write.

She put the scrapbooks, the wedding plan book, and everything else back into the box and snapped the lid on.

If Cliff hadn't really wanted to marry her, why had he asked in the first place? They'd never really been "boyfriend and girlfriend"— he'd gone on dates with other girls in college. But when he moved away to California, he'd seemed to cling to her like a lifeline—and, of course, a constant source of money when he quit whatever part-time job he was willing to take on.

Ask him.

She lugged the box back to the closet and returned to the bathroom to start getting ready for her date. She stared at herself in the mirror as a slow smile spread across her face. After all these years, she'd finally figured out how to talk to Cliff. She'd make an appointment with his personal assistant, George.

Her cell phone buzzed and started playing "That's Amore."

"Hello, George."

He didn't respond immediately, and her smile faltered.

"Anne, I—we—something has come up."

She trudged into the living room and sank into her big chair. "That's okay if you have to cancel tonight."

"Oh no, it's not about tonight—well, it is, but it isn't—" He let out a frustrated breath into the phone. "I'm making a muck of this. Here's the issue. Mr. Ballantine just received word from his agent that he's gotten a call for Mr. Ballantine to star in what's sure to be one of the biggest movies he's ever done. Mr. Ballantine doesn't want to turn it down."

Anne frowned. "Okay."

"The movie starts filming in September in New Zealand for ten weeks."

"Ten—oh. So they want to postpone the wedding?" A tingle started at the base of her skull. Postponing the wedding would mean George would be around that much longer.

"Well, no. They'd like to move the wedding up to the last weekend in August."

Anne's fantasy of George being around for an additional two or three months crashed into a heap of anxiety. "Last weekend in August? With everything we have left to do? Are they still determined to have it the same size?"

"Yes. Everything still the same, just moved up almost two months. Anne, I know this is an imposition on you. But Mr. Ballantine has instructed me to spare no expense in making it happen. Do you—do you think it can be done?"

Her stomach started churning again. Six weeks to do what was going to be difficult in four months. "Of course. But I think instead of going out for dinner tonight, we should have something delivered to my office and work on a new timeline."

The relief in his sigh was palpable through the phone. "I'll meet you at your office at six. I lo. . . . I'll pick up dinner. What do you fancy?"

Anne left the choice of meal up to him—she wouldn't be able to eat anything anyway—and bade him farewell for the time being.

So much for a leisurely, romantic dinner.

CHAPTER 25

*T*he weeks between the engagement party and Courtney's wedding sped by, even though Anne did everything to utilize every minute of every day. After a quick trip to New York to get Cliff settled into his Manhattan condo, George returned to Bonneterre to assist her with anything she needed.

He helped her avoid the media—including Kristin and Greg, the couple who'd pretended to be potential clients to try to pump her for information on the wedding. The looks on their faces when George had walked into the office and recognized them brought a smile to her face every time she thought about it.

She admired and respected him. . .and she was falling madly in love with him. She couldn't start her day until she'd talked to him on the phone, and she couldn't sleep at night until they'd prayed together to close out the day. At least once a week, they went out on what she called "real" dates—just the two of them with none of her family present—where they didn't discuss anything remotely related to their jobs.

He enjoyed spending a lot of time with her family, which was understandable, given his estrangement from his own relatives. She could be happy for him that as adults, he and his youngest brother had reconnected with each other and were now friends, even though Henry lived in Australia. George's pride in his brother's success as a barrister specializing in entertainment industry law shone through whenever he spoke Henry's name. She imagined Henry to be a lot like Forbes, explaining the close friendship between George and her cousin.

As the wedding drew closer, Anne saw more of George but spent less time connecting with him. She was past the point of no return in the relationship, yet had no confirmation George felt the same.

The memory of their conversation about whether a marriage based on friendship could survive continued to haunt her, especially given the fact George didn't exhibit any more romantic interest than he had in the beginning—saying good-bye with a kiss on the cheek, taking her hand only when assisting her in or out of the car or when they prayed over their meals.

Between the doubts over their relationship and the details of the impending wedding, Anne barely slept the week before the event. She needed every minute of each day to make sure everything was ready, every contingency plan in place, every reservation confirmed.

In the early hours of Friday morning, she tossed and turned, going over the schedule for that night's rehearsal and dinner. She'd only seen Cliff a few times since the engagement party. If she was going to resolve her past, she had to do it this weekend. She had to talk to him. No longer did she seethe with anger whenever she saw him. From the way he treated Courtney, she could tell he genuinely loved the girl. But he still had a lot of explaining to do.

Thunder shook the house, and she groaned. She couldn't understand why anyone in Louisiana would want an outdoor wedding. One of two things inevitably happened: unbearable heat or torrential rain. Or both. The weather guy on Channel Six said the rain would move through today and the weekend would be clear. She hoped for once he knew what he was talking about.

She crawled out of bed and stumbled down the hall to her home office. She jiggled the mouse, and the computer screen came alive, showing the rain contingency she'd been working on before trying to go to bed at midnight.

Why couldn't George just come out and say it? *I love you.* Did he? Maybe it was a British thing, this reluctance to be demonstrative or say the words aloud. A cultural difference. Given his loveless childhood, he might even be afraid of saying it. Yes. That was most likely the case. He loved her but was afraid to say so for fear of. . . what? Losing her?

She grimaced in wry understanding. He had as many issues with cultivating a relationship as she did. She just needed to give him time. If he could get his visa status worked out and join her as a partner, they'd have all the time they needed.

She saved the document, shut down the computer, and returned to bed, lulled to sleep by the rhythm of the rain against her bedroom windows.

❦

George rolled out of bed before the alarm sounded. He took his Bible and prayer journal out onto the back porch, along with a large mug of Mama Ketty's strong coffee, and tried to still his thoughts long enough to concentrate on God's Word.

"I know the plans that I have for you," God had said through the prophet Jeremiah. "Plans for welfare and not for calamity to give you a future and a hope."

He clasped his hands, elbows on the edge of the iron scroll table, and leaned his forehead against his thumbs. "O God, the King Eternal. I haven't always tried to follow Your plan for my life. But now I ask You to bless my steps as I walk in what I believe is Your plan in asking Anne to marry me. I love her more dearly than I ever knew possible, and she is my hope for the future. I know it was Your divine plan that brought us together. Thank You for blessing me with her. Please prepare her heart to receive my proposal. . .and to understand the haste with which I will ask her to wed with me so we do not have to part.

"As we go into the whirlwind this weekend, I ask You to strengthen Anne and give her the courage and grace she needs to speak with Cliff and finally, once and for all, forgive him. I pray You'll bless Courtney and Cliff in their new life together. Amen."

He leaned back in the chair and sipped his coffee and watched as the rain fell in sheets across the lush green yard. Even if it stopped in an hour or two, would the ground still be soggy Saturday? It wouldn't do to have the guests' chairs sinking into the newly leveled and sodded yard.

"George, what are we going to do?"

He stood at the sound of Courtney's voice. "Don't fret. It's not supposed to last the day."

In loose-fitting, blue-plaid seersucker pants and a misshapen white T-shirt with no makeup and her dark hair pulled into a ponytail atop her head, Courtney looked more like a thirteen-year-old desperately in need of loving parents than a young woman about to get married in a public spectacle. She sat in the other chair, pulled her knees up, and wrapped her arms around them.

"What are you doing downstairs? I thought we discussed how the ground floor is for employees. It's not appropriate for you to be down here. Mama Ketty or I will bring your breakfast to you upstairs—on the balcony, if you wish."

"It's boring upstairs. George, before I moved here, I was living in a sorority house just off the UCLA campus with two other girls in the same room, and nearly one hundred others in the house. I'm not used to being alone so much." She rested her chin on her knees. "I wish Cliff hadn't gone off to New York right after the party. Or at least that he'd been able to come back for longer than two days at a time. It's so hard to be separated from the one you love."

He tried not to laugh at the philosophical tone of her voice as he regained his seat. "Yes. It's hard."

She leaned her head to the side to look at him. "But you don't have that problem, do you?" She grinned. "You and Miss Anne are hardly ever apart."

His face burned and he scowled, staring out at the rain.

Courtney laughed, leaned over, and wrapped her arms around his, resting her head on his shoulder. "I'm happy for you. I'm just sad, because I have a feeling it means you won't be working for Cliff much longer, which means I won't get to see you anymore, except when we come home for visits."

He rested his right hand atop hers. "Yes. We'll always be here for you, whenever you need to get away from the chaos of life under the examining glass."

"Mama's coming back from the Riviera today. I don't think she's going to be happy with the wedding."

He squeezed her hands and reached for his coffee. "It's not her wedding, so what does it signify?"

"I don't want her making a scene. Miss Anne has worked so hard on everything, and I don't want Mama to say something to offend her."

"I believe Anne has a clear understanding of mothers of the bride. Perhaps, though, your mother's jet lag will keep her from raising too much of a stir."

"George, I can't find—" Mama Ketty stopped and propped her fists on her ample hips. "Young'un, you're supposed to be upstairs for your breakfast, not down here mingling with the hired staff."

Courtney didn't budge from her clinging position. "Oh, Mama Ketty, you and George aren't just hired staff. You're *family*."

Mama Ketty clucked and went back inside, shaking her head.

Contentment nearly burst his heart. Only one person missing and his family would be complete. Soon, though. . . He kissed the top of Courtney's head. "I don't know about you, young miss, but I for one am famished."

Instead of letting go, Courtney hugged his arm tighter. "George. Do you think. . . I mean, would it be inappropriate. . . ?"

He rested his cheek against her hair. "Spit it out, lass."

"Do you think it would be okay for you to walk me down the aisle? Do you think people would think it's weird?"

He swallowed hard. Walk her down the aisle? Take on the duty of the father of the bride? He cleared his throat. "It's your wedding. You can do whatever you wish, weird or not."

"Then I want you to walk me down the aisle. I want you to give me away like my daddy would have if he was still alive. Do you think Anne will think it's okay?"

He squeezed her hands. "We'll talk to her this morning." Despite his best efforts, his voice came out gruff with barely suppressed emotion.

"She's more like the mother of the bride than Mama. I wish. . ." She heaved a sigh. "I wish I didn't have to invite Mama, that I could have just you and Miss Anne there with me. And then when y'all get married, I'll be like your adopted daughter."

"*When* we get married?" He chuckled. "You're assuming quite a lot."

"Oh, y'all will get married. And soon, too, I figure. You may think I'm oblivbious to what goes on around me, but I know you picked up the engagement ring when we went to get my jewelry last week. So when are you going to propose?"

He didn't have to hide his smile at her *oblivious* mispronunciation. "Saturday night, after the wedding."

"At the reception?"

"Most likely. Probably after you've made your exit. She won't be able to slow down a moment before then."

"But I want to see her after you give her the ring."

"All right. I'll find a time to propose that's convenient for you." He kissed the top of her head again. "Come on. Let's go eat before Mama Ketty comes after us again."

❧

Humidity rose in nearly visible waves from the wet ground as the sun started its western descent. Anne slogged barefoot through the soggy yard toward George, holding the end of a measuring tape in one hand, cradling a clipboard in the other.

"There's nothing for it. We're just going to have to figure out some way to make the ground hard by Saturday."

George laughed and wrapped his arms around her waist from

behind. "*There's nothing for it?* Where do you pick up such idiosyncratic phrases?"

"Some strange English guy I know. He says weird things like that all the time."

He squeezed her tight a moment longer, then released her. "Has Courtney talked to you?"

"About what?"

"About me."

Anne's right eyebrow shot up. "About you?"

"Yes. She's gotten it in her mind that she wants me to walk her down the aisle." He took Anne's hand, tucked it under his elbow, and began to practice by walking her back toward the house. She released the end of the tape measure, and it snaked back toward her cousin Jonathan.

"Oh, that's so sweet. I don't have a problem with it if that's what she wants. But what will Cliff think?"

"That's the crux of the matter. I don't think he would appreciate his hired man escorting his bride down the aisle." He smiled in remembrance of Courtney's outburst of emotion this morning. "Even if the bride considers me to be part of her family."

"I guess the question then becomes, whose wishes are more important to us at this point in time? Cliff is footing the bill for this shindig but has taken no interest in the proceedings."

"I'm all in favor of giving Courtney whatever she wants."

She squeezed his arm. "I know you are. And she deserves to have someone in her life who feels that way about her."

"And she does—two of us." He sighed. "Mrs. Landry returned from France a few hours ago. Courtney's afraid she'll make a scene tonight."

"I'll do whatever I can to rein that woman in. I managed to keep her down to a dull roar at Courtney's sisters' weddings. I'll try to find some trivial—but time-consuming—task for her so she feels like she's being helpful but is out of the way. She's really not going to like the idea of you giving her daughter away. She didn't even like it when one of Courtney's sisters asked their brother to be her escort."

"Courtney has a brother?"

"He hasn't had any contact with the family since that fiasco, about three years ago. Courtney was fifteen, so she should remember it pretty clearly."

"I'll talk to her again and make sure it's what she really wants to do."

"I've always thought that if anyone in that family were ever going to stand up to that woman, it would be Courtney. She has an inner strength that most of her sisters could never hope to possess. They all let Mrs. Landry run roughshod over them. I tried to manage her, but they gave in to her demands so easily, I ended up planning the weddings to her liking rather than the brides'."

They ascended the steps to the porch behind the service entrance. Above, Anne's staff hung pink floral swags from the upper balconies that wrapped around the house. They'd be doing it all again on Saturday with fresh garlands of white flowers. Nothing but the best for their girl. Maybe in another twenty or so years, she and George would get to do this for their own child.

He stopped and pulled Anne into his arms and kissed the side of her neck.

Her hands rested on his shoulders, one hand toying with the hair at the back of his neck, a bemused expression in her eyes. "What was that for?"

He winked and took her by the hand to lead her into the house. "Just because."

At six, Cliff's limousine arrived from the airport. George instructed the butler's assistant to meet the car at the service entrance and carry the luggage up back stairs. He'd had difficulty training the Americans on the staff the proprieties that the British butler he'd hired took as a matter of course, but his efforts were proving rewarding. In the last few days with the full staff on the job every morning by seven o'clock, the house ran with English precision. Even Mama Ketty had been impressed.

Electronic planner in hand, George met Cliff in the front foyer. "Good evening, sir. Welcome home. How was your trip?"

"Long and tiresome." Cliff started up the stairs. "Have someone bring me a Mountain Dew and a fried bologna sandwich."

George nodded at the butler, who left his post at the door to relay the message to Mama Ketty. "Would you like to go over your schedule?"

His employer stopped in the middle of the wide staircase. "Yeah. I guess we have to. Come on up."

At George's request, the valet he'd hired for Cliff for the weekend had laid out several outfits across the bed. The young man followed the assistant butler into the bedroom-sized dressing closet and proceeded to unpack for their employer. George nodded his dismissal at the assistant butler and took out his stylus.

The schedule Anne had e-mailed him for the evening made up the majority of today's agenda. George read through the line items as Cliff went about the suite from bathroom to closet.

"What am I wearing tonight?" Cliff interrupted.

"Your valet has laid out some clothing here on the bed, sir." George returned to reading the agenda.

Cliff exited the closet and examined the outfits. He pointed at one and motioned for the valet to assist him in changing.

"If that's all, sir, I would like to check on Miss Courtney."

Cliff dismissed him with a wave of his hand. "Yeah. Go. Hey, boy—what's your name?"

George left him to get acquainted with his valet and went down the long hall to the bedroom suite on the opposite end. The door stood open. Courtney sat on the window seat reading, Anne in a cushioned armchair with her back to the door.

Courtney looked up and held one finger to her lips, then pointed at Anne. He walked around until he faced the chair, and smiled.

"She came in to go over the schedule with me," Courtney

whispered, "and the next thing I know, she's asleep. I don't think she's been sleeping well at night, worrying about my wedding. It was too much for her to take on by herself. She really needs an assistant."

"Yes, she does." George sank onto the window seat.

"Did I hear Cliff come in?" Courtney tried to sound disinterested, but the hurt still came through her small voice.

"He's changing." After four weeks apart, the least he could have done was greet his fiancée upon arrival. "I'm certain he'll be along directly."

"Then you probably ought to wake up Anne so he doesn't see her right off. I know he's not happy I hired her." She reached over and patted his arm. "Don't look so uncomfortable, George. Anne told me everything after the engagement party. She even offered to resign and help me find another planner. But I wouldn't let her."

He crossed to Anne and gently shook her shoulder.

Her eyes popped open. "George?"

"You have a wedding rehearsal to oversee, madam. I suggest you quit dillydallying and get to it." He kissed the tip of her nose and offered his hand.

"How long. . . ?" She looked at Courtney, her cheeks bright red.

"Just a few minutes. I didn't wake you because I knew you needed the rest."

"I'm so sorry. I'm so unprofessional." She gathered up her planner and paperwork from the small coffee table.

"No, just overworked." Courtney came over and hugged Anne. "Just in case I don't get a chance to say it again this weekend, thank you for everything. You've made every dream come true."

He heard a door down the hall and held his hand out toward Anne. "We should go."

She nodded, kissed Courtney's forehead, and followed him out of the room. Cliff's new valet caught up with them at the door to the service stairs.

"He sent me away when his food arrived. Should I just wait

271

outside the door? He's not changed clothes yet."

"Yes. Wait outside the door. Did you finish unpacking the suitcases?"

The young man nodded. "Most of it needed to go to the laundry," he said. "So I put it in the orange bags like you showed me. In England, are there really people who do this for a living? Like, all the time for one person?"

"Yes. That was one of my first positions as an adult." He squeezed the college student's shoulder. "But not a career path I'd recommend for most."

"Thanks."

George followed Anne down the two flights of dark, narrow stairs to the kitchen. The serenity above the stairs belied the pandemonium below. He and Anne had to give way on the landing between the main floor and the lower level to several young women running up with table linens and silverware. In the kitchen, Major O'Hara commanded his staff like a general while Mama Ketty directed the young men loading the china into the dumbwaiter.

They got separated by different people needing their help. He winked at Anne as she went outside to approve the setup at the gazebo.

After a few minutes, he disengaged himself from Mama Ketty's string of complaints about the hired-on linens and went to see if he could help Anne with anything in the last few moments before the bridal party started to arrive.

At the gazebo, her young cousins Jonathan and Bryan checked the sound system. George stood at the rear of the area staked off for guest seating and gave them a thumbs-up on the volume before approaching.

"Where's Anne?"

Her cousins exchanged a look. "He came and got her. Mr. Ballantine, I mean," Jonathan said. "Said he needed to talk to her."

George's heart jumped into his throat. *Lord, let her say what needs to be said. Let her forgive him, but don't let him hurt her.*

CHAPTER 26

*W*hen Cliff's hand closed around her elbow, Anne's skin burned as surely as it had from the debris from the plane crash. He led her back into the house and to the office on the main floor where she and George had spent many happy hours working side by side on the wedding. She stopped behind a tall wing chair; Cliff crossed to look out one of the two tall windows.

"Do you remember the time I invited you to go on that weekend ski trip with a bunch of my friends from the fraternity?" Cliff asked, his back to her.

She smiled in spite of her anxiety over this tête-à-tête. "I said I couldn't go because it involved flying."

"I thought it was just an excuse to get out of spending time with my frat brothers. I knew you didn't like them much. I knew you didn't like the person I became when I was around them." He turned to face her, arms crossed. "Did I ever tell you how horrible that weekend was?"

She shook her head. "Aside from breaking your arm? I had a feeling other stuff happened from the fact that you didn't really talk about it after you got back."

"All they did was drink and try to get the girls who did go into bed with them. And a lot of the girls gave in. I was so glad you weren't there to witness it all. I knew you'd be disappointed."

Anne moved around to sit in the chair. This was going to take

KAYE DACUS

awhile. "You really worried about that?"

Nodding, he clasped his hands behind his back and ambled around the room, pausing to look at objects on shelves, books, the large painting hanging behind the desk.

"Cliff, I—" Now alone with him, Anne didn't know how to start. "I'm happy for you and Courtney."

He turned to face her, surprise in his expression. "When I found out Courtney had hired you, I wondered if God was punishing me for what I did so many years ago."

Laughter bubbled up in Anne's throat. "When I found out it was your wedding, I wondered nearly the same thing."

He crossed the room and sat in the adjacent chair. "Anne, you have to understand. You were one of the few true friends I ever had. I never felt as close to anyone as I did to you. You understood me. You knew what it was like to feel alone in a room full of people. You didn't have any expectations of me." He hung his head. "And I took advantage of that friendship. I let you give and give and give—your time, your money, your friendship—without giving you anything in return. I wouldn't have made it out of school if it hadn't been for you. I wouldn't have gotten where I am today if it hadn't been for you."

Anne studied her recently manicured nails, the remaining bitterness and accusations she'd harbored for the past decade replacing her amusement of moments before.

"I wanted to marry you, Anne. Really, I did. I wanted us to get married just like you'd planned and then bring you out to California to be with me. God knows I needed you those first few years after—" He jumped up and started pacing again.

"Then why?" She gripped her hands to keep them from shaking.

He tossed his hands in the air. "It sounds so stupid now, really. When I signed the contract to make *Mountebank*, the studio hired a publicist for me. They wanted to make me into a star. When I told them I was supposed to be getting married, they went ballistic. Told me it would have to be postponed. Made me call you to tell you

274

that. I didn't want to disappoint you, Anne. And I never wanted to hurt you."

Tears burned her eyes. It hadn't been his idea to call off the wedding.

He spun and came to kneel in front of her. "They wouldn't let me call, but I could at least have the studio secretary mail letters for me."

Anne shook her head. "I never got any letters. I thought once you got your big break, you had everything you wanted and didn't need me anymore."

"I needed you, Anne." He clasped her hands in his. "I needed you more than anything. I was miserable making that movie—especially since my character fell in love with a character named Anne. I poured my heart into those scenes, the dialogue between us, because I hoped if you ever saw it, you'd know I was talking to you."

She stared at the ceiling, blinking to keep the tears from spilling out.

"When I never heard back from you, I got mad because I thought you didn't want to talk to me because I'd postponed the wedding. I hadn't wanted to think you were that shallow, but then when I got your letter. . ." Cliff shrugged his broad shoulders.

Her gaze snapped back to his. "*My* letter? Cliff, I never sent you a letter. I thought you never wanted to hear from me again."

A frown furrowed the area between his well-groomed brows. He let go of her hands and reached into his jeans pocket. "This letter."

She took the yellowed piece of paper from him. The folds were fragile, the edges darkened from years of handling. In old dot-matrix print was a brief note with what looked like her signature under it. It was dated nearly six months after he called off the wedding:

Dear Cliff,
   Congratulations on your new career as an actor. I wish you all the best as you follow your dream. I don't want to hold you back, and I feel that if we marry, that's what I'll be doing.

Please know that I will always support you from afar. Please do not try to contact me again. This is for the best.

Anne

"I didn't write this, Cliff. That's not my signature. It's a good forgery, but it's not mine." She handed the page back to him.

He folded it and put it in his pocket. "I always suspected. It didn't sound like you. You'd only typed one letter to me before that—you'd handwritten the rest of them. But I just wasn't sure."

"Why didn't you call? Or come see me whenever you came back to town?"

He stood and ran his fingers through his stylishly tousled hair. "I was going to. The first time I came back after the movie came out, I went by Aunt Maggie's house, but they didn't live there anymore. The people who did live there didn't know where y'all had moved to. I finally tracked down Forbes's phone number. I went to his office to meet with him. He told me how hurt you'd been, how you'd dropped out of graduate school just to be able to send me money."

Forbes. Anger started to rise. How dare he try to manipulate her life!

"Before you get mad at Forbes, let me explain what I told him. I told him that I wanted to see you, to apologize. He asked me if I still intended to marry you. I had to be honest with him, Annie. I'd just started dating someone else. I thought I was falling in love with her. He thought it best that we didn't see each other again. You had been my best friend. But—" He pressed his lips together as if unwilling to continue.

"But you were never really in love with me." Anne pressed her hands together and rested her forefingers against her lips.

"He thought it would hurt you more to see me on those terms than to never see me again. I'm so sorry."

Closing her eyes, she sat in silence for a long time, trying to remember when she'd stopped loving him. She'd loved the idea of being married to a handsome, talented, interesting man—the only one who'd ever shown any interest in her. But in all honesty, he hadn't broken her heart. He'd broken her trust—an emotion stronger than love.

"I forgive you, Cliff." The words, softly spoken, came from a place in her heart she hadn't felt in a very long time. "I was angry at you for so many years—especially while I was still trying to pay off all that debt, knowing how rich you were getting."

"Wait a minute! I asked my manager to have a check cut for you—I had kept a running tally of everything I owed you. The least I could do was pay you back with interest."

Anne shook her head. "Didn't get the letters, didn't get the check, either. I hope whoever that manager was doesn't work for you anymore."

Cliff started to puff up the way she remembered when he was angry. She bit her bottom lip as a smile threatened. Nice to know some things didn't change.

She stood and rested her hand on his arm. "Never mind about that. God knew what He wanted from both of our lives and that we were better off not together. And now look." She waved her hand toward the window overlooking the lawn where members of the wedding party were starting to congregate. "You do get to pay me back—with interest. You know, I never would have gotten into this business if it hadn't been for you borrowing that money and my dropping out of graduate school. Thank you."

He opened his mouth, but no words came out.

She laughed—a feeling of freedom overwhelming her. "Come on. Let's go practice getting you married."

"How did it go?" George asked when she joined him in the kitchen moments later.

She smiled and slipped her arms around his waist. "Better than I expected. I'll tell you about it later. Right now, I need to get to work."

He kissed her cheek. "Righto." He released her and pressed the button on the battery pack clipped to his belt. "Places, everyone."

Anne took the headset he offered and got wired up to be able to direct the proceedings.

Courtney's ten bridesmaids kept her busy for nearly half an hour, trying to get them in some semblance of order, while George tried to do the same with the groomsmen down at the gazebo. Once aligned, Anne clicked her headset microphone on. "George Laurence, I need to see you, please."

He appeared at her side a few seconds later. "Yes, ma'am?"

She nodded at Courtney, standing at the back of the long line of giggling girls on the back veranda. "You have a duty to perform, sir."

If Cliff was surprised to see George escorting Courtney down the aisle, he didn't let on. George returned to stand beside Anne, his hands clasped behind his back, very much the same as the position he'd maintained during Cliff's press conference. The man certainly didn't believe in public displays of affection. She wouldn't have minded if he'd put his arm around her or taken her hand. But, she sighed, they were working, and how professional would that look?

Before the rehearsal ended, George vanished to oversee the setup for dinner up on the wide front porch. Anne wrapped up a few minutes later and sent everyone in that direction.

She was stopped from following them by a bone-jarring hug from Courtney. "Thank you for everything, Miss Anne. I know this is going to be the most beautiful wedding ever, and it's all because of you."

Cliff grinned at Anne over his fiancée's head.

She smiled back at him. "It'll be the most beautiful wedding, Courtney, because you're going to be the most beautiful bride ever."

Courtney stepped back to be engulfed by Cliff's huge arm. "I hope you have lots of business cards with you tonight, Anne. Lots of the girls were asking me about you."

Anne shooed them toward the house. She set the crew George had hired to breaking down everything and followed them.

Throughout the evening, she tried to find a few minutes alone with George but couldn't seem to find him when he wasn't surrounded by people or on his way to run an errand for Cliff. She was a bit disconcerted by his inattention but reminded herself he had a job in addition to helping her, and if she knew Cliff, he kept George running at all times.

But tomorrow night. . . She sighed. Tomorrow night, it would all be over. Cliff and Courtney would be gone on their honeymoon. And she and George. . .

She couldn't wait to see what happened then.

CHAPTER 27

*A*nne watched from a distance as Cliff and Courtney fed each other a piece of the enormous cake Aunt Maggie had labored over for weeks. Cliff had insisted on being at Vue de Ciel when the cake was scheduled to be delivered just so he could see Aunt Maggie. Anne shook her head. She never thought she'd see the day when she'd be happy to witness Cliff Ballantine getting married.

Where was George? She'd only had glimpses of him throughout the evening, and he'd slipped away while Anne arranged the cake-cutting. A casual perusal of the warehouse-sized Vue de Ciel ballroom didn't reveal him.

She'd hoped they'd find a few minutes alone tonight. They needed to discuss the partnership. She wanted a yes or no answer out of him before the end of the night. Every time she'd broached the topic in the last few weeks, he'd come out with one excuse or another about his work visa. She was beginning to feel like he'd decided against it but just couldn't bring himself to tell her.

Something about the distance that still remained between them kept her from fully trusting him, held her back, made her want to retreat behind her old emotional walls and protect herself. Even talking at length with Meredith about her parents' death and the expectation she carried with her since then—that everyone who professed to love her would eventually leave or disappoint her—hadn't helped her put her fear aside.

Working her way around the perimeter of the room, she spoke to guests as she was spoken to, nodding at the service staff who caught her gaze.

As she neared the corridor that led to the kitchen, Major intercepted her.

"We're running low on caviar," he divulged in a hushed whisper. "Only half of what we ordered came in, and there is no more to be had in town anywhere—I know because I've called every grocer in a hundred-mile radius."

Anne looked over her shoulder at Cliff and Courtney. Neither of them liked caviar. They'd only put it on the menu because it was expensive and would impress people. "Don't worry about it. If it's gone, it's gone." She looked down the hall toward the kitchen.

"What are you looking for?" Major looked over his shoulder in the same direction.

"You haven't seen George in the last few minutes, have you?"

A smile spread across her friend's face. "I think I saw him headed out onto the observation deck a few minutes ago." He caught her arm as she turned to go. "Am I going to have to compete with your aunt for the privilege of catering your reception?"

Anne forced a smile. With the way things stood between them now, would there ever be a Hawthorne-Laurence wedding? "I think I can probably put both you and Aunt Maggie to work." She spun around with a wave and headed for the opposite side of the top floor of Boudreaux Tower. Although the room, with its glass walls and roof, gave a spectacular view of downtown Bonneterre, the observation deck allowed visitors to experience the view unobstructed.

George Laurence wouldn't leave tonight without discussing their future partnership—whether business or personal.

❧

"I've got to wait until the time's right. If I do this wrong, she's likely to bolt." George paced the width of the deck overlooking the twinkling lights of the sleeping city. While he stood at the top of the tallest building in Bonneterre, Louisiana, in the middle of the night, his brother Henry sat in evening rush hour traffic in Sydney, Australia.

"Look, mate. You've been in love with this woman since the first time you clapped eyes on her. You've spoken of little else since you met her." Henry paused to yell a few colorful phrases at another driver. He had adapted to his new environs quickly.

"It took me awhile, but I know Anne is the woman God created especially for me." George sighed and leaned against the waist-high safety wall. "But if I resign my post, I'll have to return to England for six months and apply for a new visa—I'll lose my years of residency toward becoming a citizen."

"So what's to keep you from just courting her until she's ready to marry you?" Henry asked.

"Because in two weeks when Mr. and Mrs. Ballantine return from their honeymoon, I'll be going to New Zealand with him for nearly three months. After that, it's off to who knows where. I'm afraid she'll give up on me. I can't lose her."

"Listen, Brother, I'm almost to the harbor bridge, and traffic is bad so I need to go. There is one idea that I don't know if you've thought of. You could always marry an American and stay in the country that way. You already have the ring for your Miss Hawthorne, do you not?"

George reached up and felt the slight bulge in the inside pocket of his tuxedo jacket. "I do."

"Well. . . ?" Henry prompted.

"What you're saying is that I should propose to Anne tonight and convince her to marry me in two weeks so that I can stay in the country?" He had a feeling Anne would say yes to his proposal, but would she want to get married that quickly?

"I don't think you'd have to get married in two weeks. I think if you got engaged and could prove it to the immigration services office, they would probably give you an extension until you do get married. That way, you can resign your post and stay there with her. At the worst, you'd have to go back to England for a few weeks until you're issued a temporary green card."

"Marriage to Anne would be the perfect solution." George paced as he ruminated on the idea. "She'll have the business partner she longs for, and I'll get to stay in the country."

"Oh, and spending the rest of your life with the woman you're madly in love with doesn't factor into the equation?"

"Well, there's that as well." Anxiety tingled through him. Would she say yes? He took a few moments after the phone call to compose himself, then returned to the ballroom in search of Anne. He had to propose before Courtney left, or the girl would never forgive him.

He didn't immediately spot Anne in the room, no surprise among seven hundred guests. He stopped a few servers, who said they'd seen her come through recently but weren't sure in which direction she'd gone.

Courtney gazed adoringly into Cliff's eyes as they glided about the dance floor. The one area where she'd disagreed with Anne had been music. Anne just couldn't convince her to have a swing band instead of one that would cover the current hit songs. When he and Anne married, he'd suggest "That's Amore" or perhaps a more traditional "Someone to Watch over Me" as their first dance. He slipped into the crowd to avoid Cliff's seeing him.

Anne didn't seem to be anywhere in the ballroom, so he went down the hall to the massive kitchen.

Major O'Hara greeted him with a wink and a smile. "Anne was just in here looking for you. I sent her out toward the observation deck a few minutes ago."

"Cheers!" George spun and headed back in the direction he'd come. She'd probably gone out the door on this side of the building. He slipped through the door and looked for the woman who stood head and shoulders above the rest. . .almost literally. He'd never imagined falling in love with a woman who, when she wore heels, stood the same height as he. Just one of her many beauties.

Finally, he found her on the observation terrace in the far corner near the emergency exit. Perfect. Hidden from the view of those inside, and far from the best views of downtown.

"Anne?"

She didn't turn.

He stopped beside her, his shoulder touching hers. "I hoped I would find you out here."

Strange distance filled her gaze when she finally looked at him. She must be exhausted. She hadn't been sleeping at all.

"I know you'll be glad when this is all over."

She shook her head. "You have no idea."

He leaned against the safety wall, facing her. "You need a long holiday."

"I can't. I have a business to run and lots of events already booked."

She wasn't making this easy. *Just do it. She's tired.* "Anne, I know we haven't been acquainted long. But I've always believed in quality over quantity. I also remember our conversation about marriage and how we both believe that it should be based on mutual respect and admiration."

Tears filled her eyes.

He smiled and reached for the ring box. Clasping her hand, he dropped to one knee with a flourish, holding the ring box toward her. "Anne Hawthorne, will you marry this man who not only admires and respects you but is madly in love with you?"

The darkness made her expression hard to read. She pulled her hand away and took the ring box. She studied the jewel for a moment, then closed the box and handed it back to him. "No."

He rose. "No?"

She gestured for him to take the box. When he didn't reach for it, she grabbed his hand and pressed it into his palm. "No."

He blocked her retreat, heated embarrassment replacing his earlier thrill. "May I have the honor of an explanation?"

She crossed her arms. Tears glittered in twin trails down her cheeks. "I was a fool to believe. . .to believe you would ever be honest with me."

"To what are you referring, madam? Please make sense!" What had changed from their stolen kiss after the wedding ceremony to now?

She pointed to the ring box. "Proposing as if you meant it. Saying you're madly in love with me to manipulate me into marrying you."

Cold anger flooded him. "Manipulate. . . ? Anne, when have I ever tried to manipulate you? I've done everything I can to prove my love to you."

She swiped at the moisture on her face. "I have to be the biggest idiot in the world. At least Cliff's actions I can blame on immaturity and bad counsel. But you? All this time you talked about honesty, about how important it is to found a relationship on trust. And all along, you were just reeling me in like the catch of the day."

"I have no idea to what you are referring." Instinctively, he handed Anne his handkerchief.

She pushed it away. "No? Let me refresh your memory. You propose, and we both get what we want: I get a business partner, and you get to stay in the country."

His heart sank. His phone call with Henry. She'd only heard one side. But she should have trusted him rather than jumping to erroneous conclusions. "Anne, you didn't hear the whole conversation."

"No. But I heard enough. This is why you've been avoiding answering me about the partnership—why you've kept me at arm's length." Her voice caught, and her face contorted as she tried to control her emotions. She shoved past him but stopped after a few feet. "I thought you really loved me. I guess you're as good of an actor as your employer. I would have been better off if you had stayed the groom!" She composed herself as she turned to reenter the ballroom.

He should go after her. Explain. Make her understand.

But how could she accuse him of trying to manipulate her? He genuinely loved her. He would never intentionally hurt her.

She was too angry right now to listen to reason. . .and he was too hurt and angry to try to reason with her. He just needed to give her a couple of days to cool off.

❧

Monday morning, George stopped in front of Anne's office, surprised to see the CLOSED sign hanging in the window. Finally, she'd decided to take a day off.

He dialed her cell phone number as he walked back toward his car. No answer. Her cheerful answering machine greeting brought him the first smile in days. "Hello, Anne. I know you may still be angry, but I would like a chance to explain. Remember what you said about misunderstandings and communication issues. That's all this is. Please call me so we can talk. I love you."

When he hadn't heard from her—or anyone else in her family—by Thursday, he decided to take matters under his own control again. Forbes's secretary ushered him into the large office.

The dark look on the lawyer's face told George everything he needed to know. "She told you her side of the story?"

"Her side? She told me what happened, yes. And to think I trusted you not to hurt her."

"It's all a horrible misunderstanding." George paced the width of the room. "She overheard a conversation I had with my brother. He and I were joking around. I would never consider marrying Anne for a business partnership or a green card."

Forbes nodded, his blue-gray eyes piercing. "Really?"

"Really!" He threw his hands up. "What do I have to do to convince you people?"

"Go home." The words were growled more than said.

"I beg your pardon?"

"You want to prove to Anne you don't want to marry her just for a green card? Go back to England. Prove you love her and not just the idea of staying in the States."

He sank into a chair and dropped his head into his hands. "Go home? I don't have a home to go to." If Henry's apartment hadn't sublet yet. . .

Forbes was right. He had to regroup, show Anne it was her, not this place, not her business, that he loved. "All right. I'll go back to England."

Forbes's expression neutralized. "I'll help you take care of things on this end—liquidating your assets, transferring accounts."

"Thanks." George stood and offered his hand. "Thanks for everything. Tell Anne. . ."

Forbes nodded. "I'll tell her."

On his way out, his phone beeped. "George Laurence here."

"Hi, George," Courtney's voice chimed through the line.

"Hello, Miss—Mrs. Ballantine. How may I be of assistance?"

"George, Cliff is going to have to cut his trip short. They need him on the movie set earlier than they thought. He wants you to meet me in Paris this weekend. *We're going to buy a villa!*"

He needed something to pay the bills while he tried to convince Anne. While this wouldn't be as grand a gesture as resigning and returning to England to live in squalor while waiting, it would serve his purpose.

"Very good, ma'am. I'll make flight arrangements this afternoon."

CHAPTER 28

$\mathcal{T}$he light clink of silver against china and the din of hushed voices reminded George of his very first meeting with Forbes. As a farewell, his friend had suggested dinner at Palermo's, bringing everything full circle.

"I've closed up the house. Mama Ketty will check in every few weeks." Emotion threatened to close George's throat.

"I'll take care of adjusting her contract. When does your flight leave?"

"Sunday afternoon at three, with layovers in Memphis and Atlanta." He pulled a copy of the itinerary out of his attaché. "Here's the schedule. I've given Henry your number in the event of an emergency."

Forbes gave the schedule only a cursory glance before folding it and sticking it in his suit-coat pocket. "Six months is a long time. When I said to take time to prove your love for her, I didn't mean *that* long."

"I know. But maybe the distance will be good for us." He grinned wryly. "And I do have all that vacation time I never take. I can be back in a trice if she decides she's ready."

Forbes chuckled. "She'll miss you, George. She probably does already."

"I hope so." He handed his friend an envelope. "Can you give her this for me? I had to at least try to explain before I left."

"She'll come around. We'll make sure of it."

"You're not going to interfere, are you?"

"*Interfere* is such a negative word, my friend. Think of it as encouraging her to reconsider her hasty and emotionally motivated actions."

Somehow, that didn't make George feel better. "Thanks."

"No problem. You realize I'm just doing this because Meredith and Jennifer have already planned your wedding, and I hate to disappoint my sisters, right?"

"Right. Tell them thanks for me."

"Will do."

For the first time in his life, George didn't want to leave a place. He had friends—no, family—who loved him. He'd made a life here in a few short months. He'd started to dream of building his future here. His happiness resided in Bonneterre, Louisiana. . . because Anne would never get on an airplane to go anywhere else. "Tell Maggie and Errol. . ." He shrugged, unable to continue. They'd welcomed him into their home and treated him like a son.

"I will."

When they parted, George barely managed to hold his emotions in check. Forbes dropped him off at the hotel where he'd stay until he took the shuttle to the airport in two days. As soon as he entered the room, he hit his knees, begging God to change her mind.

⁂

"Miss Anne, are you okay?" The bride turned, her wedding gown swishing with the hidden whisper of the multiple petticoats holding out the bell skirt.

Anne dabbed the corners of her eyes with a tissue. "I'm okay. You look so beautiful."

The young woman rested her hand on Anne's shoulder. "Thank you for everything. I know it has to be hard with your breakup and all. . . ." She bit her bottom lip.

Anne swallowed back new tears. "You're welcome, honey. Now

there's a wonderful young man waiting in that sanctuary for you. Let's get you married."

As she had every night for the past week, Anne cried herself to sleep Saturday night. Sunday, she woke up with a migraine, gave in to her self-pity, and stayed in bed. Why had she been so stupid and let George walk away? She hadn't heard the entire conversation. What if he had just been joking around with his brother? After all, George's dry sense of humor was one of the things she loved most about him. The least she could have done was let him explain.

Her anger that night had quickly melted into embarrassment, embarrassment into shame that kept her hiding out, avoiding everyone, including Forbes, Meredith, and Jenn. Tomorrow she'd work up the courage to call George to beg his forgiveness. But she needed one more day to prepare herself.

Shortly after noon, a familiar pounding started on her door.

"Go away!"

The unmistakable rasp of a key in the dead bolt followed. "Annie?"

She pulled her pillow over her head. The bed bounced and gave beside her. "Go away," she moaned.

"No. Enough of this already." Meredith pulled the pillow off her head. "We're tired of you moping around just because you're stupid enough to let the best thing that ever happened to you walk out the door."

Jenn pulled down the covers. "You're going to get up, get dressed, and go with us down to Riverwalk for an ice cream cone."

"I know I was stupid." Anne pushed their hands away. "He deserves better than me. He deserves someone who'll trust him."

Jenn grabbed one arm, Meredith the other.

"Anne." Meredith's tone stilled her. "George Laurence loves you. We saw it the first time we met him. You love him, too. But you've treated him unfairly, and you should be begging his forgiveness."

Anne closed her eyes and pressed her lips together. She knew they were right—she had no one to blame but herself if George didn't forgive her, if he didn't want to marry her now.

Regret tightened her throat. Married to George. It was all she'd dreamed of the last two months. Marrying George, working with him, restoring this house together. . .

Elizabeth d'Arcement's wedding yesterday hadn't given her the same sense of completeness she'd felt at every other wedding. A part of herself had been missing. George.

"Anne, this is ridiculous." Forbes's deep voice sounded from the doorway. "You've been avoiding me for a week, but time has run out."

Jenn and Meredith retreated, and Forbes came around to take Meredith's place on the side of the bed.

"When I agreed with Cliff that George should stand in for him, that George should keep his own identity secret, I did it never having met George before, not knowing that he's the man God created specifically for you, Annie." Forbes took hold of Anne's hand. "Once I realized that you and George had feelings for each other, the scheme was already in motion. George and I did the best we could under the circumstances. I can understand why you might still be mad at me, but if you don't stop wallowing in self-pity, you are going to lose George. And if that happens, I'm not sure I want to be around you—because you'll be miserable for the rest of your life."

Anne couldn't look at him. To her surprise, rather than try to convince her she needed to go to George on bended knee and beg forgiveness, Forbes pressed a cream envelope into her hand, kissed her forehead, and departed, taking his sisters with him.

Anne nearly wept when she saw her name in George's compact script on the envelope. Oh, she missed him. The feel of his arms around her when she was tired, his reassuring talks, the strength of his hand around hers. . .

Why, God? Why does this keep happening to me?

"I know the plans that I have for you," declares the Lord, "plans for welfare and not for calamity to give you a future and a hope."

"I love him. But I'm afraid of being hurt again."

"*For God has not given us a spirit of fearfulness, but of power and love and discipline.*"

"Fill me with that power and love and discipline," she cried out to God. "Show me how to love and be loved without fear."

She opened the letter:

My dearest Anne,

I do not know how to begin to apologize to you for any hurt I've brought you. You are the most wonderful blessing God has ever brought into my life. I was an idiot to joke with Henry about my feelings for you. You are so deep in my heart that when you're not near I feel like I can't breathe properly.

I leave Sunday for France. Forbes has information on how to contact me. As soon as I arrive, I will contact him. . .and write you.

I love you so much, I ache when we're apart. Somehow, I will manage to survive the coming separation with only the hope you will be waiting for me when I return.

Please forgive me for hurting you.

I love you, and I miss you already.

With all my heart,
George

Sunday. Today. He was leaving today. She could still stop him. He couldn't go. She loved him. She had to tell him. She wanted to marry him and spend the rest of her life with him.

Forbes. He knew where George was going. Why had she avoided Forbes all week? If she hadn't given in to embarrassment and shame, she and George could already be back together.

Jumping out of bed, she grabbed the first pair of jeans and T-shirt she could find and combed her hair back into a ponytail as she stepped into an old pair of canvas sneakers.

She ran upstairs and pounded on Jenn's door. No answer. Down two flights and pounded on Meredith's door. Same result.

She ran back to her apartment and grabbed her purse, keys, and phone, dialing Forbes's number as she flew down the stairs.

"Anne?"

"Where is he?"

"Who?"

"What do you mean *who*? George! Where is he? He said you know where he's going. I have to find him. I have to tell him not to go."

She skidded to a stop on the back porch.

Forbes climbed out of his black Jaguar and snapped his phone closed.

She jumped down the steps and grabbed his arms. "Where is he?"

Jenn stuck her head out the back window. "He's at the airport, Anne."

Forbes shook his head. "His flight for Memphis left fifteen minutes ago."

"You have his itinerary?" She snatched the page out of his hand before he had it fully out of his pocket. She looked at her watch. "His flight to Atlanta leaves in three hours. Memphis is a six-hour drive."

Forbes grabbed her arms. "Anne, there is a way."

Looking into his steel blue eyes, she saw the answer and started shaking her head. "I can't."

"How much do you love him?" His gaze bored into hers.

Her heart raced; her stomach churned. With fear's cold fingers choking her, she nodded. "I have to go."

"I'll call Rafe. He can have the jet ready by the time we get you there."

"Is that what you're going to wear?" Meredith slid out through the front passenger window and sat on the frame like the car was the General Lee from *The Dukes of Hazzard*.

"I—no—I don't know."

Forbes squeezed her arms and gently pushed her toward the porch steps. "I'll call Rafe while you put on a clean shirt and real shoes."

In less than five minutes, Anne was ready to face a fear even bigger than falling in love.

The last remaining Guidry company jet gleamed in the sun like a sparkling coffin. She was going to plummet to her death. She touched the scar on the side of her neck, the reminder of the last time she'd been on a plane.

George. She had to get to George. If he left, she might never see him again. Swallowing hard, she put her foot on the first step. Then the second. Too soon, she was hunched over, walking into the living room–like seating area.

Forbes sat on the sofa beside her and tightened her seat belt. "Do you want me to come with you?"

She shook her head. "Just tell Rafe to get this flying death trap off the ground before I change my mind."

He kissed her forehead, said a prayer for her safety, and departed.

Rafe came back and prayed with her, too, then returned to the cockpit.

She didn't stop sobbing until the plane had been in the air nearly twenty minutes. With all the window blinds closed, she could pretend she was riding in the back of the RV Errol and Maggie had rented that time they took a family trip out to the Grand Canyon. She'd just started to relax when Rafe's voice came over the intercom to say they were about to land in Memphis.

She pulled her makeup compact out of her purse. There was nothing for it. Her eyes were red and puffy, her nose, too.

Throughout the landing, she gripped the edge of the seat and prayed that if God wanted her to come home, He'd let her die upon impact. Then the wheels touched the tarmac, and the small jet coasted into the private plane section of the Memphis airport.

She nearly cried again when she saw the length of the line at the ticket counter. She kept checking her watch. Thirty minutes. Twenty. Fifteen.

Finally, with ten minutes to spare, she got to the front of the line. "I need you to page a passenger who's on this flight." She handed the woman George's itinerary.

The woman looked down at her computer screen and handed the paper back to Anne. "I'm sorry, ma'am, that flight has already boarded and pushed away from the gate. There's no way to page him."

No. So close. She'd survived the flight here. She couldn't lose him now.

"What's the next available flight to Atlanta?" Rafe asked, grasping Anne by the arm when she wavered, nausea nearly overwhelming her at the thought of boarding another plane.

"We have one that leaves in about thirty minutes. But it'll take that long to get through security, and if you have any luggage—"

"No luggage." He slapped his corporate credit card down on the counter. "Get her on that flight. First class."

Boarding pass in hand, Anne ran behind Rafe through the airport to the security gate. Only a few people milled about in front of her.

"Take your shoes off and put them in the bucket. Put everything in the bucket—cell phone, too."

She did as told, numb with fear. This time, the fear wasn't of flying. She was afraid she'd lost her only chance at happiness. If she couldn't find him in the Atlanta airport. . .

On the other side of the security gate, she waved at Rafe, slipped her shoes back on, then jogged down the corridor to the appropriate gate. At the desk, the airline employee told her to go ahead and board, as she was one of the last to arrive. She handed the boarding pass to the ticket taker and walked down the long, hollow-sounding hallway. She paused at the gaping door at the end, looking like a mouth ready to devour her, like the great fish in the book of Jonah.

She sank into the plush seat and secured her seat belt.

God, please let me find him. I have to ask him to forgive me, to come home with me.

What was taking so long for the plane to take off?

They shut the door, and the plane rolled away from the building. Then they sat.

Panic rose in her throat with each minute that passed. He had a two-hour layover in Atlanta. But she was already an hour behind him. And she'd heard the Atlanta airport was huge.

Twenty minutes later, the captain came over the intercom, apologized for the delay, and told his staff to prepare for takeoff.

Please let him still be there. Please let me find him.

An hour and ten minutes later, she rushed up the Jetway into the bustling metropolis known as an airport. She stopped at the check-in desk and thrust George's itinerary at the airline worker.

"Can you tell me where this flight takes off from?"

"That's an international flight." The woman clicked a couple of color-coded keys at her computer. "That flight leaves from E-11."

"Where am I now?"

"A-20. If you're trying to catch that flight, you'll never make it. Shows here they're already boarding."

"Can I have a passenger from that flight paged to come back here?"

"We can try. But if he's already boarded, they're not going to let him off the plane, or he can't get back on."

"Okay. Page him, please."

The woman dialed the other gate to have George paged. Anne paced. Other people came to the gate to check in for a flight to Nashville.

Where was he? Which direction would he be coming from?

Ten minutes passed. Twenty. Thirty. Past time for his flight to leave. She returned to the counter. "Did they page him?"

"That flight's already left, ma'am. The gate agent said no one got off the plane."

Anne fought tears. He hadn't gotten off the plane. "Okay. Thanks. How can I purchase a ticket to go home?"

After going through an embarrassing search as she came back through security, Anne found her departure gate and sat facing the windows, watching the planes come and go. He hadn't gotten off the plane.

Music wafted from a nearby karaoke bar. She grinned ruefully. Dean Martin. Her favorite.

Wait a minute! The man singing "Return to Me" sounded just like Dean—

She shot out of her seat and whirled, looking for the source of the music. An Asian man stood at the microphone crooning the sad ballad.

She felt someone stop behind her. Warm breath tickled her ear as someone whispered the heart-touching lyrics of the song, entreating the man's beloved to return, to forgive, to say she belongs to him. . . .

Closing her eyes, she turned, not wanting to see if it wasn't really him.

Warm, strong fingers cupped her chin. She opened her eyes, and tears escaped down her cheeks. George's warm chocolate gaze melted her lingering fear.

"I'm sorry," he whispered. "You can't know how sorry."

She touched his face, just to make sure he really stood there in front of her. Real tears dampened his real face. A sob caught in her throat as he pulled her into his arms. "They said you didn't get off the plane."

"What?"

"When I had them page you earlier. They said no one got off the plane. I thought you were on your way to Paris because you didn't want to see me."

His chuckle vibrated in his chest. "Did you ask them to see if

297

I checked in for that flight?"

"No." She gulped for air. "How did you find me, then?"

"I got here and realized I couldn't leave. I went downstairs and bought the first available ticket back to Bonneterre—this flight." He held her at arm's length. "How did you get here?"

"Rafe took me to Memphis on the company plane. I hoped to catch you there, but your flight had already left."

"You got on a Learjet and a commercial airliner just to come after me?" Emotion thickened his voice.

She nodded, drinking in the sight of him. She never wanted to be away from him ever again, ever, ever.

"You got on a *plane*—no, on *two* planes to come after me?"

Laughter bubbled up through her tears. "Yeah. Two planes." She held up two fingers.

He kissed her, his tenderness fulfilling her every dream. "Two planes."

"I had to see you." She touched his hair. He was grayer now than he'd been when she first met him. "I have a question I wanted to ask you."

He smiled and pulled her out of the path of onlookers. She hadn't meant to make a spectacle. She took his proffered handkerchief and dried her tears.

"What question did you want to ask me?"

My, my, but he was smug. "Well, I feel like we have a lot in common, and we obviously work well together." She grinned. "What I wanted to ask is: Would you consider joining me as an equal partner in Happy Endings, Inc.?"

Smugness deflated into speechless disappointment.

Oh, she couldn't resist. "I know you'll have to figure things out legally with your work visa and all."

He cleared his throat. "I—well, that is to say. . . "

She pressed one finger to his lips. "Of course, I've decided I cannot take on any business partner but my husband. So if you still want to work with me, I guess you'll just have to marry me."

He laughed and pulled her close, caressing the back of her head. "I think that's the best business proposition I've ever heard."

The touch of his lips on hers sent blue sparks through her body. "I love you," she whispered. "Always, always, always."

He traced the curve of her jaw with his forefinger, kissed the bridge of her nose, and tucked her back into his arms. "Now that's what I call a happy ending."

KAYE DACUS is a graduate of Seton Hill University's Master of Arts in Writing Popular Fiction program. She is an active member and former vice president of American Christian Fiction Writers (ACFW). *Stand-In Groom* took second place in the 2006 ACFW Genesis writing competition. She makes her home in Nashville, Tennessee.

If you enjoyed

STAND-IN
GROOM

be on the lookout for

MENU FOR
ROMANCE

Coming Fall 2009